Twilight Territory

Also by Andrew X. Pham

The Eaves of Heaven:
A Life in Three Wars

Catfish and Mandala:
A Two-Wheeled Voyage Through the
Landscape and Memory of Vietnam

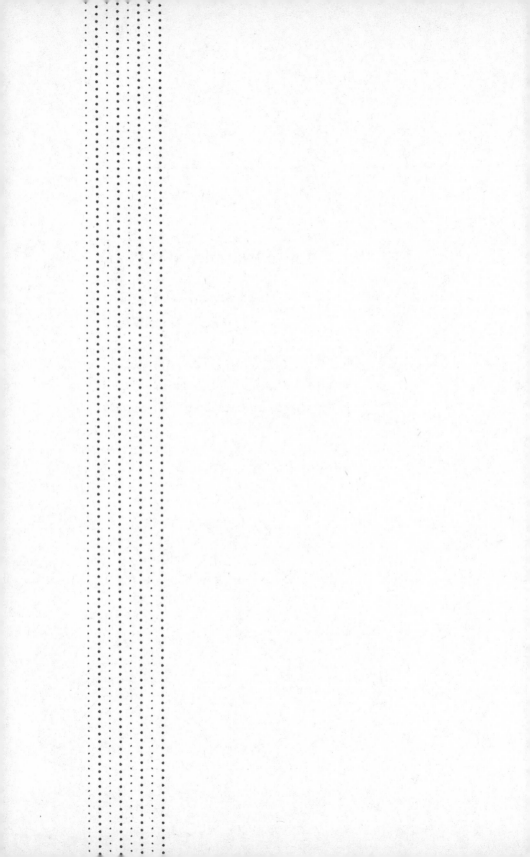

Twilight Territory

A Novel

Andrew X. Pham

W. W. NORTON & COMPANY
Independent Publishers Since 1923

Copyright © 2024 by Andrew Pham

Printed in the United States of America

First Edition

For information about permission to reproduce selections from this book, write to Permissions, W. W. Norton & Company, Inc., 500 Fifth Avenue, New York, NY 10110

For information about special discounts for bulk purchases, please contact W. W. Norton Special Sales at specialsales@wwnorton.com or 800-233-4830

Manufacturing by Lakeside Book Company

Book design by Lovedog Studio

Production manager: Anna Oler

ISBN 978-1-324-06484-8

W. W. Norton & Company, Inc., 500 Fifth Avenue, New York, N.Y. 10110
www.wwnorton.com

W. W. Norton & Company Ltd., 15 Carlisle Street, London W1D 3BS

1 2 3 4 5 6 7 8 9 0

For my wife, Srisuda,
the light of my life

CONTENTS

AUTHOR'S NOTE

THIS NOVEL IS A WORK OF FICTION inspired by some events in the life of the author's maternal grandmother.

NOTE ON TERMINOLOGY

"INDOCHINA," "ANNAM," "TONKIN," and "Cochinchina" are names coined by the French to delineate their colony without deference to the colonized. The indigenous peoples of "French Indochina" did not identify themselves by those terms, either during the colonial period or afterward. Modern Vietnam comprises 54 ethnic groups, with the Viet (Khinh people) accounting for 87 percent of the population. Most usually identify themselves by the region of their birth: north, south, or central.

During the wars with the French as well as during the Japanese occupation, numerous indigenous factions vied for power. It was a dynamic time when groups regularly formed alliances, splintered, and rebranded themselves. For this story, the majority of indigenous groups will be interchangeably referred to as "the Resistance" or the "Viet Minh."

Viet Nam, the country, is written as "Vietnam" for uniformity with global usage. "Viet" denotes both the language and the people.

Twilight Territory

PART I

Friendship

◆ 1942 ◆

The Major and the Shopkeeper

TUYET REMEMBERED THE FIRST TIME SHE MET Major Yamazaki Takeshi. An inauspicious day at the peak of the hot season of 1942. The late afternoon sun had slipped below the roofline, leaving the street in shadow. All day, the dragon-bone wind howled and showed no sign of abating. Hot and sandy, it was an unpredictable whirling thing that swept through once every few years and never brought anything good. It chafed the skin, infected eyes, and put grit in the teeth. It tore leaves and branches from trees, blew red dust into every nook and crevice. It made the dogs distempered. Few people ventured outside other than the children who played in the street, year-round, rain or shine. They were launching paper airplanes into the roiling sky.

Aunt Coi arranged a low table just inside the shopfront. "Slackers aren't earners," she said when Tuyet complained that the weather was too foul for business. Coi was forty-six years old, Tuyet twenty-eight. Coi was a diminutive woman with half-moon eyes. She had glossy black teeth, dyed for fashion as a teenager. Since Tuyet's mother had passed away fifteen years earlier, Coi had been Tuyet's mother, best friend, and confidante.

Coi hollered through the house, "Are you ready with the batter yet?"

"Coming, coming," Tuyet replied from the kitchen.

Their rented home was one half of a house, divided right down the middle by a bare brick wall, the living space consisting of three narrow adjoining rooms. The bedroom was in the middle between the kitchen in the rear and the shop, which faced the street. Ten removable planks, two meters tall, served as the door of the wide shopfront. Along the side of the house, a strip of dirt was a well-tended vegetable garden with basil, chili peppers, mint bushes, tomato plants, trellises of bitter squash, and green beans. Coi, Tuyet, and her two-year-old daughter, Anh, shared a divan in the bedroom. The only other furniture was a small dresser bought from the landlord. Coi's twenty-two-year-old son, Ha, slept in a hammock strung in the shop.

Tuyet added a ladle of rainwater to the rice batter, thinning it to the creaminess of fresh milk. She lugged the bucket through the bedroom where Anh was napping. It was their afternoon routine: baking *banh cang* dumplings to supplement the income from the shop, which comprised three wooden bins, shelves for dried goods, and some odds and ends. Jars of cooking oil or rendered pork fat, vats of fish sauce, and a barrel of low-grade rice. The kind the locals now ate.

"Don't light a fire just yet. Nobody wants dumplings in this weather," Tuyet said, stepping outside for a look.

Windows were shuttered against the hot wind. Down at the corner, a shiny black automobile turned onto their street, a dirt lane that rarely saw cars. It was the first time an expensive vehicle had graced this part of town, the children crying, "Big car! Big car!" It crawled as though the driver was trying to find an address. Boys trotted along for a peek but dared not come closer. As it drew near, Tuyet saw Japanese soldiers. Recently, there had been a strong Japanese presence in the town since they took over the Phan Thiet airbase from the Vichy French government. But it was the first time anyone saw Japanese soldiers in this neighborhood.

"Auntie, what about this big car?"

Coi held her breath when the car slowed to a stop in front of their house. She dragged her niece into the bedroom and latched the door behind them. The two women stood in semi-darkness, peering out through gaps in the door panels. Four Japanese, two soldiers and two officers, stepped out from the car. The officers entered the shop and stood just inside the threshold, removing their caps and smoothing back their hair. Both men were immaculately dressed in dark green uniforms, shiny medals, and boots. They stood at attention, square-shouldered, straight-backed, presenting themselves to an empty room. The short one was in his twenties, thin and grim-faced. The other, half a head taller, balding, rangy, and well-tanned, in his thirties.

"We beg permission to offer greetings!" said the younger officer in stilted formal Viet. "We seek a friendly visit as not to cause you concern."

Behind the door, the two women stared at each other, perplexed at the Japanese's odd phrasing. His accent was heavy but understandable. Tuyet reached for the door. Coi shook her head.

The men waited in silence. The young one cleared his throat. "Please, misses and children come out. We saw you go inside."

Tuyet whispered, "Misses and children? I think he means us."

Coi shrugged. Tuyet peeped through the crack. The Japanese seemed at ease, content to wait. They ignored the crowd gathering across the street. Tuyet reached for the doorknob, but Coi motioned for her niece to stay, took a deep breath, and went out, closing the door behind her.

"Greetings, officers," Coi said, shakily. She bowed at the waist. A simple peasant, she had never faced a ranking soldier, unsure of whether she had permission to speak or even to look at them. "Is there something wrong?"

Both men bowed stiffly. The younger officer said, "I am Lieutenant Tanaka Kenta. This is my commanding officer, Major Yamazaki Takeshi. We come to see Miss Le Tuyet."

Their friendly tone emboldened Coi. "Forgive me for asking, but what do you want with her?"

"I am a translator," replied the lesser officer, who had a

shrewd face and small teeth. He was young, but he carried himself with such imperial hauteur that Coi mistook him for the superior of the pair. He inclined his head toward the older man. "The major begs permission to speak to Miss Tuyet."

Coi bowed and retreated into the bedroom. She grabbed Tuyet's arms. "This is horrible! How do they know your name?"

"I don't know. I've never seen them before."

"What are we going to do?"

"If they want to arrest us, there's nothing we can do," Tuyet said and touched her hair, checking the chignon. She gulped and stepped across the threshold.

"Greetings, officers. I am Le Tuyet." She bowed, hands clenched firmly over her stomach.

The lieutenant repeated the introduction, and then said, "Major Yamazaki Takeshi would like to make your acquaintance. Please accept this small gift for the inconvenience of our visit."

On cue, the driver entered and placed a gift-wrapped box on the dining table.

"Um, thank you . . . sir," Tuyet stuttered, then bowed. "Forgive me, but what is this for?"

Major Yamazaki smiled and bowed.

Tanaka said, "The major saw you last Monday at the Permit Office."

"Oh, that!" Tuyet grimaced. "I'm very sorry about that. I did not mean to make a scene."

The major said something to Tanaka, who translated: "Understandable. He is not here to reprimand you."

The major stepped forward and addressed Tuyet in French, "Madame, do you speak French?"

"Yes, but not well."

"*Très bien!*" the major countered enthusiastically, his eyes brightening. He had a strong, squarish face, prominent cheekbones, and a high-bridged nose—a keel of a nose, colossal—

quite unusual, even for a Japanese. His mouth was wide and expressive, artistic. It was not a handsome face, but there was something interesting and layered about it that intrigued Tuyet.

"Let's give my translator a rest." The major dismissed Tanaka with a nod, and the lieutenant went outside to smoke.

"I appreciate the risk you took for your friend. It takes strength and courage to stand up to corrupt officials."

"Thank you, but I am neither strong nor courageous." Tuyet sighed as she invited him to sit at the table. "I am—we all are—struggling to make a living. When those officials suggested bribes on top of all the taxes and restrictions, I lost my temper."

"For good reason. You did the right thing. I would like to ask a favor of you."

Tuyet glanced at him, on guard. "It depends on what it is, Major."

"I would like you to advise me on a few civil matters."

"Me?" she said, incredulous, touching her chest. "Reporting on people like an informer."

He laughed. "No, nothing as dreary as that."

"I can introduce you to senior people who are more knowledgeable."

"That might be useful later, but for now your opinion will do."

She opened her mouth, closed it, and looked down at her hands, her mind racing. She said, "This is very sudden. I'm afraid of what people might say. May I think about it?"

"Of course, madame. I will return in a few days for your reply."

"Thank you. Please take your present with you. I have not agreed to advise you."

He simply smiled and bowed. With an elegant gesture, he put his cap back on his head, spun on his heels, and left.

"Your gift," she called after him, but he had already stepped out into the foul bluster.

The major got into the car. He smiled and tipped his hat to her. The Japanese officers were gone in a red cloud of dust. The crowd watched the car leave.

Coi was chattering, but Tuyet didn't hear a word. She stood at the door staring after the big black car. In the booming, swirling heat, Tuyet felt a strange disquiet, her eyes suddenly heavy, tired, oblivious to the goggling neighbors and noisy children barging into her shop.

"What did they want?" Sau asked in her loud, fish-market voice, their next-door neighbor a gossipy widow.

Coi gave Tuyet a look, and they set about closing up shop, bringing in display baskets of fruits, shutting the windows.

"What's that?" Sau pointed at the box.

"It looks like a box, Sau," Tuyet said, barring her way as Coi shut the door on the magpie.

"Oh, heavens, that woman! It'll be all over the neighborhood by nightfall." Coi huffed and settled onto a stool at the table.

"That's the least of my problems." Tuyet paced the room, slapping her thighs. "People are going to think I'm some kind of Japanese sympathizer."

"Aiya! I didn't think about that. I thought he was trying to get friendly with you."

"No, there are plenty of women in town. He knows where to find some pretty ones who don't need gifts."

When Tuyet first arrived in Phan Thiet from Saigon as a newly divorced single mother, a wealthy merchant had approached her with a business proposition. After a few chaste meetings, he had revealed his real aim over dinner at a fine restaurant: an indecent proposal for her to become his mistress. She had flipped a hot bowl of fish soup into his lap and given him such a public tongue-lashing that even his wife had hated her ever since. Tuyet was worried this Japanese was nosing down the same path.

She sat down across from her aunt, the box on the table

between them. They glanced at each other. Tuyet had lived with Coi since she was eighteen, when she ran away because her uncle was forcing her to marry an older man against her will. Coi fingered the sunflower-yellow wrapping paper. Tuyet's daughter, Anh, stumbled out, rubbing sleep from her eyes, and climbed into her mother's lap.

"Tuyet, aren't you going to open it?"

"I didn't accept it, so how can I open it?"

"Why not? There's no harm in looking. We could re-wrap it."

"Auntie!"

"We must know what's inside. What if it's a bomb?" She made a face.

Tuyet laughed. "If you're dying to see it, just say so."

"I'm dying!"

"Go ahead then, but I'm not touching it."

Coi harrumphed. "If you're going to act like this, go into the other room while I have a look."

"Ha! You think I'm going to fall for that? I'm keeping an eye on you."

Coi undid the artfully folded wrapping. "Look! Canned fish and canned milk and ham and chocolate and tea and candies! Smell this bag of candies, Anh. What do you think it is? Strawberry?" She handed it to Anh. "Shampoo! And soaps!" She put a bar to her nose. "Lavender!"

"Let me see that." Ten bars of imported soap. A sudden urge to bathe made her itch all over.

Anh scurried to the bedroom with the candies.

Coi hauled her back to the table. Tuyet returned the bag to the box and put Anh in her lap, the little girl on the verge of tears.

"Look, baby. It's not ours. We're holding it for the Japanese man. We can't eat what's not ours, right?"

Anh lowered her head, rolled up into a ball of misery on her mother's lap, and sucked her thumb. She was small for her age. Both Coi and Tuyet were afraid that the child would grow up to be undersized like them. They had been overfeeding her, but nothing could fill out the little girl.

Tuyet eyed the cans of milk and the other gifts, feeling both flattered and insulted. These wartime luxuries were worth more than what their shop had brought in the previous month. Tuyet chewed her lips, refraining from stuffing a bar of chocolate into her mouth. How difficult life had become since war had broken out in Europe. Two years earlier, they had been living in Saigon and her husband had been the captain of the Pan-Asia team, a star player of the country's foremost football club. They had been the toast of the town. Fancy restaurants had declined to bill them for meals. They had been invited to more parties than they could possibly attend. Now, she realized with a deep sense of melancholy that she wanted the bar of soap as though it were gold.

"Empty stomach teaches the knees to crawl." Tuyet murmured her late mother's favorite proverb.

"There you go again with your pride," Coi grumbled.

"Please, Auntie, put it all back."

"It's a greeting gift," the older woman said. "When possible, believe in the good intention of others."

"No truth more convincing than the lies one tells oneself," Tuyet retorted.

Coi waved her open hands in the air. "All right, it's your present, do whatever you want. But I think it's only fair to decide when Ha gets home. He is part of the family."

Tuyet acquiesced by raising her chin. Coi's only son was a brilliant young man. "Yes, Auntie, Ha will have an opinion. Whether we accept it or not, there will be consequences. I'm sure of it."

AT DUSK, HA pushed his bicycle through the gate and along the side of the house. The black secondhand bike was one of two luxuries he had bought with his wages. Their dining room furniture had been the first—a crude unvarnished table and wooden stools. It was his wish that the family be modern and dine properly like well-to-do people. The previous year, after receiving his Tu Tai II secondary school diploma, a major accomplishment in colonial education, Ha had been offered a good position in the provincial government, but he had chosen instead to work with the Forestry and Agricultural Services for a meager salary. He had said he did not want to condone official thievery or repression of the motherland. Everyone had thought it had been a terrible waste because for the first time in history, many Viets were given posts that had always been held by the French. With the war in Europe, there were few French-men to fill the vacancies. Even Ha's schoolmates had said he was a magnificent fool to pass up such an opportunity. But when their neighbors insisted to Coi that if she wanted to be wealthy, she should order her son to work for the government, she had replied, "I want my son to be a good man more than I want to be rich."

"What's for dinner, Mother? I'm starved!" Ha loped into the house. His huge appetite never managed to fill out his boyish frame.

"*Banh cang*, as much as you can eat," Auntie said. They couldn't waste the batter and had made a heap of dumplings to be eaten with sardine stew and chili-garlic fish sauce.

Ha pointed at the gift box. "What's that?"

Ha's father, a village tailor, had committed suicide after he had gambled away their house and savings, leaving Coi and twelve-year-old Ha homeless and destitute. At the funeral, Coi had pulled her son into her bosom. "Weep for your father, son. We will mourn him one full moon, and then we will mourn him no more. If you love your mother, then be a virtuous man. That is all I ask."

Tuyet had been eighteen then and remembered that day well

because her cousin went to bed a boy and woke up the next morning a man.

He became very quiet. He read voraciously and held himself to some stern inner compass, taking on more responsibilities than anyone expected of him. Now, at twenty-two, he spoke and carried himself like someone twice his age. Ha was serious, driven, and idealistic, though given to bouts of melancholy, which he hid from others by walking in the forest.

"MOST OF THAT," Ha said, gesturing at the box, "isn't available on the black market. Our Japanese friend must have access to some very exclusive stores. A man of rank."

"I don't care if he's royalty," Tuyet snapped.

"So you think this could be an overture to romance?"

"I hope not."

"Don't underestimate your beauty and charm," he said wryly, trying to keep a straight face.

She smacked him on the back of the head.

Ha yelped. "A thousand apologies! Seriously, now, let's say he wants to meet you. How could he do that? Would you like it if he chatted you up in the street? Maybe sent a dowager? But that would be too much, especially since you had never seen his face. I can't think of any other way. If I were him, I would have done the same."

"Oh, really? What a strategist you are. I thought you haven't even asked a girl out yet," Tuyet said, arching an eyebrow.

Ha blushed. He was clumsy when it came to girls—the one thing he couldn't glean from books.

Coi intervened. "The major had to come here himself. It's the honorable thing to do when a man courts a woman."

"Nobody said anything about courting!" Tuyet cried, a bit too shrill, to her own dismay. "Don't you go jumping to conclusions, Auntie."

"Friendship, that's right. My error." Coi rolled her eyes.

Tuyet ignored her. "I wonder why he brought a Japanese translator. I always see the French and the Japanese using Viet interpreters."

"Japanese are proud and discreet," Ha said with the sweeping generalization of an unseasoned youth. "The major wouldn't want to involve a Viet interpreter in his private affairs."

"When the major returns, I'll tell him it's too risky for me."

"It might be dangerous to reject a Japanese. We don't even know what he wants. Let's think this through." Ha rubbed his chin, elbows on the table. "We don't know a thing about him. I'll ask around. He could be a dangerous character. Never offend someone making a friendly gesture."

Tuyet glanced at her cousin, who sounded very mature. Although he was six years her junior, he was becoming the head of their household. He looked so much like his father, the kindly eyes and the pensive expression. It was easy to underestimate him.

Nightmares

MAJOR YAMAZAKI TAKESHI HAD ARRIVED IN INDO-china two months earlier to take command of the Phan Thiet airbase. The post had been given as a reward for his service in the Second Sino-Japanese War, though he suspected it had more to do with him saving a general's life. That act of bravery had wounded him in battle and put him in the hospital for multiple surgeries. He was still suffering from his injuries, but considering the easy life he was enjoying in the fishing town, he knew he would gladly save the general and be wounded all over again.

He had slept well enough during the first two months in the convalescent ward, buoyed by painkillers and sedatives. The mind had held out until the body healed, and then it had begun to fragment. Nightmares breached his sleep. He came to expect them. He returned to a familiar city almost every night, to the same scene of destruction, trapped beneath a starless, impenetrable sky.

IN HIS DREAM, he plunged down a dark, muddy alley, hurling ahead toward a cleft of gray, careening off mossy walls. Something was chasing him, not far behind, keening cries of pursuit jabbing at his back. He had to reach somewhere, across the burnt-out city. The sky flashed dull orange. White whips of lightning fractured the night, electric stitching on storm clouds. Far off, sporadic cackle-pops of gunfire. A spark brushed by his face, a firefly, on fire, a throbbing red dot.

He reached an open square. Gray snow was falling. He

looked up. Black clouds burned, peeling sheets of flame. Ashes drifted down. Shadows shifted, splotches of ink stretched, forming shapes, spilling over hills of rubble. From shattered buildings poured hundreds, thousands of skeletal figures, pale ghosts, walking cadavers. Starving night creatures staggered forth to scavenge the debris of that dead city.

His pistol. The holster was empty. He had to cross the city. He started across the square, splashing through puddles. The water rose and the ground became sodden. He was wading through a knee-deep swamp. Something snared his ankles and dragged him down. Bony hands tore at his clothes. He sank to his chest in a cesspit of churning body parts, limbless torsos, severed hands, bloody legs thrashing, flopping like fish in the throes of death. Something slithered into his mouth. He fought for air. His screams choked in his throat; nothing escaped but an indistinct warble, a muffled gurgle, unheard.

The night opened like an abyss. He fell in.

TAKESHI JERKED AWAKE, dripping in a pool of sweat that had soured the bedsheet. His head throbbed, cheek clammy against the pillow. A swampy taste in his mouth. His throat dry, hoarse, his limbs leaden. He felt wearier than the previous night. His left shoulder creaked, protesting his effort to rise. He fingered the scar between his nipple and collarbone. The bullet had punched through his left shoulder and out the front. Raising his elbow higher than his ears was painful. Shrapnel had mangled his right leg. A long-distance runner in his prime, he barely managed an ungainly jog with his stiff knee, which bent only halfway. Whenever a storm approached, his knee ached. He managed with medicinal herbs, morphine when he could get it, alcohol, and heavy doses of stoicism.

He rose from his narrow bed, banged his knees against a chair, and fumbled for a match to light the oil lamp on his desk.

He padded in his slippers over to the dresser by the window and put on his clothes, folded on a bamboo rack. The shelves held few personal items: a small oil painting, paintbrushes, several seashells, and a small box of books wrapped in wax paper to preserve against the humidity. He poured some water from the pitcher into the basin on the dresser, washed his face, and with a damp towel wiped his chest, shoulders, and arms. He stared at his reflection in the mirror, feeling as old as he looked.

Out of habit, he checked his pocket watch. He had had an unfailing sense of time since childhood. His father had set his internal clock to wake at predawn on the purple edge of night. The old man had drilled into his only son the importance of completing a quarter of the daily chores in the first three hours before taking breakfast. Takeshi donned the practice hakama, cinched the obi tightly around his waist, and laced up the bamboo armor. He grabbed his bokken and headgear and stepped outside.

Lieutenant Sakamoto Ryota waited for him in front of the main house, which served as the officers' quarters. The camp was still asleep, dark barracks lining the west side of the airstrip. Yellow kerosene lamplight spilled from the mess kitchen where cooks were preparing the morning rice. Sentries walked their rounds along the perimeters. In the wooden tower, little more than a crow's nest, the silhouette of a sentry against the glowing sky.

In silence, they lumbered toward the practice field, an odd pair of friends, one lanky and tall, the other stocky and short, nearly the same age, born on opposite sides of the same island, Hokkaido. Neither man broke the silence. On a patch of barren ground, they went through a routine of stretches, calisthenics, and kata exercises. The motions, the cuts, the parries, the sweeps as old as time, second nature since they were boys. As early sunlight needled through the trees, the aging veterans sparred, their grunts, cries, and the violent bokken *clack-clack-clacks* sounding across the fields.

··· 3 ···

Invitation

A<small>MONG GODS AND SERVANTS, NO SECRET IS SAFE.</small>

Ha learned from a maid working at the Japanese base that Major Yamazaki Takeshi had previously served in Manchuria. Respected by his men, Yamazaki was known as a skilled pilot and able administrator. He regularly chartered small boats for fishing excursions.

"They say he's a man who always gets what he wants," Ha told Tuyet and his mother over dinner the next evening. "So, if he wants advice, we can introduce him to a few smart people. If he wants you, it's unwise to hurt his feelings by rejecting him outright. You let him come around but don't be nice to him. Don't dress up. Make yourself unattractive. That should cool him off sooner or later. It's better to let a man change his own mind about these things."

"You're pretty smart for someone with no experience."

"Is that a backhanded compliment? How sweet-and-sour of you."

"You're such a pain." Tuyet pinched him.

"Ow! Listen. It's a part of my plan. First, don't offend him. Accept his present politely but discourage him from bringing more gifts."

"I'm in favor of this plan," interrupted Coi. "Go on, son."

"Second, you must invite him to dinner."

"I'm trying to get rid of him. Why would I want to cook him dinner?"

"We can't afford to make a meal good enough for someone like him," Coi muttered. She knew their shop ledger ran dozens of pages because half of the customers bought on credit. The other half hardly bought anything at all. Since the beginning of the Japanese occupation of Indochina, their shop had grown increasingly bare. Fresh eggs, yams, fruits, rice, and a few meters of rough cotton cloths—the bulk of their stores— came from those who could not pay their debt with cash.

"We can sell or trade some of these gifts for food," Ha said.

Tuyet went to the kitchen.

"Don't you want to hear my plan?"

"Keep talking. I'm boiling some water. If we're keeping the box, I'd like a cup of tea to go with the chocolate."

"Good idea!" Coi sprang to her feet and went about setting cups and plates. Anh shrieked and pranced around the room clapping her hands. She had been sniffing at the strawberry candies since the previous day.

"I should have known," Ha cried, slapping his thigh. "Both of you wanted to keep the gifts all along. You only want a reason to ease your consciences!"

MAJOR YAMAZAKI arrived the next morning with two twenty-five-kilo bags of first-grade jasmine rice and two kilos of white refined sugar. Tuyet and Coi had changed out of work clothes into blue *ao dai*, traditional long dresses with trousers reserved for formal occasions.

"Thank you for these gifts. I am very flattered that you think my opinion is worth your time," Tuyet said in French as she poured him a thimble of tea. "Please don't bring any more gifts. It's very generous of you, but it puts me in an awkward position."

"Are you worried about what people say?"

"Absolutely. We're from the north. A scandal could make life here difficult for us."

"What constitutes a scandal?"

"An unmarried woman seeing a man for gifts. People can be very judgmental."

"Ah, I understand."

"I've been propositioned before, and I had to humiliate the man in public to redeem my honor. This is a pretty little town, but it has its share of scandals."

"What do you mean?"

"It's not for me to say," she replied, not relishing the thought of explaining sordid things. "If you really want to know more about this place, I'd like to invite you to dinner with some knowledgeable elders. If they become acquainted with you, things will go easier for me."

"That makes sense," he said with a smile. "I am honored to accept your invitation."

4

Magnate

THE MORNING BREEZE FADED. POCKETS OF COOL-
ness wafted from the canopy of the banyan trees. At the mag-
nate's mansion, the manicured garden of hibiscus and wine
rose was quiet, save for birds chirping in the trees and the soft
rustling of leaves. Servants knew to respect silence until the
master stirred. In the west-facing suite, the two occupants were
awake, a Viet girl sitting by the window, an old Frenchman
splayed belly-up in bed.

A haze of cigar smoke filled the over-furnished bedcham-
ber, which was the decade-long labor of his estranged wife,
whose taste leaned toward Victorian antiques with touches of
the baroque. The curtains, her pride and joy, had battens of
intricate fabrics in hues of coral and lavender, commissioned
in London. She had collected an expensive set of chairs, upholstered benches, an oak armoire, gilded mirrors, and a four-
poster bed befitting a baron. Thick carpets had traveled from
Persia to England to France and thence to this end of the South
China Sea. Since her departure from the colonies, not a single
item had been shifted a centimeter or undergone more than
regular dusting. Mandarin porcelain vases, framed sepia photos of the Ferauds arrayed on the teak dresser, oil paintings of
pastoral Provence, memorabilia and souvenirs, both big and
small, having lost their purpose, sat forgotten.

Propped up in bed, naked among the crumpled sheets, Gaspard Feraud checked the stump of his cigar and puffed. He
had once been a moderately handsome man in a barrel-chested,
outdoorsy manner. But at sixty-three, he was a portly figure,

wrecked by decades of indulgence, a hoary mountain of flabby muscles long gone to fat. He kept most of his hair save for a space on the crown of his head. He had one lazy, drooping eyelid, and a pair of mean eyes, dark buttons pressed into a doughy face shored up by a double jowl and a scraggly salt-and-pepper beard. Vein bursts radiated from his bulbous nose, forming a reddish-purple mosaic across his cheeks. His huge ears with the mangled ridges and lumps fascinated his servants. They whispered that such extraordinarily large lobes indicated longevity, someone not soon to leave this earth.

Feraud had spent a lifetime in Indochina, thirty-five years as a second-generation colonialist, having arrived on the coattails of his father, a high-ranking official under Governor-General Jean Baptiste Paul Beau. He had inherited his father's vast plantations and branched out into business and manufacturing. His wealth and power would have continued to grow if it hadn't been for his carnal appetites. When news of war with Germany reached the colonies, his wife left him and returned to France to live with her daughter and grandchildren. Her departure, intended as a reprisal for her husband's infidelity, had the opposite effect. Gaspard Feraud experienced a minor revival because for all practical purposes, he had become, once again, a bachelor of considerable wealth, a feudal lord free to revel in his pleasures.

Draped on the white windowsill, the naked girl sat, one leg straight as a beam, ankle extending a slender foot, pointed toes with the tan lines of sandal straps. Her other leg was drawn close, foot near her smooth buttock, the raised knee bent to support the elbow of her outstretched arm, the small, fluted hand with long fingers dripping languidly from a slack wrist. Her other arm was bent, and her hand held her opposite shoulder, forming a triangular nest in which she rested her head as she gazed out the window.

The girl was sixteen, her frame as lithe as a dancer's, her bearing as untutored as a child's. Her silky, fair skin had a green undercast. She had a delicate face with high cheekbones and brown cat-eyes common to Central Highlanders. She stared at the branches, unblinking, searching for the chirping birds with an idle feline curiosity.

Tsk. Tsk. He clicked his tongue, summoning her. She unfolded her limbs and rose to her feet, transitioning with a youthful alacrity that pleased him. Her face was blank. Her eyes understood what he wanted, the expected routine. She crossed the carpeted tiles with the flat-footed strides of a sandal-wearer, naked without awareness or pretense of seduction. Her narrow hips did not sway, her small breasts too firm to bounce, her adolescent pubis barely a shadow between her legs.

She clambered onto the bed, peering into his eyes for a brief moment. She swung her leg over, astride him, hands on his shoulders, her smooth arms bridging them. He took her hands and pressed them against his ravaged cheeks. He tasted her fingers, engulfed them with his mouth. His ivory nicotine-stained fingernails traced the lines of her ribs, the elegant compactness of a girlish body. A soundless giggle, she squirmed, arching her back. Her long hair, black as wet coal, cascaded behind her, the ends sweeping the rounded mounds of her buttocks. He drew her to him and buried his face in her breasts. He pushed her back a little, the girl pliant, following his cues.

He fingered the furrow of her taut abdomen, her shallow navel. He dragged his hand upward and traced the lower half-parabola of her left breast, spiraling to the pink nipple, the size of a shirt button, hard like a tapioca nugget. He pinched it. She emitted a startled gasp, eyes wide open. He thumbed her birdlike collarbone and the notch at the base of her throat. His fingers around her fragile neck. In his palm, the quick flutter of her breaths, the pulsating arteries and, also, his own power. She trembled. He released her and stroked the firm outer part of her thigh. With his hands, he urged her onto her knees, still astride him. As she rose, his fingers strayed into the soft part of the inner thighs, up toward where she was moist. He tasted his fingers, a salty sweetness, a faint, nearly undetectable trace of musk, the scent of blooming youth that preceded womanhood.

She felt him stirring and reached down to help him but was unable due to the massive bulge of his gut. He scooted downward to flatten his back and to diminish his protruding belly. He noticed that it was getting warm, perhaps too warm for physical exertion. In the hot season, he knew he succumbed easily. She took hold of him. He repositioned himself. They fumbled, each move more distracting than the last. His blood was pounding, reddening his face. He was sweating, fretting that his lust was conspiring with his aging body to betray him. That tangent veered him from the moment and sent his thoughts careening into a series of potholes.

She looked up at the slowly turning ceiling fan and then at him. He nodded. She leaped off the bed and darted to the control switch on the wall. The ceiling fan accelerated, wobbling on its axis, whipping up a stronger breeze. She was on top of him again, but he was flagging. She went to work to restore his passion, diligently, perhaps too mechanically.

Sighing, he surrendered to her manipulation. His thought strayed to the first time he had seen her, in the previous season, at the tail of the monsoon, a lingering glimpse from his automobile as it crept down the congested road, muddy and reeking of ceremonial incense. She was standing in a wedding procession, partially hidden by the bride and groom, who were posing for a group photograph in front of the home, surrounded by their family. She wore a lilac blue *ao dai*, a distant cousin of the bride, relegated to the rear.

This virgin came to him as most of his girls had, through Madame Ngu, a professional matchmaker and procurer, part dowager and part enforcer. One of Madame Ngu's many talents was her specialization in converting good girls from respectable family into mistresses for wealthy colonialists. For decades, since the arrival of the first French diplomats, it had been a common practice for Frenchmen to order the wives or daughters of their Viet underlings to come to their beds. Those who wanted women not directly under their control approached mediators such as Madame Ngu to facilitate the transaction. Madame Ngu was among the best in the business, and Feraud was one of her most demanding and frequent clients. She had fulfilled all his requests except for the latest one—Miss Mai-Ly, the daughter of a local restaurant owner, a virgin whose beauty made Feraud hoarse with thirst and gave him sharp pangs every time he set eyes on her.

The thought of his latest obsession pulled Feraud out of his reverie. He looked down at the obedient girl, the simple peasant daughter, between his legs and felt a wave of disappointment. His lust dissolved; a sober clarity came into his eyes. It was hopeless. Each new conquest brought him diminishing pleasure. It had become a lifelong addiction, and his palate had dulled, though not his desire. He needed the forbidden fruits, nubile, virginal princesses.

Exasperated, he groaned, dismissing her with a perfunctory flick of his hand. "Go back to Saigon."

"It's Saturday," she said in French, in a soft girlish voice, astonishingly sweet with the Hue accent—which ironically was the harshest of the local dialects. "Mother Superior doesn't expect us back in the dormitory until suppertime tomorrow."

"Go today."

"Did I do something wrong?"

"I'm busy," he grunted, not looking at her.

"You told me to come for the weekend."

"I'm telling you to go now."

She recoiled, cocking her head, perplexed. She remembered Madame Ngu's advice: *Old men's attention is old men's stamina—slow to rise, quick to fall.* She had been warned. Monsieur would eventually find another girl, a new distraction, and she would be free.

"You're finished with me," she said in a plaintive voice.

"I'm not finished with you," he replied in a tone that said that he was.

Her lips tightened to a thin line. Silently, she gathered her belongings, eyes downcast, picking up pieces scattered around the room, one by one, a crumpled cream dress with navy silk ribbons, a leather book satchel, pink undergarments, a straw sun hat, clutching them to her bare breasts, two fingers hooking the straps of her student sandals. She did not check the room for overlooked items or pause to dress. Goose flesh appeared on her arms.

His eyes followed her to the door. She paused at the threshold, glanced back once, a fleeting motion, and was gone. A fine gem, hard-won and well-cherished for a brief season. He had taken her virginity, nurtured her in his ways, taught her a few things about life and a number of things about sex, and left his marks on her. In his vanity, he might assert that she had developed, as some girls did, a little genuine affection for her master. The door clicked closed behind her. It did not matter now. He had little control over his fickle virility or his wandering thoughts. Confronted with the ravages of time, he reached for his cigar and allowed himself a moment of self-pity.

A few minutes later, he found solace in, of all things, the flip-flop sounds of his long-suffering maid who was deliberately announcing her approach with her indoor sandals. Bui, a widow in her mid-fifties, had been a part of the household since Feraud bought his first house in Saigon, which was right after the birth of his daughter, twenty-four years ago. She had witnessed his family's glories and woes with few words, a discreet and reliable servant who was privy to things Feraud never shared with his wife and also to things his wife never shared with him. These days, he appreciated Bui for her skills in managing his girls and her ability to keep a neutral face with regard to his appetites—not that he had ever cared for the opinions of others. He could tell from the pace of her sandals that things had gone smoothly: Bui had dispatched the girl, sent her away with her allowance, and summoned the driver to take her to the bus station.

A knock, the door opened, and a small, thin-faced woman entered with a silver coffee tray, her sandals suddenly soundless. Bui had an ivory complexion that was nearly ageless. She was compact in body and efficient in movement. Her eyes had a placid intelligence. Her mouth, the colorless lips, was a joyless line. She wore no makeup or rouge. Her hair was, as always, pulled back from her blunt forehead in a tight chignon, seemingly lacquered and nailed to her symmetrical skull by a pair of silver stakes.

Without a glance in his direction, she placed the coffee tray on an end table by the window. "Breakfast is ready on the terrace. Police Chief Leroux has arrived," she said. "Would you like him to wait for you?"

Feraud, still immodest on the bed, replied without turning his head. "Serve him first. I don't want him in a cranky mood."

"That's what he said."

"Bastard," he groused. He needed the man's assistance with the acquisition of his next obsession.

Feraud wiggled to the edge of the bed to prepare for the dismount. Swinging his legs over the side, he leveraged himself into a sitting position. Hands on knees, he heaved to his feet with a grunt. He put on his burgundy silk robe and went to sit in a chair by the window with his coffee.

"Shall I get your bath ready?"

He nodded and turned stiffly toward the window. His eyes roamed the branches for the sparrows that had caught the girl's attention earlier. Silence. They were gone now.

Behind him, barefoot servants padded quietly into the chamber, hauling pails of hot water to fill the bathtub.

5

Kim Long

KIM LONG, THE BEST RESTAURANT IN PHAN THIET, was renowned for its fine cuisine and its ability to secure the best of the daily catch, year after year, regardless of weather. It was one of the few businesses that catered successfully to both natives and colonialists, including the recently arrived Japanese. The well-organized establishment comprised three shopfronts, or half of a two-story commercial building in the center of Main Street, a stone's throw from the municipal town market. An elegant piece of calligraphy in Nom script near the front door played on an old proverb: *An inch of time is an inch of gold. An inch of gold cannot buy an inch of time, but it can buy a feast divine.*

In her late thirties, Yen Long, the proprietress, was arguably one of the most striking women in town. Her oval face, high forehead, delicate nose, and rose-petal mouth were of classical beauty. Her skin glowed like pink alabaster, nearly translucent. That evening she was dressed in a burgundy *ao dai* with embroidered flowers, her hair in a modern style, exposing her graceful neckline.

"Good evening, Major Yamazaki. Welcome, Lieutenant Sakamoto, Lieutenant Mori, Second Lieutenant Ishigara. We are honored by your visit tonight," Yen said in Japanese, bowing. Fluent in French, she had recently picked up just enough Japanese to welcome her new guests.

The four officers returned the greeting with equal formality, drawing the attention of the entire dining room, two dozen tables of Viet and French patrons, representing the town's elite.

While the French were generally cordial and reserved toward the Japanese, the Viet were respectful and friendly. They were in awe of the Japanese for showing no deference whatsoever to the colonial ruling class. In fact, it was a vicarious pleasure for Viets to see how the French behaved in Japanese presence.

Ignoring the crowd, Yamazaki inhaled the enticing aromas of food and declared in French, "Something smells wonderful. They say you can't get to heaven without dying, but I say, this comes pretty close."

"Major, you say that every time," Yen replied with a gracious smile, switching to French without missing a beat. "Please, this way, your usual table is ready."

YEN'S HUSBAND, Minh Long, was a stocky, balding forty-five-year-old chef-restaurateur with a square jaw, wide nose, and perpetual smile. He wore gold-rimmed spectacles, behind which his sparkly eyes revealed both mirth and worry. He had the assured, dignified manners of someone who had grown up in the service industry, someone whose face was always set inscrutably in a mask of hospitality. A third-generation restaurateur from a Hanoi culinary family, he had worked in every capacity in the family business, from scullery hand to sommelier to sous chef. Fifteen year earlier, when his father died, leaving the restaurant to his elder brother, Minh had decided to move south to seek his own fortune. He had traveled nearly the length of the country when, passing through Phan Thiet, a beautiful girl—a merchant's daughter—had caught his eye, and that, as he was fond of telling everyone, had been the end of his wanderings and the beginning of his good fortune.

Minh quickly changed the disk on the gramophone, choosing instead a Spanish guitar record the major liked. He rushed up the stairs to greet the officers in Japanese, swinging open the brass-trimmed double doors to a spacious wood-paneled room

with an elaborate screen, decorated with carved ivory tusks
and mother-of-pearl artifacts. He folded window shutters to let
in the cool evening breeze.

After seating the guests, he poured the first round of sake
and waited as they tossed back the rice wine. As usual, the
major announced that they would enjoy whatever the chef saw
fit to serve.

"Major, if I may, we just received a new shipment of wine
today. Some very special vintages. Would you like to see it?"

"Of course, that would be delightful!" Yamazaki brightened,
leaping out of his seat. Friday dinner at Kim Long was always
the highlight of his week. None of his men cared for wine, but
that never stopped him from enjoying his favorite drink.

Built with granite and marble quarried in Hoi An, the wine
cellar was one of the town's exclusive institutions, open to
only the wealthiest. It was a long, spacious chamber lined with
floor-to-ceiling racks of bottles, well appointed with leather
armchairs and a long counter made of wooden barrels. Kim
Long Cellar was also the foremost wine purveyor of the province. Five open crates of wine stood on the floor, with a row of
bottles lined up on the counter for inspection.

"These are the best of the lot. Some of them are peaking
now," said Minh, preparing the tasting glasses. He had been
trained by a top sommelier in Hanoi.

"I didn't know there are still shipments coming into port."

"A few here and there. Where there is demand, there is always
a supplier. My son bought these from dealers in Saigon."

"Bourgogne, thirty-three," Yamazaki read from a bottle of
pinot noir with a sailboat label.

"That's a lovely wine. Very rare."

"How much will it set me back?" Yamazaki asked with
mock trepidation.

"Tonight, not a single piaster, monsieur," Minh declared and
took the bottle from him. With a flourish, he broke the seal and

uncorked the bottle. "Compliments of the house for one of our most esteemed patrons and a true wine connoisseur."

Yamazaki put his nose to the glass and was in the vineyards of Bordeaux. He tasted berries, oak, nightshades, orange peel, and lavender. His mind flew back across the years to the one summer he had spent in the French countryside as a struggling artist. He sighed. "Oh, that is exceptional."

"Thank you, monsieur."

"You have a rare talent. I look forward to every meal here."

"Thank you for your kindness," said Minh with a deep bow. He continued, in a matter-of-fact tone. "Unfortunately, our restaurant will be shutting down by the end of the week, and I may be rotting in jail sooner than that."

Yamazaki frowned, taken aback, for he genuinely liked the man. He suspected Minh had brought him down here to share something important. "Here, let me pour you a glass. Drink up and tell me about it."

"Only if you insist, monsieur. I don't want to burden you with my problems," Minh said, taking the glass with an unsteady hand and quaffing it like water, his mind elsewhere. He braced himself against the counter. "You know my daughter Mai-Ly just turned sixteen. A smart girl with a good head for school. I'm very proud of her. She wants to go to university. It's a shame she's too pretty. Matchmakers are already calling about suitors. One dowager has made a particularly odious offer."

Yamazaki nodded. "Go on."

"Hmm . . . there is no civilized way to say this," Minh said in a tense voice. Massaging his temples, he moved his tongue from side to side in his mouth and cleared his throat, and finally, he blurted out, "Monsieur Gaspard Feraud has demanded my daughter. He wants her for a mistress, to turn her into one of his playthings."

"Can you refuse the swine?"

He answered with a pained smile, twisting the rag he was

holding. "If I don't deliver my daughter to him in three days, his underlings will shut down our restaurant. His police chief will arrest me on trumped-up charges. My family would be at his mercy. I can't . . . I just can't bear the thought of Mai-Ly in the hands of that monster."

"I've heard that Chief Leroux is Feraud's man."

Minh grimaced bitterly. "Feraud got Leroux that post. He is the town's baron. God knows he has ravished enough wives and daughters of so many poor municipal workers. He has fathered three half-Viet children, whom he won't acknowledge."

"Power and corruption go hand in hand."

"A truth as undeniable as the day, monsieur. Let me offer you three interesting facts. First, he is extremely wealthy. Second, he is a major financial backer of Free France. Third, I know where he keeps his fortune."

"This wine exudes a complex terroir," Yamazaki said, arching an eyebrow. He refilled both their glasses. "You have my full attention, monsieur."

Minh met Yamazaki's eyes squarely, dropping all pretense. "Forgive my boldness, Major. I am a desperate father. I have a proposal that can save my family and make you a very rich man."

6

Dinner

ON THE EVENING OF THE BIG EVENT, HA CAME HOME early with his boss, Supervisor Xuan, a wiry man in his late thirties with a scraggly beard that failed to hide a puckered scar from ear to jaw. He was of average height, browned chestnut by the sun. He had intelligent eyes, a flaring nose, and beautiful white teeth.

He greeted Coi and Tuyet warmly, giving them a jar of superb honey from the cliffs of the Central Highlands as he showered them with compliments. "This is a lovely shop. What a tidy little home you have here. You're a lucky man, Ha, to be living with these kind ladies."

"Thank you, Mister Xuan. I'm so happy you are his supervisor." Coi beamed, liking the stranger right away.

Two other guests arrived. Khinh, an acerbic seventy-five-year-old great-grandfather, was an elected neighborhood elder, known for his integrity. He had been one of the many thousands conscripted and sent to France during the Great War to serve Mother France. Lang was a middle-aged local labor leader who spoke passable French. He was a gregarious character and a successful fisherman.

The men moved the furniture and rolled out the dining mats while the women returned to their work in the kitchen at the rear of the house. Coi, Tuyet, and neighbor Sau were putting the finishing touches on the five-course meal. Coi and Tuyet had decided to hire Sau to help with the cooking, knowing that gossip about the evening would appear in more favorable light if the magpie was included in the festivities.

In the street, a large, respectful crowd had gathered to get a glimpse of the black sedan rolling up to the house. The crowd bowed as Major Yamazaki and Lieutenant Sakamoto, both in uniform, stepped from the vehicle. The Japanese returned the bow. Tuyet, Coi, and Ha greeted them at the door. Sakamoto presented Coi with flowers, a box of sweets, and five bottles of sake. Tuyet invited everyone inside as two soldiers stationed themselves at the front door.

Introductions were made and the men settled in a circle on the mat. Tuyet served the sake and retreated to the kitchen with Coi and Sau. The men praised the sake and thanked the major for his generosity. Delighted that everyone spoke French, Yamazaki asked Khinh about his experience in Europe during the Great War. Happy to hold court, Khinh had had decades of practice in retelling his stories. Conversation was lively, but as soon as the group discovered the one thing they all had in common, the talk shifted to fishing.

The women placed dishes on the dining mat. Tuyet described each course in detail for the guests: pork belly stewed with carrot, radish, and hard-boiled eggs in a caramel sauce with coconut water, with a side dish of pickled cabbage; tamarind sea bass soup with tomatoes, taro stems, and bean sprouts; stir-fried beef with pineapple, chilies, and onions; grilled aubergines simmered with garlic and chili; and shrimp salad rolls with a lime-chili sauce. The feast was received well by all, and the meal progressed easily under the warm glow of the kerosene lamps as dusk deepened into night.

A breeze came through the front door. Outside, the crowd dispersed. Children played hide-and-seek in the dark street, their singsong chants and laughter filling the air. Sated, the men fumbled with their tobacco.

"Will Japan liberate us from the French as well as the Chinese?" Xuan asked Yamazaki.

"I believe so, but it would be untrue to say imperial help comes without a price."

The men nodded at one another, appreciating his honesty. Xuan said, "I don't want to spoil this fine evening with politics. Let's go fishing when you have a day off. I'd like to hear your thoughts on some political ideas."

Yamazaki nodded. "Yes, thank you, I would enjoy that."

Lang added, "I have a good boat. Let me be your skipper!"

Tuyet brought out a pot of jasmine tea. Sau placed a platter of artfully carved fruits at the center of the mat. The major sipped his tea, looked at Tuyet, and nodded as though he knew she was waiting for the right moment.

Tuyet cleared her throat and announced, "I would like to thank everyone for coming tonight. As you already know, Major Yamazaki came last week to ask for my opinion about some civic matters."

The major said, "Two weeks ago, I saw her in the Permit Office lecturing a corrupt clerk. I was impressed with her courage and wanted to ask her some questions."

Tuyet continued, "I'm flattered, but I am not comfortable speaking with him. I do not want my neighbors to have the wrong idea, so I'm introducing him to you, the community leaders. You can be more helpful to him than I."

The men squirmed, realizing belatedly the real purpose of the meal. The major's face was unreadable.

"My family and I are from Hanoi. We came here without friends or family. These kind people welcomed us. Without their goodwill, we would not have a life here," she said and paused, feeling both grateful and exposed in equal measure.

Khinh and Lang nodded in agreement. Xuan agreed sagely as though he was one of her close neighbors.

"A woman meeting with a Japanese officer would start ugly rumors. She would be shunned by her neighbors. This could make life very uncomfortable for her," she said. "As for myself, I am recently divorced, so I have an aversion to men in general."

Khinh looked as if a fish bone was lodged in his throat. Lang examined the bottom of his teacup. Sakamoto, a stoic, sat perfectly still. Ha smiled awkwardly. The major gave the slightest nod as though acknowledging her without conceding anything.

Yamazaki said, "I beg your forgiveness. It was not my intention to create difficulties. I withdraw my request." He gestured to the others. "I will seek the opinions of these men instead. However, as you are also a shopkeeper, I have decided that I will come here as a customer. I don't see any harm in that. No one can fault a shopkeeper for selling goods to a customer, Viet, French, or Japanese. Don't you agree?" He fixed his eyes on the men. "I'm confident that as upstanding men of your community, your opinions are respected by all."

Khinh and Lang exchanged wary glances, sensing a trap. The elder one nodded and the younger one shook his head. Then they changed parts. Finally, they corrected themselves and bobbed their heads in unison.

Sau muttered to Coi, "Those fools are going to snap their heads clean off, jerking it every which way like that."

Xuan said, "That sounds fair and logical to me. I suggest the neighborhood elders encourage the local folks to be more understanding."

Yamazaki grinned broadly. "Excellent. The matter is settled then. Let me buy some supplies here."

Tuyet said, "Major, that's really not necessary. Our shop is tiny; we don't have much to offer."

"That is for the customer to decide. Now, I thank you for your hospitality and for this delicious meal. I have enjoyed this evening with all of you."

He rose to leave, and everyone stood up. Bows and thanks were exchanged. Flustered, Tuyet escorted the officers to their car. Outside, the major turned to her and said with a wink, "This public supper was a brilliant idea. Now the burden of propriety is on them. Well done!"

Tuyet's mouth dropped open. Speechless, she watched the

Japanese drive off. She didn't know what to make of the evening, but she was impressed at how relaxed and easy Yamazaki had been sharing a peasant meal with commoners. There was something worldly about the major. Whatever else, she did not sense meanness in him.

"HEAVEN AND EARTH!" Sau flapped her hands at the ceiling and snorted. "What a thick-skinned devil! I wouldn't have believed it if I hadn't seen it myself. Shameless!"

Lang shrugged. "When you're the boss, who is going to shame you?"

Coi wrung her hands. "What are we going to do now?"

Face beet-red from the wine, Khinh motioned for Lang to help him to his feet. "Let's not worry. We know you did everything you could. You can't be blamed for his attitude. But, for what it's worth, he seems like a decent fellow. I don't think he'll try anything unkind."

Lang added, "Mister Xuan and I will take him fishing and talk some sense into him."

Khinh left, supported by Lang and Xuan on either side. Coi paid Sau for her help, handing her a bar of lavender soap and a share of the food to take home. With the guests gone, they closed up the front of the house. Exhausted, Coi, Ha, and Tuyet lay down on the dining mat.

Coi asked her son, "Your friend Xuan has a northern accent. Where is his birth-village?"

"Ninh Binh."

Tuyet said, "Your supervisor came just to connect with the major."

Ha shrugged. "It will be useful to have someone like him to advise the major."

Tuyet shook her head. "There is something shady about him.

Is he working for the communists, the nationalists, or those religious nuts, the Hoa Hao?"

It was a chaotic time. Groups changed names and affiliations constantly, joining forces and splintering just as easily. The French, whom the Viet had accepted as invincible and nearly as untouchable as demigods, were now kowtowing, fearful of the Japanese, who behaved like the tyrannical Viet nobles. All the factions were throwing their support to one side or the other.

Ha replied in a conciliatory way, "Xuan is a respected member of the Viet Resistance."

Tuyet said, "Please don't bring strangers to the house again. I don't want people to think that we're involved with any group."

"Oh, sister, there you go again, being an old-fashioned northerner, suspicious and inhospitable."

Tuyet did not reply. It was unwise to look too far ahead. The patterns were only beginning to form, but she sensed an aura around Ha, Xuan, and Yamazaki, as if their destinies would be linked for better or for worse.

7

Coup

A VIOLET HAZE FILLED THE PREDAWN SKY. MAJOR Yamazaki's black sedan swung onto the main road, followed by a jeep and a covered truck with a squad of soldiers. Behind the convoy, a long hedge of fog-like dust hung in the still air. Muted shadows crept along the fields. The main highway, an obsidian marvel of colonial engineering, stretched straight through the sparsely inhabited country. Not a single motor vehicle in sight. Peasants were trekking into town on foot, bicycles, and oxen carts laden with corn, watermelons, and pineapples. Along the side of the road, women shouldered yoke-baskets full of produce, walking as though on invisible legs, their dark trousers melding seamlessly into the twilight, their bluish-white tunics floated ghost-like in the indigo air. They moved at a brisk pace, a cadence of steps matching the sway of their loads to ease the weight. All around, harvested paddies were dotted with scraggly clumps of trees and hardy palms. A low range of dark green mountains loomed far to the west. The fresh morning air was laced with a thread of brininess from the sea, hidden behind a low rise of land to the east. Closer to town, rows of shacks and bungalows lined the road.

The convoy passed the south gate and continued along the main road through the residential areas where smoke from cooking fires had begun to rise. By the fish sauce factories, a cloying odor of salt and decomposing fish hung in the air. The motorcade passed the town market, unnoticed by vendors setting up their stalls, to continue north onto the metal bridge across the greenish-brown river bisecting the town. It formed a natural boundary between poor and rich, commercial and governmental, indigenous and colonialists. Poverty and labor to the south, wealth and power to the north, the way the wind blew, so to speak. The only working-class district on the north side was home to roughly a hundred French nationals, retirees, teachers, merchants, sailors, and soldiers. The convoy went down a wide road with provincial offices and turned onto a tree-lined avenue of stately villas, the grandest of which was the Feraud mansion at the end of the street, a white forty-window rectangle, embellished with columns, iron railings, and a gabled roof.

The sentry in the guard box was encouraged at gunpoint to swing open the gates, and the cars drove slowly up the gravel path to the white mansion at the top of the rise. Lieutenant Sakamoto ordered the detachment from the truck. They fanned out, moving through the flower garden. In neighboring properties, dogs barked. As the major's sedan stopped in front of the manor house, a gray-haired servant came out and, beholding the soldiers, shrieked. A trooper punched him in the mouth and frog-marched him back inside by the scruff of his neck.

Yamazaki lit a tobacco pipe at the top of the steps while his men swept through the mansion, kicking doors as they checked the rooms. Sounds of furniture being overturned. A woman screamed. Someone cursed in French. Two sharp pistol reports. Moments later, Sakamoto exited the house, saluted, and informed Yamazaki that a bodyguard had been wounded. They had gathered the servants in the main room and found Feraud in his bedroom. Yamazaki ordered Sakamoto to fetch the medic for the wounded man and to take Feraud to the main sitting room.

Meanwhile, Yamazaki ambled about in the marbled foyer, inspecting the armchairs, the sofas upholstered in red velvet, the Persian carpets, the gilded mirrors, potted ferns, a marble sculpture of a girl, and a magnificent crystal chandelier. It brought to mind an upscale Parisian brothel.

Yamazaki and Sakamoto followed the hallway to the storage room next to the kitchen. There, Yamazaki checked Minh's hand-drawn map of the mansion. The access to the cellar was hidden within a walk-in closet. Sakamoto kicked in the door and switched on the lights. The two men descended a flight of creaky wooden stairs. The cellar was a long, whitewashed chamber, six by twelve meters, cool and dry as the house sat on a rise with good drainage. Cabinets and wine racks lined the walls. They discovered several crates of rifles and pistols, metal boxes of ammunition, cases of wine and liquors, a comfortable pair of leather chairs, and a desk with a shortwave radio. Yamazaki walked over to a large painting of a matador with a bull and took it down to reveal a steel safe built into the wall. Everything was exactly as Minh had described it. Yamazaki grinned, confident about the contents of the safe.

As YAMAZAKI and Sakamoto strolled into the main sitting room, Feraud bellowed in his gravelly voice, "Major Yamazaki! What's the meaning of this?" He was seated in his undershorts with his bathrobe open, in an armchair by a long table, flanked by four soldiers.

"Monsieur Gaspard Feraud," Major Yamazaki intoned. "You are detained under suspicion of conspiracy against the Imperial Japanese Army."

Feraud jumped to his feet, face flushed with outrage. "Are you mad? You invaded my home in direct violation of the agreements of our governments!"

Soldiers forced him back into his place and bound his wrists to the back of the chair. Glaring at the Japanese, Feraud slouched, his belly protruding like a stuffed leather sack.

The major studied the Frenchman with a long, searching look. At the beginning of the occupation, he had met this Frenchman and several of his colleagues at a formal function.

He remembered noting the man's arrogance. Yamazaki said, "Monsieur Feraud, my apologies for the intrusion. You have a safe in your wine cellar. I need to see its contents, so you will have to open it for me."

Feraud gasped. "How . . . how do you know about that?"

"It's not important."

"I have not done anything wrong. I demand to see the chief of police."

"Your pet Leroux is useless here."

"This invasion is unlawful."

"That depends."

"On what?"

"On what is in the safe. If I find proof that you are a Free France organizer, I will seize the contents of your safe. If I find no such evidence, then I will offer my apologies and we will leave you as you are. No harm done."

"Go to hell!"

The major did not reply. Scratching his big nose, he strolled about the spacious room, perusing the library and the array of artwork. The sun was rising in the trees outside the window. He stopped in front of a large painting and inspected the somber scene of an exquisitely detailed schooner, running with billowing sails, crashing through frothy waves beneath coils of thunderclouds.

Looking back from across the room, he said, "With some effort, my men can open your safe. No doubt about that. However, as proof of your innocence, I would prefer that you open it willingly."

Feraud retorted, "You take me for an idiot?"

"One that needs to be persuaded," Yamazaki said and nodded at his lieutenant.

Sakamoto threw a short hook, knocking Feraud's head sideways. Feraud coughed. Blood trickled from his nose. He cursed and spat. Sakamoto wiped the spittle from his face with a handkerchief. Next, he landed a quick combination on Feraud's head. He took a step back, reviewing his handiwork, then landed another flurry at the man's mouth and eyes. Blood ran down Feraud's chin onto his neck and chest. Sakamoto paused to wipe his knuckles.

Left eye swelling, Feraud chuckled. "What a champ! Untie my hands. I'll show you how to punch, you miserable midget!"

"You are too tough for your own good, monsieur," Yamazaki said, dismissing Sakamoto. "Let me introduce you to our interrogator, Lieutenant Kitamura."

A slight officer stepped forward and saluted. He was a soft-spoken man, small in stature with slender hands like a woman's. He had a long, sad face with narrowly set eyes and tiny, sharp teeth. He gave an order. Soldiers yanked Feraud to his feet, stripped off his bathrobe, and flipped him, belly up, onto the table, handling the big man like a side of pork. They spread-eagle roped his wrists and ankles to the table legs.

Wheezing, Feraud growled and jerked against the restraints. Out of breath, he froze, overcome with disbelief.

"I'm a French citizen. You can't do this to me!" Feraud rasped, craning his head to see soldiers setting up a kerosene burner and readying a kettle. His hair rose at the nape of his neck. Sweat streamed down his face.

Kitamura stood over the Frenchman, distaste rippling across his face. His nose twitched. The Frenchman reeked of musky cologne, tobacco, alcohol, sour milk, and perspiration. He took a knife and quickly cut off Feraud's undershorts, leaving him naked. Kitamura picked up the now boiling kettle.

Yamazaki spun on his heel and said over his shoulder, "Just let him know when you've had enough."

"Damn you son of a bitch! You dirty dog. Who do you think you are? You slit-eyed shit picker, you have no idea who I am. You're not going to get away with this."

With a soft sigh of disapproval, Kitamura poured scalding water on Feraud's mouth, but the Frenchman turned his head, so it splashed instead on the side of his face and neck. He howled and convulsed so violently that the table rattled beneath him.

The major strode briskly through the door. Blood-curdling shrieks followed him down the hallway. He saw torture as routine in warfare but lacked the stomach for gore, and he didn't want his subordinates to notice this weakness.

THE FRENCHMAN broke within half an hour, emptying both bowel and bladder. The malodorous mess dribbled off the table, splattered the soldiers' boots, making it unpleasant for everyone. Boiling water was rarely employed in interrogation because it rendered the skin unusable for repeated application, but Kitamura faced two considerations: time constraint and his own desire to inflict long-lasting agony. There was a very good chance the wounds would become infected and cause protracted suffering and even permanent damage.

The handcuffed Feraud took a few wobbly steps and crumpled to the floor, his doughy face a knot of agony. Two soldiers lifted him to his feet and helped him into the corridor. Stark naked, Feraud stumbled on discolored legs and swollen feet, his huge gut hanging low, hiding his ruined manhood. He yelped as they forced him roughly down into the basement.

"He soiled himself," Kitamura said apologetically to his commander.

"Proceed," Yamazaki grunted, averting his face.

Feraud waddled bow-legged, wincing at every step. The skin on his calves, thighs, and crotch had blistered and turned bright red. One of his eyes had closed completely, swollen like a ripe fig. His face was dripping sweat, snot, and tears. Bracing himself against the safe, he turned the combination wheel with trembling fingers and pulled open the heavy door.

Yamazaki looked at the safe's contents and nodded his satisfaction. He picked up one of the heavy leather ledgers on the upper shelf of the safe and flipped through the pages. "I will need to question you about these accounts, but first, my men will take you to the washroom."

8

Petits Blancs

WHEN EVERYONE HAD CLEARED OUT OF THE CEL-
lar, Yamazaki filled a leather bag he had found with the safe's
ledgers, documents, bundles of cash in large denominations,
and a small gem box with several dozen diamonds, rubies, and
emeralds. Rows of red silk sachets were stacked neatly on the
two bottom shelves. He picked up one, pulled the drawstring,
and shook the contents into his palm: five thin gold slabs, each
weighing two hundred grams, a kilo per pouch. He ran his
hand over the magnificent hoard, whistling under his breath,
then put ten kilos of gold in the bag. Poking around the cellar,
he found a sturdy wooden crate. A tingling sensation rushed
over him as he was packing the gold hoard. The enormity of
the fortune dumbfounded him. All his dreams seemed to be
about to come true—the life he was meant to live when the war
was over. The vision was surreal and intoxicating.

The dream was his for the taking and so he took it—a simple decision that did not jar his moral compass. Capturing the
enemy's war chest was his duty. Claiming a healthy portion of
the loot for himself was his right. It was standard practice to
take one's cut before sending the loot up the food chain. First,
take plenty but not too much so as not to draw suspicion. Second, share the bounty generously with the subordinates to keep
them quiet. Third, hide one's share well.

THE UNMISTAKABLE crack of a carbine shot came from
above, followed by a commotion of shouts and heavy boots.

Yamazaki hurriedly bagged the gold but had to stop when Lieutenant Mori came thumping down the stairs to announce that French troops had arrived. He grabbed the leather bag and lugged it upstairs, where he ordered two men to guard the cellar entrance. Sakamoto ran down the hallway, following Yamazaki into the foyer.

"The prisoner escaped, sir!" Sakamoto reported. "We left him alone to use the toilet. He escaped through a hidden door. We are chasing him to the creek behind the property."

Yamazaki cursed.

"This is my mistake, sir. I take full responsibility," Sakamoto said and bowed, face ashen. "I request to stand down and accept my punishment, sir."

"No, denied. I ordered his toilet break."

"I'll send a search."

Yamazaki paused and scratched his nose, looking out the window at French troops who had surrounded the mansion. "No, call them back. Let him go. The cavalry just arrived. If we catch him now, we'll force them into a fight. I don't want this to escalate into a major incident. We got what we came for."

"Yes, sir!"

Yamazaki put the bag on a side table and strode out the front door.

A squad of French troops and local gendarmes had taken up positions behind the trees. Their four vehicles were parked on the driveway thirty meters in front of the mansion. He spotted Captain Moreau of the town garrison, a slim soldier in an untidy uniform standing behind a sedan with portly Police Chief Leroux, who was an unmistakable figure in a white linen suit. On either side of Yamazaki, his men had taken defensive positions around the building.

Leroux shouted, "Major Yamazaki! I demand you release Monsieur Feraud immediately."

"Good morning! Your boss just escaped out the back. If you want him, you'd better find him before my men do."

"You expect me to believe that?"

"Come inside, have a look. He fled through a hidden door in the bathroom."

Leroux paused, said something to Moreau, and climbed into the passenger seat of the sedan, which roared off straight across the lawn, through the flower garden, around the side of the building.

Yamazaki ordered his men to stand down. Moreau did the same.

"Captain Moreau, please come inside. I need to show you something."

Moreau hesitated, then ordered his men to wait.

THEY WENT TO the dining room. Moreau slouched over to the bar and helped himself to a whiskey lowball. Streaks of sunlight fell on the long mahogany table, dividing it crosswise into alternating bright and shadowed sections. They sat across from each other and fussed with their tobacco—Moreau his cigarette, Yamazaki his pipe. They smoked in deliberate silence.

"You on your side of town, I on mine. I thought we were doing so well, Major," Moreau said, sipping his drink. Completely bald and clean shaven, he was in his late thirties but moved and talked like an old man.

"Little has changed, Captain. From where I'm sitting, it's a fine day. I have proof that the owner of this mansion is a Free France financier and organizer," he said. When Moreau did not respond, Yamazaki took the leather ledger from the satchel and placed it on the table between them. "I think you might recognize many names in this book, including your own."

"Is that surprising?" Moreau asked, the smile draining from his gaunt face.

"Not particularly. You have never struck me as a Vichy sympathizer."

"I'm not. I've given blood and sweat for my country," he replied in a level tone, devoid of bravado or passion. His melancholy gray eyes were deep-set in a weathered face with lines carved by years of war in Algeria. After several long, languid drags on his cigarette, he asked, "What do you want me to do?"

"Nothing. Do absolutely nothing."

Moreau paused and raised an eyebrow, tossing back his whiskey as he digested the implication. "How are you going to deal with Chief Leroux?"

"I'm not. Leroux has a handful of deputies, but against me, he is as helpless as his boss."

"Are you going after Feraud?"

Yamazaki inspected his fingernails. "No, that's a tedious task I will leave to the Kempeitai."

"What about the ledger?"

"It will disappear. It's my insurance to make sure that everyone in this ledger behaves," Yamazaki said with an easy smile. "There is other evidence I could turn over to the Vichy authorities and the Kempeitai."

"How do I know you won't do that later?"

"You don't know our secret police very well, do you?" Yamazaki chuckled dryly. "The Kempeitai are nasty bastards. I don't want them rooting around in this town. They will ruin everything. This is the only decent post I've had after years in the trenches, and I intend to enjoy it in peace until this war is over, one way or another."

A roguish smile crept across Moreau's nicotine-stained lips. "We do have something in common, you and I."

"I believe so." Yamazaki nodded in agreement.

He knew Moreau was in a devoted domestic relationship with a Viet woman and their two children—a social taboo that defied the colonial hierarchy. The brass had planted him in this backwater with no chance of promotion. Moreau was one of Indochina's *petits blancs*, too poor to return to France, incapable of gathering wealth in the colony, doomed to labor and bleed for the empire. The captain was like one of those embittered veterans, his fighting days behind him.

"I like peace and quiet," said Moreau.

"Then simply do nothing."

Yamazaki withdrew a red silk sachet from his pocket, shook the gold slabs into his hand, admired them a moment, then put them back into the pouch. One by one, he took four more sachets from the leather bag and stacked them on the table—five kilos of gold.

"I've never liked Feraud," admitted Moreau.

Yamazaki pushed the heavy stack across the table. "Now you have five more reasons to dislike him."

9

Treasure

THE SEVEN-YEAR-OLD KAWASAKI KI-10 BIPLANE
climbed toward dawn. In the open cockpit, Major Yamazaki
Takeshi banked away from the airstrip toward the sea. Sunlight glinted off his goggles, the white scarf around his neck
whipping in the propeller wash, the wind balmy, like feathers
on the skin. He inhaled the morning air and was back in his
element. On his starboard, the crown of the sun was peeking
over the dark rim of the ocean. Below, the fields were still partially shrouded in shadow, even as the western foothills were
afire at first light. Wings of white herons lifted off a pond to
glide over the green expanse of coconut palms. High above,
dawn streaked the clouds with hues of gold and cayenne.

He followed the coastline northward, cruising at three hundred meters over a fleet of fishing skiffs. Several boats with
motors dragged white ribbons across the satin water. On the
wide beach, teams of village women and children were hauling long nets ashore. Closer in to town, fruit tree foliage grew
dense, partially hiding thatched dwellings as within the town
gate, the houses had tiled roofs, gray with dried moss. Larger
buildings stood crowded together in the town center. Around
the main market were two-storied shops. In the better neighborhoods with tree-lined avenues, white and yellow villas were
covered with terra-cotta roofs. A group of four large buildings
belonged to the Catholic church, the longest rectangular structure a school run by the nuns. Along the water, dense, organized rows of round fermenting jars, like sand balls hocked

up by tiny beach crabs. Here and there, among the greenery, spiderweb plumes of smoke rose from small fires.

The winding river was at the year's shallowest. Beyond the old lighthouse, the shoreline curved east, swinging the sun into Takeshi's eyes. He climbed, pulling the nose up just enough to block the glare. Over the coconut palms of Mui Ne village, he turned north, crossed the stubby peninsula, and continued up the open coast. A patchwork of dull green, grass brown, and dusty copper rocks stretched far and flat across an arid tableland that sloped down almost imperceptibly to the dunes-edged sea.

For the rush, he took a deep breath and looped the biplane. Slamming the throttle forward as he hauled back on the stick, Takeshi climbed as high as the old bird could go, stalled, and then kicked over into a roll and dived toward the beach, skimming the treetops, then skipped his wheels across the hard sand.

The main Saigon base was merely a hundred and forty kilometers to the southeast from his position, and the next airstrip was only two hundred kilometers to the north. Short enough distances to make his current base irrelevant from an operational standpoint. Fortunately, the Imperial Air Service had declared Indochina a no-fly zone and had enforced this rule by seizing control of all airports. Sheer luck had landed Takeshi in Phan Thiet, one of the dozens scattered along the serpentine country with a three-thousand-kilometer coastline.

He flew over six fishermen's huts, continuing a few kilometers along the coast to the halfway point to a settlement to the north. The land was scrubby, with low bushes and a few gnarled trees, scant vegetation for grazing. Circling twice, he verified that the area was deserted: no cattle, no herders, no clam diggers. On the flat sea, not a single vessel in sight. In months of flying over this area, he had never seen anyone near the desolate bluff that rose thirty meters above the beach. It was devoid of trails or any sign of human activity. Near the top of the bluff, there was a depression, a small hollow, hidden from view in all directions, no line of sight to the ocean nor the mountain. A person might work for hours without fear of being observed from afar.

HE MADE a third wide sweep of the area, flying low, nearly at stall speed, for a final close look. Satisfied that he was the only human here, he put the plane down gently on the hard sand near the end of the beach and killed the engine. He traded his goggles for a brown fedora and grabbed a short shovel, a metal toolbox, and a rucksack. Trudging through the sand, he made his way inland through thorn scrubs and took the easiest route up a rocky slope. The rucksack and the box were heavy with gold, and he had to rest a dozen times before reaching the top of the bluff.

His initial impulse had been to bury the hoard in the mountains, but the physical difficulties of getting in and out of the forest had been daunting. Moreover, he likely would have picked up a tail regardless of any precautions. The jungle sheltered unseen inhabitants, hunters, trappers, bandits, and renegades. That set him to thinking about burying the gold somewhere accessible, near the airstrip. He quickly ruled out this idea because at the base, there were too many eyes. The most worrisome detail was how long his command here might last. Easy posts such as this one were often poached by sons or nephews of generals. Reassignment could come at any time, without warning. After much thought, he decided that the gold had to be buried in a remote place with more than one route of access. Although he had given half of the gold to his superiors and shared a good portion with his men, he still worried that the Kempeitai might come looking for his treasure. He decided to keep some of the gold and hide most of it. He hoped he had enough to bribe the brass if they were ever tempted to give his post to someone else. Luck had put him in Phan Thiet; gold might keep him there.

He climbed to the top of the largest boulder, which had a long crack splitting a meter down its face. Through a notch formed by the crack, he sighted the highest knoll, two kilometers to the west, fixed the direction of his compass, and rigged up a guideline with metal stakes. He measured out twenty meters along the cord and marked the spot. As a backup, he triangulated the spot using his compass. A few numbers, simple, easy to remember. He did not want to rely on a map, which could be lost or stolen. He expected to retrieve his treasure in a year or two after the war was over.

Shedding his flight jacket, he started digging. In fifteen minutes, he had a knee-deep hole, and he was sweating through his shirt. He wanted to go deeper but struck a rocky layer. He placed the gold-filled toolbox into the hole, opened the lid, and added all the gold sachets from the rucksack plus a pouch of gems. He knelt and looked down on the fortune in the ground. It meant a sum that could buy a modest man like himself a lifetime of luxury. He would never need to work again.

Since the first day he had been drafted, six years earlier, he had hoped for little more than survival. After nearly dying in battle, he now saw life passing by without giving him what made it all worthwhile: love, family, fatherhood. He also knew, from his months in the rehab ward, the misery of living with a crippled body. Whether or not the empire would be victorious at the end of this infernal war, he was certain that it would be dog-eat-dog for veterans trying to earn a livelihood when it was all over, let alone support a family. There was a fate worse than death.

Anxiety, doubt, and happiness coalesced in his mind. He dug into his breast pocket for a notebook, scribbled some lines, tore off the page, and placed it on top of the stacks of gold slabs.

> *seeds of gold to earth,*
> *all hopes and fears but a dream*
> *what will be will be*

Smiling at his schoolboy effort but pleased nevertheless, he closed the lid, shoveled a little dirt over the box, put a large rock on it, and filled in the rest. He tamped the soil down and placed an oval stone over the spot, knowing that the earth would compress a little after rain. The stone would mask any subsequent depression. Using a branch, he brushed away all traces of his labor and footsteps, then gathered his belongings, retreated to the boulder, and surveyed his surroundings. Walking along the cliff, he found the section that had a shallow landing, a flat stone slab, jutting out two meters below the edge. It was a shorter but more treacherous route down to the beach. He lowered himself to the slab and from there began to descend, scrabbling among the boulders. At the bottom, he walked around the foot of the bluff back to his biplane. The sun was climbing as he glanced at his watch. The ground crew would be expecting him back soon.

10

Water Cart

THE DAY WAS HOT AND GRITTY. TUYET STOOD AT her front door, squinting down the street against the afternoon glare. She took a handkerchief from the waist pocket of her blue work shirt and dabbed perspiration from her nose and forehead. Her lips were chapped. What would she give for a burst of rain! They had long drunk the last of their precious rainwater and had depended on the water cart for more than a month. Although a meter of brackish water still remained at the bottom of the well, it was only good for washing and even then, the water left an unpleasant chalky residue. Much of Phan Thiet was in a depression. It had been a marshland before the ocean receded. Its groundwater bore traces of the sea. Every home had large tanks to collect rainwater. During the dry season, those who could afford it bought water from wells outside town.

"You see him yet?" Sau, the portly magpie neighbor, squawked from her hammock next door. "Do you want to split a block of ice? I can send my boys down to the ice factory."

"Thirsty for a cold lemonade?"

"You bet! I've got the best lemon tree in the neighborhood, and you've got the Japanese's white sugar. We can work together, eh?"

Tuyet smiled. With Sau, it was never an equal trade. "I wonder what is taking Mister Binh so long."

A commotion at the far end of the street. Little boys ran from house to house, bearing news. People came outside, craning their necks, talking about an accident. Tuyet stopped one of the neighborhood kids: Binh's water cart had been hit by a truck on the main road.

Coi handed Tuyet their first-aid basket and said, "You'd better go and have a look. You too, Sau. You're a midwife. I'll mind the shops."

TUYET AND SAU grabbed their hats and hurried down the street, keeping to the shaded side with a throng of curious neighbors going in the same direction. Two turns down a side street brought them out to the main road where a large crowd had gathered, packed four deep around the overturned cart. The ox was still entangled in the yoke, one hind leg skewed at an unnatural angle, its bloody entrails spilling out in coils on the dirt. It was bellowing in agony, thrashing about, slamming its horns into the ground, maddened by pain. Bystanders were calling for the beast to be put out of its misery. A woman told them that Binh and his grandson had stopped the cart by the side of the road to deliver water to a customer. A military truck had swerved to avoid some dogs and had accidentally hit the ox. The driver, a Viet soldier, had stopped briefly, then driven off without further ado.

Tuyet and Sau pushed their way through the crowd to Binh, who was on the ground, grasping his ankle. His teenage grandson was frantically trying to help the ox. Sau had people move Binh farther from the overturned cart and was probing him for broken bones.

"Nippon! Nippon!" the children shouted.

The crowd parted as the black sedan pulled up. The crowd shuffled, moved back, forming a wide circle. Major Yamazaki and his adjutant stepped out.

"Oy! Isn't that your Japanese friend?" Sau asked.

Tuyet glared at her. Sau didn't notice.

The major greeted them. Tuyet explained the situation, saying that Binh wanted to end the animal's suffering. Yamazaki nodded and gave an order. The adjutant drew his pistol, stepped up to the thrashing animal. Two shots into the ox's skull and it was over. The crowd heaved a sigh of relief.

Binh's grandson sobbed over the ox for it had been his companion since childhood, the only inheritance his parents had left him. Binh wailed that his poor family would now starve. Tuyet told Yamazaki that Binh had lost his only son and daughter-in-law a few years earlier in a building site accident. He lived with his wife and their two grandchildren, this teenage boy and his younger sister. Binh had a small farm outside town with a freshwater well. In the planting season, the ox pulled his plow; in the dry season, his water cart. Losing the ox was a disaster for the family.

Yamazaki sighed. "This is a very unfortunate situation. Tell him that the Japanese army would like to purchase this ox. We will pay him enough to buy another animal. As a goodwill gesture, we will pay to have his cart repaired."

Tuyet glanced at the major, surprised by his generosity. She bowed and translated what had been said. Binh was stupefied, so she had to repeat the offer. The old man was beside himself with gratitude and started kowtowing to the major, touching his boots.

Kneeling down, Yamazaki touched the old man's shoulder and shook his head. To Tuyet, he said, "Tell him, no thanks needed. Your karma has found you."

She translated and the words passed through the crowd with a ripple of approval. Elder Khinh arrived and Yamazaki greeted the old man with the proper measure of respect as he asked Khinh to help Binh find another ox for his cart and set a fair price. The meat of the ox should be given to the neighbors and the town's orphanage. The major took a thick stack of bills from his adjutant and handed it to Khinh. Words of gratitude were exchanged. Impressed by the dignified air of ceremony, the crowd bowed to the major, who bowed in return. Tuyet was speechless, for she had never seen such a thing before.

Yamazaki thanked Tuyet and Elder Khinh and drove off in his sedan. The people smiled and waved as the car pulled away. Tuyet told a rickshaw man to take Binh and his grandson to the hospital. Elder Khinh had some men see to the ox and the cart. There was much praise for the Japanese and the unexpected outcome. Every family in the neighborhood would have meat on the table that evening.

A dust devil swirled in the street. Tuyet shielded her face and hurried home, leaving Sau to supervise the butchering of the ox. Her mouth was dry, her throat parched, but her shirt was drenched in sweat from standing in the hot sun. As she passed a tailor's storefront, she caught herself smiling in a mirror. She had been moved by the way the major had handled the situation.

SEVERAL DAYS after the accident, Major Yamazaki sauntered into her shop, dressed in field khakis. He chatted amiably as though he had already forgotten about the accident. Tuyet was feeling a little cross for having had to wait so long for him to turn up. He bought some cigarettes and a whole jar of hard candy displayed on the counter, which he then passed out to the children who had become quite friendly with him.

Tuyet gave him an envelope. "Here is the money left over from the purchase of the ox and the repair of the cart. Elder Khinh negotiated a good deal for another ox for Mister Binh."

"Please donate the money to the orphanage on my behalf."

She smiled. "That's very kind. Thank you."

"Not at all. It's self-serving. I'm trying to impress you."

She made a face. "I see that the truck driver who hit the ox is now working for Mister Binh. Did you have anything to do with that?"

"I had a little talk with Captain Moreau. We thought it was a fair arrangement until the old man's leg is healed."

Tuyet said, "Captain Moreau. I know his wife. She's a beautiful woman from Hue. They have two children."

"I have not met his wife, so I cannot comment on her beauty," he replied with a playful grin. "Would you say she's even more beautiful than you?"

She rolled her eyes, refusing the bait. "Well, your generosity earned the respect of the townsfolk," she replied and lowered her head.

He dismissed it with a wave of his hand. "You translated. I wouldn't have known what to do without you. Your French is excellent."

"Thank you. I'm a little rusty. You speak it almost like the French."

"A couple of years in any country will give anyone the language," he replied with a shrug. "Did you learn French in school?"

"It's a required subject from primary school through secondary. My French could have been much better if I'd completed my studies."

"What happened?"

"It's a long story."

"Go on, please, if you don't mind. We have time."

"I'll give you the short version," she said resignedly. "My father died when I was eight years old. My paternal grandparents took me from my mother because they were rich, and she was poor. My uncle became my guardian and I lived in his household for ten years. He arranged for me to marry one of his business associates without my knowledge. I couldn't go through with it. I was already involved with someone else. My uncle disowned me, so I had to drop out of school. Young, broke, and homeless, I eloped with my boyfriend. We moved south to build a new life in Saigon."

"You must have loved him very much."

"First love."

"First love can sometimes chart the trajectory of a lifetime."

"I was just a foolish eighteen-year-old."

"Who has not been foolish at that age? It's one of the few privileges of youth."

"Hmm." Tuyet canted her head, a little smile coming to her face. "What foolishness did you get up to in your youth?"

"Let me save that story for another time," he said with a wink and rose to leave. "Right now, I'm trying to impress you."

Tuyet laughed quietly, shaking her head at his back.

After the sedan had driven off, Coi emerged from the bedroom. "What was all that about? And why are you smiling?"

"Nothing."

"Don't tell me. You're enjoying these visits."

"I don't know. He's unusual, in a rather weird way."

Coi understood Tuyet's unease. She had heard whispers in the neighborhood. Some people were becoming jealous and suspicious. Others were urging her niece to wheedle favors from the major. The path ahead was narrowing, perhaps too quickly for her niece to make up her mind.

They went into the bedroom and sat on the divan where Anh was sleeping. Tuyet kept an eye on the store through the open doorway. Her daughter woke from her nap, crawled into Tuyet's lap, and was at once fast asleep again. Coi put her hand over Tuyet's. The afternoon heat was stifling. In the corner of the room, entangled in a web, a fly buzzed violently. Anh jerked in her sleep, her arms flailing. Tuyet hummed the one melody she knew best, the one her mother had sung to her:

Mother brought you a fish, but you were sleeping
The old cat ate it, the skinny cat was beaten
The little cat got blamed, the crow lost his tail.
The bamboo pole has notches, the grasshopper has legs
My child was sleepy.

PART II

Courtship

⌐ 1942 ⌐

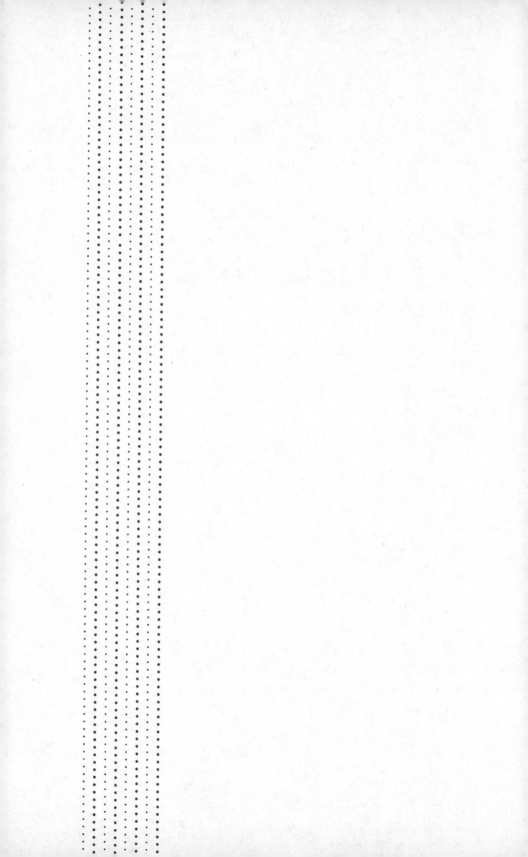

11

Mui Ne

A DAY OF MANIC BRIGHTNESS. FEATHERY CLOUDS fanned across the sky. Gulls wheeled above a flat blue sea. Ripples fluttered on the beach, chased by quick-footed sandpipers. Colossal dunes gleamed white in the afternoon sun, swollen undulations as far as the eye could see. The air was dry, with a pristine clarity that revealed the long, uninterrupted curve of the desolate beach to its scimitar tip five kilometers away.

A squad of Japanese was pitching a canvas pavilion on the beach. Cheerful soldiers in white undershirts bustled about with hand towels wrapped around their heads. Some were hauling baskets, food crates, and kitchen implements from the trucks. In the makeshift kitchen behind the white tent, Tuyet and Coi were busy around trestle tables, prepping fish, squids, shrimps, shellfish, and vegetables with two Japanese cooks. Little Anh watched a young male assistant stirring a large iron pan over an open fire. Along the shore, Ha and Second Lieutenant Ishigara were swimming, barely popping their heads out of the water.

The major and Lieutenant Mori were galloping their horses along the beach, exploring the coastline. Yamazaki wore a brown fedora, white short sleeves, and pleated trousers. The older Mori surprised everyone with his American Western regalia, replete with a ten-gallon hat, vest, denim jeans, leather chaps, and cowboy boots. They drew up next to Lieutenant Sakamoto, who was casting a line from the beach with his long bamboo fishing pole. Yamazaki dismounted, handed the reins to Mori, and went to play with Tuyet's daughter.

The major gave Anh a pink butterfly-shaped kite with a long ribbon tail. Tuyet and Coi sat on a straw mat, watching Anh struggle to launch the kite. The major pulled off his boots and ran with the girl riding his back. Anh towed the kite aloft, screeching joyously as it squiggled upward into the sky.

Coi said, "Look how he plays with Anh. He's good with her."

"It's all too complicated for me."

Coi clucked her tongue. She gathered her niece's long hair and began braiding it.

Tuyet twisted the jade bracelet on her wrist. It was a family heirloom, her mother's single valuable possession. *The longer you wear it, the greener it becomes*, her mother had said. On her deathbed, she had slipped it onto Tuyet's ten-year-old wrist. *The purer your heart, the deeper the color.*

"You seem to enjoy his visits," Coi persisted. "He behaves like a gentleman. He brings us useful little gifts."

"He doesn't make me laugh . . ."

"Like Khoi?"

Tuyet flinched. Her ex-husband's name still needled a tender spot deep inside.

"That was thoughtless of me," Coi whispered, squeezing her niece's shoulder. "It's nice if a man can make you laugh, but it's better if he can make your heart smile. And I know he does that for you. I can see it in your face."

"He's eccentric in a good way."

Coi sighed. "It's such a nice day. When are you going to talk to him?"

"Waiting for the right moment, Auntie."

THEY GATHERED for lunch under the pavilion. Sea breezes stirred white cotton shade awnings. The chef and his assistant brought out a colorful bounty of seafood in a giant iron pan. Yamazaki introduced his paella with a note of pride, a recipe from his travels in Europe. Tuyet said it was one of the best things she had ever tasted. He beamed, explaining that he had brought the saffron all the way from Spain. He opened another bottle of red wine from Bordeaux. She grew more blissfully drunk with each glass, and she couldn't stop grinning. Fruits and flowers blossomed in her mouth and made her feel wonderfully heady. It stirred a yearning to see exotic places that produced such eloquent flavors.

Yamazaki said little but smiled the entire afternoon. He was happy, and Tuyet found that she was too. It struck her as peculiar, in a pleasant way, that they had stepped out of reality this afternoon, here on an empty beach, wearing European clothes, eating Spanish food, sipping French wine. For a moment, she could imagine a world without war. Tuyet squinted at the major, trying to picture him in a civilian setting as a clerk or a teacher, but it was difficult. There was too much she didn't know about him.

The festivities wound down slowly. Some of the men napped on the sand. Ha led a group to the tide line to dig for clams. Yamazaki and Tuyet lingered over the wine. She had reached a pleasant stage of giddy drowsiness.

"Your dress is very beautiful," he said, looking into her eyes.

"Thank you, Major."

It was a white Parisian summer dress with tiny blue flowers she had bought in Saigon before her daughter was born. She had been happily married the last time she wore it. The previous night, she had laid it out on the divan and then decided against wearing it, only to change her mind in the morning. She felt that avoiding the dress meant that she was still chained to the past.

"Call me Takeshi," he insisted. "I am Major Yamazaki to everyone. Please, I would like to be Takeshi with you."

She smiled and nodded, blushing a little, to her own vexation. In the harsh afternoon light, he looked much older than his thirty-six years. Sunspots splattered across his cheeks and forehead. Lines crinkled his brows. The dark patches beneath his eyes gave him the look of perpetual exhaustion.

They strolled along the beach. Foamy ripples erased their footprints. Wine-drunk, she floated lightly on her feet, feeling giddy. He said she was made of heron-bones, slight, graceful. She snorted and skipped ahead to pick up pretty shells. Tuyet carried them in a fold of her dress. He was smiling, holding his wrist behind his back, strolling in the sunlight like an office clerk on lunch break.

It was the first time they were alone, not another person within hearing distance. She ventured a personal question: "Do you miss your home?"

He thought about it and replied, "A boy misses home; a man remembers it."

"And a woman?"

"A woman makes a home."

Tuyet tilted her head. "Do you miss your country?"

"As much as you miss Hanoi."

"Hanoi is not across the sea."

"Sea, land—same. Distance and time."

She paused without comment, her dissent passive. "What do you remember about Hokkaido?"

He gazed toward the sea, his long sigh almost inaudible. "In Hokkaido, there are mountains, rivers, plains, marshes, lakes, ocean, and all the seasons. We have everything."

"Did you want to leave Hokkaido?"

"When I was a young man, yes. To see the world, to run away from home. Not for this." He batted vaguely at the air, meaning the war.

She asked him about his childhood.

"I am the only child in my family. I was born in the middle of the night during a cyclone. My father went down to the bay to fetch two buckets of seawater to bathe me, to put salt into my veins. But it also put wanderlust into my bones. My mother never forgave him for that. I remember sailing with my father, just the two of us. I was five. He tied a rope around my waist so the waves couldn't take me. When I was seven, he took me on my first overnight sail. When I was twelve, he gave me my own sailing skiff."

As he reminisced about the ocean and a volcanic mountain called Fuji—which he had climbed to the snowline with his father—the stiffness slowly faded from his shoulders. He seemed to step away from his official duties. His eyes sparkled. His hands unclasped from behind his back and became expressive as his mind rambled. It was the most she had heard him utter at once.

"Ah, I must be boring you, talking like a fishwife," he cried, for she had barely said a word.

"I like to listen. I hardly know you."

He cocked his head and stated rather plainly, "You are still afraid of me."

"A little."

Silence fell on them. They struggled up the steep face of a dune, ankle-deep in unstable, sliding sand. Takeshi offered his hand and pulled her to the top. His palm was coarse, his fingers hard with the sort of sinewy strength common in fishermen. They reached the wind-sharpened ridge and he let go of her hand.

"Fear is not necessary," he said.

"It's natural; the weak fear the strong."

Tuyet was young, but she was not blind. The Japanese were as brutal as the French, and their taxes were even higher. It was peaceful here, on this beach in Mui Ne, but the whole world was at war. In the north, bombs were falling. In the south, Viet soldiers rioted in multiple provinces. Her neighbors' voices swirled inside her ear: *People are envious and suspicious of his interest in you. They will call you a whore if you become his woman. Can you live in this town when he is gone? Will you survive if the Japanese lose?*

"If you want to end our friendship, I will honor your wish," he promised, seeing fear on her face. "It will sadden me, but I will not come to your shop again. You never need to fear me. I give you my word."

She bowed.

He turned to her, head tilted sideways. "How long has it been since I first came to your house?"

"Nearly two months now."

"It has not been entirely terrible, no?"

"We've had some good conversations. You are a good man, Takeshi. You could find someone better."

An old village proverb said the difference between a lame ox and a single mother was that a butcher would pay something for the ox. This was a country of widows, single mothers, children, and the elderly. The most able-bodied males were always conscripted for labor, went to war, or sought work far from home. Many never returned, leaving the women behind. When Tuyet married a professional athlete, she thought she would never be in this position. The bitterness of squandering her youth on the wrong man was still fresh. She thought it must be possible, wise even, to lead a simple celibate life. She was still young enough to convince herself.

"Don't worry about me. I'm not an innocent boy." He smiled. "Who do you think I am?"

She guessed that he had reached the height of his military career but longed for a simpler life. Tuyet answered, "You are an intellectual, but a fisherman at heart. People say you are an honorable soldier. Your men respect you. Someday, when the war is over, you will go home."

"Is that all?"

"That's all I know."

They reached the top of the highest dune and sat down

next to each other. He frowned at the sea. "What else do you want to know?"

Tuyet let out a drunken laugh, which sounded silly to her. The wine had loosened her tongue. "A woman does not want; she needs to know all there is to know. Even then, maybe it's still not enough. Her life isn't hers alone."

A long silent moment. He said, "Words cannot map the heart."

"Then tell me one thing, Takeshi, if nothing else. Why me?"

He stared off into the distance. Crying gulls circled above the rising surf. In the distance, their canvas pavilion was a white speck on the sand.

She sighed to herself. *Never ask a man for more than he can willingly give.*

He said, "You remind me of someone I once knew, a long, long time ago . . ." His eyes clouded over. Conflicted emotions flowed just beneath his skin. "Her name was Hirumi. She was twenty-two. It was a lifetime ago." The words caught in his throat. His face changed, and it was as if she was looking at a younger man, on whom the scars of tragedy were still fresh. His voice hushed, hollowed. "We were to be married. She fell ill and died suddenly before our wedding. I could not stay in Hokkaido after that. It was impossible. I signed on to an ocean liner as a deckhand. A year later I landed in Europe. I had a little money saved. I drank. Traveled and painted. For a time, I lived like a madman."

The stories tumbled out of him as if they had been pressing against his throat. He talked about his first love. The dissolute years in Paris afterward, the wanton drinking and reckless living as a struggling artist. Then, he had been a lonely man wandering through Spain, Morocco, Algeria, and Italy. Loneliness eventually turned him back home. His father fell ill. He helped his father until the old man's health improved. At his mother's urging, he entered university "to make something of myself before it was too late." He graduated and was drafted and was sent to Manchuria. After six long years in the military, he was rewarded with this non-combat post in Phan Thiet.

Sunset crept onto the beach. The calm, glittering surface of the sea yielded to twilight. Shadows stretched and twisted on the dunes. Wild colors swirled across the sky on the horizon, the smear of a brewing storm. The wind strengthened and brought his scent to her. Her eyes grew heavy.

"I am not Hirumi . . ."

"I want you as you are. My feelings are true," he said, touching his chest. "In time, you will know."

His simple words resonated and struck some deep fiber in her.

Long years of sorrow and isolation had prepared Tuyet. Her heart turned toward him. He spoke a language she knew well, the language of loss and loneliness. From her earliest memory, Tuyet knew what it was to be without family. She was unaware that she suffered the universal hunger of orphans, a profound yearning to be loved, to be wanted. It rendered her vulnerable.

12

Rendezvous

DARK CLOUDS STACKED ABOVE THE CITY AS EVE-
ning fell. The train groaned into Saigon station, trailing a black
plume of smoke. Its shrill whistle blasted flocks of sparrows
from the treetops. The air was baked with the muggy odor of
an impending downpour. Clay dirt, kicked up by foot traffic,
glowed like gold dust in the slanting sun. Foremen rallied shirtless coolies from their stupor to line up handcarts in rows along
the track. On the platform, a crowd surged forward, scanning
passenger cars for familiar faces. As the locomotive screeched
to a halt, the clamor of arrival seemed almost festive.

Japanese troops in pond-green or beige uniforms clomped
down the platform with the swagger of conquerors, having
defeated the combined forces of the Americans, British, Dutch,
and Australians in a three-month campaign. With control of
the Dutch East Indies firmly in their grasp, the Imperial Japanese Army (IJA) secured vast oil fields, vital for the Japanese
war machine. Troops passing through the Saigon hub had few
precious days of leave before transferring to other theaters in
Southeast Asia.

Passengers gave them a wide berth. Porters wove through
the throng with suitcases and trunks balanced on their heads.
Handlers caught baggage tossed through windows. Peasants
jumped down from flatbeds where they had been riding atop
cargo piles of sacks and boxes, pulling the cargo down along
with them. People abandoned the chaos with the determi-
nation of insects. A burlap bag tore open, powdering the air
with cinnamon.

Tuyet stepped off the third-class car with her valise and woven basket, relieved to be free after a five-hour journey from Phan Thiet. Sweat pasted the blouse to her back. She brushed soot from her sleeves and wound up smearing it. She mopped perspiration from her brow with a handkerchief. Dark clouds rumbled above the station. People surged toward the exits, baggage handlers shuffling after them. Tuyet spotted her friend Ly standing by the ticket booth.

Sheathed in a robin's-egg-blue silk *ao dai* and dark merchant pants, Ly was quite tall and thin-boned, a figure of elegance. The twenty-six-year-old widow still possessed a self-contained girlishness which Tuyet found endearing. Her pale olive Hanoian skin stood out from a crowd of dark Saigonese faces. She had kind eyes set in an oval face. A single mole beneath her left eye foretold a life of many sorrows.

"Sister Tuyet!"

Both threw their arms around each other, ignoring the stares at their public display of affection. They were best friends, closer than sisters.

"Careful, I'm covered in soot."

"Never mind. I've missed you!" Ly squeezed her, then held Tuyet at arm's length for inspection. "You look beautiful!"

"I gained a little weight."

"Fresh love is all cream and sugar," Ly crooned salaciously. The last time the best friends had bidden each other farewell, one had been a widow, the other a divorcee.

Not long in the past, their futures had been bright; both had been happy, married, and wealthy. Ly's husband, Dinh, her childhood sweetheart from a rich Chinese merchant family, had inherited his family's fortune. He had bought a French villa in an upper-class neighborhood in Saigon. An avid football fan, he had befriended Tuyet's husband, Khoi, who was captain of the premier team in the national league. Dinh and Ly had hosted weekly dinner parties for Khoi's team and their loyal socialites. To capitalize on Khoi's fame, Dinh had used his connections to help him set up a sports clothing business. The two men had played tennis at the country club while their wives shopped, indulging in the leisure life of Saigon's upper class. When Ly gave birth, Tuyet was at her bedside for a fortnight to nurse, cook, and perform the duties of a sister. A year later, Ly did the same for Tuyet when she delivered Anh. These rites of blood sisterhood had bonded them for a lifetime.

Now Tuyet put her arms around Ly and squeezed, grinning. "Did you wait long?"

"I had the afternoon to buy groceries," said Ly, nudging her chin toward Ben Thanh Market across the street. A caravan of handcarts finished moving goods from the train to the market, which was in the final stages of closing down. Sanitation crews raked garbage into big piles. Food sellers stacked their tables and stools.

"That's a sweet color on your cheeks, Ly."

"My new rouge. It will look even better on you tonight." She checked her wristwatch. "We have two hours to get you bathed and peacocked gorgeous for your special dinner date." Ly winked.

"Psst!" Tuyet blushed. She had decided to escape hometown scrutiny by meeting Major Yamazaki in Saigon, her familiar stomping ground, and backed by her best friend. "Did you check with Big Sister Van about having Japanese officers at her club?"

"She said not to worry. The French have flexible backbones these days; they'll bow to anyone."

"Wonderful! The major requested a French meal. He lived a few years in Paris and misses the food."

"I've missed Van's duck confit!" moaned Ly.

"And champagne with chocolate cake. I'm starving!"

"Why are we standing here drooling? I got us a rickshaw."

Ly threaded her arm through Tuyet's and went out to the parking area.

"What happened to your Citroën?"

"I was lucky to sell it last year while people could still buy petrol," she said with a pragmatic shrug. The sedan had been her most treasured possession. "It's impossible to drive any-where with these awful fuel rations now."

Rickshaws, resting pitched forward on their bars, lined two deep outside the station. Young boys working as touts trot-ted alongside travelers, tugging at their sleeves, asking their destinations, and offering to carry their luggage. Old pullers usually served only local neighborhoods. Strong, younger ones accepted fares to the city limit. Ly's rickshaw sat far away from the crowd, already loaded with a basket of produce and a jack-fruit the size of a piglet. A shirtless old man in black knee-length pants and bald with a fringe of white hair around his ears greeted them with a deep bow.

"Good heavens, Uncle!" Tuyet said, surprised to see the old puller from Ly's neighborhood. "I thought you'd be retired by now."

"Me too, ma'am, but my stomach ain't retired from eating, so here I am. It's cruel how the appetite hangs on even when the teeth are gone," he said, flashing a gummy grin. "Till then, I thank you for the fare if you don't mind my plodding feet."

Bowing, Tuyet chuckled. "Plod away, Uncle."

They climbed aboard and sat side by side. Tuyet's valise rested across both their laps. The old man lifted the bars, bal-anced his rickshaw, then called another puller nearby for a boost. Together with some effort, one pulling, one pushing, they rocked the rickshaw into motion. Slowly, the old man built momentum until it rolled along at an easy jog. His bare feet made soft pitter-patter sounds on the pavement.

The breeze put a smile on Tuyet's face. Although she was fond of the countryside, Tuyet was a city girl at heart. She was in love with the wide avenues, tall trees, great buildings, endless streets, and alleys. She could never see them all, though the possibility of it excited her. Restaurants, markets, cafés. Nightclubs, country clubs, and churches. The French had built Saigon to be the jewel of their Indochinese empire. She found it a splendid place to live, the city where she had come of age.

Ly smiled mischievously. "Secretive sister, tell me all about your new man."

Tuyet pointed her eyes at their puller, who certainly could overhear them.

Ly made an exasperated noise and motioned for Tuyet to whisper in her ear.

"He's not my man."

"You haven't *neared* him!" she exclaimed, meaning sex.

"Mmm!" Tuyet egg-eyed Ly and pinched her arm. "I haven't even kissed him!"

Ly giggled, a throaty, scandalous sound that made Tuyet's ears burn. "When was the last time you kissed a man?"

"Khoi," Tuyet muttered, remembering, eyes blinking rapidly. It had been almost three years ago. A look of surprise passed over their faces.

Their lives had unraveled at nearly the same time. Ly's husband had died in a car accident, leaving her bankrupt with his gambling debts. That month, while consoling her best friend, Tuyet had discovered that Khoi had a mistress, a nineteen-year-old cocktail waitress, who was pregnant with his child. Her world had crumbled.

Old friends had avoided them, treating their bad fortune and marital infidelity as contagious diseases. Tuyet and Ly had clung to their friendship, two single mothers in their twenties, social outcasts, neither wealthy nor employed. After divorcing her husband, Tuyet had taken her baby and moved in to live with Ly for half a year until her cousin Ha had secured a job in Phan Thiet and urged Tuyet to join him and his mother.

The sky rumbled. Rain crashed down. Both women reached back and pulled the canopy over their heads. Ly found a tarp behind the seat and draped it over the valise and their legs. They huddled close, holding hands, and watched the puller. Without breaking stride or flinching at the cold rain, nor glancing back at his passengers, the old man hunched his shoulders and quickened his pace. His drenched trousers stuck to his lean legs like a second skin. The monsoon onslaught drummed the fabric canopy like so many fat fingers.

◆

"SOLDIERS ARE the neediest type of men. They're lonely, far from home," said Ly's grandmother. She was standing in the hallway outside the bathroom, one hand on her cane, the other on the door frame. She was lecturing her granddaughter and Tuyet, who had locked themselves inside. "They feel their mortality."

"So do single mothers approaching their thirties!" Ly retorted from the other side of the door.

Ly rolled her eyes. Tuyet struck a provocative pose. They burst into fits of giggles. They had bathed, and Ly had helped Tuyet wash her hair. They were fussing with their makeup, sharing the mirror above the sink.

Granny harrumphed and rapped on the door with her cane. She declared in an ominous voice, "They're quick to get you into bed."

"And quicker to run off to war!" added Ly's mother, limping with her bad knee up the stairs and down the second-floor hallway.

Having lived under the roof of the Tran women, Tuyet knew the barbs and rhythm of their chatters. After the creditors had sacked their holdings to collect on her late husband's debts, this dilapidated villa in an upper-class suburb and two rental properties in a middle-class area had been all that remained of Ly's family fortune. Ly lived in the sprawling villa with her three-year-old daughter, her mother, and her grandmother.

"Aiya, Ma!" Ly opened the door and tossed her mother an exasperated look. "That's vulgar, the both of you!"

Ly dragged Tuyet out of the bathroom by the hand. They dodged the scowling matriarchs, ran down the hall, and ducked into Ly's bedroom. She slammed the door shut behind them and drove the bolt home.

Ma hollered after them, "You two are behaving like hot-blooded teenage girls."

Granny grumbled loudly, "My bones ache when it comes to the Japanese."

"Oh, Granny!" Ly shouted, continuing the conversation through the bedroom door. "Everything aches when you're seventy-seven!"

"Don't you sass your grandmother!" warned Ma as the pair shuffled a few steps down the hall, then laid siege outside Ly's chamber.

Granny rapped her cane on the door. "Those sneaky little devils want us to exchange a French yoke for a Japanese yoke."

Ma chimed, "When that happens, people will hate Jap collaborators."

"Ma! She's in love," said Ly. "Now, please leave us alone. We're already running late for the gala. The taxi is going to be here any minute."

Ly turned on the radio. French big band blared out. Ly and Tuyet waltzed around the bed laughing, oblivious to the matrons stewing on the other side of the door.

Le Jardin Rouge

LE JARDIN ROUGE—THE RED GARDEN—SAT IN the middle of Pasteur Avenue, east of downtown. It was a grand two-story mansion with white columns and steep rooflines, illuminated by a hundred red globe lanterns. In the garden of roses, bougainvillea, and wisteria filled with water fountains and gazebos, waiters in black velvet jackets served guests at tables covered in white linen. An ornate wrought-iron fence fronted the property. It was Saturday night, and luxury automobiles lined the road, still slick from the afternoon rain. Drivers milled about on the footpath, smoking, watching the arrival of the dinner crowd.

A black Citroën taxi pulled up curbside and an attendant opened the door. Ly stepped out in a form-fitting violet gown, her hair fashionably coiled above her head. Tuyet followed in a sapphire-blue wraparound dress, a soft silk cut that flattered her petite stature. Her hair was twisted into a bun and pinned with ivory combs. Click-clacking on their heels, the pair proceeded around to the rear and entered the building by the rear door. They went down the hallway past the men's restroom and the kitchen. Cooks greeted them warmly. Hitching up their dresses, they climbed the stairs to a private dressing room on the second floor. Two women were fixing their faces in the large vanity mirror by the window.

"Sister Oanh, Sister Giang!" Tuyet and Ly shrieked with joy. The four women collapsed into hugs and giggles.

"I haven't seen you since you left town," Giang cried with her arms around Tuyet.

The friends exchanged news as they touched up their makeup in front of the mirror. Café owner Oanh, voluptuous with a magnificent head of permed hair. Schoolteacher Giang, slender with a serious oval face and long hair in a single thick braid down her back. She was the best dancer in the group. Both women were divorcées, single mothers in their late twenties. Neither spoke much Japanese, but both were curious about Japan and Japanese soldiers in particular.

"Greetings, my beauties!" Madame Le Van rasped in her familiar whiskey voice as she swept into the room. The folds of her vermilion dress rustled like leaves. The fifty-year-old proprietor of Le Jardin Rouge was a flamboyant widow with an appetite for young Frenchmen. She had inherited the property from her late lover, a rubber plantation owner, and turned it into a famed nightspot for the well-heeled.

Behind Van was a short Japanese matron in a solid blue evening dress. "Before we go down to meet the men, I'd like to introduce you to my dear friend Madame Nagano Yuki. She is a translator with the International Trade Bureau. She generously offered her services. Thank you so very much, Yuki-san."

"Please, Sister, don't mention it." Yuki bowed, her hands folded in front of her. She had a melodic voice with traces of a Japanese accent. "It is my honor to be your translator this evening. I know Major Yamazaki, so I can guarantee that his officers are gentlemen. You will have an enjoyable evening."

YUKI AND VAN sat them at a white linen table under a pergola in a private section of the garden. A maestro in her element, Yuki arranged the seating in such a way that the pairings came naturally: Yamazaki with Tuyet, Ishigara with Ly, Mori with Giang, and Sakamoto with Oanh. Handsomely dressed in matching tuxedos, the men had been coached by Yuki and knew how to carry themselves. She conducted the meal with ease, creating drinking games to relax the guests. She teased them as though they were teenagers. Peals of laughter rolled around the table. The hors d'oeuvres and aperitifs set the mood. The courses came, one after another in steady procession.

After dessert, Yuki announced that it was her bedtime. The entire table rose to offer compliments. Van walked Yuki out to her vehicle. The head waiter relocated the party to the main hall where the band was just warming up.

Le Jardin Rouge was filling with Saigon's trendy upper class, an even mix of French and Viets, with a handful of wealthy internationals. The band was playing. A dozen couples were spinning on the dance floor. A waiter showed them to one of the tables reserved for special patrons. Tuyet felt self-conscious. The crowd watched as the Japanese escorted their guests to their seats. Yamazaki ordered champagne.

Tuyet asked him privately, "Do you mind everyone staring?"

"The French? They can't help themselves. They are unhappy about us crowding their colonies. Now, we're in their exclusive club. The more they stare, the sooner they will get used to it. Does it bother you? I thought you liked this place."

"I do. Van is like family. Ly and I used to come here often."

Yamazaki winked at her, grinning. "You're full of surprises! I thought you were a homely shopkeeper. I'd never dare talk to a Saigon socialite."

"Homely!" Tuyet bristled.

"Would you like to dance?" He rose quickly to his feet, pulling her to the floor.

As the pair started dancing, the other officers followed Yamazaki's lead and led their partners to the floor. Mori proved himself to be a gifted dancer, to the delight of Giang. Sakamoto knew only the waltz and performed like a drill sergeant. Ishigara, the youngest and most athletic of the group, was a fast study under Ly's tutelage. The way she looked at Ishigara made him grin like a boy. The whole party spun around the floor for several songs until Sakamoto, drenched in sweat, asked Oanh for a rest. Ishigara begged Ly for a break too. He and Sakamoto returned to the table while their partners ran off to the powder room. Sakamoto signaled the waiter for a bottle of sake.

"Over there," Ishigara said to Sakamoto, glancing over to the bar where three Frenchmen were drinking. Their suits looked shabby.

"Those apes?"

"I don't like the way they've been staring at us. It makes me itchy," Ishigara said.

Sakamoto nodded. "They're watching the major."

As the song came to a close, they saw Yamazaki and Tuyet leave the dance floor, heading toward the powder room from which Giang and Oanh were emerging. Tuyet went in and Yamazaki proceeded down the hall. Immediately, the three Frenchmen peeled away from the bar, one after the other, walking casually in the same direction. A look passed between Ishigara and Sakamoto. They were both out of their seats, moving swiftly through the crowd.

YAMAZAKI HAD drunk too much. The evening was going splendidly. He couldn't remember the last time he and his men had enjoyed themselves so much. Walking down the hallway to the men's restroom, he noticed an oil painting, an excellent copy of Degas's *Dance Class*, and paused. Paris, the food, the music, the art, the theater, he missed it all. Some memories were murky, yet others survived with sharp details, potent enough to touch and taste. At his elbow, a rotund Frenchman cleared his throat, asking to pass. Yamazaki apologized and stepped aside, allowing the gentleman to move by him. The stranger reeked of freshly sprayed eau de toilette, sweet and flowery. In the restroom, a teenage attendant offered Yamazaki a towel, which he declined. He went directly to the urinal, oblivious to the three Frenchmen who followed him inside. By the time he sensed assailants behind him, it was too late.

Someone clubbed him over the head.

ISHIGARA GRABBED a steak knife from a dish cart and hurried down the hallway, Sakamoto right behind him. Foot traffic from the kitchen delayed them, and they lost sight of the Frenchmen. Edging past the waiters, they ran to the men's room. The toilet attendant was backing away from the door, wide-eyed with fear. He pointed them into the room. They burst in as the assailants were dragging Yamazaki from the urinals.

Without warning, Ishigara lunged at the closest man and knifed him in the ribs. Sakamoto charged the second man, driving him into one of the toilet stalls. Both men crashed through the door of the stall, fighting as they fell. The third man reached for a gun in his shoulder holster. Ishigara knifed his first opponent again, rolled away, and came to his feet. Leaping over the unconscious Yamazaki, Ishigara tackled the third man before he could fire. They tumbled on the floor, wrestling for the pistol. Ishigara's knife clattered across the tiles. A shot went off like a thunderclap. The mirror above the sink shattered in a shower of glass. The man with knife wounds grabbed Ishigara's foot.

In the toilet stall, Sakamoto twisted his opponent's arm backward, dislocating his shoulder. He slammed the man's head into the ceramic toilet and dropped him, unconscious, to the floor. He came out of the stall as the gunman broke free from Ishigara and fired at Sakamoto. The first shot missed; the second struck him in the thigh. Sakamoto toppled over. Ishigara grappled with the gunman and stomped the face of the other. The gunman turned around, and Ishigara kicked the pistol from his hand. It skittered across the floor toward Sakamoto, who picked it up. The disarmed man fled. The assailant with knife wounds tried to escape, but Ishigara grabbed him from behind and choked him unconscious.

TUYET HEARD the first shot, standing in front of the mirror in the women's restroom. It was a muffled crack, but the other women heard it too. They all ran out, and Tuyet followed. The band was still playing, though some of the dancers had stopped. People were looking toward the men's restroom. The second shot rang out in loud snapping claps. She had a terrible feeling and started down the hallway without thinking. Several waiters had stopped in the corridor, looking toward the men's restroom and the back door at the very end of the hallway, the very same entrance she and Ly had used earlier. She pushed through the crowd and saw a Frenchman yanking on the door, which was made with heavy-duty wrought iron and metal mesh. It didn't budge. The door, normally left open during dinner hours, had been locked once the dance began to prevent patrons from skipping out on their bills.

The Frenchman turned and charged down the hallway, straight at them. Tuyet stumbled back against the people behind her, unable to get out of the way. He barreled into Tuyet, knocking her out of his path. Her face slammed into the wall. Stars filled her vision. Tuyet fell, landing awkwardly. Pain shot up her arm. Another person tripped and fell on top of her. In the stampede, someone kicked her in the head.

14

Surrender

THREE IN THE MORNING AT THE CITY HOSPITAL. At the front entrance, bathed in syrupy yellow lights, two male orderlies squatted on their haunches curbside, smoking cigarettes. The nurses had just finished their last round. The ward was dark and quiet. The front waiting room by the reception desk had four wobbling ceiling fans to stir up stuffy air.

Tuyet was sitting on a long bench, resting her bandaged wrist in her lap and pressing a cold pack to her forehead with the other hand. Her left cheek was puffy and bruised. Ly sat next to Tuyet. Giang and Oanh had taken a taxi home because they had to work in the morning. Out front, Mori and Ishigara pulled up in a sedan, returning from their interviews at the police station.

A tired doctor in his thirties and a nurse came out to meet the group. The nurse spoke Japanese and translated for the doctor. "Mister Yamazaki has a concussion. Mister Sakamoto was very lucky. The bullet only grazed him. Have the medic change the bandages daily, and check for infection."

"There were two injured Frenchmen," Mori said. "Are they here?"

The doctor shook his head. "The French use a different hospital close to the cathedral."

The nurse handed Mori packets of painkillers and antibiotics. A few minutes later, another nurse wheeled Sakamoto out from surgery. The right trouser leg had been cut away. Sakamoto's thigh was bandaged. Behind him, Yamazaki came out with a white bandage around his head. The nurse advised them to stay, but they bowed and smiled knowingly. They had been through worse.

The six of them piled into the black Citroën. Mori drove with Ishigara and Ly next to him, Tuyet in the back with Sakamoto and Yamazaki. The windows were down, and they took in the cool night air, scented with roadside greenery.

Yamazaki asked Tuyet, "Does your wrist hurt?"

"It's just a sprain," she said. "Why did those men attack you?"

"I made powerful enemies when I raided the home of that rich Frenchman, Feraud."

"Are you still in danger?"

"No. I promise you that will never happen again," he replied without elaborating.

Hearing the finality in his voice, Tuyet knew it was neither the time nor place for questions. "I'm thankful you're not badly injured."

"I'm very sorry about all this," Yamazaki whispered.

Tuyet shrugged and smiled. "This doesn't change the wonderful evening we had beforehand."

Speaking up, Yamazaki translated for his men. They cheered. Sakamoto said something and bowed to Tuyet. Yamazaki chuckled. "He said you have a rare insight. You remind him of his mother."

"*Arigato gozaimasu, Sakamoto-san,*" Tuyet said with a bow.

Yamazaki asked, "May we take you and Ly home now?"

Tuyet replied, "Ly and I think it doesn't look good coming home so late like this. Can we go somewhere and wait for dawn? The doctor said you shouldn't sleep for a few hours yet. We can go home in the morning."

Sakamoto moaned that he was hungry. Tuyet directed Mori down deserted avenues, winding through the sleepy city and back to Ben Thanh Market. All-night snack vendors lined the streets, their oil lamps dotting the darkness. Their carts and yoke-baskets filled the air with the aromas of barbecued meats

and fried dumplings. Piles of produce were stacked high curbside as suppliers and distributors were already trading before
the market opened. Tuyet and Ly bought a selection of hot sesame fritters, barbecued duck, steamed buns, sweet soybean
milk with lotus seeds. And bags of fresh fruits.

THE VILLA was in one of the wealthiest districts, four
blocks from Saigon Cathedral. Gravel crunched underneath as
the sedan rolled up a curved driveway to the sprawling two-
story building. Warm light poured from windows as though a
party was in progress, but there was no one except the middle-
aged butler who greeted them outside. Mori helped Sakamoto,
who was on crutches. The butler, Ishigara, and Ly took the
food into the kitchen.

Yamazaki led Tuyet into the foyer. She gasped at the glittering crystal chandelier and the expensive furnishings.

"This is a palace," she said softly, as though not wanting to
disturb the inhabitants.

"Too bad it's not mine," he whispered, glancing
furtively about.

"Oh, what a relief!"

He chuckled. "A friend owes me a favor. These villas are
allocated for the use of diplomats and generals. I'm punching
above my rank here."

They went to the main sitting room. Tuyet settled on the sofa
and watched Yamazaki open the windows. A fragrant breeze
drifted in from the flower garden. He talked absentmindedly
about the many properties in Saigon that had been taken by
the Japanese army. This villa had five bedrooms, a library, and
a wine cellar. Tuyet yawned and hinted a tour in the morning
would be lovely. He thumbed through a stack of records, pulled
out one particular album, and played a piano sonata on the

phonograph. Ly brought them a tray of food and, with a wink, said that she was eating with the men in the kitchen.

He removed his jacket and kicked off his shoes. They sat side by side with their backs against the sofa. Picking at the food, Tuyet examined his face in profile, the gaunt hard lines, the keel-like nose, the strong chin. His scent was distinct—a mixture of tobacco, cologne, and sandalwood. She leaned a little closer. Her arm brushed against his. She felt the warmth of his skin. They sat still. He put his hand over hers. The world felt remote, as distant as dawn.

He gestured for her to remove his head bandage. She obliged and checked the stitches. The bleeding had stopped. He touched the bruise on her cheek. She looked into his eyes and realized then that it had been a long, gradual surrender, incremental steps from the day they met. It was undeniable, the terrifying sense of loss that had come over her when she saw him unconscious on the floor. Her eyes grew heavy. She tilted her face toward him as he leaned in for their first kiss.

15

Exile

ON A GLOOMY SECTION OF THE SAIGON RIVER, A
police sedan bounced through muddy puddles. Bright head
beams swept back and forth across the dark, winding road.
The air was wet, cool. On the right, brief expanses of moonlit
water, a rippling slate-gray flashing between the obsidian curtains of trees. Plantation manors lined the road, separated by
stretches of woods.

Behind the wheels was a baby-faced deputy. A burly sergeant
in the passenger seat. Both Frenchmen sat in silence. Their eyes
fixed ahead, wary of their cranky boss sprawled angrily across
the seat behind them. Inspector Mercier was a stringy man in
his late fifties, a mere shadow of his younger, more powerful
self. His once handsome face had turned angular and hawkish.
His dragoon mustache was streaked with gray.

Barely into his first hour of sleep, he had been roused by
his sergeant, much to the distress of his wife, who had been
unwell. The assault at Le Jardin Rouge had been instigated
by one of the Brotherhood's own senior members, Gaspard
Feraud, whom he had personally installed in a luxurious safe
house. Feraud's audacity was astounding. The secretary of Free
France had personally tasked Mercier with cleaning up the
mess. Feraud was endangering everyone.

Mercier lit a cigarette with his lighter and held the guttering
flame to his wristwatch. Less than two hours to sunrise. It had
been a long night, and somebody was going to hang before
it was over.

"Bastard! What a goddamn fool," Mercier muttered.

The vehicle turned down a drive and came to a gate with a modest brass sign: La Maison du Lotus. It was an upscale club, discreetly located on the outskirts of the city, with an exclusive clientele of wealthy colonialists. The old watchman recognized the inspector, a frequent guest, greeted him politely, then opened the gate. Sounds of laughter came from one of the poker halls. They continued around to the rear of the property to a brick bungalow perched on the riverbank. They parked at a distance. Mercier and the sergeant walked up to the front door while the deputy circled to the rear of the house.

A maid answered the door. They found Feraud sitting in a dimly lit chamber. The windows were cracked open. The windless night left the stale air in the room cloying with herbal unguents, disinfectants, cigar smoke, and stagnant sweat with an undertone of urine. Like a drugged steer, Feraud turned his head and regarded them with bloodshot eyes. He nodded, one hand holding a glass tumbler of whiskey, the other a cigar. He was dressed in a white silk short-sleeved shirt and a blue sarong wrapped around his lower half. His wounds were seeping through the fabric. The second- and third-degree burns on his legs and groin had become infected. The doctor feared permanent damage to his manhood.

The sergeant proceeded to search the bungalow. Mercier nodded, went to the bar, poured himself a drink, and sat down by the bay window opposite the brooding Feraud. The inspector glared at him and kept sipping at his whiskey until he got a firm grip on his anger. "That was an unbelievably stupid thing to do."

"It was," Feraud admitted. "I apologize."

"You've endangered all of us."

"I received an urgent tip. The Jap was vulnerable. There was no time to spare," Feraud explained, puffing his cigar. "You will be well compensated, Inspector, as soon as I get my hands on that son of a bitch."

"Forget the gold. They have already divided your treasure chest a hundred ways."

Feraud shook his head stubbornly. "That Jap is no fool. I know from a good source he kept most of it for himself. I'll find the gold and I'll find the bastard that betrayed me to the Jap."

"I'm telling you, forget about the gold. He still has your damn ledger with our names in it. Your vendetta will put all of us behind bars."

They paused at the sounds of scuffling from another part of the house. A piece of ceramic shattered on the floor. A moment later, the sergeant and his deputy came into the room, frog-marching a disheveled Frenchman between them.

"Look what we caught climbing out the window," the sergeant said. "This must be the missing survivor."

"Tomblin," Mercier said in a tone of dismay. A knuckle-headed bottom feeder. No wonder, he thought, it went sideways so badly. All the capable men were long gone, off to fight in Europe or Africa.

"Inspector Mercier," Tomblin said, forcing a smile. "It has been a while."

"I see you've managed to put your foot in shit again."

Tomblin quipped, "True, whenever I smell shit . . . there you are."

The sergeant drove a fist into Tomblin's gut, folding the man in half. The sergeant said stiffly, "Manners."

Holding his stomach, Tomblin wheezed, "We almost had that Jap bastard."

"You have one dead from a cracked skull and another in the hospital with knife wounds," Mercier said, brushing his dragoon mustache with a finger. "The moment the doctor patches up your man, the Kempeitai will get their hands on him. What do you think will happen then?"

Feraud hurled a lengthy string of colorful expletives at Tomblin. He turned to Mercier. "Inspector, you have to free that man."

"I can't. He is under heavy guard," Mercier said, spreading his palms. He had already planted a man in the hospital to ensure that the patient did not survive the surgery, but he kept this fact to himself. "Those bloodthirsty Kempeitai are on their way here as we speak. Yamazaki is going to make you pay for that attack. That sadist Kitamura will finish the job he started on you."

Feraud blanched. "You have to get me out of here."

"It's time for your exit plan."

"No, take me to another safe house," he said, pleading.

"Orders from above, effective immediately."

Feraud slumped in his chair. He hadn't left the colony in fifteen years. Outside, in the inky trees by the riverbank, a koel bird cried three times, long and mournful. Friends and allies had distanced themselves. His connections, once eagerly sought, were now a liability. There was still one person he could count on: his younger brother, a wealthy businessman in Macau, a neutral Portuguese territory.

"Exile," he mumbled as though trying on the word for fit.

"Don't be dramatic. Leave for a few months until things quiet down. Here are your papers," Mercier said and handed an envelope to Feraud.

"What about him?"

Mercier turned to Tomblin. "You should join Monsieur Feraud for this trip."

"It's somewhere far, isn't it?"

"It's for your safety and ours."

Tomblin took a moment to mull over the idea. He ran his tongue over his lips, eyeing the room. He shook his head, his jaw set. "I have a girl and a house. I'll take my chances here."

There was a tense silence. Mercier saw the gears turning in the man's head. Tomblin was a gutter crook with neither honor nor allegiance. If such a man proved unwilling, no amount of money or threats could keep him on course.

Mercier knew from experience that sometimes, it was best to decide on their behalf.

Mercier nodded. "Very well, Tomblin. I see you've made up your mind. Go on, get out of here."

Tomblin relaxed visibly but made no move to leave. "Monsieur Feraud, I will need the balance you owe us."

Feraud bristled. "You don't deliver, you don't get paid!"

"I've lost a man. I need to compensate his family."

Mercier cleared his throat. "Tomblin has a point."

Feraud snarled, "Stay out of this. It's none of your business."

Mercier nodded, then told Tomblin, "Proceed with my blessings. Collect your pay however you want."

Tomblin's eyes widened. The corner of his mouth curled up in a sneer. He rushed at Feraud, who pawed for a pistol hidden under a cushion. Tomblin knocked it from his hand. The gun clattered to the floor, and the sergeant picked it up.

Tomblin grabbed Feraud's hand, almost in a friendly manner, isolated the thumb, and bent it backward. Feraud yowled. "Pardon me, monsieur. I'm going to break your fingers one by one until you pay."

"You cannot allow this, Mercier!"

"I'm staying out of your business, per your request."

Feraud surrendered a small red pouch. While Tomblin counted the gold, Mercier cut a quick look to his men.

Tomblin clucked his tongue. "That was too easy."

"On your way, Tomblin," Mercier said, motioning for his men to step aside.

"Bon voyage, Monsieur Feraud," said Tomblin.

Without warning, the sergeant came at Tomblin, beating him repeatedly with the baton until he crumpled. The sergeant and his deputy dragged the unconscious man out.

Mercier picked up the satchel, surprised at the weight. "This is a considerable sum."

Feraud held out his hand. "Do you mind?"

Mercier resisted the urge to smash his fist into Feraud's florid face. The Brotherhood of Free France had taken great risks to protect him. Whatever his fault, Feraud was still one of them.

"Consider this a cleaning fee," Mercier replied, pocketing half the gold.

Feraud snatched the pouch, grating his teeth. "What are you going to do with Tomblin?"

"I gave him a choice, but he made the wrong one."

"The Kempeitai will make him talk."

"He won't. Somebody has to hang for your crimes, Feraud," Mercier said darkly. "Let's go. The fishing boat is waiting in the harbor. You'll need to hurry to connect with the cargo ship en route."

PART III

Family

1942–1945

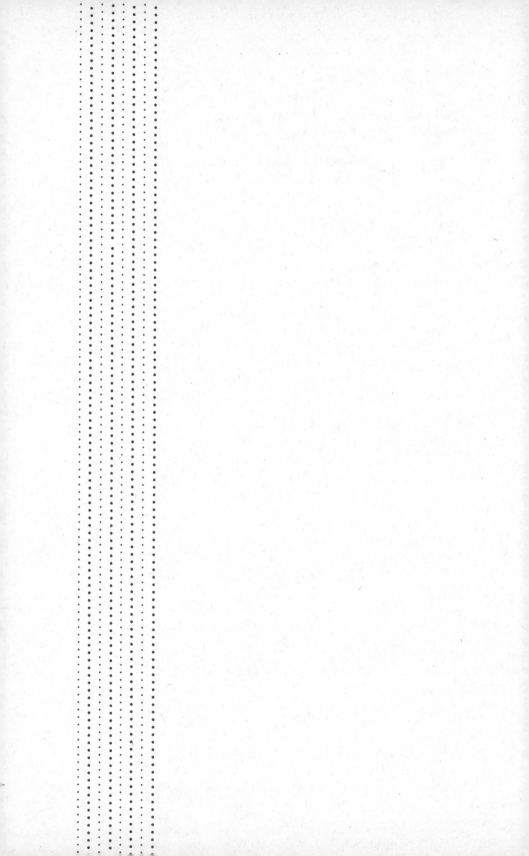

16

Yellow House

TUYET WAS A KEEN OBSERVER OF SIGNS AND A devout follower of the Lady Buddha. She had a dream about a toddler playing in a sunlit stream. A few months later, she discovered she was pregnant, which meant that her baby would be a water sign child, arriving in the Year of the Goat. Rather than telling Takeshi, she confided in her aunt. They went to the Rose Shrine of the Lady Buddha. The seer-nun read her palm and said that a whirlwind of change was upon them, the channel of destiny irrevocably carved. There would be love and joy, but there would also be suffering and darkness. Above all else, the child would be unusually gifted.

After Tuyet told Takeshi about the pregnancy, he proposed and she accepted, choosing love over omen. Takeshi wanted a grand party after the wedding, but Tuyet insisted on a modest private event. It was her only request, so he gave in. She explained that an elaborate wedding would only invite gossip. After all, it was her second marriage. She did not tell him that she was afraid of the spirits and needed to guard her happiness against evil winds. An intimate ceremony, she said, would be more meaningful. To this, Takeshi merely smiled, saying that it was bad luck to begin a marriage by arguing about the wedding party. They exchanged vows in an intimate ceremony, conducted by the village headman in Tuyet's home. The reception was attended by only twelve people. They did, however, at Tuyet's suggestion, send gifts of rice, roasted pork, scallion noodles, and sweets to the entire neighborhood.

With some of the gold he had taken from Feraud, Takeshi

bought his new wife a sun-bright yellow house with a terra-cotta roof and tall windows trimmed in white. It was sur-rounded by fruit trees and a flower garden. When he showed it to her, she smiled, saying she had always wished for such a home. She also told him that she had had a dream of their son playing on a swing beneath a starfruit tree. Surprised, he took her hand and led her to the rear of the house where there was, among the trellises of wisteria, a grand old starfruit tree. "It needs a swing," he said. Tuyet laughed, patted his arm. She told him not to worry. It was a very good omen.

The house was on a tree-lined street in an affluent part of town, three blocks from the main market. Built in the colonial villa style, it had four bedrooms, one sitting room, a Western-style kitchen, and a cozy terrace with white-tiled balustrades. A low redbrick wall topped with wrought-iron railings enclosed the property. The previous owners, gardening enthusiasts, had laid out every square meter of outdoor space with camellias, jasmines, vegetable patches, fruit trees, and herbs.

The house was somehow too beautiful, so much above her place in society that Tuyet had a premonition that it would not be her permanent home. This gave her a measure of vicarious pleasure, as though she was wearing expensive jewelry on loan. Since childhood, nothing had come easily, so she always felt that whatever she got without shedding sweat and tears hadn't been truly earned. Without this "earning" process, owning something was neither complete nor fulfilling.

Tuyet delayed the move three weeks, insisting that they needed an auspicious date. She was not in a hurry because she loved her rented place in the working-class neighborhood. It was the first home she had chosen for herself, the first business she had created for her family.

"How are we going to load all your stuff onto that oxcart?" asked Sau, waving her hand at the shelves of goods and the bins of rice. It was moving day, and the magpie neighbor had come over to lend a hand.

Tuyet and Coi were piling their bags and boxes at the door, and Mister Binh and his grandson were loading them into the oxcart. The whole family was moving to the new place. Anh was taking leave of her vegetable patch at the side of the house. The family's belongings were meager: a couple of handbags, two boxes of clothing, and some baskets stacked with kitchenware. The only furniture they took was the dining table and stools Ha had bought with his first paycheck and, therefore, was too attached to leave behind.

"I'll get some boxes for these dry goods," Sau said on her way out.

Tuyet stopped her. "It's not necessary, Sister. We're not taking any of it with us."

"What do you mean?"

"This is all yours. We're leaving you the shop—a gift for being such a good friend and neighbor," Tuyet said, clasping Sau's shoulders.

"No! You're joking. Don't you make fun of me," Sau exclaimed.

"You deserve it. Here is the permit for the shop. You'll need this too," Tuyet said, handing her the ration card. "Just go to the Permit Office and transfer it to your name."

Sau gushed and dabbed her eyes, sniffling that life had been so hard. No one had ever been so generous to her. The shop would nicely complement her cooking business.

"That's everything, I think," Mister Binh announced at the door. His leg hadn't fully healed from the accident that had killed his ox. "There is more room in the cart if you'd like to take something else."

Coi gathered her yoke baskets and said, "No, that's all we have. Thank you so much for taking a day off to help us, Uncle."

"Don't mention it. I can move you a hundred times and still be in your debt. Thank you for letting me do this. I know you could have had your husband order an army truck for the move."

Tuyet shook her head. "It wouldn't feel right, and it wouldn't look right. We came here humbly, and we want to leave the same way. You don't owe us anything. We're family. Good neighbors."

"That we are!" he enthused and clapped his hands. "You can count on us anytime."

"Likewise for us, Uncle."

AT LUNCHTIME one afternoon a week later, Tuyet and Coi heard a ruckus outside the front gate of the Yellow House. Someone was rattling the metal grating and shouting for Tuyet. They hurried out to find Sau, their old neighbor, ranting about some injustice.

"They won't renew it!" Sau shrilled, shaking with anger. "Those crooks, they won't renew the shop's license!"

Tuyet ushered Sau inside and Coi handed her a bowl of rice, insisting that she join them for lunch. Huffing, Sau sat on the straw dining mat where Tuyet and Coi always ate when the men weren't around. Sau was too upset to eat. They poured her a glass of honey-hibiscus tea to calm her down.

"Where is Mister Two?" Sau managed to ask, using the man-of-the-house honorific for Takeshi. "I hope I'm not interrupting anything."

"He's at the base every day. Ha is also at work. It's just us ladies having lunch," Tuyet replied, slipping a morsel of meat into her daughter's rice bowl, urging Anh to eat.

Coi said, "Tell us what happened."

Early that morning, Sau had queued at the Permit Office to request a change of ownership for the shop and to have the ration card updated. The clerks had sent her from one desk to another, each raising more problems, but suggesting some "tea money" would resolve them. After she had emptied her purse, she was sent to face an arrogant man, who insisted on a ridiculous sum because the shop had been moved from Tuyet's old rental to Sau's house.

Tuyet's nostrils flared. "Sister, I will sort this out. That's a promise. Now, let's enjoy our lunch. He ruined your morning, but don't let him spoil your appetite. Look at this fat spotted perch we got at the fishmonger's this morning. It'd be a shame to let it go to waste."

AFTER THE MEAL, Sau and Coi cleaned up while Tuyet went to wash her face.

"Why don't you change into something nice?" Coi suggested. "Put on some jewelry, maybe a pearl necklace."

"Why? What's wrong with what I'm wearing?"

"You look like a peasant."

"I am a peasant."

"So, he's going to treat you like a peasant."

"He can try!"

Tuyet went into the bedroom to exchange her dark blue peasant shirt for a fresh identical one from the dresser. They had spent the morning in the kitchen pickling and cooking. Allowing herself two generous pumps of the perfume bottle, she grabbed a framed photo on the dresser and shoved it into her satchel.

THE PERMIT OFFICE had been there less than two years. It had been created at Japanese decree, initially to monitor the movement of commodities. However, with ever-expanding functions, it had become the largest department in the building with a dozen clerks and secretaries. Now, its primary directive was to secure, track, and control commodities requisitioned by the Imperial Japanese Army. All merchants, traders, and vendors, large and small, had to apply for permits to purchase staples and other consumer goods. Anyone caught selling them without a permit could be fined or jailed.

The clerks had returned from their lunch break and were at their desks, clacking away on typewriters and thumping rubber stamps. There were no chairs or benches for the public. A dozen sad-looking petitioners were queued up, squatting in rows along the walls facing the formidable banks of desks. Sau led Tuyet to her tormentor's desk and was about to squat, but Tuyet pinched her. The portly middle-aged clerk recognized Sau. He motioned for her to come forward, bypassing the queue.

"Are you ready to pay the fees?" he asked, scribbling something on a document. His cheeks were pockmarked, his mustache trimmed. Looking through his wire-rimmed spectacles, he regarded the women with the condescending air of one secure in a lifetime position.

"Let me introduce you to Le Ngoc Tuyet, the original permit holder." Sau held out the document, pointing at Tuyet's name.

His face turned sullen. "So she is, but it's still not transferable."

"Mister Hao Hong, you are wrong, and you know it," Tuyet said rather loudly, making heads turn. "Let's stop this silliness. She has paid this office tea money five times over this morning already."

"Listen, little lady. You are out of line. How dare you come in here and raise your voice at me!"

Raising her head, Tuyet addressed the whole office at the top of her voice. "Pardon me, but this concerns everyone who works here. All of you will want to know why the Japanese auditors will be visiting this office shortly."

On cue, Sau wailed in a mocking tone, "Oh, heavens, heads are going to roll!"

Tuyet removed from her satchel a framed photograph, popped out the supporting stand at the rear, and placed it on his desk. "Believe me," she said. "I am sorry to resort to this, but you have left us no choice."

"What?" he blurted, suddenly unsure of himself. He took a close look at the wedding photo, a Viet bride in a Viet *ao dai* and headdress and a groom in a Western suit. The groom looked to be Japanese. The stocky soldier, next to him, was a Japanese in an Imperial Japanese Army parade uniform.

"That's me and that's my husband. And this woman here is my neighbor. She catered our wedding. I'm giving the shop to her. I've already checked, so don't lie to me. There are no rules or fees associated with a simple transfer of ownership."

The room hummed, scandalized. While most of them didn't know Tuyet, they had heard about the Japanese commanding officer marrying a local woman. Another clerk whispered something to Hao, who jerked upright in his seat, looking as though lunch had soured in his stomach.

Tuyet said, "I would like to speak to the office supervisor."

A secretary hurried to an office at the rear of the building and returned with an older balding man in a white short-sleeved shirt and spectacles. The secretary had informed him of the situation because he came forward, head bowed, beaming an ingratiating smile. He said he was Truong Luu, the Permit Office supervisor.

"Mister Luu, this is not the first time I have had a problem in this office. A few months ago, I had an argument with another of your clerks. Over there, Mister Tran." Tuyet pointed at a man in the corner trying to hide behind his desk.

"I'm so sorry about your trouble. Please accept my sincerest apology. We will have the paperwork and a new ration card done at once and delivered to the shop within the hour. I'll make sure all Missus Sau's money will be returned as well."

Sau heaved a sigh of relief, but Tuyet was not finished. She said, "Your clerks were putting the squeeze on a single widow with three children. Have you no shame?"

"It's terrible. I will discipline them. You can count on me."

"Do you take me for a fool? You are all in it together." She scowled, shaking her head. "I know foot-dragging and bribery are common everywhere, but this is daylight robbery of the poor. I will not tolerate it. You've seen the Japanese chop off the hands of thieves and whip people in the market for minor offenses. What do you think they'll do to crooked officials they trusted to carry out their mandates?"

His voice trembled. "Please, madame, I beg your forgiveness. It won't happen again. Times are hard."

Tuyet searched his face for any sign of sincerity. All the typists had stopped. No one spoke a word or made a sound. The room became so quiet she could hear onlookers crowding the front door. Inside, she was shaking with anger, but she didn't have it in her to hurt people even in revenge.

"Times are hard for everyone, Mister Luu, harder even for the people you cheated," Tuyet said, loud enough for everyone in the room. "I will let this pass, but I'm holding you responsible for the behavior of your people. I promise you if this office continues to extort the poor, I will introduce you to my husband."

Walking through the park on the way home, Tuyet slumped down on a bench and buried her face in her hands, quaking with a blend of fear, anger, and adrenaline. She had never faced down a crowd like that before. Sau was elated, electrified by the way Tuyet had scolded the haughty officials.

"I can't believe you just did that!" Sau cried gleefully.

"Neither can I!"

"Is your husband going to be upset about you using his name?"

"He won't like it, but he believes in fairness."

"Then what are you worried about?"

Face flushed, Tuyet gasped. "Everyone is going to hate me for being a bully."

Sau slapped her big thigh and said gleefully, "Trust me, they'll love you!"

EVERY GOSSIP was part storyteller, and a good storyteller never had qualms about stretching the truth a little if it improved the story. Sau was among the best. She crafted a thrilling tale, painting both Tuyet and herself as heroines against corrupt officials. Within a day, the story had traveled around town, growing more fanciful with each telling, and so, Le Tuyet, the Major's Wife, instantly became a household name, beloved of the townsfolk.

A new chapter of her life began. People greeted Tuyet in the street. Women chatted with her at the market, seeking her advice or assistance. Hardships had taught her empathy for the weak and the poor. It was not long before she blossomed into a champion of the common people.

17

First Son

IT WAS THE YEAR OF THE HORSE. HE WAS THIRTY-six years old. Three full cycles of the Chinese Zodiac. His wishes had been fulfilled within twelve months. Everything had come easily. For Takeshi, 1942 had begun with him rising from his convalescence bed to receive a medal of valor and a prized post in a seaside paradise. Perchance, he had found love with a beautiful woman who made him feel alive again. Now, she was carrying his first child. He owned a house and a luxury car. And a king's ransom in gold had fallen into his lap. At times, it felt like a dream. As the Year of the Horse drew to a close, Takeshi was apprehensive about waking up.

His fears were not unfounded, his intuition not wrong about the momentum of the war. As 1942 flowed into 1943, the tide had turned for the Axis Powers. It had already turned for the Japanese, months earlier in the Battle of Midway. In the last days of the year, news came of Germany's catastrophic defeat by Russia at the Battle of Stalingrad. The veteran Yamazaki had grown cynical of the rosy outlook High Command was relaying to the troops. He knew the end was approaching.

ON APRIL 7, 1943, in the Year of the Goat, Tuyet, assisted by her midwife, successfully delivered his son at home. Takeshi named him Kei—"jubilation"—to mark his fatherhood. Tuyet chose his middle name, Huy Hoang, for "glorious" to counterbalance the turmoil the seer-nun had predicted. As a precaution, she insisted that they use the baby's shortened Viet name,

Hoang, to confuse angry spirits that had been offended by the Japanese, who were, even by Takeshi's admission, becoming crueler by the month as the tide of war turned against the empire.

Over dinner one evening, Tuyet told her husband about seeing dozens of panhandlers at the market. She found it immensely sad that the war had made so many people destitute to the point of begging for food.

"It will get much worse!" Takeshi warned, drinking his second bottle of sake. "We must be prepared."

"Is that why you've been working so hard?" Tuyet asked, attempting to catch his eyes across the candlelit table. Fuel rations provided the town's power station a mere three hours of electricity after sunset. They were having a late dinner alone, Coi and the children already asleep.

He lowered his voice. "We have some logistics problems at the base. I'm very busy in several business ventures. I need a steady stream of revenue to keep the bosses happy at HQ. My post is safe as long as I line their pockets every month. Generals need to eat, too."

"I wish there were something I could do to help. I know you are working very hard to take care of us." Tuyet sighed.

Since their wedding, they had been living in bliss: a new baby, a new home, family meals, occasional trips to Saigon, cocktail parties, and dances at Le Jardin Rouge with friends. Takeshi purchased a farm in the countryside, with plans to build a vacation home there. Tuyet had begun volunteering at the temple as well as the orphanage. She regularly made donations to charities. Over the year, she earned a good reputation among townsfolk, even though she was married to a Japanese officer.

He held her hand and said with a sad smile, "Bad news at the office. I received orders to transfer half of my men to New Guinea. The fighting is intense there. If we lose our foothold in New Guinea, and it looks very likely, it will be terrible."

Takeshi thought that 1943 would be a year of mounting losses for the Imperial Japanese Army. The empire had been on the defensive for months, draining its dwindling resources to hang on to gains won in the opening moves. From all directions, Allied forces were advancing steadily toward Japan. They already had recaptured half of New Guinea with relative ease while inflicting massive Japanese casualties.

"Will the empire win this war?" Tuyet asked.

He paused and looked at her. "Never repeat anything I say to anyone."

"Of course. It's just that we hear so much positive news on the radio."

"Propaganda. When they attacked Pearl Harbor, our generals planned for victory within six months. Look where we are, two years later. Except for Admiral Yamamoto, those old fools never spent much time outside Asia. They thought fighting the peasant Chinese was the same as warring major industrial powers." He sighed, shaking his head in disgust.

She noticed more gray in his hair, even on his chin and chest. Since they had moved into the Yellow House, it had slowly dawned on Tuyet that her husband was a man with divided loyalties. His worldly travels had made him unsettled from the start. The places and things he had seen had opened his eyes, making him ill-suited for military life.

He continued, talking into his cup, slurring his words. "These proud old generals use troops like ammunition. You can't order new soldiers from a factory!"

He gulped his sake, emptying the bottle as he asked her for brandy, and fumbled for his pipe. His face was beet red, flushed with alcohol, but she did not stop him for she saw he needed the deep rest that only a boozy slumber could bring.

"You're worried about your men going to New Guinea," she said softly, disquieted by his note of finality.

"Remember their war slogan? *A million deaths!*" He croaked

a bitter laugh. "Our damn generals! A country willing to sacri-fice a million lives needs ten million miracles."

A haunted look came over his face as his thoughts drifted to places and memories he had never shared with her. "This is the beginning of the end."

"How much worse can it get? Hospitals don't have medi-cine. Farmers lost half their crop to requisitioning. Those with food to sell can't transport it to market because of petrol short-ages. Even the fishermen can't get enough fuel to go to sea. And prices keep shooting through the roof."

He laughed derisively, his eyes glinting. "Worse than you can ever imagine. What seems impossible today, may be inevitable tomorrow."

"Is that why you are working with all sides?"

"I am making as many allies as I can so you and the chil-dren have money and people to rely on if I get sent to the front line . . . if something happens to me."

◆

AND SO it went, the gradual decline of Japanese con-trol over the war as well as Vietnam. Over the next eighteen months, the Imperial Japanese Army suffered massive losses on all fronts. Meanwhile, Vietnam descended into chaos as fam-ine and starvation spread throughout the country, eventually claiming more than a million lives. Then in early 1945 the Jap-anese launched a preemptive strike against the Vichy French in Vietnam.

18

Bright Moon

"CEASE FIRE! DO NOT ATTACK THE GARRISON!" Major Yamazaki screamed into the radio. "Captain Tanaka, that's a direct order!"

A garbled affirmative came back against a background of rattling gunshots. Gnashing his teeth, Yamazaki held back from scolding his second-in-command over the air. He repeated his order, telling Tanaka to wait for him. Lieutenant Mori was at his side, along with a radio operator and two second lieutenants handling logistics. It was midmorning.

"Have my plane ready on the runway. Immediately."

"With fuel and ammo, Major?" a young ensign asked.

"Just fuel, half tank. Now. Run!"

Mori asked, "Do you want a co-pilot?"

"I don't need one. There will not be any fighting if I can help it. Radio and tell them to clear the road. I'll be landing there shortly."

Mori relayed the order. He said, "I wonder how the fighting began at the garrison."

"Probably because Tanaka was looking for a fight," Yamazaki growled, stomping out the door. "It was a mistake to let him lead the operation."

Mori mumbled, "What can you do? He's the admiral's son."

Yamazaki was already running into his quarters for his flying gear. He paused to think, grabbed a few things, and stuffed them into a small canvas satchel. It had been a bloodless coup so far. He'd be damned if Tanaka would turn it into a bloodbath.

EIGHT HOURS EARLIER, High Command had launched Meigō Sakusen—Operation Bright Moon. The plan had been on the table for several weeks, ever since the French had picked up six American airmen shot down by the Japanese and had refused to turn them over to the Imperial Japanese Army. When Japanese troops prepared to storm the Saigon Central Prison to forcibly take the American pilots, the French had smuggled them out.

With signs of French defection being imminent, High Command put all bases on alert and ordered troops to be stationed at every French garrison throughout Indochina. At two A.M. on March 9, 1945, Yamazaki deployed his men, using all available transport at the base. Under cover of darkness, at two thirty A.M. Lieutenant Kitamura walked into Phan Thiet Prison and ordered unsuspecting Viet guards to open the gates. By three A.M., Japanese troops had rounded up all of Phan Thiet's 121 French residents, dragging some from their beds in their pajamas. At first light, eight inmates, all convicted murderers, were led into the prison yard for execution. Kitamura beheaded them one by one with his katana. Other prisoners were pardoned and released. The prison became a holding pen for the captured French men, women, and children.

THE MORNING AIR was dry and hot, the breeze chafing. Bright blue sky with fleecy white clouds. Yamazaki banked the plane and circled the garrison once, Frenchmen and legionnaires in bunkers, Japanese troops in fortified positions on the outside. Peasants were fleeing in fear. He lined up and landed gently on the road, shut off the engine, then strolled across the space between the garrison and his soldiers' positions. Captain Tanaka and Lieutenant Kitamura came to attention and saluted. Yamazaki brushed into the tent and demanded a report. They stood around a table with a hand-drawn map of the garrison, which had been designed to defend against poorly armed rebels. Not a trained army. Tanaka reported the dispositions of his men, announcing that they could overwhelm the garrison in half an hour or simply destroy it outright.

"Tell me about the gunfight," Yamazaki snapped.

"Five men tried to sneak out the back of the bunker. We stopped them. They fired at us as they retreated. My men returned fire. We wounded or killed several of them. That was when I radioed to request permission to attack."

"Good work, Captain Tanaka," said Yamazaki grudgingly, relieved that Tanaka hadn't started the fight. "I will meet with Captain Moreau. High Command ordered us to exhaust all peaceful options first."

"But . . . but we must teach them a lesson," stammered Tanaka, bristling with indignation.

"If he doesn't surrender, you can have your battle," Yamazaki replied and left the tent, ignoring Tanaka's protestations. He strode across his men's line of fire and headed to the garrison.

"Captain Moreau! Captain Moreau!" Yamazaki called out.

"Bonjour, Major Yamazaki! Nice landing," Moreau shouted in cheery French, stepping out of the guardhouse.

"A word, please. Over there," said Yamazaki, pointing to a bamboo platform with a thatched roof in the middle of the rice fields, erected by farmers as a place to rest and have lunch.

He led the way. Soldiers on both sides watched as their commanders walked across earthen dikes to the shelter about two hundred meters away. They settled on the platform in clear view of both the garrison and the Japanese. A bottle of brandy and two metal tumblers came out of Yamazaki's satchel.

Yamazaki raised his mug. "To our mutual health."

Moreau smiled wearily. "To our mutual health."

They sniffed, sipped, smacked their lips in appreciation, and sipped again. Yamazaki said, "That's the last of the good stuff from our friend Feraud."

"So we've arrived at another crossroad."

"It would seem so."

"Tragic, but fitting somehow, if you don't mind my saying so."

"Only a fool denies the truth."

"Touché."

Yamazaki inhaled the fragrance of rice ready for the harvest, fat grains on drooping stalks. Looking at that crop, one would never imagine the millions starving up north. He asked, "Are your men injured?"

"Four wounded, one seriously."

"My apologies. Captain Tanaka did not have permission to attack."

"I allowed my men to leave," said Moreau, raising his chin and giving a little shrug. He downed his brandy hard. His bald round head, red with sun, gleamed with sweat. He was in bad shape, gaunt, his face clammy, eyes feverish. Involuntary tremors wracked his thin frame.

"Drink up while the drinking is good," said Yamazaki as he refilled Moreau's mug. Yamazaki knew that Moreau was an opium addict who only smoked at home, the pipes prepared by his wife. Moreau had been at the garrison for five days, so Yamazaki reasoned he must be suffering withdrawal.

"Please surrender. You don't stand a chance against us."

"What if I don't?"

"We'll set fire to those dry fields around the garrison. While you choke on the smoke, we will mortar the garrison. Then we will bomb you from the air. This is the good scenario."

Moreau sat stone-faced, hiding the fact that they were running low on food. They had only several hundred rounds of ammunition, a case of grenades, and even fewer mortar rounds. The war was going very badly for the Vichy French.

They hadn't been resupplied in months. Live-round practice had been suspended long ago to conserve ammunition. A firefight would deplete them in minutes.

Looking unmoved, Moreau asked, "And the bad scenario?"

"The IJA has its own protocol, which is what my second-in-command is eager to implement. We would proceed to execute the Frenchmen captured last night. If that doesn't persuade you to surrender, we would bring your families here to the garrison so you can watch. Tanaka and Kitamura would behead them one by one until you surrender."

"I don't believe you would execute the innocent," Moreau observed, scowling.

"I won't, but Captain Tanaka will," replied Yamazaki. "If you refuse to surrender, I must yield field command to Tanaka or his father the admiral will have my head. The war is reaching a climax and poor Tanaka is very hungry for blood and glory. If you fight and lose, there will be no mercy. He will execute all survivors."

Moreau replied defiantly, "We can hold long enough for reinforcement."

Yamazaki shook his head in sympathy. "There is no one to come to your aid. We already captured nearly all the garrisons. A scattered few are still fighting in Nha Trang and up north near the Chinese border. Go check your radio."

"What guarantee do I have that you won't kill us the moment we surrender?"

"My word," he answered, fixing the other man's eyes for a long spell. "I swear on my honor that your men and their families will not be harmed. My wife will see to it that your family has everything they need until this situation is resolved."

"What do you intend to do with my men?"

"I have orders to disarm and confine your men at the garrison until further notice. That should not surprise you since

Governor Admiral Decoux has been refusing to cooperate with General Tsuchihashi."

"France has been liberated. When the Allies defeat the Germans, they will be coming here. Decoux knows it's suicide to collaborate with the IJA now."

"And Tsuchihashi knows it's only a matter of time before Decoux orders an uprising against us."

Moreau acknowledged the point with a grunt and topped off their cups with more brandy. The Colonial Army, the Tirailleurs Indochinois, and the Foreign Legion outnumbered the Japanese occupation forces by two to one; however, the Vichy French of Indochina had neither the willpower nor the desire to resist. French forces would fight the Japanese to regain control of the colony but not for Vichy France, subservient to the fractured German empire.

Moreau sighed. "We're only pawns."

"Pawns that haven't suffered. If the war is to end, it will be decided elsewhere, with or without us fighting. I do not need to spill your blood now. Please, for the sake of your family, don't force my hand."

Moreau produced his tobacco pouch from his pocket and gestured to Yamazaki, who declined by taking out his pipe. They smoked in silence. Moreau had backed the Japanese major three years earlier. Thus far, he did not regret it. He knew things might have been much worse, but, fortunately, Yamazaki was an honorable man. The major had been generous, almost kind, especially during this past year when the country was starving. Yet, he had still made sure Moreau's garrison remained adequately supplied.

"Damn it, Moreau!" he cried, his patience wearing thin. "Lay down your arms, and I will permit your wife daily visitation rights. She can bring you whatever you need, as much as you need," he said, alluding to the opium. Discreetly, Yamazaki removed a cotton pouch from his pocket and, while reaching for the brandy bottle, slid it across to Moreau. He added, "And a little something for you to start over again once this is all over."

Hearing those words, Moreau felt his resolve crumble. Finally, he surrendered to common sense and the survival of his family. Loathsome Vichy France wasn't worth the sacrifice. The French captain had spent the past five days in the garrison mulling over the possibilities of his wife taking another husband or selling her body to feed their children. He held out his mug for more brandy and swept up the pouch in the same motion. Safely inside his shirt, he knew it contained a small stick of opium, the size of his little finger, wrapped in wax paper, and several familiar red silk sachets of gold.

"Ah, the spoils of war."

"You're a veteran, you know how it is," Yamazaki replied, holding the other man's gaze. "Enough for a comfortable retirement, whatever happens."

With a cynical smile, Moreau nodded. "What are you buying?"

"Your life. And I give it back to you. I do not want your death on my conscience. You helped me once. I am returning the favor."

Moreau chewed his lips in grim silence. At length, he stubbed out his cigarette and extended a clammy hand. "I have your word?"

"On my honor," replied Yamazaki, reaching out and sealing their deal.

19

Spoils

THE MORNING AFTER OPERATION BRIGHT MOON,
the sun had cleared the treetops, but the normally bustling
downtown streets were quiet. The market empty, most shops
closed. Beggars nowhere to be seen. The dusk-to-dawn curfew had ended but the townsfolk were expecting a clash.
Tuyet hired the neighborhood cyclo to visit Captain Moreau's
wife. The cycloman pedaled slowly. On his handlebar, the bell
clanged hollow warning to no one. They crossed the deserted
bridge without meeting anyone. Nearer the government buildings, some civil servants were scurrying about with stacks of
documents, but the offices seemed abandoned. Trash littered
the area. A few customers milled about outside a bakery. At
sidewalk cafés, small groups of well-to-do retirees sat sipping
coffee with an air of too-old-to-care.

On the near side of the river, two "colonial" areas were
inhabited mostly by the French. The section closer to the sea
was one of sprawling opulent estates of merchants, plantation owners, and ranking colonial administrators. The other
inland section was a hardscrabble neighborhood of small bungalows and row houses inhabited by *petits blancs*, craftsmen,
and soldiers.

"*La rue des petits café au lait.*" The cycloman chuckled,
swerving to avoid a boy playing in the street. A rowdy ball game
was under way. A dozen mixed-race children scrambled about.

Street of little ones like milky coffee. A quaint slang, Tuyet
thought. Their skin tones ranged from pink to beige to ruddy
mocha. The offspring of poor whites and indigenous partners.

The Imperial Japanese Army had left these children unmolested at home with their Viet mothers. They had herded the purebloods with their French parents into the town's prison.

The captain's house sat at the end of a tidy road of brick bungalows on small plots. Tuyet had met Moreau's wife, Tam, at temple festivals. They had both volunteered at the orphanage. Tam was hanging laundry in the side yard of the house with the help of her seven-year-old daughter and five-year-old son. The children bowed, respectfully greeting Tuyet.

"I'm so sorry," Tuyet said, bowing to the younger woman.

"No, Sister, we're not responsible for what soldiers do," Tam said, touching Tuyet's forearm.

SIPPING TEA in the living room, the two women exchanged pleasantries. Tuyet glanced over the mix of Viet and European furnishings, judging the younger woman to be a sensible homemaker. The worn tile floor was immaculate, windowsills spotless, the ceiling corners free of spiderwebs. Vases of flowers and potted orchids made the room fragrant, but tobacco smoke with the sweet, medicinal whiff of opium had seeped into the walls.

Tuyet set her teacup down and said, "I hope all this will soon end peacefully."

"Who knows how this war is going to turn out or what they will do to one another. Please, thank your husband for not attacking the garrison."

"He said your husband would have done the same for him," Tuyet said. "I know the Japanese are losing the war. I never thought it would come to this."

"My husband expected something would happen, but he didn't know what or when," Tam replied calmly. "But what could he do? Orders go down, not up."

"True, they seem to understand one another." Tuyet nodded.

"My husband sent me to ask you to head up the kitchen crew at the garrison. The job comes with a salary and vouchers for food. Also, pick five more women as your assistants. You'll be able to see your husband daily and bring his opium."

"Oh, thank you!" Tam said. "I know my husband is suffering without his pipe."

Tuyet pressed an envelope of money into Tam's hand. "Take this. If you need anything, come directly to me. I'm here to support you. We'll get through this together."

Eyes lowered, Tam struggled to mask her emotions. In a choked voice, she said, "Big Sister, I will never forget your kindness as long as I live. If the day ever comes that you need me, I will be there."

TUYET TOLD the cycloman to detour through the wealthy neighborhood by the government quarters. She still couldn't quite believe that the French had been arrested and imprisoned like common criminals. For generations, they had ruled the country like demigods. Japanese audacity forced her to see a new reality.

They were startled by a burgundy red automobile thundering past. There was only one of its kind in town, and it belonged to the owners of Kim Long restaurant.

"Follow that Citroën," she said.

"Madame? It's too fast."

"Just keep going. I think I know where it's heading."

Continuing down the avenue, they came to a checkpoint manned by Japanese soldiers. The Citroën stopped briefly and was allowed through. They lost sight of the car as it turned at the next intersection. Japanese soldiers stopped the cyclo. A young corporal greeted Tuyet, recognizing his commander's wife. Tuyet bowed and greeted him in Japanese. The soldiers beamed. They were there to protect the homes from looters.

The corporal waved them through. She saw few people, mostly servants. At several large estates, Japanese soldiers were carrying things out, cataloging them, and loading them into trucks.

They found the Citroën at the Feraud mansion. A stooped gardener was trimming a hedge, oblivious to visitors as well as to the strange events taking place in his neighborhood. Tuyet greeted him, but he did not respond. The cycloman let Tuyet down behind the Citroën where Yen Long and her daughter Mai-Ly were standing. Yen wore a sleeveless cheongsam, a glittering peacock-green sheath dress with ruby trim that emphasized her slim figure. Her daughter was an even more beautiful version of Yen but with a gentler, softer face.

Yen smiled, radiant. "Sister Tuyet, I told Mai-Ly that it was you!"

They exchanged greetings. Tuyet and Takeshi had been regular patrons at the restaurant. Tuyet wanted to know whether the mansion was for sale.

"Mister Chu already bought it. Do you know him?" asked Yen. "He was Feraud's accountant."

"Yes, my husband also uses his services."

"The tax office seized the property recently. He bought it for next to nothing."

"That's brazen!"

Yen shrugged. "Feraud is probably dead. If someone had not bought it, sooner or later, looters would have taken everything. Besides, if the Allies start bombing here in the south, this may all be rubble next month."

"What are you doing here?"

"Shopping! Mister Chu is selling everything. He said the Ferauds have a good art collection. Will you join us?"

"It feels strange picking over his belongings," said Tuyet, shaking her head.

"Oh, Sister, you shouldn't feel anything but joy. Think of all the girls he abused, the lives he ruined. It's a blessing he's gone."

The front door opened and a portly Chinese man in dark trousers and white long sleeves waddled out. He had narrow, quick eyes in a round beatific face, a fine pencil mustache, and a double chin. His broad, friendly smile was marred by his small sharp teeth. He wore a gold watch and gold-rimmed reading spectacles.

"Missus Long, what are you doing out here?" he shouted. "Aren't you coming in?"

"Good morning, Mister Chu. Sorry to keep you waiting. I was just chatting with Sister Tuyet."

"Oh, Madame Yamazaki," Chu said with a deep bow. "Good morning. I didn't see you."

"Good morning, Mister Chu," said Tuyet, forcing a smile. She was unsure whether he was mocking or complimenting her, for no one had ever called her by her husband's surname.

A second-generation Chinese immigrant, Yim Chu was one of the town's top accountants. Since the early days of the colony, the French had been importing Indians and Chinese to manage their finances and trade, effectively keeping power, knowledge, and wealth out of the hands of the Viet. Thus, these "outside Asians" had become the overseers of the colonized.

"How is Major Yamazaki?"

"Very busy, same as always."

"Good to hear," he said. "Are you looking for some art or furniture?"

"No, I saw Yen's car and just stopped by to say hello."

"Come in anyway, pick a painting with my compliments. No charge."

"Oh, I couldn't, but thank you. I'm late for an appointment," she blurted and hurried back to the cyclo.

Mai-Ly walked back with Tuyet, waiting until her mother had gone into the house with Chu. She said, "Aunt Tuyet, I'm not supposed to talk about this, but if it hadn't been for your husband, my life would have been very different. I just wanted to say thank you to you and your husband. I hope I can repay him someday."

"Just live a good life." Tuyet smiled.

As she bade Mai-Ly goodbye, she had a disquieting premonition that the owner of the mansion wasn't dead. His aura still lingered about the estate.

◆

IN MAY, Germany surrendered to the Allies. Japan found itself isolated, its resources depleted. Defeat was imminent. Takeshi worked frantically, traveling between Nha Trang, Phan Thiet, Vung Tau, and Saigon. Tuyet knew he was involved with the Resistance through her cousin Ha and his supervisor Mister Xuan. She rarely saw her husband more than once a week and knew almost nothing about what he was doing, other than that he was preparing for what might come after the war.

From May to mid-August 1945, Vietnam descended into worsening turmoil. With the French still imprisoned and the Japanese facing catastrophic defeat, there was no central authority to keep law and order. Over six long years of occupation, the Japanese had drained the country's resources. Even in the later stages when their supply lines had been disrupted by the Allies, the Japanese continued to impose high delivery quotas on farmers, stockpiling food, only to leave much of it to rot in warehouses while a million peasants died of starvation. The north bore the brunt of this. Protests and riots broke out in many provinces. Bandits ruled the highways, raiding villages with impunity. In cities, people were robbed in broad daylight. Gangs multiplied, emboldened by chaos. In the power vacuum, political and religious factions thrived and maneuvered against one another with attacks, kidnappings, and assassinations.

———

GIVEN THE chaotic and difficult circumstances, Coi and Tuyet were fearful that burglars might think the Japanese major might have hidden a fortune at home. Tuyet knew Takeshi had somehow become wealthy at his post, but she was oblivious to the details. They had an easy life of plenty even during the worst periods. She never asked him how he managed this, and he never told her. Besides, it was tradition for the man to handle external financial affairs while the woman managed the household budget. It was beneath a husband to ask his wife about family expenditures, and a wife did not presume to question or advise her husband on his earnings and investments. Takeshi never asked about his wife's lending ventures and Tuyet never inquired about her husband's business dealings. She sensed that he wanted it kept private, and she did not want to put herself in the position of judging him.

◆

ON AUGUST 6, 1945, an American B-29 bomber named *Enola Gay* dropped the world's first atomic bomb on Hiroshima, instantly killing eighty thousand people. Three days later, on August 9, another B-29 bomber named *Bockscar* dropped a second atomic bomb on Nagasaki, killing forty thousand. Even then, Imperial troops remained dug into the beaches, prepared for battle. Meanwhile, the Soviets declared war on Japan and sent more than one and a half million troops into Japanese-controlled Manchuria. Both the American atomic bombs and the Russian offensive forced the Japanese Empire to its knees.

20

End of Empire

AN AUGUST MONSOON FLOODED THE TOWN, TURN-
ing streets into murky canals. Life came to a standstill as water
stood several feet high in much of the neighborhood. People
huddled inside, staring out into the deluge. Day after day, dark
clouds off the South China Sea hauled in heavy rain. The river
that divided the town had swelled to several times its usual
width as it swept to sea fallen trees, bobbing islands of hya-
cinths, broken bamboo rafts, buffalo carcasses, and thatched
huts. A beggar encampment along the bank had slid into the
current and had been dragged under. Bodies drifted out to
open waters, so no one bothered to inter them. Corpses piled
up at temples, the ground too soggy for burial, the firewood
too wet for funeral pyres.

Late one afternoon, the sky let up, the last of the raindrops
dripping from the eaves. Sudden silence startled the town. People stepped outside, heaving a collective sigh. Birds took wing,
a chorus of song erupting from the green canopy, flashing over
the rooftops. Chickens scattered in a frenzied feast of bugs and
earthworms. Dogs scampered about marking territories. Cats
ventured out, shaking their wet paws irritably. Windows and
doors were flung wide open to air out musty houses. While the
weather held, women with satchels over their shoulders hurried
out on errands.

Coi, Tuyet, and the children came outside to work. The sun
pierced through the linty clouds. Steam rose off the ground,
wet musk of the earth. Stagnant puddles fringed the house.
On the south side stood a pond, its beige surface covered with

dead insects. From tree to tree, black, red, and brown ants marched up trunks, crossing branches. The garden was gone, flower beds obliterated, trellises knocked over and broken into pieces, ground-level vegetables swamped. Weeds thrived, having cropped up to calf height almost overnight. Coi and Tuyet dug drainage channels while Anh and Hoang splashed about, catching little frogs as they picked up debris.

The front gate creaked.

"Uncle Ha!" the children shrieked. Ha was pushing his bicycle through mud, his sleeves rolled up to the elbow, pant legs bunched around his knees. He was completely soaked.

"It's over! It's over!" Ha yelled, grinning from ear to ear.

Anh and Hoang wrapped themselves around his legs. They knew he always came home with presents for them. He picked them up, one in each arm, and spun them around until they squealed. He hugged his mother in a rare display of affection.

"Ma, it's over!" Ha cried. "Haven't you heard? It's all over the radio! The Japanese surrendered. The war is over."

"What?" Auntie and Tuyet cried in unison.

"The war—it's truly over. Japan surrendered."

"It's over?"

"*It's over!*"

The whole family cheered and splashed about in the flooded garden, dancing until they all collapsed, exhausted, on the porch steps. Coi and Tuyet grinned, speechless with relief.

At that exact moment, Tuyet saw a scrim of cloud drifting across the lowering sun. Golden, liquid light engulfed them. She had a moment of crystal clarity as time pooled like syrup. The silken air was rich with scents of renewals. On the branch of a starfruit tree, one gold-billed magpie preened its wings, fanning its long blue tail to dry. Nearby in the foliage, a spider-web sparkled, a necklace of raindrop diamonds.

Coi saw it too and smiled; the crow's-feet clawed deep in the corners of her eyes. Five-year-old Anh pointed at the web, thrilled. She had that rare ability to be content. Two-year-old Hoang watched his sister intently. His head tilted at an angle as if in perpetual curiosity. Ha stood over them, arms folded across his chest, a smile on his lips, a lock of unkempt hair over an eye. Veins on his forearms popped out like cords, his muscular legs bulging, as strong as a porter's. Tuyet's bookish cousin was now twenty-five: a strong, confident man, yet untouched by defeat and heartbreak. In a sudden leap of intuition, she saw a decade of sacrifices, sorrow, and exile awaiting him. Destiny was imprinted deeply. She saw it the way a river sensed the distant sea.

YOUNG MEN RAN down the street, from house to house, shouting that the war was over. People came out, wandering with the dazed look of the convalescing. At the street corner, a small group of royalists had gathered around a dignified old man who was hoisting the flag of Emperor Bao Dai, a horizontal red band on a yellow field. Across town, political and religious groups convened and debated the future.

For the first time in a century, the country found itself in a sudden power vacuum. From Hanoi to Saigon, political factions began vying for power. Some allied themselves with the French, who remained imprisoned by the "surrendered" Japanese. Others looked toward Americans or the Chinese. A few royalists hoped for the powerless emperor to emerge and lead the country. The Resistance bartered with the Japanese for arms and support. Alliances were forged and broken in a matter of weeks. The stage was being set for the first Indochina war.

21

French Mob

MA-BAO, A GREASY BAKERY IN THE FOOD ALLEY across from Ben Thanh Market, was Tuyet's favorite bun shop in Saigon. Shaded by taller buildings, it was a popular afternoon hangout for tea and the news. Office workers, housewives, and shopkeepers sat on stools crammed around crude wooden tables. Everyone was talking loudly. A disorderly queue gathered by one wall and meandered out the door, two dozen customers waiting for rice cakes with minced pork, sweet barbecued red pork, and bean paste. At the rear of the shop, a range of five-tiered bamboo steamers billowed clouds of mouth-watering aromas.

It was late September 1945. Tuyet had only arrived in Saigon the day before. She was shocked at the sheer abundance of food everywhere, in markets, in eateries, on the streets. Even though most of the country was still in the grip of famine, Saigon had been flooded with food, almost magically overnight, displaying a vast array of every sort of edibles as though the war years had been only a bad dream.

"Do you think the wholesalers have been hoarding all this time?" Tuyet asked.

"Of course," Takeshi said, sipping his tea. His jaw was smarting from a tooth extraction. "You'd be surprised at how resourceful people are when they want to be. Smugglers have had a free run this past month, yet most of the goods and staples were here all along, right under our noses."

Tuyet fed him a piece of cake. "Here, try this red bean cake. No one else makes it like this."

Takeshi was dressed in the civvies he had worn to his dental appointment. He took a bite and winced as he tongued the space where the tooth had been. "That was the third one I have had pulled in this country."

"The dentist said you should cut back on your whiskey and tobacco. They weaken your teeth," Tuyet said primly, mildly nagging him about his excesses. She was dressed in her favorite lavender *ao dai* and was looking forward to seeing her best friends, Ly and Van, for dinner that evening. She hadn't been to Saigon since the New Year.

Takeshi grunted and made a face, incapable of imagining life without a few vices, especially now when he had so many new problems. How to secure his secret fortune? Leave it buried in Mui Ne? Take it back with him to Hokkaido? Japan, at the mercy of the Allies, did not seem like a good haven. Lately, he often wondered about that pervert Feraud. There had been no sign of the Frenchman, not even a whisper on the underground network. It was rumored that Feraud had met his death, but Takeshi didn't believe this.

Seeing his thoughts were far away, Tuyet smiled. "I think you like going to the dentist."

A commotion in the street came closer. Car horns blared wildly on the main thoroughfares. A noisy convoy of vehicles converged on the city center as the crowd rushed out to look. Takeshi and Tuyet followed. Several vehicles halted at a major intersection, blocking traffic. One screeching sedan plowed into a row of parked bicycles. Bedraggled Frenchmen spilled out from a truck. They cursed and yelled randomly at anyone. Two men protested the damage to their bicycles. A group of Frenchmen descended on them, beating them savagely. The British Indian Army troops, the new authority in Vietnam, had vanished as though wanting no part of the chaos. Thousands of French civilians and soldiers were now swarming into the city's central district. Some wore threadbare army khakis, others filthy shorts and undershirts, all of them emaciated. Shop-keepers came out to gawk alongside pedestrians, shocked at the awful spectacle. A handful of loyalists managed a feeble cheer for the French.

Tuyet asked, "What's happening?"

"The British released them from the internment camp." Takeshi sneered. "You see the rifles they're carrying? Those are Lee-Enfields. General Gracey has re-armed the French with British weapons."

"Did you expect the British to support the French?"

"Not to the point of arming them and turning them loose like this on the city."

"I can't blame them for being angry," Tuyet said. She did feel some sympathy for the Frenchmen. Five weeks had passed since the Japanese surrender, and the French had been released only today.

"You will see some nastiness very soon, my dear. This riot is about to get ugly."

At that moment across the street, two freed legionnaires hurled a park bench through a liquor store's window, shatter-ing the glass. Dozens of men swarmed to loot, whooping glee-fully. People stopped, mouths agape, transfixed by the sight of the French mob. Rowdy men hauled out crates of whiskey and started guzzling the booze in the street. A man popped a bottle of champagne and showered his compatriots with it. Some sat down on the curb and ate food they had stolen. The pandemonium rolled outward like a wave as the once civilized Frenchmen vented their rage by vandalizing businesses, rob-bing shops, and attacking anyone in their way.

"Let's go," ordered Takeshi as he stopped Tuyet from return-ing to the bakery. "Leave the bags! Run!"

He dragged her away from the bedlam. They dodged through a crowd surging in the opposite direction toward the commo-tion on the main avenue. The French mob spilled into the alley, drawn by the smell of fresh bread and barbecued meats. Scuffles broke out as marauders pushed aside protesting vendors and gorged on whatever they could lay their hands on. The crowd panicked and scattered.

Shopkeepers began shutting doors, but these were promptly kicked in by the mob. Street vendors fled, abandoning their carts. Pedestrians stumbled, slipping on the wet pavement. Frenchmen knocked over fruit carts and newsstands. A charcoal grill ignited a kiosk. Pistol reports rang out. Men dragged restaurant patrons into the street and beat them.

Takeshi said, "We won't make it back to the hotel. Is there a safe place near here?"

"Le Jardin Rouge."

An incredulous Takeshi turned to her. "It will be full of French!"

"They adore Van. They will go there to celebrate. No one will see us if we go through the back door. It's not far."

They paused, indecisive, backing up against the wall to let others pass. Takeshi surveyed the mounting madness and rubbed his nose, weighing their chances. He nodded for Tuyet to go forward. She trotted into the warren of alleyways that riddled several city blocks, the working-class slum rarely visited by the French. Within minutes, people had swarmed into the labyrinth as residents barricaded themselves inside their homes.

Emerging onto a street, they waited for a lull in the traffic. They dashed into another alley on the far side. Halfway across, Tuyet saw soldiers kicking a well-dressed businessman on the sidewalk. Sirens howled on the next street. A bonfire of tables and chairs roared three meters high in the middle of the road. A group of Frenchmen was hauling furniture out of a posh restaurant and hurling it onto the fire. The proprietor and his wife were on their knees, pleading with the vandals. Tuyet in her sandals ran as fast as she could, and Takeshi struggled to keep up with his aching knee.

A shriek. Tuyet halted at the T-junction. A few steps away on her right, two Frenchmen had a teenage girl pinned to the ground. They were tearing off her clothes. A scrawny bearded man restrained the girl's arms while a much larger brute knelt between her bare legs, pressing down on her naked belly with one hand while fumbling to undo his trousers with the other. Both heard Tuyet's gasp and turned.

Takeshi dived by Tuyet in complete silence. Yanking his pistol from its shoulder holster as he thumbed the safety catch, he closed half the distance before the bearded man released the girl and lunged for a rifle leaning against the wall. Takeshi's slug hit the man just above the ear, his head bursting like a dragon fruit. The girl screamed and clawed at the throat of the man looming on top of her. He sat up on his knees, mouth agape, staring at the smoking barrel of the pistol. He uttered a pitiful cry, shielding his face with his hands. Takeshi fired twice into his chest, knocking him backward.

Shocked, Tuyet averted her eyes but not before catching a strange, placid look on her husband's face. The executions had been swift and professional, emotionless, like shooting wild animals. It was chilling. Tuyet shuddered. Pushing the thought from her mind, she rushed over to the girl.

"Are you hurt?" Tuyet asked, helping the teenager with her pants. She signed the unspoken question at the girl.

"No. No, I'm fine. He didn't," she said bravely, pulling her torn shirt over her breasts. Her mouth was bleeding.

"Hurry, we have to go now," Takeshi said.

The urgency in his voice made Tuyet look. A soldier had entered the far end of the alley and was peering in their direction, whence the sounds of gunshots had come. He backed away and called his comrades. The girl grabbed her student satchel off the ground.

"Halt!" the soldier shouted as he waited for reinforcements. They fled as more men entered the alley. As they rounded the corner, another group of Frenchmen was moving toward them, no more than fifty meters away. Left with no choice, they escaped in the only direction available.

"Follow me," the girl cried, sprinting ahead. "This is my neighborhood!"

The crack of a rifle. A bullet zinged overhead and ricocheted off a wall. Takeshi returned fire. They ran after the girl through the winding alley. The buildings were closing in and the roofs began to overlap. They ducked under clotheslines, hopped over trash piles. Takeshi pulled down a stack of crates to slow their pursuers. The girl waited for them at the next turn, beckoning them to hurry. The chase was rounding the corner. People retreated into their houses. Stinging smoke filled the air.

The girl took several turns and stopped at what Tuyet thought was an alcove. It was a meter-wide maintenance gap between two buildings. A narrow space, deep in the shadows, cluttered with bamboo scraps and piles of broken bricks. She rolled a thick bundle of bamboo poles aside, which revealed a small opening. She squeezed through sideways. Tuyet fumbled blindly after her, feeling the bare bricks, clumps of cement. Beneath her feet, broken tiles, rubbish. She stepped into a puddle, gagging at the stench of raw sewage.

Takeshi wriggled in, forcing himself through the tiny opening. The hem of his jacket caught on the bamboo. He tugged at it, but it was stuck. Takeshi jerked, ripping the fabric. The bamboo poles rattled back into place.

They froze, peering out through the gaps. Confused shouts rang up and down the alley. The rabble careened around the corner, shouting obscenities. Two soldiers stopped directly in front of them. One knocked over bins of bottles, searching under a heap of trash. Tuyet fought the rising panic in her throat. Her breath roared in her ears. Takeshi leveled his pistol at the bamboo blocking the opening.

"Which way did they go?"

"They were right in front of us."

"Search the houses!" a bald man commanded. "You and you, check the street!"

Fists pounded on doors nearby. Women screamed as soldiers burst into their homes. Somewhere farther down the alley, residents fought back. The men ran in that direction. After the sound of boots receded, the girl led them to the other end of the maintenance corridor. They climbed over a low wall into a small courtyard, which was shared by several homes. An old couple were squatting next to a charcoal stove, preparing dinner.

"Uncle, Auntie! The soldiers are after us," the girl said to the couple.

"Child! What happened? Your face . . ." the woman cried.

The white-haired man motioned them into the house. "Run quickly!"

The girl said to Tuyet, "We can pass through their place to get to mine. It's in the next alley."

Through a windowless two-room dwelling, they exited the front door onto a parallel alley, barely wide enough for two walking side by side. The girl went to the house directly opposite and tried the door. It was locked. A middle-aged woman opened the door, and the girl collapsed into her mother's arms, bawling about what had happened. Takeshi and Tuyet followed them inside and locked the door.

After taking a moment to catch their breath, Takeshi and Tuyet peered through the shutters. This alley was quiet. The pursuers would have to go a long way around to get here. The house was four meters wide, ten deep. It had two rooms, a sleeping loft, and a small patio at the back, which was used for cooking and bathing.

"We should try to get to Van's," Tuyet said.

"Wait it out. This is a riot, not a manhunt. The mob will soon be distracted. We'll leave when it's dark."

"Please stay," pleaded the woman. "You saved my only

child. It's the least I can do." She ushered them up the wooden staircase to the loft. Straw mats, pillows, and rattan baskets took up most of the space. The daughter pointed at a bamboo ladder up to the roof via a trap door, telling them to go up there if soldiers searched the house.

The mother said, "There's a broken water tank on the roof. We don't use it anymore. You can hide there."

"Thank you. We will leave as soon as it's dark," Tuyet said. Takeshi nodded.

"We are in your debt. Our home is your home, now and always," she said. Mother and daughter went below to lock up the house.

Takeshi took Tuyet's hand. She leaned into him, their clothes damp with sweat as they gazed out over the rooftops. Gunfire cracked across the city.

Tuyet sensed a dark tide rising. "Does this mean what I think it means?"

"If you want peace, prepare for war," Takeshi replied.

She sighed, wishing it were not so. They had discussed two scenarios. The first was a smooth transition into civilian life— the desired path. In the second scenario, Takeshi would retain his command until the last possible moment. Then he would slip away into hiding to avoid forced repatriation to Japan. Tuyet would ready the household for relocation. Cousin Ha would help the family reunite somewhere, sometime, somehow. Tuyet had never thought it might come to this.

Takeshi gestured toward the north and said, "There is a Japanese post about a kilometer from here. We'll go there after dark. We can use their transport out of the city. The Resistance will retaliate. We don't want to be caught in the crossfire."

22

Southern Resistance War

SATURDAY, SEPTEMBER 24, 1945. TWO NIGHTS after the French riot, Takeshi and Tuyet were safely back in Phan Thiet. As he had predicted, violence broke out in Saigon as Vietnamese groups retaliated. Under cover of darkness, well-armed bands rumored to be Binh Xuyen mafia, Cao Dai religious sectarians, as well as other rogue elements "eluded" the Japanese guards and invaded the Cité Héraud district of Saigon, also known as the Eurasian Quarter, inhabited by twenty thousand French, Europeans, and *métis*—mixed-race people. The gangs were reportedly loosely associated, united for the purpose of revenge for the French riot days earlier. Going house to house, these Vietnamese bands beat men, women, and children, taking more than three hundred hostages and killing half of them.

An hour later, British Gurkhas arrived to find Japanese soldiers standing inactive, having done little or nothing to stop these atrocities. The Japanese claimed they were behaving similarly to the British, who had withdrawn when the French mob had rampaged unchecked through the central district two days earlier. The incident became known as the Cité Héraud Massacre.

The following day, the Viet Minh and other groups set fire to Saigon's central market district and unsuccessfully attacked Tan Son Nhat airfield. Over the next week, they clashed with British troops, seizing public utilities. The Viet Minh had, only days earlier, controlled many of these strategic locations but had been tricked into relinquishing them to the supposedly neutral British, who soon turned over control to the French.

In early October, realizing war was imminent, British major-general Douglas Gracey brought in reinforcements and ordered Japanese troops to join French and British forces to quell the Viet Minh uprising. After weeks of fighting, the Viet Minh lost a thousand men, more than ten times the combined losses of the British, British-Indian, French, and Japanese troops. They had been roundly defeated in almost every engagement even when they had the tactical advantage of position and number.

After the Imperial Japanese Army's High Command committed huge numbers of troops against the Viet Minh, thousands of disillusioned Japanese veterans deserted, deeming it dishonorable to join their erstwhile enemies to kill former allies. Many simply merged into the general population or somehow made their way home to Japan. Yet others went over to the Viet Minh to fight the British and French.

Among those contemplating defection was Major Yamazaki Takeshi.

23

Homecoming

THE RIVER'S MOUTH WAS WIDER THAN GASPARD Feraud remembered. It spanned several kilometers like an inland sea. Standing on the deck of a freighter headed into port, he watched the smooth water change from dark blue to a silty brownish-green, and soon, he caught steamy scents of earth and jungle. But the overwhelming stink was that of engine exhaust from a dozen ships plying the deep channels toward the Port of Saigon a fair way upriver. Each vessel was belching thick oily coils of black smoke that hung in the humid air. Ferries, produce barges, merchant junks, and skinny sampans with moth-like sails crowded the waterway with its radiating maze of tributaries.

Tipping the brim of his hat, Feraud squinted at the hot pearl throbbing on the overcast sky. He was sweating under his white long-sleeved shirt. His beige travel suit hung loosely on his once robust frame. Complications from the burns he had suffered presented other health problems. He had become a heavy drinker and a morphine addict. He had lost fifteen kilos. His health had not recovered even after three years in Macau, but his fortunes had. He lived for one purpose. Revenge.

The ship siren bellowed, and a flock of red-breasted parakeets dispersed from the mangroves. White herons stood unperturbed on floating clumps of water hyacinth as wind gusts rippled across the wide sleepy estuary. On both banks, the land was flat, the shores lined with corrugated iron shanties, a couple of yellow villas, and dense vegetation as far as the eye could see. On the distant horizon rose tall plumes of gray smoke, smearing the canvas sky like soot stains.

"The Brits took their damn bloody time," said Jacques Renier, standing against the railing next to his cousin Feraud, who was ten years older, richer, and taller. Average in height, Renier was barrel-chested with the build of a farmhand. Middle age had thickened his belly but kept his power undiminished. His finest feature was a perfectly round head, completely bald and shiny. He had the scarred face of a boxer, lumpy, squarish, centered around a bulbous nose, underscored by a proud handlebar mustache.

"They're too busy pushing their noses up the asses of these Americans," Feraud muttered, thinking about the timeline of events. The war had ended in Europe in mid-May. Hirohito had surrendered on August 15. It was now October, and the accursed British, ever so grateful to the Americans for joining the war, were still reluctant to let France reclaim the crowning gem of her colonial empire.

Renier fanned himself with a piece of cardboard. His skin was flushed. His clothes were sticky with sweat, his socks soggy. "Is it always this hot?"

Feraud turned and repeated the question in an amused tone to his Indian valets, Vihaan and Samir, two trusted brothers in their twenties. They had been his employees ever since Macau.

"This is the cool season, monsieur," replied Vihaan in French. He was the elder of the pair. He spoke four languages.

"God have mercy."

"You'll get used to it, monsieur," added Samir, who was taller and stronger than Vihaan.

"If the break-bone fever doesn't get you first," added Feraud.

"What on earth would bring a Frenchman here?"

"Gold, land, women. In that order," Feraud said, looking ahead. His eyes were sharp and clear, fixed on the port a couple of kilometers away.

"I'll take the gold and rent the women. You can keep this infernal country." It was his first trip away from Europe. Fifty-seven years old, an age when men began to value the familiar over the new.

"Can't you smell?" Feraud raised his head, sniffing the wind like an old hound. "That faint sharpness right under the tropical rot, cousin. Take a deep breath. That's called opportunity. It's everywhere."

"You can have it. I'm here to do a job," Renier remarked, mopping his brow with a handkerchief. A retired police inspector and a widower, he had come to Indochina to forget the family he had lost during the war. And to make a fortune for his retirement.

"Right you are, cousin. Help me get that slimy Jap and you'll never work another day in your life."

Renier nodded. He thought the chances of recovering his cousin's fortune fair to good. With two decades of law enforcement under his belt and years in the French Resistance fighting Germans, he was a doggedly resourceful investigator with a lucky star.

A weathered junk drifted past with a handful of pigtailed Chinese in black cotton tunics. One struck a gong in greeting. Several passengers on the freighter waved. At their backs, a sullen steward yelled at people to mind their luggage and stay clear of the cargo deck. Excitement mounted as they coasted by British warships anchored at mid-channel and approached a long queue of ships of various sizes.

INSPECTOR MERCIER was waiting for them on the dock. After a brief introduction, a jolly British official whisked Feraud's party through inspection and walked them out to the busy processing area, bypassing long queues of sailors and passengers. Mercier led them to two black sedans parked along a rusty row of warehouses. Samir and Vihaan helped the porters load the baggage.

"I did not expect you back so soon," Mercier said, holding the car door for Feraud as he motioned for Renier to take the front seat next to the driver. He nodded toward Vihaan and Samir to take the second sedan.

"Did you expect me at all?" Feraud asked in a mocking tone.

"Who can say? There have been so many losses," replied Mercier. He walked around the car to take the seat next to Feraud. "I see you have done well in Macau."

"You seem to have done poorly here."

"The camps did that to everyone," Mercier replied as he opened the window to catch the breeze. They wove around trucks and out the port, heading toward the city. Mercier's face was gaunt, almost skeletal. His dragoon mustache was scraggly and streaked with gray. His mouth a mess, his teeth rotting. "Two weeks ago, I was living on one mildewed bowl of rice a day and sleeping in a hammock in a stinking hut. My wife almost died from beriberi."

"I guess you spared me that."

Mercier shrugged. "We sent you off to save ourselves."

"I know."

"The tides of war, who can foresee them?"

"Isn't that the truth!"

"No one on the council thought it would come to this, not even Bouchard."

"And how is the chairman of our brotherhood?"

"Bouchard is gone, executed in the camp for insulting the commander."

"Poor bastard."

Mercier looked out at the crumbling houses lining the road. His voice was dry. "We lost many. Marceau was already on his last legs before the coup. He went first, heart failure. Virgnaud died of dengue. Baptiste had a stroke and was bedridden

for a month, shitting himself to death in a hammock. Your
police chief, Leroux, died last year, some sort of fever, I heard.
Molière, his wife, and their three children died of dysentery a
month after the surrender. The Allies let us rot in camp for five
long weeks. All for nothing!"

Feraud cursed and slumped back in his seat. Before his mind's
eye, the faces of people he had known for decades appeared.
In exile, he had dreamed of a grand homecoming, feted by
friends and enemies alike. His dream reception morphed into a
funeral, the guests long gone. Mercier, a shadow of his former
self, had survived. The inspector was an efficient gofer with
encyclopedic connections. With Mercier and Renier, he could
still achieve his goals.

Renier and Mercier talked about the reconstruction of
France. Mercier's wife was yearning for her home in Provence.
They talked about the vineyards and lost vintages of the
war years. At checkpoints along the road, British Indian
troops glanced at Mercier, then waved him and his entou-
rage through. Mercier explained that the British had imposed
restrictions after widespread violence following the French
riot. Saigon, the glorious capital of French Indochina, was
sinking into anarchy. Administrative and social services had
collapsed. The Viet Minh had seized power. The Japanese
were still fully armed, some openly supporting the Viet Minh.
Colonial French forces, newly released from prison camps,
were sickly, defenseless. Out of necessity, General Gracey had
had to arm French companies with British rifles so they could
defend themselves.

Renier had suffered much while fighting the Germans. He
felt removed from the colonial struggle. He was far from home,
taking in the dense tropical air for the first time. The lush countryside captivated him. He gawked at diminutive peasants in
their mollusk palm hats. There were bony shirtless men laboring in crushing heat, shriveled women with obsidian teeth car-

rying heavy loads in yoke-baskets. Children played naked in the red dirt.

Ben Thanh Market, the largest market in the country, had been torched, parts of the roof caved in. Mountains of charred debris had been piled around the perimeter. Scruffy-looking gendarmes in white short-sleeved shirts and crumpled kepis were supervising brown men loading trash into garbage trucks. People moved lethargically, their words dull in the steamy afternoon. Along the main avenues, trees were bare, their trunks blackened by fire. All the shopfront windows had been smashed. Glass shards glittered like gems on pavement. At intersections, blackened shells of burnt vehicles had been pushed aside. Street sweepers looked up as they passed. A woman was splashing water on the sidewalk to keep down the dust. A delectable scent of fried pork mingled with the stench of animal remains in the trash piles.

"Have you found a suitable dwelling for me?" Feraud asked.

Mercier chuckled. "I did more than find you a dwelling."

"You found that bastard accountant?"

Mercier nodded smugly. "With pleasure. That bottom feeder Yim Chu built himself a real estate empire. While the Japs had us locked up, Chu sent loan sharks into the camps. You can imagine the deals he was able to make with starving people."

"Where is that bastard?"

"Here in the city. We're going to see him now at your new house."

"How?"

Mercier laughed aloud. "He thinks he is meeting a prospective buyer."

"Mercier, you have outdone yourself."

They turned onto a gated drive. A lush canopy of shade trees covered much of the sprawling property. Gardeners were working in the flower garden. Feraud recognized the two-story mansion, its expansive double wings, tall windows, and the water fountain with a Grecian statue, a palatial compound compared to his villa in Phan Thiet.

"This is Bolton's place," Feraud remarked. The owner was one of the wealthiest men in his circle of acquaintances.

"Bolton met his maker. His widow took his ashes back to France. Chu bought this place from her for mere pocket change."

A maid greeted them at the front door. She walked Mercier, Renier, Feraud, Vihaan, and Samir through the marble foyer and down a bright hallway to the study. Trailing behind the others, Feraud pulled down the brim of his fedora to hide his face. Yim Chu was sitting behind a large oak desk, sifting through a stack of papers. He stood up, smiling, dressed in a navy-blue pinstriped suit with a paisley necktie. He came around the table with his hand outstretched.

Mercier said, "Monsieur Chu, this is Monsieur Jacques Renier and his cousin . . ."

They shook hands and Chu turned to face the other man, who took his hand in a firm grasp and slowly looked up. Feraud removed his hat.

Mercier continued, "Whom I think you know."

Chu's face froze with horror. He tried to back away, but the other man held his hand in a powerful grip. He mumbled, "Monsieur . . ."

"Have you forgotten my name already?"

"You . . . you!" Chu staggered backward against the desk, his face bloodless. His mouth puckered.

"Who has gained the most from my misfortune?"

"Monsieur, what are you talking about? I thought you were dead," Chu sputtered, trying to free his hand.

Feraud punched Chu with an overhand hook that snapped his head back. The plump Chinese fell. The maid shrieked and fled. Vihaan and Samir caught her at the door. Feraud walked around to the other side of the desk and placed a knee on Chu's chest. The Frenchman's face was flushed red. His mouth twisted in a snarl. He rained more blows down at Chu's head. Then, he stood up and began kicking Chu in the torso. Mercier shouted for him to stop, but Feraud was beyond hearing. Mercier and Renier dragged him away.

"Easy there. He's no good to you dead," Renier said, restraining Feraud by the arm.

Feraud growled at the unconscious man, "You will pay, I swear it. Before you die, you will pay for all of it, every insult, every pain, every minute, every piaster."

PART IV

Trials

— 1945–1946 —

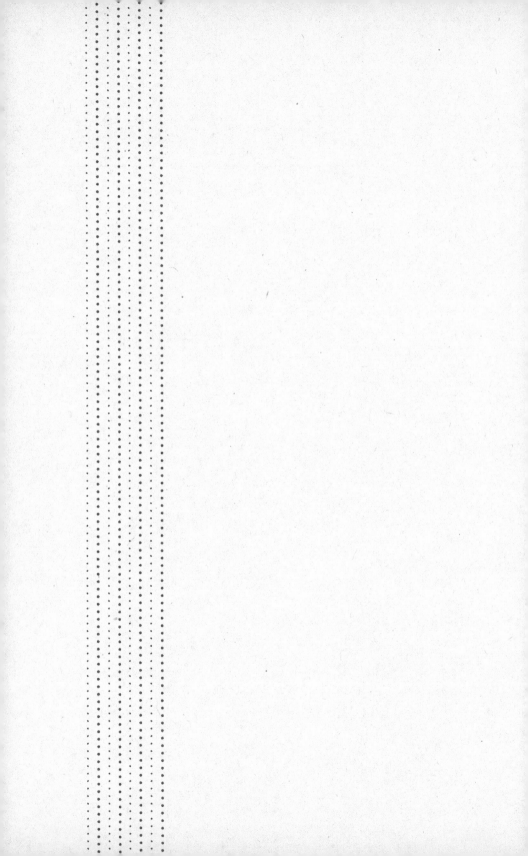

24

Departure

FLEEING THE FRENCH RIOT IN SAIGON, TAKESHI and Tuyet returned to Phan Thiet, ahead of the next wave of violence as the Viet Minh retaliated against the French mob. Unlike Saigon, Phan Thiet remained quiet. The Viet Minh had retreated and allowed the French to take control of the town without a fight. The Japanese withdrew to the airbase to wait for the handover.

Two weeks after Tuyet arrived home, Ha turned up unannounced in the middle of the night. He had got in through the rear fence from the neighboring property. He woke his mother, who roused Tuyet. They became apprehensive when Ha asked her to shutter all the windows as he turned down the oil lamp on the kitchen table, reducing the flame to a tiny bead of light.

Fear pinched Tuyet's belly. She said, "I didn't expect to see you for another week."

"Big Brother Ki sent me," Ha said, using Takeshi's honorific of elder brother-in-law and his Viet nickname. "He told me to move you to the safe house."

"What happened?" Tuyet cried.

"Gaspard Feraud isn't dead. He's back in Saigon and caught Yim Chu. We got the news from one of our people who works for Chu."

Tuyet gasped. "Is that the accountant who bought Feraud's mansion?"

Ha nodded. "Chu has been buying properties at fire-sale prices from Frenchmen while they were in detention."

"What a devil! We have to warn Long and Yen," Tuyet said, thinking about their daughter Mai-Ly.

"I've already told Long. He is leaving the restaurant to his in-laws and moving his family north to Hanoi."

"Do you think Feraud will go after Takeshi?" Tuyet asked, fearing that her husband was too preoccupied to worry about this new threat.

"Ki said they can't get to him at the airbase. They are probably watching the house, hoping to ambush him or take you hostage."

"Oh, heavens!" Coi cried as she went to the window.

"Don't do that! If they know that we know, they might do something rash," Ha said. "Pack your things, then get some rest. In a few hours, the farmers will come to town for the morning market. We can slip away then and make it to the beach. Song will be there with his boat."

Coi said, "I'll pack some clothes for the children. Tuyet, you take care of your husband's things."

"I almost forgot. Brother Ki asks that you bring his swords and his diaries," Ha added.

Tuyet groaned, head in her hands, resting her elbows on the tabletop. "There's so much stuff. I thought we had months yet."

Coi pulled Tuyet to her feet. "Pile everything else on the floor here. We'll decide what to take with us. What we can't, we will have our friends keep it for us."

Tuyet hurried around the house, a basket in one hand, the oil lamp in the other, trying not to wake the children. She gathered her savings, gold, jewelry, and legal papers. She went through the photo albums, taking out some pictures and putting them into a waxed envelope. Hurriedly, she leafed through the pages of her files, reviewing all the outstanding loans that were now unlikely to be repaid. Two sets of civilian clothes and a warm coat for Takeshi went into her satchel along with clothing for herself and a comb and her ivory brush. The diaries she wrapped in an oiled cloth with Takeshi's pair of ancestral swords. Remembering his ivory collection, she took out his two favorite carvings, tiny pieces hardly bigger than her thumb, one a dog, the other a fisherman in a boat.

She went through the desk drawers, scanning old letters, accounts, receipts, permits. What to keep, what to discard. She picked up odd things in their bedroom. This too bulky, that expensive but unnecessary. She wasn't sure whether she was fully awake. It felt like one of those loopy dreams in which she kept forgetting what she had already packed and what she still needed to pack. Every time she got halfway out the door, she turned back to fetch something else. What to take, what to leave? What had she forgotten? None of it mattered. Suddenly, she wondered whether they were making the right decision. She remembered talking with Ly in Saigon. Ly had been thinking about leaving to join Ishigara in Kyoto after his repatriation. Ly's mother and grandmother would follow once they had settled in a new home. Tuyet envied and admired her best friend's audacity.

She made one last round through the house, touching each piece of furniture: the rosewood bed Takeshi had commissioned, Hoang's crib, the collection of precious china Takeshi had bought in Cho Lon, gifts from friends, Takeshi's library, framed photos, her many beautiful *ao dais*—oh, how she had loved those long afternoons choosing fabrics and standing for intricate fittings at the dressmaker's shop. There was the matching pair of porcelain vases from the Ly Dynasty that Takeshi had found and Tuyet had spent a whole day haggling over in a sweltering warehouse. So many things she had thought important and desirable no longer warranted a second glance. Three years, such a short period but enough to collect a truckload of possessions.

"Are you all right?" Coi came into the room, putting her arms around Tuyet. "I know you love this house."

"It feels so wrong slinking away like this." Tuyet sighed, shaking her head. "You know, Auntie, I never dreamed about us growing old in this house, but that did't keep me from wishing we could live a long time here."

Coi shushed her. "Remember all the good things. You came here a young woman; you leave a lady. Wherever we go, we take with us the scars and the karma we've earned."

Tuyet went back to the armoire. Among the dozens of tailored dresses, she chose a robin's-egg blue *ao dai* with embroidered water lilies over the front; this simple gown she had worn on many dates with Takeshi. It was fine Hoi An silk. So light and thin, it folded to practically nothing, she reasoned, feeling calmer, and tucked it into her bag.

TWO HOURS till dawn. It was pitch-black outside. Coi set the altar with tea and fruits. Tuyet dressed the children. Everyone took turns lighting incense and prayed to Lady Buddha and their ancestors for protection. All dressed in black clothes and sandals. Ha led them out the back door, Little Hoang on his mother's back in a sling. Anh held Coi's hand. They slunk across the dark backyard and through a gap in the fence in the neighboring yard, which fortunately was unoccupied.

They waited at the side of the house while Ha went out front to watch the road. Mosquitoes buzzed in Tuyet's ears. She felt strangely unreal, leaving home like criminals. Looking back at the house, she saw only the rooftop and wished she could see it one last time in daylight.

An oxcart came down the street and stopped. At Ha's signal, they climbed into the back and lay down. Ha covered them with a tarp, then joined the driver on the bench. Hoang complained the cart smelled of fish. Coi shushed him. In the ensuing silence, they all hugged together tightly. As the oxcart lumbered through town, Tuyet shivered in a cold sweat.

UNDER THE paling moonlight, a briny breeze rustled coconut palms as the oxcart arrived at the shore. The beach was purple-gray, creamy, paste-like, a bright band between the coconut palms and the dark water. Song, the fisherman who had sailed regularly as Takeshi's charter, met the cart and walked them down to the water where a boat bobbed in the shallows. Farther down the shore, stick figures were putting boats to sea with the early tide. Tuyet and Coi waded toward the boat. Ha and Song carried Anh and Hoang on their shoulders.

The boat motor coughed and sputtered. Ha climbed aboard, then hauled in the anchor. It swung out to sea, pitching up a salty spray that seared their nostrils. Water trickled down their necks onto their chests. They huddled for warmth. The children giggled as their bottoms bounced on the hard planks. Anh dangled her arm over the side and slapped the waves. Coi clutched Hoang firmly and placed him on her lap. The boat tilted, left, right, up, and down. Tuyet vomited over the side. She sprawled among the nets and ropes at the bottom of the boat, moaning, shivering, and wishing it would all go away. Ragged clouds drifted by like dirty cotton in the predawn darkness. Daybreak unfurled across the sky, and an hour later, the engine stuttered and died.

"What's wrong?" Coi asked, alarmed.

"Out of fuel," Song said, checking the tank. "Don't worry. The wind is in the right direction."

Song and Ha raised a grubby tarpaulin with many patches. Wind filling the sail, the boat listed to one side and began making headway over the undulating water. Ha sat next to Tuyet, his face gaunt with exhaustion.

"Can you tell me where we're going?" Tuyet asked.

"One of our people has a large farm not too far from the coast. You all can stay there until Brother Ki can join you."

"When is that? Did he say?"

Ha shook his head. "Very soon, hopefully. He has joined the Resistance to train our recruits. His expertise is essential to us."

Tuyet turned sharply to her cousin. "It isn't just training, is it? I know Takeshi. He's not the type to sit by while others fight."

Ha lowered his gaze. "He's a good commander. Men follow him."

"Promise me you'll look after him."

"I will guard him with my life. You have my word."

25

Rogue

FISHERMAN SONG STEERED HIS BOAT OVER THE white rollers, between the reef, and into the sheltered bay. The previous day, he had delivered Tuyet and her family safely to a cove ten kilometers north of here. Now, he was serving her husband and his men. Sitting on open benches in front of him, the four Japanese officers—his regular fishing charter— were in a quiet mood, perhaps a little tired from fishing since before daybreak. By the expression on their faces, he doubted it had anything to do with the day's poor catch.

News of fighting and violence had reached Phan Thiet and even he, a backwater fisherman, knew that the Japanese were being dragged by the Brits into a brewing war against their former allies. Thinking about the impending catastrophe depressed Song because he truly enjoyed taking the major and his friends fishing. The tidy income he earned from being their guide would come to an end, but this was about more than money. It was natural, he told himself, that men would have formed bonds after years of fishing together. It was such a shame he couldn't have found a decent catch for them today.

The men jumped over the side and pulled the boat through the turquoise shallows, dotted with slick black boulders, to the sandy beach. Yamazaki and Mori carried the fish basket and their supplies up to the tree line. Ishigara and Sakamoto wedged the bow anchor into the sand. Song dropped the stern anchor. The men stripped to their undershorts and waded in to wash. Shirtless, barefoot, and still in their undershorts like schoolboys, they went about the routine of gathering wood for a fire at their usual spot under the coconut trees.

A white towel tied around his head, Mori squatted by his cutting board, preparing sashimi. Ishigara and Sakamoto grilled fish and prawns. Yamazaki uncorked a big jug of rice wine, filling their mugs to the rim. As they drank and ate beneath coconut palms, the sun had traveled halfway to its zenith.

Mori said, "You know what I'm going to miss the most?"

Sakamoto guffawed. "The women?"

"Women are women, same-same everywhere," Mori said. He waved expansively over the group and the ocean. "I'm going to miss fishing in water that doesn't freeze my balls off."

Ishigara snorted. "You sound like my grandfather. Always worrying about his balls."

"We had good times here." Yamazaki smiled. His thoughts lingered over the many fishing days they had enjoyed during the past three and a half years. He was saddened to think that it was all coming to an end.

"Even when the fishing was poor, the drinking was good." Young Ishigara chortled.

Mori toweled his face and sighed. "And those dances. I like to dance while I still have the legs for it."

Sakamoto said reassuringly, "Don't worry, your old lady is waiting to dance with you at home."

"My wife is a fine woman, but she's no dancer. But she does make the best ramen in the prefecture. Come for a visit. I will give you all the ramen you can eat."

"You'll regret that! I'll eat your restaurant out of business." Sakamoto laughed, patting his big belly.

They bantered about what life would be like at home. There was hope, for the news was that the Americans did not massacre and plunder as had been expected—as the Imperial Japanese Army had routinely done in the conquered territories. The Americans were, inexplicably, helping Japan rebuild.

Relieved, many Japanese soldiers were looking forward to going home.

"The sea was rough, but I'm glad we went out today," Mori said. "Who knows when High Command will order us to fight?"

Sakamoto grumbled, "I wish the Brits would wrap it up. I'd like to put the whole war behind me. I'm looking forward to seeing my drafty hut and my leaky boat again. "

Ishigara was stretched out on his back, hands behind his head, gazing at the sky. "I can't imagine facing my father. The shame. I don't know if I will be able to bear it."

Sakamoto shook his head. "He'll be happy to see you. Every father wants to see his son come home alive."

"You'd be surprised at what you can bear when you have a woman who loves you," Mori added.

Ishigara nodded. "Yes, I'm sure you are right. I just hope Ly will follow me back to Japan."

Yamazaki said, "Don't be so glum. You're young, you still have a full life ahead of you."

"I hope so, but it feels like we're doomed to serve the French and turn on our friends. It's bad karma. I don't see a way out."

Sakamoto nodded. "If we back the Brits and the French, the Resistance has no chance. They are unorganized, untrained, and practically unarmed. At the rate they are losing men, the Viet Minh may be wiped out in a month."

"The Resistance can recruit thousands more. They may run out of ammunition, but they won't run out of men," Yamazaki said. "It's too bad the Americans are siding with the French. Ho Chi Minh is already leaning toward the Communists. This will certainly push him in that direction. Who else can he turn to?"

Mori groaned, "This could be a long and ugly war."

"I don't know how long the war will continue, but I know I don't want to serve French interests," Yamazaki said.

"Neither do I," echoed Ishigara.

Yamazaki faced his men, searching their faces in turn. "This is the reason I brought you here today. I have an important announcement. But first, I have gifts for you." He took out three leather purses from his rucksack and presented one to each man. "This is a tidy fortune to keep you, Mori, fat and warm in your twilight years. For the rest of you, use it to start a new life, new adventures."

Each of them had been given twenty-five gold slabs in red silk sachets. Expressing heartfelt gratitude, the men soon grew pensive. Over the years, the commander had rewarded them generously, but the sum in their hands now opened new possibilities for their postwar life.

Sakamoto looked up at Yamazaki. "Is this what I think it is?"

Yamazaki nodded. "It's time. I'm leaving my command."

Mori smiled sadly. "I had a feeling you wouldn't be on the repatriation ship. Thank you again, Major, for your generosity. Winters are hard at home with many mouths to feed."

A surprised Ishigara blurted, "Are you deserting, Major?"

"Resigning without approval," replied Yamazaki with a smile. "My oath was to serve the emperor and Japan, not the French or the British. Now that the war is over, and we have surrendered, my life is my own. My mind is made up. I will do as I wish."

"You will join the Viet Minh?"

"Yes."

"Then I will come too," Sakamoto declared without hesitation. "You will need someone to watch your back."

"Thank you for your loyalty, old friend, but you have watched my back long enough. I want you to go home. You deserve it. You belong in your village, fishing with your family. That's all you've talked about for years. It would make me very happy to know that one of us made it back to our ancestral land."

A sad look crossed Sakamoto's face. In a plaintive voice, he said, "I never imagined returning without you."

"Look in on my mother. Tell her I will be home as soon as I can."

"It will be my honor," Sakamoto declared.

They grasped one another by the forearm. They had survived many battles together. There was too much that needed saying, so they said nothing.

Mori blinked rapidly, cursing his watery eyes. "Major, what are we going to do without you?"

Yamazaki grinned. "Mori, you go home and help your wife with the ramen shop. Better yet, sell it and go live somewhere warm. You have enough in that pouch for a very comfortable retirement. That's an order!"

Mori snapped to attention and saluted. "Sir, yes, sir!"

Ishigara asked, appalled, "Are you leaving us right now?"

Yamazaki nodded. "My Viet comrades are waiting beyond the hill. I sent Song ahead with my duffel bag so I could have this time with you."

Ishigara's shoulders sagged. "What will we tell Captain Tanaka?"

"He thinks I'm taking a day off to see my family before reporting to Saigon for new orders. I'm not expected back for a week."

"I want to join you, Major," Ishigara said.

Yamazaki shook his head. "I must go alone. I don't want my actions to affect anyone else later if things take a turn for the worse. You have found happiness with Ly. Don't throw that away."

26

Viet Minh

DRESSED IN PEASANT'S BROWN SHIRT, BLACK TROUsers, and leather sandals, Yamazaki climbed the hill, a rucksack on his shoulders, feeling buoyant, intoxicated half with rice wine, half with freedom. For the second time, he was radically changing the trajectory of his life. At the top of the ridge, he paused and lifted his face to the sky, his keel-like nose sniffing the breeze. On the beach around the cooking fire, a hundred meters below, his men were on their feet, staring after him, bewildered like stranded passengers. They snapped a salute in unison. Yamazaki returned the gesture, turned sharply on his heels, and continued inland, committed to his course.

Under a shady tree squatted fisherman Song, who had returned from his errand and was sharing a bottle of rot-gut with Comrade Xuan. Starting back to his boat, Song bade Yamazaki a gruff farewell, mumbling something about needing to take the others back to port. Xuan glanced toward the trail behind Yamazaki as though expecting more arrivals. Yamazaki shook his head.

Xuan hid his disappointment behind a bright smile. "Your men must be looking forward to getting back to Japan. Aren't you eager to go home, too?"

Yamazaki looked away. "Every man who goes to war takes it home with him. I'm in no hurry."

Xuan waited, but the major's face remained impassive as he set off, taking the lead. Xuan picked up Yamazaki's canvas duffel bag and fell in behind him. He did not press the matter.

They walked in silence. The trail led them to the paved provincial road where twelve men were waiting. The Resistance fighters were all local villagers except for Taa and Tee, Montagnard twins who served as forest scouts. An old man and his teenage grandson were tending an oxcart. Xuan introduced Yamazaki as Ki, using his nickname. Xuan and Yamazaki rode on the cart bed. The others walked with hoes over their shoulders, bantering like farm workers behind the oxcart as they traveled on the deserted coast.

After half an hour, they turned onto a rough wagon trail toward the northern foothills. The cart slid into a deep rut, breaking the axle cotter pin. The wheel was damaged. They unyoked the ox and lifted the axle onto a wood block. Xuan ordered the baker and the blacksmith to help with the repair while the others continued to their destination, a kilometer up a dirt track. Leaving his heavy duffel bag behind and shouldering his rucksack, Yamazaki led the way with a glance at the sun high overhead.

THEY CAME to an abandoned farm. Yamazaki led them to the hill behind the house and showed them a cave overgrown with bushes. They cleared away the nettles and brambles to find a large boulder blocking the entrance. Using wooden staves, they levered the rock aside to reveal a low opening barely a meter wide, just big enough for a man. On his knees, Yamazaki probed the sandy ground and found the tripwire, which he followed back to a grenade mounted on top of a reconfigured landmine. Xuan held a flashlight while Yamazaki defused the bomb.

Xuan chuckled. "I'm glad you insisted on coming, Ki."

Yamazaki winked. "It's a little tricky if you don't know what you're doing."

Inside the cave, Yamazaki showed Xuan stacked crates of small arms and ammunition, confiscated from several garrisons during Operation Bright Moon. When news had come that the British were taking charge of the handover in the south, Yamazaki had hidden the weapons here, anticipating British maneuverings to return the colony to the French.

A JEEP and an open truck carrying a French platoon rumbled down the main road. The men working on the oxcart by the trailhead heard them coming. The carter told the others to get their weapons and disperse into the woods. He fetched his ox but couldn't decide whether running off with the animal might look suspicious. The French might pass by without noticing him, whereas an unattended cart would look odd in the middle of nowhere.

The blacksmith and the baker grabbed their rifles from the cart and scampered into the tall yellow grass toward the trees. Lingering, the teenager called out, "Grandfather, you too. Come!"

"Too late," the old man said, standing beside his ox holding its rope.

The two vehicles stopped just beyond the wagon trail. They backed up, and French soldiers leaped off the truck. Approaching the cart, a métis corporal with a narrow angular face barked, "Old man, what are you doing here?"

"I was on my way home when I hit a spot of bad luck," the old man replied, gesturing at the damaged wheel on the ground.

"Don't you know the inter-village roads are closed?"

"I didn't know, Honorable Mister," cried the old man, bowing deeply, sensing that the French-Viet métis was an irritable fellow. "Please, I beg your forgiveness. I'm just an ignorant farmer."

The lieutenant, a middle-aged Frenchman with a red beefy

face, scoffed at the explanation and ordered his men to search the area. The whole platoon fanned out along the dirt road. An Algerian paced the area, scanning the ground for clues.

The métis scowled. "You didn't lift the cart onto the block by yourself, old man."

Flustered, the farmer wrung his hands but did not reply. A soldier clambered onto the cart bed and poked at the pile of hay with his bayonet. The Algerian pointed at the tracks, saying that a large group of people had been there recently.

"Tell your men to come out," said the métis.

"Some villagers came through earlier. They helped me lift the cart," he insisted.

He slapped the old man hard, sending him to his knees. "Tell them to come out!"

"There is no one here. Please don't hurt me."

The soldier dragged Yamazaki's canvas duffel bag off the cart and scattered its contents on the ground. They searched through the clothes, army boots, charts, two Japanese books, and some toiletry items. The lieutenant ordered his men to take up defensive positions. Another found a metal case, opened it, dumping several magazines and fistfuls of cartridges on the ground. The lieutenant drew his pistol and pointed it at the old man.

The métis shouted into the trees, "Come out now or this man is dead!"

CROUCHING IN the bushes, they watched the old man being beaten. The teenager turned to the baker, who looked to the blacksmith, who shook his head firmly. The boy made a soft choking sound, a tormented look on his face. The blacksmith gave a hand signal to pull back into the trees and crawled away, the baker following close behind. Hands white-knuckled on the rifle, the boy did not retreat. His whole body vibrated, bloodlust rising to his face. A good shot with his MAS-36, he was confident he could hit the lieutenant and maybe one or two more. But then what?

"Last warning. Show yourselves!" the métis shouted.

The boy hadn't budged. Taut with outrage. The stock of the rifle firm against his shoulder, the iron sight square on the lieutenant who had cocked his pistol. A gunshot rang out. The old man screamed, clutching his leg. The boy squeezed the trigger just as the lieutenant turned. The round struck the Frenchman in the arm. The next instant, a stream of bullets sprayed the bushes around the boy, none hitting him. He panicked and ran for better cover. Too late, as the following volley slammed into him. He was dead before he hit the ground.

Cursing, the lieutenant turned around and shot the old man in the head. The frightened ox bounded into the trees. The platoon leader ordered his men to search the boy's body.

THIRTY METERS AWAY, the baker and the blacksmith were hiding behind a fallen trunk. They heard orders in French instructing the men to move through the underbrush. Soldiers advanced warily, guns sweeping side to side.

The baker raked his fingers through his thinning hair, moaning, "Poor kid! What am I going to tell his mother?"

The blacksmith grabbed him by the scruff of the neck, hissing into his ear, "Shut up! You're going to get us both killed."

The baker sniveled, "Let's find our group. Leader Xuan will know what to do."

"No. If we rejoin our team, we might lead the enemy to them."

"The tracker will lead these devils up the road anyway," whimpered the baker.

"True. Then we must delay them as long as possible so our comrades can do their job."

"They must have heard the gunshots. Leader Xuan will send someone," replied the baker, hoping for a quick exit.

"Sure he will, and we don't want them to walk into a trap, do we?"

The baker sighed. "I suppose not."

"Let's split up. Shoot sparingly. When you run out of ammo, try to rejoin the group."

The baker checked his cartridge belt. A dozen bullets. He gulped and said ruefully, "That won't last long."

"Remember to pick a retreat route before shooting and never fire more than one shot from the same spot. Keep moving and keep them guessing. Don't be a hero."

"There is no chance of that."

The blacksmith said, "Good luck, Brother."

They crawled away in different directions as the soldiers were fanning out among the trees.

THE DISTANT gunfire ceased. Xuan said to Yamazaki, "I'll go look, but we can be sure the oxcart is gone. Prepare to destroy whatever we can't carry on foot."

Yamazaki nodded. "Send me a signal as soon as you know the situation."

Xuan instructed two men to load the weapons into yoke-baskets. To the others, he gestured at the rifles. "Arm yourselves and follow me."

They hurried back down the wagon trail, running with the flat-footed stride of sandal wearers. Gunshots echoed in sporadic bursts around the low hills. Halfway to the oxcart, the sharp-eyed twins spotted the French through the foliage. A platoon was advancing up the road on foot with a truck following in support. An African legionnaire walked in front, inspecting footprints in the wagon tracks. Xuan gave a hand signal, and they melted into the trees on both sides.

Xuan followed the tracker with the rifle sight and waited until the Algerian had come within thirty meters. Even at this distance, he knew his poorly trained men had little chance of hitting anything. He dragged his sleeve across his sweaty brow, slowing his breathing, ignoring the flies buzzing around his face. The long scar on his face itched as it always did just before a fight. His finger tightened on the trigger. Focus on the shirt, not the man, he reminded himself. Sometimes, the prey sensed the predator.

The shot startled birds from the trees. The bullet slammed into the man's chest, knocking him sideways. Xuan's men opened fire, wild volleys that hit everything except a target. The enemy returned a hail of bullets overhead. Xuan crawled to the twins, who were shooting from behind a fallen log.

Digging into his pocket, Xuan found his treasured cigarette lighter, a present from Yamazaki, and handed it to the twins. "Start a couple of fires in that dried grass over there. Build up thick smoke. The crosswind will carry it into their position. It'll give us some cover. When I give the retreat signal, you two stay behind and cover the retreat. Buy us some time. Here, take my ammo belt. We will go up through the hills and regroup at Maternity Rock. Find your way there. Don't follow us through the farm and don't lose my lighter. I want it back!"

They scurried away. Xuan sent another man back to Yamazaki with a message to destroy the surplus weapons. He gave covering fire from several positions to confuse the enemy. For the moment, it was a stalemate. The poorly trained Resistance fighters hadn't hit anything. The French couldn't pinpoint them hidden in the forest. But Xuan knew their advantage would be lost as soon as his men ran out of ammunition, which would be very soon, judging by the frenetic rate at which they were firing.

Smoke drifted through the trees. Fires were spreading not far to his left. Cries of warning rose among the French as the smoke thickened, and coughing erupted from the direction of the fires. Xuan gave a sharp bird cry. His men on the other side of the track repeated it. He made eye contact with one of the twins and signaled his retreat.

The twins stayed behind to delay the enemy while the rest of the group pulled back to the cave with Xuan. They found the baker, who reported three dead: the blacksmith, the old man, and the boy. Xuan ordered his men to retreat into the hills. Shouldering yoke-baskets heavy with loads of explosives, guns, and ammunition, they climbed up the hills to the north behind the farm. Xuan and Yamazaki hauled cases of cartridges into the abandoned farmhouse, a timber and thatch structure. They placed the cases on top of the bed and built a fire under it. As they ran back to the cave, they heard the gunfire tapering off to silence. Next, they heard the truck laboring up the road.

Yamazaki said, "There are fifty kilos of dynamite in the cave. This fuse reel should give us about three minutes. We'd better run for it."

"Light it! They're almost here."

Yamazaki shouldered his backpack, lit the fuse, grabbed his rifle, and ran after Xuan, who had already vanished up the wooded footpath behind the cave. At the edge of the trees, Yamazaki turned and saw the army truck and a platoon of soldiers. Wisps of smoke curled up from the thatched roof of the house. He dashed up the trail as the fire in the bedroom set off the first shell. French soldiers dove for cover, firing at the deserted house. A moment later, the stacks on the bed exploded, sending thousands of rounds in all directions.

Yamazaki soon caught up with Xuan on the wooded slope above the farm. Breathless, they paused and peered through the foliage at the bonfire. The explosion from the cave blew outward like a massive cannon shot, raining the nearby field with rocks and debris. The ground shook. When the air cleared, the bodies of several dead and wounded soldiers littered the ground. Cries of agony drifted across the hillside.

Xuan whistled and said, "There's no turning back now. You're in the Resistance!"

"We're in for a long fight," Yamazaki replied grimly and started up the hill.

27

Coexistence

AT THE POTSDAM CONFERENCE IN GERMANY IN
July 1945, the Allies had agreed that China should move more
than one hundred fifty thousand troops into Vietnam to disarm
the Japanese and control the country north of the sixteenth
parallel. The underpaid, undernourished, and ill-disciplined
Chinese troops looted and plundered from the northern border
to Hanoi, wreaking further havoc on a country already devas-
tated by Japanese occupation and famine.

From October 1945 to January 1946, the Viet Minh fought
a losing war in the south against the British-led coalition of
British and British Indian troops, French regulars, French
legionnaires, and the Imperial Japanese Army. After joining
the Resistance, Yamazaki Takeshi participated in several Viet
Minh engagements against French forces. In early November
1945, he visited his family at the safe house, located on a plantation in the highlands owned by a Viet Minh supporter. Satisfied that Tuyet, Coi, and the children were safe, he immersed
himself in the cause of the Resistance. At Xuan's recommen-
dation, Yamazaki went north to Quang Ngai Military Academy, where many experienced Japanese officers—defectors like
himself—were already training the Viet Minh's peasant army.
Yamazaki chose the academy primarily because he did not
want to face fellow Japanese in battle.

By late 1945, the British-led coalition had pushed the Viet
Minh into the remote countryside, effectively crushing the
Resistance. Wrapping up the British campaign at the end of
January 1946, General Gracey handed over the southern part

of the country to the French general Jacques-Philippe Leclerc. Weeks later, the northern part of the country was traded to the French by Chinese generalissimo Chiang Kai-shek, who had earlier vehemently opposed the recolonization of Vietnam. Thus, in one spectacular swoop, France regained its colonies.

With the French firmly in control, the nascent Democratic Republic of Vietnam (DRV) quickly fell into disarray. Factions within DRV became polarized between the two leading groups, the Viet Minh and the Nationalists. The former was generally popular with the peasantry, the latter with the middle and upper classes.

Faced with an unbreakable deadlock, Viet Minh general Vo Nguyen Giap launched "the Purge," a vicious campaign to eliminate all opposition within DRV ranks. He sent Viet Minh assassins to deal with specific individuals throughout the country. From March to May 1946, hundreds of Nationalist leaders and organizers were summarily murdered, some killed in secret, others butchered in front of their families.

Abandoned by the Americans, deceived by the Brits, and betrayed by the Japanese as well as the Chinese, the Viet Minh adopted Communist doctrines. In July 1946, temporarily allied with the French, Viet Minh troops attacked the Nationalists' headquarters in Hanoi. Simultaneously, French armored troops surrounded the area and arrested those who had escaped the massacre. Viet Minh and French troops drove the remnants of the Nationalist army into China and into permanent defeat, killing tens of thousands.

With the opposition groups eliminated, the Viet Minh faced the French alone. The two sides controlled the country in an uneasy coexistence. Tension escalated through the fall of 1946. A misunderstanding in Hai Phong resulted in Viet Minh militiamen killing twenty-three French soldiers. North of Hanoi, six French troops were killed days later. On November 23, 1946, the French retaliated by butchering more than six thousand men, women, and children in a single day, bathing the streets of Hai Phong in blood. Fighting soon spread throughout the country.

At the end of the year, as the war was under way, Yamazaki yearned to be with his family. He quit his instructor position and volunteered for a mission in the south. He left Quang Ngai under new identity papers. Yamazaki was now Vo Van Ki, a language professor born in Saigon to a Vietnamese mother and a Japanese father. During his time at the academy, he had improved his Viet language skills so he could pass himself off as a native in simple exchanges. In mid-December 1946, Yamazaki set off on a trek south to Phan Ri with Senior Comrade Xuan and a group of newly trained Viet Minh cadres.

28

Cousins

AT NOON, A GRAY SEDAN DROVE UP TO GASPARD
Feraud's mansion. It halted beneath a royal poinciana. Inspector
Jacques Renier and his spy, Vo Phong, walked up to the door. A
butler showed them through the spacious home to a wide veranda
at the rear where the master usually greeted his daytime visitors.
It was cooler there than in the house. Mopping his bald pate with
a handkerchief, Renier asked the butler for his usual drink. There
he stood, arms akimbo, scowling at the rose garden, his magnificent handlebar mustache twitching. He could barely contain his
excitement at the first break in the Japanese case.

A few minutes later, a petite woman with an ivory complexion appeared with a tray of iced beverages. Her colorless lips
curved up ever so slightly—a smile. "Good afternoon, Inspector. Mekong Cooler, four lumps of sugar, pickled lemon, and
pickled plum, with two shots of rum. Is that correct?"

"Good afternoon to you, Bui," he said as he took a sip. "You
have a good memory. Excellent. Don't you think so, Phong?"

"It's very refreshing," Phong replied politely.

"Thank you."

Renier nodded toward the house. "It's lunchtime. Isn't
he up yet?"

"As you know, the master has been feeling poorly. He will
be out shortly. You can ask him yourself," Bui said and made
a quick exit.

Renier stroked his mustache, admiring the woman's tact-
fulness. No wonder she had been Feraud's domestic right
hand for decades. He marveled at how she had shown up at

the Boltons' mansion in Saigon and immediately resumed her position as the manager of Feraud's household. How Bui had learned about her master's return was a mystery. Feraud had been beside himself with relief to see his most faithful aide. Renier wished he could find someone like Bui. After a year in Indochina, he remained a bachelor. His interest in women was minimal. Roughly twice a month when the biological urge arose, he visited the gentlemen's spas to relieve the pressure. Once his needs were satisfied, he desired neither female conversation nor female attention. For thirty-five years, his late wife had provided all the companionship he needed, and he felt that hiring a companion now would defile her memory.

He turned to the creaking sounds of a wheelchair from within the house. Through the windows, he saw two beautiful teenage girls pushing Feraud through the library and out onto the veranda. Feraud was unwashed and unshaven, still in his night robe.

Glancing at the stranger, he asked Renier irritably, "What is it?"

"Are you all right?" Renier inquired.

"No! I'm in a goddamn wheelchair," Feraud snapped. "Gout. My blasted feet."

Renier nodded sympathetically. "Cheer up. I bring you a gift. We have another lead, a solid one."

"Unlike all the leads you've dredged up this year?"

"Judge for yourself." Renier gestured at the Viet man standing silently nearby. "This is Phong. He arrived this morning from Phan Ri. Let him have a look at those photos."

Dismissing his nubile attendants, he told Bui to fetch a box from his office. Renier explained Phong was a police spy who had infiltrated a Viet Minh cell in a fishing town north of Phan Thiet. A southerner, Phong was dark and thin, and, although he had a stoop in his posture, was about the same height as Renier. He was a Catholic, in his late twenties, clean-shaven with a short schoolboy haircut. Bowing, he greeted Feraud in French.

"Where did you see the Jap?" asked Feraud.

"Yesterday, he arrived in camp with a squad from the north. I could tell he was Japanese. Even though he spoke fluently like a Central Highlander."

Bui returned with the box. Feraud opened it, took out two photographs, and handed them to Phong. "These pictures are two or three years old."

Phong scrutinized them and said confidently, "Yes, that's him. He's thinner now, but that big nose is unmistakable. I have no doubt he's your man. I spent all afternoon yesterday showing him around our camp."

"How long is he staying?"

"A few days. I tried to find out, but they're secretive about that type of information."

Renier asked, "How many men are in the camp?"

"Twenty-five, including the new arrivals."

Renier said, "I'll need a platoon. I have a tracker with a pair of good hounds. Do you still have some of his clothes?"

Feraud rummaged through the box and took out a crumpled and soiled shirt. It had been found at the major's house after his family's escape, which had been right under the noses of Renier's men as they waited outside to capture Yamazaki. Since then, they had lost track of the major and his family. With the trail gone cold, Feraud had turned his attention to rebuilding his fortune, seizing opportunities presented by France's recolonization effort. As quickly as he had regained his old station, he had fallen into old habits, which soon brought on various ailments, including high blood pressure, jaundice, and gout.

"The shirt hasn't been worn in a year, but the hounds should be able to pick up his scent," Feraud said, tossing the garment to Renier. A cold excitement came over him. "Go now. Bring him back to me alive. I have waited long enough."

29

Flight

NGUYEN LINH AND HIS WIFE, BI, WERE IN THEIR sixties, both staunch Resistance supporters. They owned a large farm with their four grown sons. Their clan comprised five families, altogether twenty-seven adults and children. The farm grew a wide range of crops and various fruit trees. They also raised cattle, hunted, and trapped wild game, for their remote property abutted the forested mountains.

Since leaving Phan Thiet a year earlier, Coi, Tuyet, and her children had been living with the Nguyens as part of their extended family. Tuyet and Coi had their own thatched bungalow, but they cooked and ate together with the others. Anh and Hoang had four playmates the same age and enjoyed an easy life with other children on the homestead. Coi and Tuyet busied themselves with farm work and became fast friends with the Nguyen women. They felt safe and contented even though Ha and Takeshi were rarely around.

When Coi received a message that her son and Takeshi would be coming, she and Tuyet decided to host a feast to mark the family reunion. Tuyet bought a pig. The men butchered the animal and the women cooked it. As they could only eat a portion of the fresh meat, the rest was made into sausages, cracklings, bacon, and ham. For the feast, they made barbecued pork, scallion noodles, catfish soup, sour pork salad, and Coi's special fried spring rolls.

At sunset, the whole clan gathered at the main house for the party. The dogs were begging for scraps around the grill pit when they heard something in the distance. Yapping, the pack bounded off downhill to the road, wagging their tails.

"I think it's them," Tuyet said to Coi. They wiped their hands and walked out front with Mister Long and Bi.

The dogs escorted Ha and Takeshi back to the house. Takeshi gathered Tuyet in his arms and whirled her about. The children danced and skipped around their parents, squealing. Ha hugged his mother, who was ecstatic every time her son returned safely.

Ha groaned, "I'm hungry. We haven't eaten since morning."

Long said, "You're just in time for dinner."

"That's my boy." Coi laughed, tousling her son's hair. "His timing is always perfect when it comes to mealtime."

They gathered on the lawn, where straw mats had been laid out end to end in a long row for thirty-three people. The atmosphere was rowdy as the men set about jugs of rice wine. Tuyet ate little, fussing over her husband. She had not seen him for four months. He had become leaner and darker but was in excellent shape.

Takeshi talked about his past few months at the training camp and the long trek south with Xuan and his men. They had met up with Ha at a camp near Phan Ri and there they had trained recruits for two days. Xuan had stayed with the squad while Takeshi and Ha had left early that morning to visit the family.

Night fell as the dinner went on. Torches and oil lamps were lit. Then, the dogs started barking, hackles up, glaring down toward the road. Three men on horseback galloped up. The Nguyen men ran for their weapons.

Ha jumped to his feet, peering into the darkness. He shouted, "It's Xuan."

Xuan pulled his mount to an abrupt halt and swung down from his saddle, panting. Tee and Taa, the Montagnard twins, dismounted. Xuan shook his head at Takeshi and Ha. Tuyet felt an ominous twinge in her belly.

"Our unit has been ambushed. We lost everyone!" Xuan gasped as he sank to his knees.

While Xuan had been out on reconnaissance with the twins in the late afternoon, a French platoon had raided the camp, killing six men. They had seized five, including the man who had driven Ha and Takeshi earlier that day. A village lad, who had served as a lookout, had warned Xuan and the twins as they were returning to base. They had barely avoided capture.

"We are in immediate danger. You should leave this place at once," Xuan said.

Ha gnashed his teeth. "We've been in that place for weeks. It couldn't be a coincidence that they hit the camp two days after your arrival."

Xuan said, "I think there's a mole among your recruits. Someone has been on the lookout for a Japanese deserter. They've posted notices about big rewards in every town about Japanese deserters wanted for war crimes."

"Do you think they're after Brother Ki?" Ha asked.

Xuan nodded. "This was no regular army raid. They had with them a French inspector with a professional tracker. They had dogs sniffing through all the tents. Leaving is your only safe option."

Tuyet felt dizzy. Things were spiraling out of control faster than she could have ever imagined. She turned to her husband. "Can we go to Saigon and stay with my friend Ly or Van?"

Takeshi said, "That's not a good idea."

"Why?" Tuyet objected.

Ha shook his head. "The French have checkpoints inside and outside every town. Staying with your friends will put them in danger. For now, our best chance is to move the family deeper into the interior until the situation improves."

Long turned to Bi. She nodded. He said, "There is another way. We have a hunting hut deep in the mountains. You will be safe there."

Xuan added, "Good idea. You'll be closer to HQ."

Tuyet, Coi, Ha, and Takeshi thought this over. Tuyet and Coi nodded. Takeshi agreed. Long's son would take the family up to the hut while Ha and Takeshi tried to divert the pursuers by backtracking to the T-junction where they had left the truck. The twins would join Ha and Takeshi. Xuan said he had to alert other Resistance units.

Long asked, "You are going to lead them in a different direction?"

Takeshi nodded. "Right; those hounds will bring them straight here."

"Then what? You can't outrun them."

Takeshi glanced at Ha and the twins. An unspoken understanding passed among them. He said, "We don't intend to run. We intend to take revenge for our fallen brothers."

"I'm with you, Brother Ki," Ha grunted, sparks in his eyes.

The twins said, "For our brothers. Blood for blood."

30

Ambush

BY THE LIGHT OF A HALF-MOON, TAA AND TEE LED them, moving with the sure-footed ease of game hunters. They were Gai-rai tribesmen from the Central Highlands and had been mountain scouts for the Resistance for more than a year. On his back, each carried a woven basket of dynamite and other supplies. Ha and Takeshi followed with backpacks of ammunition, food, and water. By three A.M., they approached the junction where the truck had left Ha and Takeshi the day before. Turning off the dirt road, the four men entered the pitch-dark woods. The twins made torches. Once at the river, they continued downstream in the water to mask their tracks and scents.

The river was thirty meters wide with dense vegetation on either bank. They sloshed through the shallows, swatting at mosquitoes and bugs drawn by the torches. They came to a crude bridge of fallen trees lashed together with rope. They went across the bridge to the other side of the river, where they stopped and built a fire. Squatting around the flames, they ate a meal of rice balls and fruits.

Taa said, "The T-junction is on the other side of the bridge and up that hill about two hundred meters. Brother Ki and Ha, you will need to go up and leave a fresh spoor for the dogs. Take off your shirts and wipe rocks and tree trunks with them. Try to piss along the way as much as you can. Dogs always follow the freshest scent."

Takeshi nodded. "You mentioned a good place for a trap. Is it far from here?"

"Right there," Taa said, pointing to a scree below a ridge about a hundred fifty meters away. In the pale moonlight, the pebbles glowed gray like a frozen waterfall. The gravel pit where they were sitting was a semicircle about thirty meters across, gradually narrowing as it sloped uphill toward a rock chute. "The trail follows the tree line, up through that gully. It's the only way over that ridge in this part of the river. If we go up that way, they have no choice but to follow us."

HA AND TAKESHI cut branches and wedged them into a pile of boulders to make a blind about halfway up the slope. They waited, resting behind their cover, for an hour. A little after dawn, they heard heavy vehicles rumbling through the foothills. The groan of engines echoed through the forest. A minute later, Tee came barreling downhill and across the log bridge. Dogs were barking not far behind. He paused at the campsite and kicked over some leftover food, tipping the teapot into the fire, which sent up a hissing cloud of steam. He grabbed his rifle and dashed up to where Ha and Takeshi were hiding.

"Good job. The dogs picked up your scent," Tee said, grinning.

"How many dogs? How many men?"

"Two dogs with a French handler. Two other Frenchmen and a full platoon of Viet troops."

Ha waved him onward. "Hurry, go join your brother."

STRAINING THEIR LEASHES, the hounds pulled the handler across the log bridge. Soldiers fanned out on both sides of the river. A French sergeant squatted beside the smoldering campfire, poking at the hot embers. A burly man in safari khaki and a colonial pith helmet tottered over the bridge. He was followed by a tall, slight Viet in white short sleeves and black trousers. When the pair reached the campfire, they inspected the ground with the sergeant and the hound handler. They picked up the teapot, feeling its still-hot surface. The excited dogs pulled the handler uphill.

BEHIND THE BLIND, Ha stiffened and muttered bitterly, "There's our mole, Phong. I recruited that traitor myself."

"I remember him, the disillusioned bourgeois."

"He's mine," Ha said through clenched teeth, sighting the man down the barrel of his rifle.

Takeshi scowled, for they had agreed to kill the dogs with the first shots. He knew Ha was good with a rifle, but his young brother-in-law had never been in battle or killed anyone. Takeshi sighed to himself; no man went to war without getting blood on his hands. This was as good a reason as any to kill a man. He placed a hand on Ha's shoulder and nodded. Ha adjusted the sight on his rifle. The range was almost a hundred meters. Takeshi turned and looked up at the ridge fifty meters above and behind him. He could not see the twins, but he knew they were watching, ready with the dynamite.

"Wait. They're coming up to our position. Let the dogs clear those bushes. On my signal," Takeshi whispered, sighting the approaching animals down the barrel of his rifle. "Ready. Aim. Fire."

In the silence, gunshots cracked like thunder. The lead dog collapsed, shot through the chest. Phong, the traitor, doubled over, a bullet in his gut. Even before they fired again, soldiers scattered for cover. Another bullet struck Phong's shoulder. Takeshi's second shot missed, but it made the handler drop the leash. The other hound charged uphill directly at them. Salvos raked the hillside. Ha and Takeshi ducked for cover. A moment later, Takeshi peeked out and saw a sleek brown form crashing through the branches and leaping at his head. He brought up his rifle just in time, and the hound's jaw clamped down on it.

Both man and beast tumbled backward. He let go of the rifle and rolled away, drawing his pistol. Ha shot the dog in its hind-quarters. Takeshi put a bullet into its head. Both took positions behind the blind and returned fire on the enemy below.

The chatter of infantry rifles continued until the sergeant stopped it. The handler whistled for his hound.

Takeshi shouted in French, "Your dog is dead."

"Bastard! You killed both of them!"

"What do you want me to do? Pet them?"

"I swear you will pay for this!"

The Frenchman uttered a string of expletives.

Another voice boomed from below. "Major Yamazaki. Is that you?"

Takeshi peered through the leaves and spotted the pith helmet behind a tree stump. "Who is asking?"

"Inspector Jacques Renier."

"Enchanté."

"Enchanté, Major." Inspector Renier chuckled and half rose from his crouched position. "Surrender and I will guarantee your safety."

"I'm safe where I am. Thank you, Inspector."

"Come now, Major. If you cooperate, I can provide passage to Japan for you and your family. You won't go home empty-handed."

"Who hired you?" Takeshi asked, as he turned quickly to fire at some movements on the left. He continued, "It would be easier to talk if your men stop trying to outflank me."

Orders were relayed below. Renier called out, "Monsieur Feraud hired me to recover what you took from him."

"Unfortunately, the gold is all gone." Takeshi signaled for Ha to creep up to the next position on higher ground, closer to the rock chute. "Do you think I would be here if I still had it?"

"I'm not paid to consider that possibility."

"Are you paid enough to die, Inspector?" Takeshi slung the rifle over his shoulder and drew his pistol.

Renier laughed aloud. "There is no chance of that. I have another platoon coming any minute now."

"Thanks for the warning."

Takeshi fired two rounds at the handler's position and dashed up the incline. The handler spotted the retreat and followed him. Ha fired several shots, but the handler was moving too fast, not bothering about safety. Below, the sergeant rallied his men in pursuit. Volleys of rifle fire whined over Takeshi's head, striking around Ha's position. Bullets slammed into the trees and ricocheted off boulders. Takeshi reached Ha. They ran along the tree line toward the gully, following exactly where they had practiced earlier. Taa and Tee covered them as they scampered up the exposed section of the chute, forcing the handler to take cover in turn. Grabbing at exposed roots on the hillside, Ha and Takeshi reached up over the ridge. Taa threw a Japanese stick grenade. It sailed overhead, tumbling end over end.

"Grenade!" The handler threw himself on the ground.

It detonated behind him, lower down the hillside, injuring several soldiers. Ha, Takeshi, and Taa opened fire on the attackers. Tee lit the fuse to the dynamite, and they all rushed away from the ridge. The hissing red-white flame ate its way up the fuse, snaking down over the rocks and into a crevice where three bundles of dynamite had been wedged behind large boulders. The first explosion heaved dirt and rocks outward. Two more followed in quick succession, shaking the whole hillside. A billowing blast of dust and stones engulfed the entire slope. Reverberations rumbled like an earthquake, a deep drawn-out groan with the grating sound of loosened rocks. A loud clatter of heavy stones, then the hillside slid downward, covering men and crushing trees like matchsticks.

The inspector fled for the bridge along with several soldiers. A car-sized boulder bounced and crashed onto the bridge, clipping the inspector as it broke apart the logs, pitching everyone into the water. Small rocks and pebbles rained down on the river.

A slab of the hill had been sheared off, exposing bare earth, stones, and tree roots. As the smoke and dust cleared, most of the platoon lay injured or crushed under piles of debris. A handful of survivors were swimming for the far bank of the river. Moans of the injured drifted up the slope.

The wounded wailed, sobbing loudly. Ha shuddered, peering down, scanning the riverbank. He saw Phong, curled up in a fetal position, inert, his body missed by the landslide. Not two meters away, a boulder had landed squarely on a soldier, smashing his head and torso. His legs splayed out from beneath it. A muffled sound drew Ha's attention to the right side of the slope. A bloodied arm rose from between two large stones, the hand deformed. The injured man screamed, waking to his horrific reality. The sound raised the hairs on Ha's head. He froze, blood draining from his face.

Tee bit his lips as he reloaded his rifle. He crossed over the ridge, descending like a mountain goat, bouncing from boulder to boulder. The screaming stopped as Tee crouched and spoke to the dying man. Tee lowered his rifle into the gap between the rocks. A single sharp report echoed off the slopes. A brief silence. Other injured men began to plead for a merciful death. Tee emptied his rifle, granting four more quick endings.

Ha fell on his knees, retching. Taa patted him on the back and said, "Every time you feel bad for killing the enemy, all you need to do is remember what they did to your brothers."

Tee returned with the weapons of the fallen. Takeshi gulped from a water flask, then passed it around. They decided to leave the injured for the platoon that was supposedly on its way. Takeshi said it was unlikely the troops would pursue them with their French masters dead.

"I saw the inspector crawl out on the other side of the river," Tee said. "His leg looked injured, but he was alive. Do you think he has reinforcements coming?"

"It might be a bluff. It doesn't matter. Without the hounds, he won't get far," said Takeshi, getting to his feet and shouldering his pack.

Taa started up the incline. "Let's go. We have a long march ahead of us."

31

Trek

UNABLE TO SLEEP, TUYET ROSE IN THE EARLY hours and went outside to stand in the dark field. Stars were fading as an indigo glow rose over the eastern horizon. Roosters crowed for the coming dawn, rousing birds in the trees. She wondered what Ha and Takeshi were doing. Clutching the Lady Buddha pendant at her throat, she prayed for protection.

The whole clan was present for a farewell breakfast of hot tea and sweet coconut rice. Dabbing at their eyes, Coi and Tuyet thanked their hosts. They had become quite close to the Nguyens. Bi gave Coi her homemade preserves, a glass jar of fermented fish, and a jar of shrimp paste.

"A little heavy, but it should last you a long while. Eat it and think of us."

"We're going to miss all of you," Coi said, holding the other woman's hands.

Tuyet's voice quivered. "We couldn't have made it through this year without you. You took us in like family."

"You are family!" cried Bi. The other women echoed that sentiment, throwing their arms around Tuyet and her aunt.

Tuyet gave each family two gold slabs wrapped in red velvet. The men hemmed and hawed, but their wives accepted the gifts, knowing there would be hard times ahead. Linh announced that his eldest son, forty-five-year-old Lam, would be leading the trek and his four grandsons, one from each family, would be accompanying them as porters. No one said goodbye, for it was considered bad luck at the start of big journeys. *Never tempt the spirits.* It was better to pretend those leaving were only stepping out for a moment. Blinking back tears, everyone put on a happy smile, and the party set off into the murky dawn.

Lam, the clan's second in command, was a stocky, pragmatic man with a square face, dark watchful eyes, and a salt-and-pepper beard. He had served seven years as a rifleman in a French-trained regiment. The experience had turned him into a staunch opponent of the colonial regime. Whistling, he sent his two dogs up the trail as he lumbered after them, humming a cheery tune. His twenty-two-year-old son, Bien, followed, humming along. He was a carefree version of Lam, so far untouched by war. Both carried back-baskets, wielding machetes to clear the path. Coi came third with her yoke-baskets, then in single file came Anh, Hoang, and Tuyet, who had a large cloth satchel and a sling in which to carry Hoang when he tired. Truc, Vu, and Mot brought up the rear. They were strapping lads in their early twenties, squarely built with wide shoulders and powerful calves like wooden cudgels. They all had their grandfather's broad face, flaring nose, and white teeth. Each carried yoke-baskets of staples and dried goods. They were armed with three old Lebel hunting rifles.

The departure had been sudden. Grateful that her children were too young to understand, Tuyet gulped down an awful feeling that she would never see the Nguyens again. Tuyet could not help her thoughts returning to the perils Ha and Takeshi were facing at that moment.

In the distance, the forest stood dark against the dawn. The trail was rocky, overgrown by weeds. After walking an hour, they spotted water shimmering beyond the trees and followed the trail down a steep slope to the rocky bank of a small creek.

The water was smooth, clear like a mountain pond. Small fish were darting over the mossy bottom. Downstream, bushes and grass grew on small rocky islands inhabited by white cranes. Colorful birds flitted across the morning sky, ringing the forest with their songs. A lemon sun cleared the treetops. Lam placed some food by a tiny stone shrine and lit three sticks of incense as he said a prayer to the river god.

They crossed the creek by a rope strung from one bank to the other. The water was chest-deep midstream, so the men had to cross several times carrying the baskets on their heads. Bien and Truc carried the children across on their shoulders. Tuyet helped her aunt because Coi was so short, the water coming up to her chin.

They rested on the other side to wring out their wet clothes. Lam led them up the trail at a leisurely pace. Good progress was made in the first two hours. Coi and Tuyet were fit from working on the plantation the whole year. Anh and Hoang had developed tough feet, having turned into rambunctious urchins much like the other farm kids, Anh now six and Hoang three.

At mid-morning, Lam called a break in a meadow with a tiny stream. They weren't tired yet, but he said they needed to conserve their strength, urging them to eat bananas and peanuts for energy. Tuyet said she wasn't hungry, but he replied that by the time she was, it would be too late. They cooled their feet in clear water. The children soon forgot any tiredness, skipping among pools trying to catch tadpoles.

Back on the trail, shafts of light slashed through the canopy. The jungle began to steam, the dense canopy trapping the humidity. In the gullies, the scents of lush vegetation with its hint of decay were overpowering. Tuyet could not comprehend the direction of their trek, yet Lang advanced without trouble, hacking efficiently at the dense vegetation with his machete, leading them through thorny shrubs, tangled undergrowth, and curtains of tight vines draped from high branches. The dogs barked, chasing creatures from their path, once alerting Lam to a python.

Tuyet marveled at the many shades of green—at skyward-reaching trees, bushes covered with bright crimson blossoms as big as a dinner plate, and moss carpets sprinkled with tiny violet flowers. Everywhere, the high-pitched drone of insects. Dragonflies zipped about. The jungle echoed with harsh caws of birds and screeches of monkeys. Anh spotted a red giant centipede with brilliant orange legs. Long-tailed blue and red parrots glided overhead. White butterflies swirled like snowflakes in a verdant fern tunnel. As one, they all stopped in their tracks and sighed.

A city dweller who had been quite unaware of the flora and fauna beyond her garden, Tuyet gaped, speechless. She meant to ask the name of one or other plant or creature, but by the next break, fatigue had wiped all that away, and what she now wanted was a nap. In some places, the undergrowth was so dense there was nowhere to sit. They rested every half hour, setting themselves down right on the trail. Hoang begged to be carried piggyback, and Tuyet obliged. Anh developed a blister on her foot, which Coi popped with a needle, then swabbed with ointment. Although still a little girl, she had marched on without as much as a whimper.

When they finally stopped for a noon break, Tuyet and the children were exhausted. Lam handed out food his wife had wrapped in banana leaves: hard-boiled eggs, rice balls with dried fish and chili paste, meat cakes, green mangoes, and candied coconut. Tuyet was so tired she could barely eat. After lunch, everyone napped. Squadrons of flies buzzed around Tuyet's head. Gnats bothered her nostrils and ears. She had to breathe through a scarf wrapped around her face. Mosquitoes feasted on her neck and ankles. Vu passed around a small bottle of strong-smelling herbal oil that was somewhat effective against the mosquitoes but not against anything else.

"How much farther to where Ki is meeting us?" Tuyet asked Lam.

"Hard to say in kilometers. If we're lucky, we might make

it by nightfall." Lam mopped his brow, adding, "We have to make it by nightfall."

"Why?"

"The last portion of the trail is over an exposed ridge with no place to rest. Too dangerous to hike in the dark."

THE TERRAIN BECAME rugged and steeper, the path narrow. Vegetation thinned. The trees now were shorter, more stunted. Anh's stamina surprised everyone. She never complained. Hoang fell asleep on his mother's back. Lam cut Tuyet a pair of bamboo walking poles to help her balance. Marching on, he rolled a cigarette, lit it, and smoked without breaking stride. The others struggled behind, huffing and grunting.

"Oy," Coi called out to Lam. "Slow down, you old goat!"

He turned, made a face, and bleated. Everyone laughed.

Their progress was painfully slow as they had to stop and help one another over several treacherous scree slides. Some were precariously steep. Around several bends, Tuyet glimpsed blue sky that made her think the top was near. But when they proved to be only more ridges, she just became sullen. She slipped on a rock and painfully stubbed her big toe. Scolding herself, she focused anew on her feet, taking one step at a time. Sweat stung her eyes, soaking her clothes. Her son had dozed off in the sling, pressing against her like a warm sack of cement. Dust mixed with sweat made her leather sandals even more slippery. She had to take them off and go barefoot. Although she drank water until she felt bloated, she was still thirsty. They paused to rest at a switchback. Vu handed out salted plums, which helped her with the maddening thirst.

Tuyet called out to Lam, a few meters ahead of her, "Are we going to make it by nightfall?"

"I think so."

"How soon will we get there?

"Soon."

"How soon?"

"Really soon."

"Are you sure?"

"Sure."

"How far is it, really?"

Lam chuckled and kept walking. His son, Bien, turned, saying as if comforting her, "The more you dwell on it, the farther it becomes. It's not too far. You can make it."

Bien heard Tuyet groan. He retraced his steps, took Hoang off her back, and arranged the boy in the sling on his own chest, then continued forward. He smiled at her encouragingly.

Tuyet's face was flushed, feverish from exposure. Her hands were chafed from gripping the bamboo walking sticks. Blisters burst open on the soles of her feet. She bent over, stretched her back and shoulders, took a deep breath, and got a second wind. She plodded onward, eyes to rocky ground, no longer peering upward in search of false summits.

Yellow and orange wildflowers dappled grassy slopes as hawks soared on thermal currents. When Anh's legs gave out, the young men took turns carrying her. Tuyet's left hamstring and right calf began to twitch, a sign of onsetting cramps. Lam had noticed and called for a brief break. Coi massaged Tuyet's legs as she lay on her back, grimacing at the sky. The dogs licked her hand.

Seeing her distress, Lam set a more moderate pace and gave the group a five-minute break every twenty minutes. Tuyet fell asleep at each stop. Her mind detached from reality. She stopped thinking about the climb and accepted the agony.

"We're here," Lam said suddenly.

Tuyet blinked and stumbled up the last few steps. She stood dumbstruck on a windy ridge, a narrow, flat place barely five meters wide. Glowing orange in the waning light, the peak loomed two hundred meters above her. She dropped onto the grass. Delirious. She looked out over the green ranges. Her husband and cousin were still down there somewhere. Evening approached. The sun straddled the range to the west; the valleys filled with shadows.

As NIGHT FELL, they built a small fire behind a pile of boulders. Coi and Tuyet cooked up a rice stew made by boiling rice with dried pork sausage, dried mushrooms, and dehydrated radishes. Lam added herbs and wild greens that he had gathered along the way. Tuyet poured in two spoonfuls of fish sauce concentrate.

"I smell dinner!" someone cried coming over from the trail. The Montagnard twins approached with their baskets of rifles. Ha followed them into camp.

Coi hurried to meet her son. "Are you hurt, Ha?"

Avoiding eye contact, Ha greeted his mother then sat down, staring into the fire without speaking. Coi handed out bowls of porridge. The twins helped themselves to seconds. Ha did not touch his food. A few minutes later, Takeshi limped into camp. Tuyet threw her arms around him. Lam assigned the watch, then told everyone to get some rest. Another half day of hiking still lay ahead of them in the morning. Coi watched her son, her face betraying a mother's worries.

Takeshi whispered to Coi, "We had a hard battle. Your son became a warrior today."

She turned her face away and wept in silence.

32

Fountain

THREE DECADES EARLIER, LINH AND BI NGUYEN
had built the hut as newlyweds. They had used it for hunting
and trapping, for game had been plentiful in those days: wild
boars, deer, leopards, and tigers. They had earned a good living
from the wilderness between planting and harvesting seasons.
Now that they were too old for the trek, their adult children
came with their own families for the annual summer hunt.

Lam, his son, and his nephews set about helping Takeshi to
make repairs to the hut. Tuyet and Coi cooked and cleaned. Ha
and the twins stayed only one night, continuing to the Resistance headquarters deeper in the mountains the next morning.
On the second day, Lam showed Takeshi the best hunting and
fishing spots and how to find his way about in the surrounding
wilderness. On the third morning, the Nguyen men set off for
home, promising to return with supplies in a few weeks' time,
leaving their two dogs to guard the refugees.

The first week passed in a blur of activity as the family busied themselves setting up a new home. The first chore was to
evict the hut's current residents: hornets, spiders, ants, and
scorpions. Next, the jungle had to be trimmed back, the garden
reclaimed. For three days, they cleared weeds, slashed bushes,
and chopped firewood. Next, they re-planted the vegetable garden. For a farmer like Coi, no house was ever a home without a garden.

From the second week and onward, chores claimed most
of the daylight hours: cooking, cleaning, washing, gardening. Early in the mornings, Coi, Tuyet, and the children went

to gather wild greens, fruits, mushrooms, bird eggs, bamboo shoots, and any other edibles. After lunch, Coi stayed with the children for their nap. Takeshi and Tuyet hiked a short way up the mountain to a spring-fed pond for their afternoon rest. In the evenings, when Coi and Tuyet were busy cooking dinner, Takeshi played with the children.

Food was plentiful. The camp had bananas, mangoes, forest plums, fish berries, milk fruit, mushrooms, and edible roots. For starch, they had the rice they had brought up from the villages. Although they found several bamboo groves, they could only eat so many shoots, for boiling out the bitterness took a lot of firewood. The dogs earned their keep by alerting the family to snakes and other creatures that roamed at night. Mountain lychees had ripened the week they arrived. Crimson-skinned lychees, a wild strain, were superbly tangy. They had thicker, leathery skin over a large seed with a gossamer layer of translucent meat and tart nectar, the flavor enhanced by the harsher mountain environment.

"My mouth is numb," Tuyet announced after she had eaten so much that the citric juice hurt her tongue.

"I'll save some seeds to plant in the lowland. In a few years, we'll eat until our bellies burst."

"I have a feeling I will never eat these again," she said with a strange look on her face.

Coi did not notice her niece's expression. "Of course, you will. I can grow anything from seed."

Tuyet closed her eyes, looking inward. Something told her that someday she would tell her descendants about these magical fruits. Months later, while carrying a bag of seeds down the mountains, Coi would cross a river and accidentally drop it in the water.

Life in the wilderness suited Takeshi. He shaved his head completely and looked younger. He hunted small game and dwarf deer, and fished almost daily. Before sunrise, he slipped down the trail with his poles, a jug of water, and a lump of sesame rice wrapped in banana leaf. At lunchtime, he would reappear, sweaty, sunburned, and carrying a basket of fish. Wherever else he went, he always returned at dusk for supper around the campfire.

On clear, breezy nights, the whole family lay down in a silky meadow, side by side, engulfed by the scent of honey grass. Fireflies sailed overhead like fairies. Takeshi told his children the names of stars, recounted myths and adventures of little alien children on distant planets in other galaxies. They linked arms and imagined the world turned upside down so they might fall away into space, speeding toward the stars. The game terrified Hoang. It made him dizzy. Clenching his mother's hands, he whispered that the darkness was too big. If he let go, he would never find the others again among all those points of light.

DAYS SLIPPED into weeks; weeks became months. Quiet contentment filled their glade. They went about their days as though they had spent their entire lives here. Monotony lengthened the minutes, hours. Summer heat made the air sultry, redolent of forest scents. The routines of daily life in the wilderness absorbed them, the outside world forgotten until the porters arrived with their supplies.

Cousin Ha visited too, unannounced, accompanied by a pair of high-ranking cadres who wanted to meet Takeshi. Ha brought little gifts: rice whiskey and tobacco for Takeshi, clothes for his mother, candies for the children, and jars of fermented fish paste he knew Tuyet liked. He also brought news to share around the campfire.

"Our men are fighting all over the country. But the French are too strong. They have regained control of all the cities and ports," he said.

"We're secure in our mountain stronghold," the dour-faced

cadre hastened to add confidently. "We retreat to train our forces. When the moment is right, we will strike."

The older cadre added, "We hope with your help, Major."

"Of course, the Resistance will always have my support. I fought side by side with you before, and I'll do it again," Takeshi said, reminding them of his service. He was mildly irritated that the commander did not address him as brother, cadre, comrade, leader. A member of the Resistance! To some of the hard-liners, Takeshi was still an outsider.

"Very good. Comrade Ha will tell you what we need."

"It's an honor," Takeshi said with a bow. "When can our people return to their homes?"

"HQ will inform everyone as soon as they know," replied the younger cadre. He did not admit that the Viet Minh had been pushed into the mountainous wilderness that ran the length of the country. Some cadres were hiding among the rural population, carrying out hit-and-run raids—the sole option for an ill-equipped force consisting primarily of peasants.

Takeshi poked at the fire, adding another log. He knew that when dealing with hardened fanatics, the less said, the better. There was a long silence.

Ha cleared his throat. "Our forces have started attacking garrisons. The French are mounting massive reprisals."

The younger man snapped, "We can handle anything they send against us."

Takeshi read apprehension in their faces. The Viet Minh were in desperate need of resources and allies.

◆

THERE WAS a dark cleft in the mountain face three hundred meters up from the hut. Hidden behind stunted scrubs and vines was a cave, a shallow rock chamber, about eight meters deep and six meters wide. Its position offered a panoramic view of the forested range to the northwest. Spring water seeped out from bedrock, forming a clear, refreshing pool that filled half the entrance. The overflow trickled downhill past the hut below.

In the sweltering afternoons, Tuyet and Takeshi slipped away from camp and climbed to the cave. They undressed and washed their brown tunics and black trousers in the stream, then spread them on rocks to dry. The cold pool, clear as glass, shocked them to life. They splashed, laughed, played like children, reveling in the giving and taking of small pleasures. Tuyet rubbed, scraped, and kneaded his arms, legs, and back. Takeshi lathered soap into her hair, spreading it out on a flat stone like a sheet of black fabric, rinsing it until it was silky, like wet moss. Life was perfect at the mouth of the cave, content, removed from responsibility.

IN THE HEIGHT of the dry season, each day arrived hotter than the last, the night offering little respite. A shimmering blanket of air covered the mountains. The sky was a milky blue alabaster, veined with fraying threads of cloud. The sun, a merciless white orb, pressed down with unrelenting force, the breeze, a breath from a withering furnace. Cicadas screamed in the unforgiving heat, a keening note of agony that silenced all birds and beasts.

They slept at the edge of the emerald pool entwined atop a thick mat laid over a slab of granite, sheltered from the sun. Their naked bodies were smooth-limbed, compact, tanned, like driftwood on the rocks. This was their private place, above the world, beyond the known. They belonged in this picture, part of the scenery as though they had always been here. Naked savages by the fountain of youth.

It was a new phase with its unique flowering of strength and appetite. Every afternoon—this place in those mid-hours,

196 Andrew X. Pham

in the eye of the infinite sun—they made love in the feverish heat, wet, musky, salty. He was rough and precise, sometimes unimaginably tender. Always the invisible cicadas, as inseparable from the tableau as the sun, cried a singular piercing note, to drown everything.

At times, the cicadas ceased as abruptly as they had begun. In that startling silence, the lovers surfaced from their slumber into a fog of lethargy. Minds drifting, bodies listless. They talked to fill the eerie emptiness, to mark time, to remember there had been a world before this. They were sprawled on their backs, her head pillowed on his arm, staring at the roots and vines dripping from the cave ceiling, their skin pressed against cool stone. His thoughts roamed backward and forward. Sometimes, he remembered his helplessness, and it upset him.

"Do you regret ever meeting me?" he asked.

"Regret means choice."

"What does that mean?"

"After the first time you came to my shop, I had a dream about us."

"You never told me."

She hummed and nibbled at his chest.

He traced her naked ribs with his fingers. "Do your dreams tell you what the future holds for us?"

"It doesn't work like that. In hindsight, dreams unveil what I already know. In foresight, they show me the prominent thread of destiny."

"There is no choice, then."

"A fortuneteller once told me: 'The lines not yet read can be rewritten.'"

"What does that mean?"

"What you want it to mean."

Without looking at him, she knew he was smiling. His voice became playful as he spoke of travels, how he wanted to show her the world, all of its luxury. She allowed herself to be swept along on the tidal flow of his enthusiasm. His imagination blazed, and she stoked the flames. He talked about Scotland, London, Paris, Barcelona, Rome, the Sahara, a year on safari in Africa. These were places she'd only seen pictures of in books and magazines, and as she listened he raced forward, leaping ahead, a season, a year at a time. A decade charted in a steamy afternoon.

He had a confession: "I thought you would resent me for this hard life."

They lay on their sides facing each other. She ground her knuckles into his palm, like mortar and pestle. With a little shrug, she said, "You have not broken my heart. I have no reason to resent you. A hard or an easy life, that's destiny."

He reached for her. She realized with a sharp pang that this was the pinnacle of their love. Life was uncertain. Danger lurked in darkness. It would never be so perfect again. In the trees, a lone cicada sang a shrill note. A chorus replied.

Matsuo Bashō's lines rose like silvery bubbles from the dark depth of his mind:

> *The cry of the cicada*
> *Gives us no sign*
> *That presently it will die*

PART V

Tragedy

→ 1946–1947 →

33

Dawn of Endings

TUYET REMEMBERED THAT SHE HAD BEEN AWAK-
ened on that pivotal day, in her thirty-third year, by a lullaby
her mother used to sing. It drew her from slumber and left her
at the last sweep of night when silence had blanketed all but
the chirring crickets. She recognized the omen. An irrational
panic rose in her throat, her chest hollowed by a looming sense
of loss. In the recesses of her mind, storm clouds churned, and
she heard the soft clicks of doors closing. She wept in silence,
her knuckles pressed into her teeth.

Outside the awning window of split bamboo, ragged clouds
passed before a sickle moon hooked high in the branches of
the longan tree. A breeze from the woods rustled across the
dry fields, carrying into the small room musty, bitter scents of
undergrowth and decay. A season turning. A tremor beneath
her ribs. Tuyet resisted the urge to reach for Takeshi, an arm's
length away, the bed suddenly as wide as an empty plain.

Takeshi slept shirtless, on his back, his wiry, corded arms
at his side. He was gaunt, and tanned to a deep shade of teak
from fishing. Beads of sweat dotted his skin, trickling down his
limbs. Even in repose, he looked shipwrecked, the last Japanese
in the province.

A rooster crowed. Takeshi opened his eyes. Tuyet dabbed
the sweat from his chest with the cuff of her sleeve. They faced
each other, exchanging breaths.

"Were you dreaming?" she whispered.

"You were in my dream," he replied.

"Mmm."

"I saw you in my home by the sea, in Hokkaido. Our children were playing on the beach."

"Were we happy there?"

"Yes, very."

"Are we happy now?"

He paused. He had passed the midpoint of life, with its morning aches and minor injuries. He could taste it in his mouth.

"You're not happy." She knew everything about homesickness.

"I did not say that."

She hushed him, fingertips to his lips. She could feel his loneliness. A life, even one readily sacrificed for love, could not be lived solely within the walls of a house. His yearning for home was palpable.

He squeezed her hand. "Let's take the ship to Hokkaido. You will see why I talk so much about the mists of Kushiro. I will catch delicious fish for you in that cold ocean. My father needs to bless his grandson. We can return when there is peace, when it's safe. The longer we stay here, the harder it will be to leave. The fighting will only get worse."

"Someday, we'll go. Someday." Half promise, half evasion. A dose of desire, a fathom of fear. Not something she wanted to face. She curled into him, nestling her head in the crook of his neck to stem his sudden flight of fancy. Japan seemed so far away, foreign, unreal. She was afraid, she was selfish. It was not in her to leave friends and family. She was not ready. She could not imagine living in a foreign land.

He sighed. "I love you, but you are a very stubborn woman."

"Yes, and you're a buffalo."

"We're a pair."

"My hero."

"I am a fool."

"Never."

"I don't know anything." The colonial conflict grew more

meaningless to him with each passing day. He wanted to retrieve his buried gold and take the whole family to Japan with him.

Four months earlier, they had moved down from the mountain hut to this small village in a border area people called the Twilight Territory, a swath of land between the towns and the wilderness, controlled by neither the French nor the Resistance. They had bought a small homestead consisting of a thatched bungalow, a few sheds, and a fruit orchard on the outskirts of the village. It was a temporary arrangement that allowed Coi to stay in touch with Ha.

He shook his head. "I really don't know what tomorrow will bring. Do you?"

When Tuyet could not be truthful, she retreated into silence. She placed her hand in his and pressed her knuckles into his cupped palm, mortar and pestle, their private sign.

Indigo dawn wedged into the dark horizon. Bickering starlings fluttered in the trees. In the other room, Coi stretched her limbs, rising from a hard divan she shared with Anh and Hoang. She fumbled with the back-door latch, shuffled outside, and washed her face at the rain cistern beneath the eaves of the house with much clattering of buckets as if to remind Tuyet that it was a market day and they had to make an early start. The children slept on undisturbed.

"Stay," Takeshi whispered.

Tuyet fought off his hands. "We need supplies for the shop."

She set her feet on the floor, but he sat up and caught her from behind. He pulled her into a crushing embrace with his rangy arms of knots and cables, of scars and sun-bronzed flesh. The callouses on his palms pressed into her hard as pebbles. Her head lolled back against his, the stubble on his chin rough against her skin, his breath hot on the nape of her neck in long exhalations, tender as whispers. She drew in his scent, the saltiness of tears still on her lips. Night dissipated around them like a slow-moving fog, leaving their limbs awash with the lilac luminescence of predawn.

THAT WAS HOW she remembered him, how she remembered them.

In their last hour of happiness.

Despite all the hardships and heartbreak, they were still whole then. They had all that could be good and kind and sweet between two people. They were perfect in those final moments.

And, she believed, some parts of them, some part of their spirits, remained there, unassailable by the evil to come.

That was the art and the tragedy of dream-walking. One did not ask "what if" after reality had unfolded. It was not in the dream-walker's lexicon. Things, events, parts of life played out like déjà vu. It had always been too late. They had been here before. It was inescapable.

34

Conscription

IN THE MUTED TWILIGHT, THE FAINT DIRT ROAD lay across the grassy swale like a satin ribbon. Copses of stunted trees hoarded lingering night, foliage heavy with dew. This was a sparsely populated country. Separated by rice fields, rough homesteads of thatch-and-mud houses were scattered along the rutted road. Coi and Tuyet walked side by side, shouldering yoke-baskets of fruits from their orchard: mangoes, green guavas, and the early pickings of custard apples. The small market served only two nearby villages, so the baskets were light, for any unsold fruits would have to be carried back the same four kilometers.

"Let's have a bowl of *bun rieu*, Auntie," Tuyet said. Tuyet had not grown up in the countryside, and so she missed the variety of food available in town.

"You enjoy your noodles. I have my boiled yam." Coi snagged a sprig of wild mint and held it between her black-lacquered teeth. Her sandals were in the baskets. She preferred to feel the earth beneath her feet, soles as tough as seasoned hide, toenails like chips of ivory.

"You know I don't like to eat alone," Tuyet pleaded, struggling to keep up with her aunt. "If we sell all our fruit, will you have a bowl with me?"

Clucking her tongue, the older woman quickened her pace. A lifelong ascetic, she denied herself even the smallest luxuries. Yet she would skip a meal to buy treats for the children. She rarely allowed Tuyet to buy her anything. Over the years, Tuyet had given her four jade bracelets as nest eggs, but Coi had sold three of them one by one the moment someone came to her with a tale of woe. Suffering had made Coi sensitive to the pain of others. When Tuyet scolded her, she shrugged, saying, "Pretty stones won't earn me merit in the next life, but a kindness in this one will. Tell me, do you want to be reborn into another life like this one?" Tuyet could only throw up her hands crying, "Oh, Auntie, why is it that we are so good at poverty?"

THE SATURDAY MARKET was an informal affair for peasants in the buffer zone between the town and the mountains. It drew local farmers and village shopkeepers. Peddlers from town came with bullock carts full of spices, fabric, medicines, bundles of incense sticks, and a variety of manufactured products. Some bartered for local produce and livestock for resale in town. Children swarmed around the carts, gazing at dolls, kites, and candy jars. That day, three bare-bottomed little boys marched gamely through the crowd, sucking on homemade lollipops of hardened rice syrup on bamboo sticks.

Tuyet and Coi lowered their baskets at their usual spot next to a pork seller who had displayed his wares on a mat of fresh banana leaves: piles of cuts of meats and innards, and one whole hog head, pink, beady-eyed, and startlingly manlike, staring through a halo of buzzing black flies.

Nearby, a blacksmith was sharpening blades on a wet grindstone. His young daughter had set out an array of knives, spades, pickaxes, and hoes on a burlap sack. The field rang with the singsong cries of sellers, the full-throated laughter of southerners, and their sparkling banter. Squealing children darted about, chasing each other. Vendors were hawking sweet coconut rice, roasted ears of corn, and field crab noodle soup. Tuyet's stomach groaned at the sweet aromas of fatty pork sizzling over hot coals. The brisk hike had sharpened her appetite, but she decided to wait. She should not have to wait long, for shopping at rural markets was quick and friendly because, first, there was not much to buy and not much money to spend, and second, the fair price of food was common knowledge. Most of the buying and selling happened in the first hour, and people usually left before the sun had climbed halfway to noon.

Shoppers turned their heads to the western end of the field at the sound of approaching automobiles when two jeeps and two trucks rounded the bend. A collective gasp went up across the field, and the crowd promptly dispersed. Those near the eastern end of the market took to the road away from the convoy; some ran into the rice field to the north, but most fled into the woods to the south. Without a word, Coi and Tuyet shouldered their baskets. The smartest vendors ran off, leaving everything behind. The tumult turned to pandemonium. Handcarts and tables were upended. People scrambled toward the trees, pushing, shoving, tumbling over others, trampling the fallen. The uneven field became a tangle of limbs, baskets, and poles.

Soldiers jumped from the trucks and began chasing the peasants, shouting for them to stop. The jeeps had veered off the road and were bouncing over the uneven ground in a flanking maneuver. Soldiers hit people with rifle butts. Coi and Tuyet had dropped their baskets and were sprinting toward the woods when a man banged into Tuyet, knocking her to the ground. She lost both her hat and her sandals. Coi turned back and pulled her to her feet.

A French officer, standing up in the jeep, fired his pistol into the air. Some people stopped; others kept running. Submachine gunfire raked across the path of those making for the trees, clumps of soil popping up right in front of Coi and Tuyet. Everyone dropped to the ground for cover. Down on her stomach, Tuyet saw the man who had crashed into her escape into the bushes.

They were surrounded, being herded back toward the road where they were ordered to sit. Several soldiers were gathering food and items from the market. Everything, including live chickens and baskets of fresh meat and fish, was loaded into one of the trucks. No one dared protest the thievery.

A tall métis corporal, half-French, inspected the captives. He had a café-au-lait complexion, an angular face, a high Caucasian nose, and deep-set hazel eyes. He wore threadbare ill-fitting beige khakis, the sort issued to indigenous troops.

"Imbecile! Don't you know how to form a proper line?" he yelled and booted a youngster in the rear, sending the teenage boy sprawling. He pointed at a mother holding a crying baby. "Quiet that baby right now!"

They separated the men from the women, had them squatted in rows. Two corporals went among the captives, selecting healthy men and women, leaving the frail and elderly. Vendors who had come in bullock carts showed their identity cards, proving that they were not local residents. They were allowed to return to their carts.

A short soldier motioned with his weapon for Tuyet to join the group of captives waiting by the road. Coi stood up to follow her niece, but he pushed her back down saying she was too old.

"Please, let me go in her place," Coi said. "She has young children!"

"Sit down and shut up, old woman," he snapped and pushed Tuyet forward by her elbow.

"Take care of the children, Auntie," Tuyet called over her shoulder as the soldier roughly shoved her along.

Tuyet climbed onto the back of the truck, where she stood crammed shoulder to shoulder with other captives. She quickly moved toward the side rails to keep from getting crushed in the middle. One man refused to climb into the truck. Two soldiers beat him with their rifle butts until he collapsed. He was lashed with ropes to the side of the truck like an animal. No one else resisted. When the truck was full, they lined up the remaining captives in two columns and ordered them to march down the road. One of the jeeps brought up the rear.

"Please, Honorable Officer," pleaded an old man who had not been conscripted. "Where are you taking them? I have to tell my daughter where you are taking her husband."

"Have a heart, young man," begged another elder. People clamored to know where they were being taken.

"Don't you have a family? Mother, father?"

"Can't you help us? Aren't we all Viet people here?"

Finally, the corporal replied, "Those in the truck are being taken to the garrison for work. Those people on foot are going to Crystal Creek to repair the bridge the Viet Minh destroyed last week. If you want to help them, bring food and clothes to the garrison or the workers' camp at the creek."

THE TRUCK LURCHED into motion. People standing in the bed fell against one another. Slammed against the railing, Tuyet cried out in pain as she fought to stay upright. Looking back at the crowd, she did not see her aunt. In the field where the market had been, chaos prevailed: trampled fruits, smashed jars of pickles, mounds of white noodles souring in the sun. The butcher's table had been turned upside down, pink heaps of innards and meat scattered in the grass, the hog's head on its side with its beady eyes seeming to laugh at the mess. Cawing blackbirds descended on the remains, picking through the spoils, brazen like scavenging dogs.

The convoy returned the way it had come, kicking up a cloud of dust. Old women and children trotted after them. Tuyet spotted her aunt among the stragglers. She called her name. Coi was jogging, picking up speed until she was running as fast as her short legs could carry her, hands outstretched as though she wanted to climb onto the truck. Her hat flew off.

She ran until she had left everyone else behind, but the convoy pulled farther and farther away. Her legs finally buckled, and she crumbled in the dirt, sobbing. Tuyet wept, her vision blurred by tears. Around her, the cries of the wretched rose in a long wail.

Tuyet shivered. At last, all her premonitions were taking form.

35

Search

TUYET HAD SAID HE LACKED ANY SENSITIVITY beyond the visceral. The spirit world only touched him in his nightmares. He was spiritual but without the spirits. In their hurried lovemaking that morning, he had failed to notice her anxiety. He remembered that her lips had been salty but promptly forgot it, focused on his own needs. Afterward, he had gone back to sleep, warm, sated, oblivious to the timbre of her farewell or to the way she had lingered, uncharacteristically, at the threshold. For him, that decisive day had unfolded as one more ordinary day.

Takeshi brewed a cup of strong black tea and thought about dishes he might cook for the family that evening. It had become his market-day routine because he liked the way his wife beamed when she enjoyed his food. At dawn, he woke the children, had them wash their faces, and told them to prepare for a mushroom hunt. Anh clapped her hands, for she loved spending time in the woods. The dogs danced in circles, infected with her excitement. Nunu, the calico cat who had come with the house, looked down from the kitchen shelf, yawned, and dismissed them with a flick of her tail.

They left through the back door. He strapped on his machete belt and lifted sleepy Hoang onto his shoulders. The boy was uncommonly smart for his four years, but he was also very frail and small.

Anh commanded the mother dog with a firm index finger. "Stay, Mimi. Stay! Guard the house."

The walnut-brown mutt retired to a spot on the patio next

to the cooking pit. She and her year-old pup were new addi-
tions to the family, given to them by their neighbors as house-
warming presents. The pup, Momo, bounced from the house
and plunged into the trees beyond the orchard. Anh skipped
after him, a woven basket riding on her hip, clutching a small
paring knife in her hand. Seven years old, she fancied herself a
princess in commoner disguise. She did not know how to joke
or tease, but she had an endearing smile, a special skill with
animals, and a prodigious memory for things that grabbed her
interest, such as searching the woods for things to eat.

Takeshi followed, carrying a walking staff, his son riding
his shoulders. Hoang wiggled impatiently, urging his father
on. They hiked through the dew-laden forest that glowed with
the honeyed light of dawn. The puppy chased a black squir-
rel through the green undergrowth. It leaped onto a fallen log
covered in moss and scampered up a tree. Anh squealed when
she discovered a cluster of mushrooms and squatted to harvest
them. Outraged by the intrusion, a koel bird scolded them from
the branches of a fire-blossom tree.

A game trail meandered down to the bank of the river where
on a gravel bar, a muntjac deer looked up, then, bounding
around a bend in the river, vanished into a curtain of light that
slanted through the trees. The stream gurgled, rippling over
smooth black rocks, flushing clear as fluid glass through calm
pools where emerald dragonflies with ruby eyes skimmed over
spearweed and butter lilies. Anh pointed out the dragonflies to
her brother, saying that the previous night she had ridden them
in her dream. The boy groaned enviously. Takeshi put his son
down and waded into the bracing cold water. Checking his basket trap, he found two juvenile moon carps, finger length, with
bony, translucent bodies.

Anh said, "Papa, may I have them?"

He nodded. "What will you do with them?"

"I will raise them in the rain barrel. They are a pair, so they won't be lonely."

He remembered a fairy tale about a girl raising a magical moon carp in a well and something about a wish being granted. "Ah, oh . . . I know—"

"Shhh! Don't say it, Papa!" she cried, shrill with panic. "You'll spoil it."

He nodded solemnly, a finger over his lips. He let her hold the basket in the stream while he walked up the bank to a bamboo grove. He chopped down a bamboo stem as thick as his thigh and fashioned a small pail from a section of it. Filling the container with water, he put the carps in it.

"Thank you, Papa!" Anh said, thrilled.

"Hmm, I suppose we will be having chicken tonight."

"Yakitori?" Anh asked.

Perking up, Hoang said, "Papa, may I have the wings?"

"Yes, son."

"Granny likes wings too," the boy said. "We have only one chicken?"

"One is plenty. Perhaps you should share one of the wings with Granny. You can give it to her yourself."

"Good idea, Papa," he said. "Do you think she will bring back some peanut taffy from the market?"

"Have you been a good boy?"

"Of course, Papa! You know I have," Hoang replied indignantly.

He chuckled. "Then she probably will, but remember, you should not expect it, and don't ask for it."

"Expectation cheapens the gift," the boy declared, quoting one of his father's sayings back at him.

He patted his son's head, struck by the boy's precociousness. *My father would be so proud if he could see his grandson,* he thought wistfully. *What would he say if he heard you speak three languages?* He glanced at his stepdaughter, who was too shy to ask for anything for herself. "Daughter, would you like a drumstick?"

"Ooo! Please, Papa." She clapped her hands, excited at the prospect of getting to gnaw on her own drumstick. She gave him two large cinnamon cap mushrooms. "For you, Papa!"

"Good job. Thank you."

She curtsied, glowing. "May I have extra teriyaki sauce on my drumstick, Papa?"

"For princesses, always extra!" He winked.

She giggled.

The sun was dancing in the stream like so many jewels, there for the taking, none for the keeping. His heart brimmed as he embraced his children. The joys of family and fatherhood had come to him most unexpectedly in this strange, impoverished place. Year after year, until the past few months, he had been too busy, preoccupied, driven. He couldn't remember spending an entire day with his children.

WHEN THEY HAD a basket full of mushrooms and young bamboo shoots, they went home to a light breakfast of the previous evening's rice with leftover clay-pot catfish. They played in the orchard, picked guavas. For lunch, he made an onion omelet with freshly steamed rice topped with morning glory. While the children took their afternoon rest, he killed and feathered the oldest hen in the coop, then carved it up into three portions, one for the steamer, one for the soup pot, one for the grill. Steaming the breast, he set it aside for Coi, who would turn it into meat floss. The torso and thighs went into the soup pot with onions, mushrooms, and bamboo shoots. The drumsticks, wings, and some odd bits he marinaded in a homemade teriyaki sauce. Once the yakitori began sizzling over charcoal, his mouth watered so much he couldn't resist breaking the wax seal on a new jug of sake. Mimi and Momo sat at rapt attention, drooling. *You don't tell, I won't tell.* He chuckled to himself. He selected two skewers of meat to share with the dogs.

THE DOGS sat up, ears perked. In a blur, they darted around the house without barking. The children followed. *They must be home*, he thought. He removed the yakitori skewers from the grill and got to his feet, dusting himself. That was when he heard her chilling wail.

Aunt Coi stumbled to the back of the house, followed by the children, and collapsed at his feet, gasping incoherently. Her bare feet were bleeding, her pants and shirt torn and soiled, her hat gone. She had run all the way home empty-handed. "Legionnaires at the market!" she blurted, sobbing. The children fell into her arms, huddling on the ground. The dogs crowded in to lick their faces.

He felt light-headed, dizzy, gooseflesh rising on his neck. He had to sit down, unable to comprehend what he was hearing. "Where is she? Where is Tuyet?"

"They took her!" Coi wailed. "They took everybody!"

"Where? Where did they take her?" he asked, seizing Coi by the shoulders.

"The garrison." Tears streamed down her face.

Hands trembling, he wobbled on his feet as though someone had punched him in the gut. He grabbed the jug and gulped down the sake. In the bedroom, he climbed up into the rafters to get a metal box from a hidden space in the thatch wall dividing the room. From the box, he took a revolver, a box of cartridges, a roll of piaster notes, and twenty slabs of gold. The box back in its place, he checked the revolver, then divided the gold and the money, putting half into a canvas satchel and the other half in a silk pouch.

He found Coi with the children still weeping. Pressing the silk pouch into Coi's hands, he said, "Take this and spend it as you see fit. I might be gone some time. Send word to Ha and Xuan. Tell them I'm going after Tuyet. I'll leave messages with our contacts along the way."

"I'll warn Ha and Xuan, but I'm coming with you," she replied, wiping her face with her shirttail. "The children can stay with the neighbors for a few days. I have to go with you. You cannot pass for a Viet."

She limped inside to get her things. When she saw the meal they had prepared on the table, she sat down heavily with her hands over her mouth.

"It's not safe, Auntie," Takeshi said, touching her arm.

"What can they do to an old woman?"

Shushing her, he took the medicine basket from the shelf and knelt at her feet beside the divan. Anh brought him a tin basin of water, Hoang towels. He told the children to go outside and mind the soup pot. He began cleaning and dressing Coi's wounds. It was the first time he had seen cuts on her thickly calloused soles. She tried to push him away, but he wouldn't have it.

"Auntie, you're not an old woman. You have half my strength but twice my stamina and the heart of ten men."

He had seen this tiny woman carry yoke-baskets twenty kilometers up a mountain trail, rest long enough to eat a meal, and return the way she had come, armed with nothing more than her will, her wit, and a small paring knife. Against bandits, tigers, snakes, and evil spirits, she claimed protection from the Lady Buddha. He never doubted her, for saintly souls often were thus safeguarded.

"What if someone finds out that you're Japanese?"

"Exactly. That's why you can't be seen with me. It's easier for one man to travel and hide. It's safer this way."

"Don't worry about me. I can take care of myself," Coi said defiantly. She rose on her bandaged feet without even wincing as though to prove a point. She stood all of one hundred forty-five centimeters tall.

He didn't argue. "I know. I'm thinking of the children. If something happens ... you are all they have. Take care of them. Please, Auntie, I am counting on you."

Coi pursed her lips, weighing the risks at length, then nodded. "But if I don't hear from you tomorrow, I will come after you."

36

Garrison

STANDING UP IN THE TRUCK BED WITH THE OTHER captives, Tuyet watched the road as they rounded the bend and the town gate came into view. A row of peasants lined the side of the road, waiting to be checked by soldiers. She had passed here only once since moving to the area, but Aunt Coi made the trip to town twice a month. She recognized the guard shack with its sandbag barriers and beyond it, a line of shabby huts, eateries, and shops.

The garrison loomed three hundred meters behind the checkpoint, sitting in the middle of a rice field. A plantation owner had lived there before it was converted into a military base. The two-story brick villa with whitewashed walls and a terracotta tile roof served as the office space and officers' quarters. It was flanked by four large buildings and several huts, housing three platoons, two Viet and one French, and conscripted coolies. The entire compound, roughly the size of one and a half football fields, was ringed by a tall mesh fence topped with barbed wire.

The vehicles pulled inside and parked at a dusty gravel lot next to the barracks. The swaggering half-French soldier, whom the captives had already nicknamed Halfwit, ordered everyone to sit in the yard in front of the dining hall, which was a large open veranda with a high thatched roof. Tuyet squatted with the other women. She counted forty-two conscripts, thirty-five men and seven women including herself. Tuyet wrinkled her nose at the faint reek of sewage and urine that hung over the garrison. A small crowd had gathered outside along the barbed wire fence, staring at the new arrivals. Viet soldiers shooed them back, threatening half-heartedly to lock them up in the tiger cages next to the guardhouse.

A giant bare-chested Moroccan lumbered out from the villa, barking orders. Coolies trotted to the truck to unload what the soldiers had pilfered at the market. Fresh produce was carried to the kitchen behind the dining hall; dried goods to the warehouse on the other side of the villa; live chickens to the barn at the rear, by the latrine row. The hog squealed as it was dragged to the pen at the rear of the compound. A platoon of disheveled Viet troops in threadbare beige uniforms with old carbines assembled in front of the barracks next to the parking area. Across the yard, one European and two African legionnaires came out of the barracks. The European lieutenant climbed into the jeep with the Africans as he motioned with his hand. The Viet platoon leader ordered his men into the truck. The jeep driver beeped the horn twice, the trucker honked once, and the patrol rolled out of the gate.

Tuyet glanced at the dozen off-duty soldiers lounging in the dining hall, a slovenly bunch of French, North Africans, and Viets. Few wore anything resembling a uniform save their boots and trousers. Many were shirtless, sweaty. Viet troops wore tattered uniforms in various shades of brown, from dark tan to bleached ivory. They had been issued one new uniform upon enlistment, so now most of their clothing was tattered secondhand bought with their wages.

Halfwit hung about the hall, fawning over the Europeans. He gestured toward the female captives, made a joke, and snickered. The men laughed and craned their necks to leer at two teenage sisters squatting near Tuyet. A shiver of fear passed among the women. Instinctively, they huddled closer together.

A tall Viet man with a clipboard strolled from the villa to address the group. "Greetings, friends and neighbors. My name is Liem," he said. Liem wore a white short-sleeved shirt, dark trousers, and leather sandals. He spoke the southern dialect with a thick Central Highland accent that was difficult to understand.

"I am the administrative secretary to the garrison commander. I apologize for your sudden conscription. I know some of you have questions about why you're here. Let me assure you it's for the noble purpose of building our country. Your duty is to serve your country and Mother France."

The captives looked down at the dirt under their feet. The woman next to Tuyet rolled her eyes. Everyone knew that service to Mother France was just another way of saying the French didn't want to do the dirty work themselves. The colonizers paid so poorly no one wanted to work for them. Previous attempts to force Viet troops to do coolie work had resulted in mass desertion. The French solution to the labor shortage was to conscript peasants. An older woman raised her hand and asked about informing her family.

"Do not be concerned about that, good friends and neighbors. We will take your name and notify your village chief. Your family will be proud that you are doing your duty as good subjects. The sooner these projects are completed, the sooner you can go home."

He read aloud a list of rules from his clipboard. Small infractions were subject to whipping. Major violations were punishable by imprisonment in the tiger cage. Anyone trying to escape would be shot on sight. He called them out one by one, asked a few questions, and then assigned each to one of three groups: skilled male laborers, unskilled male laborers, and female kitchenhands. Since few villagers had documents of any sort, Tuyet gave an alias she had been using and was told to join the kitchen crew.

A HEAVYSET, round-faced woman with graying hair introduced herself as Second Sister, the senior cook. A large birthmark shaped like a mango covered her cheek from her left eye to the jawline. She led the women past the side of the hall to the kitchen building behind the dining area, ignoring the cat-calls of the soldiers. The kitchen was divided into two parts. One was walled on three sides to vent smoke from a bank of cooking pits. The other was for preparing food and for wash-ing dishes and laundry. The brick building behind the kitchen had three rooms, two used as a pantry, one as the women's dor-mitory with metal bars on the windows and a reinforced door padlocked from the outside.

Second Sister had them meet six other women who were preparing the midday meal, telling them their duties, includ-ing gardening, laundry, sanitation, and general housekeeping for the legionnaires and officers. She added that the staff now numbered fourteen including herself, so the workload should not be too heavy. After a brief exchange about basic rules and routines, she promptly put them to work on the midday meal.

AFTER THE SOLDIERS had been served their lunch, the women ate with the other coolies, sitting down with their bowls in the shade around the compound. Following half an hour of washing the dishes, they were allowed an hour of rest. Most just lay down in the shade for a nap until Second Sister roused them for work with an older male overseer, who ordered them to dig a latrine trench by the fence on the north side of the bar-racks. Tuyet picked up a hoe and began hacking at the hard earth. The orange clay had been baked by the summer sun. Each hoe stroke chipped off a fist-sized clump. Her shopkeep-er's hands began to blister, her thoughts turning to her family. Aunt Coi must be almost home by now. She prayed Takeshi would not do something rash. Without a hat, Tuyet became dizzy and vomited the little food she had eaten for lunch. One of the women shoveled it away with the loose dirt. A Viet sol-dier sitting in the shade ordered them to keep working. They pickaxed, hoed, and dug for another hour until they were sum-moned back to the kitchen to prepare the evening meal.

There, Sergeant Valle was perched on a stool next to the butcher's block. A balding, florid man of muscular build gone fat, he cultivated a bushy mustache. A blood-smeared apron was draped over his paunch. He had just finished carving up a side of beef and was sweating profusely from the effort. Tow-eling his face, he took a swig from a bottle of wine while the kitchen help filed in to squat before him.

"Bonjour!" he said in French with a friendly smile. Speaking slowly, he waited after each sentence for Second Sister to trans-late. "Welcome to my kitchen. I am Sergeant Valle, and the kitchen is my domain. I am the master here. The big Moroccan over there is Corporal Berrada. You can call him Ali. He is in charge of supplies. You have met Hai, our kitchen manager." He gestured at Second Sister, mistaking her title for her name. "Mo and Uyen are my assistants. You are to obey these three women in everything. Learn from them."

"Now, listen carefully," he continued, wagging a finger. "I run a clean and punctual kitchen. I don't put up with laziness and tardiness. You will work hard, but you will eat well here." He took a slug from the bottle and dragged the back of his palm across his mouth. "I have cut up a good side of beef. Hai will tell you what to do."

With that, he nodded and grinned, pleased with his speech. He hoisted himself to his feet and toddled off with his bottle to the hammock strung between two trees in the vegetable gar-den. Second Sister outlined what was to be done to Granny Mo and Uyen, who were to ready the ingredients. Granny prepared French fare while Uyen cooked Viet. They divided the work among the women. Right away, they split the kitchen help into four groups, each made to squat around several heaps of food. Cutting boards to hand, they were glad that they would be working in the shade.

One of the younger women asked, "Second Sister, why did they grab us?"

"Free labor," she replied. Second Sister had worked for the French garrison since before the Japanese occupation and had returned to her job when the French had been put back in control by the British. She had been at the garrison since long before Valle. "When they conscripted laborers in town last month, a huge riot broke out. So now they do it in the countryside where people are Viet Minh sympathizers anyway."

"We're not Viet Minh sympathizers! Our families have farmed on our land for generations."

Another woman grumbled, "It's just an excuse to do whatever they want. Who's to stop them?"

"How will our families find us? How will we get home?" sobbed the teenage girl, the youngest of the captives. Her older sister put an arm around her shoulders. Silence fell over the group.

"Let's get this meat trimmed and marinated," Granny Mo said, clapping her hands. The old woman was working at the garrison to be close to her only son, who was an enlisted man there. "Over there, you ladies be quick with those potatoes. We'll make a stew for the whole camp. Plenty of bones to make some noodle soup too." She added on a lighter note, "The sergeant is not so bad. When there is plenty, he lets us cook whatever we want for ourselves."

"He's not like the French regulars," Uyen said. A humorless woman, she was the workhorse of the kitchen, as solidly built as any farmer, with strong arms, a wide back, and powerful legs. Valle had hired her himself.

"What do you mean?" Tuyet asked.

Without looking up, Uyen replied flatly, "He doesn't force himself on women."

Tuyet stared at Uyen, but Uyen was already chopping the meat, not adding another word. Tuyet turned to Granny Mo, who said nothing, which in a way said everything. In one corner of the kitchen, a moon-faced woman stopped working. She hugged herself, rocking back and forth on her heels.

A pall of silence fell over them. They eyed one another apprehensively, but none spoke for to speak of evil was to summon it. Tuyet shuddered as she stared at her palms, at the deeply scored, intersecting lines, these wrinkly hands that might have belonged to someone thirty years older. Since childhood, she had been ashamed of her hands, these balance sheets carried over from a previous existence. Here, along the edge of her palm, the markings of five children; there, the contorted lines of love. At the center, the compelling triangle of destiny revealing two seasons of surrender and two of daring, marred by crisscrossing choices and tragedies.

37

Bandits

DUSK SUFFUSED THE TRAMPLED FIELD IN PEWTER gray. The deserted market looked blighted, devoid of life and color. The woods were dark, impenetrable. Scavengers were picking over the market area. Stray dogs were nosing beneath a broken trestle for meat scraps. Crows cawed in protest as they took wing.

Takeshi was prowling the grounds, prodding at debris with his staff, looking for what he did not know. He felt an urge to talk to someone but thought better of it. His shirt was drenched in sweat from running. The mosquitoes were beginning to swarm. He drank from his water flask, deciding to push on toward the next village. It was too dark to run, so he walked briskly, mindful of vipers that sometimes lay coiled patiently along the roadside. He thought about what could be happening to Tuyet, but when he felt panic rising, he forced himself to focus on what he should do next. He had to contact the local Resistance agent, the village blacksmith.

Clouds drifted across a starry sky. A sliver of moon hung low on the horizon. Smoke from cooking fires drifted like wraiths above the village. As he neared the cluster of huts, he caught the aroma of fish being fried in garlic. Yellow beads of light winked from thatched houses a few dozen meters off the road. Dogs sensed his approach and started barking. One paced alongside him, growling and snarling, alerting every mutt up the road that he was coming. He whistled a tune, keeping a firm grip on his staff. People stood in lamp-lit doorways, watching the road. A man called out a tentative greeting. Takeshi grunted and continued, for he did not want to be questioned. It was clearly impossible to pass unnoticed without a back-country guide.

Branches rustled behind him: something moving fast through the underbrush. Out of the corner of his eye, he saw two large dogs closing in, four meters away. Instinctively, he swung the staff in a swooping arc overhead, hitting one of the dogs with a loud crack. It yelped and beat a hasty retreat. The second dog barked at a safe distance. A couple of people stepped from their houses, peered at the stranger on the road, and called out, asking his name. He lowered his head and quickened his pace.

CROSSING THE MEADOW between the main village and the blacksmith's home, Takeshi had an uneasy feeling. He neither heard nor saw the blacksmith's pair of ridgeback mongrels. He stopped under a tree and watched the yard from a distance. From previous visits, he knew the lot was a mess of broken machinery, odd pieces of farm equipment, rusted coils of barbed wire, heaps of scrap metal, broken plows, and oxcarts in various states of disrepair. Weeds and vines had overgrown much of the junkyard. A faint glow emanated from the hut's windows. He heard low voices. Something or someone was in the workshop behind the main dwelling.

He whistled a bird call through his fingers. No reply. He leaned his staff against a tree, took out his pistol, and crossed the road, moving closer for a look through the window. Carefully picking his way through the maze of scrap metal, he heard something to his right and froze.

"So you're the one stirring up the village dogs," said a man in a falsetto voice. He stepped out from the shadow, sighting down the barrel of a rifle. "Put the gun on the ground very slowly, friend."

Takeshi paused, sensing danger in that voice. He complied, putting up his hands. "I'm looking for the blacksmith."

"So were we," said the other man, keeping the MAS-36 rifle leveled at Takeshi. He called toward the house, "I told you boys something was coming down the road."

Two figures emerged from the hut: a teenage boy carrying an old Lebel rifle and a squarish brute in his thirties holding an oil lamp and a machete. The light fell on the leader, a handsome man in his mid-twenties. They were unshaven and grubby, in black clothes with ropes for belts and rough cord sandals. Takeshi knew at once they were bandits.

"Put the bag down," Leader ordered.

Brute picked up the pistol and wedged it in his belt behind him. Boy took Takeshi's satchel and upended it onto the ground. Brute set down the oil lamp, and the pair squatted to examine the contents.

Takeshi asked, "Where's the blacksmith?"

"Uncle Den was conscripted today," Leader replied.

"Did they grab him at the market?"

"No, they came here for him. Killed his dogs too."

"Are you with the Resistance?"

Ignoring the question, Leader said, "You speak our language very well for a Japanese. I have met some of your countrymen in the Resistance. Who are you?"

"My name is Ki. I'm with the Resistance," Takeshi replied, using his nickname. "My wife was conscripted at the market today."

"Son of a monkey!" cried Brute. He held up a stack of gold slabs.

Leader's face broke into a smile. He said, "This rich Japanese might be one of those deserters with a price on their heads. Tie him up."

Boy went into the hut for a rope. Brute put the gold back into the satchel. He came over and, without warning, punched Takeshi in the stomach. Takeshi doubled over. His hand went to his waistband, closing around the hilt of the rice-blade knife.

As Brute reached for him, Takeshi drove the knife upward into the man's torso. He felt the thin blade pierce the flesh, lodging between the man's ribs. Brute froze, moaning as he looked down at the knife. Ducking under Brute's arms, Takeshi reached for his pistol wedged in the other man's belt.

A shot rang out. Hot pain searing his side, Takeshi crumbled to his knees, pistol in hand. Leader was working the bolt of the rifle, loading another round. Takeshi thumbed away the safety on his revolver and fired, hitting Leader in the arm. The man screamed, nearly dropping his rifle.

Boy ran out of the house and stopped short, fumbling with his rifle. Takeshi scrambled away for cover. Boy fired, the bullet slamming into a wooden barrel.

Takeshi took cover behind a woodpile, fired at Boy, and missed. Boy retreated into the house. Leader grabbed the satchel off the ground. All three bandits went for cover.

"You got me, but I got you too!" Leader shouted.

"Let's finish it, then," Takeshi replied. Blood was trickling down his waist. He fingered the wound. Perhaps a grazing shot, not too bad.

A muzzle flashed from the shadow. The bullet whizzed high overhead. He heard the bandits talking among themselves, but he could not make out the words. He fired at a movement near the house. Two shots came back in his direction.

He heard movement and the labored grunts of the wounded men. They were moving. Sounds of footsteps receded toward the rear of the house. The bandits were retreating with their loot. Three shadows detached themselves from the main structure and were shuffling toward the bushes. Too long a shot for a handgun. He let them go and sank to the grass, clutching at the searing pain in his side.

He knew he had rushed into action without a plan, and this was the price. His gold in exchange for a bullet. He fumbled for the tobacco pouch in his pocket and rolled a smoke. His hands shook as he tried to light the cigarette. What a mess, he thought. Perhaps his run of luck had run out at last.

A koel bird called from the road. A familiar sound. Takeshi cupped his palm and cawed.

A moment later, a voice shouted from the road, "Who is visiting?"

"Your cousin from the mountains," he replied, using the pass phrase.

"Where are you?"

"Over here."

Four teenagers stepped out from the roadside shadows. They picked their way carefully across the salvage yard and found him sitting on the ground, holding his side. One of the boys removed the hood of the lantern. They saw his bloodied shirt.

"Mister Ki, you're wounded!" cried the tallest, a sixteen-year-old boy.

"It happens in a gunfight," Takeshi replied, puffing on his cigarette.

"Is it bad?"

"I don't know, but it sure hurts a lot," he said. "It's good to see Resistance youths on patrol tonight. It has been months since I came to your gathering. I'm sorry I forget your names."

"That's Mong and Luu. This is my brother Quyen, and I'm Tri. We heard the gunshots. What happened?"

"My wife was conscripted today. I came looking for Uncle Den, but instead, I walked in on three burglars. They robbed me right in front of his house. They got my money, but I wounded two of them," he said, waving his pistol toward the woods. "They fled that way, out the back."

"Aiya! Your wife was taken, and now you're hurt. What rotten luck!"

Takeshi smirked. "Good luck never comes in pairs, misfortune never comes alone."

"A lot of families suffered today. Uncle Den was conscripted, too. The French took around sixty people from the villages around here. I'm glad you got those bandits. I'm sure they had been planning to break into a few other houses tonight."

Another boy said, "Those aren't the only lowlifes hiding in the woods. We had better warn everyone."

"Right," said Takeshi. "Can you help me get home?"

Tri and his brother pulled Takeshi to his feet. "Let's take you to the healer first."

Takeshi hissed with pain. "Yes, please!"

38

Blue-Eyed Demon

TUYET'S THIRD NIGHT IN THE GARRISON. IT WAS pitch-dark in the women's cell. She had settled on her sleeping mat. Eleven members of the kitchen crew were quartered in this large room, sleeping side by side on the floor. The senior crew had mosquito nets, newly conscripted ones only old cotton sheets to cover themselves. Someone was sobbing quietly in the far corner of the room.

Footsteps approached. The padlock rattled. The door creaked open. Two Frenchmen appeared on the threshold, one a bald oaf in a filthy undershirt, the other a gangling man with a thick beard. The bearded one came into the room, holding a kerosene lantern to their faces.

"You two," said the bald one, grabbing the teenage sisters. He waved at Tuyet and the four other new conscripts. "Come!"

No one moved. The brute cursed and dragged the shrieking sisters through the door. The bearded man hauled the women to their feet and pushed them outside, where the barracks were lit by kerosene lamps, small oases of yellow light that drew halos of buzzing insects. The men herded the women across the dark yard toward the main building. Groups of French and African legionnaires were rolling dice. Someone strummed a guitar. They whistled at the women. Across the yard, Viet troops sat, watching in sullen silence, their cigarettes glowing red holes in the blackness. At the gate, guard dogs barked. Fear wrung Tuyet's insides into a knot. Her legs were shaking, so she could barely walk.

The two men took them into the villa and made them climb the stairs to the officers' quarters on the second floor, where they shoved each woman into a different room. Tuyet found herself in a small bedroom with a sleeping cot, table, and chair and a metal trunk lit by a kerosene lantern dangling from a hook. Geckos clung to the ceiling. The room was stifling. It reeked of stale smoke, sweat, and dirty laundry. Clothes lay strewn over the cot, empty bottles and cigarette butts on the floor. On the table, documents, maps, and a tin plate with a crust of bread and a lump of cheese crawling with ants. She picked a soiled shirt off the floor and draped it over the chair. A tingling sensation pricked at the back of her neck. Tuyet glanced out the door. Guards sat at the end of the hallway. She scanned the room for a weapon but found nothing. Heavy footsteps echoed in the hallway.

Frenchmen looked into the room as they staggered by. A tall man stopped and stared at Tuyet, an unlit cigarette dangling from his mouth. He leaned on the door frame, filling it with his bulk, his head barely clearing the entrance. Lieutenant stripes on his unbuttoned shirt. The pistol belt still hanging from his hip. He rummaged through his pockets, found a lighter, put it to the cigarette. He held in the smoke, smiled, then let it curl out through his teeth and nostrils until it almost masked his face. He toyed with the lighter, flicking the cap open and shut, turning it in his fingers. He had huge hands, those of a worker. He cocked his head to one side and smirked, the cigarette in the corner of his mouth. In his mid-thirties, he had a long striking face, freckled, a blade-like nose, square jaw, a cleft chin, and deep blue eyes. His wavy red hair was long, unkempt, matted at the crown where his kepi had been.

She could smell his day-long sweat, the reek of bitter tobacco. She averted her eyes. Her hands trembled uncontrollably. A Frenchman like him, a lieutenant, she reasoned, did not need to force himself on a woman. Drunken shouts echoed down the corridor. She flinched. His face transformed as he pushed the door shut behind him.

Tuyet backed away. Her heart hammered wildly in her chest. Grinding the cigarette under his boot, he slipped his ammo belt off one shoulder, then the other, tossing it into a corner. He shrugged off his shirt and pulled his stained white undershirt over his head. His muscular torso looked milky against the ruddy-copper hue of his arms and face.

Screams echoed down the hall, shrill shrieks like a hog being butchered. Her stomach clenched in vertigo. For an instant, she wavered, and then she dashed around him for the door.

He caught her, pinning her arms behind her in a bear hug. "Where are you going?"

"No, monsieur. Please!"

"You speak French."

"I beg you, monsieur. Please, don't do this. I'm married with children."

"Hush, my little dove."

He laughed, lifting Tuyet off her feet as if she were a child. He embraced her, his face close to hers. In a flash, she took in his startling blue eyes as he tried to put his lips on her mouth. She twisted away. When he pressed his beard into her face, she bit his chin. A mouthful of hair, oil, ash, and tobacco. He yelped, releasing her. He touched his chin, the fingers coming away with blood. Any good humor fled from his face. She backed away as he made to grab her again. A spark of fear made her lash out. He was twice her size, but she wasn't thinking. Survival instinct took over. His first blow, open-handed, was a crack across her face. It spun her backward. Light exploded over her vision. She was on her side, on the ground, the taste of blood in her mouth. She crawled away on hands and knees, ears ringing.

He hauled her up by her hair. She slapped at his arm. His meaty palm slapped against her face. Stunned, her legs buckled, and she dangled like a doll by her hair. He swiped the tabletop, pushing papers, maps, cups, and plates onto the floor. As he lifted her up and sat her on the table, she bit his forearm. With all her strength, she dug her nails into his face, clawing deep into the flesh. Four long gashes opened on his cheek. Blood ran down his chin. He roared. His arms rose and fell like pistons, pummeling her with mechanical savagery. Fists rained punches on her body. She curled up into a ball, protected her head with her arms. The blows banged like wooden mallets on her head, shoulders, and arms, beating her into numbness. His fists found her head. Her left eye was a crimson orb. Her nose and lips were bleeding. Her vision blurred white. Her heart was breaking in her mouth. Ocean waves crashed in her ears.

The hounds were baying in chorus. Darkness hardened on the rice plain. An owl sailed across a blade of moon. A lifetime of light drained from her.

39

Coolie Agent

NIGHT HAD SPREAD A WHITE VEIL OF FOG OVER the rice fields, leaving the air soft and damp. A pair of herons took wing, gliding away like ghosts trailing milky streamers of mist. Roosters called to the morning, yet an hour away. On the winding dirt road, Coi shuffled after her guide, Nhung. She minded her injured feet on the rough ground, the yoke-baskets swaying lightly on her shoulders.

Nhung was a strong twenty-one-year-old woman, one of the many young people her son Ha had recruited for the Resistance. With a plain round face and a perky nose, she was highly intelligent and as dedicated to the Cause as Ha was. The two had become close friends. When Takeshi had arrived home wounded two days earlier, Coi had gone to Nhung for her help.

Crossing the last rice flat, the two arrived at the city gate with their yoke-baskets just before dawn to join a throng of farmers and merchants taking their goods to the market in town. Oxcarts were already queued up at the barbed-wire barrier, the animals grazing by the roadside. A teenage boy was napping astride a rare white water buffalo. Coi and Nhung walked up to the head of the throng where a group of people squatted by the gate. An old man spat out a red wad of betel nut chew. At his feet, a young boy was playing with a spinner made of flattened bottle caps and string. Peasants were hugging themselves and stamping their feet, trading news.

Two Viet soldiers yawned, leaning on the guard shack, waiting for the hot-drinks woman to brew their morning coffee using a charcoal stove carried in her yoke-baskets. The smell of chicory coffee turned a few wistful heads. A teenage girl with a basket of banana cakes on her hip walked over to the soldiers, urging them to buy. The older man made a face, complaining about eating the same thing every day, as the other struggled to roll a cigarette. People were milling about waiting for opening time. No one, including the soldiers, had a watch, and the wind-up table clock in the guardhouse had long since died of rust. The soldiers sipped their coffee, passing the single cigarette leisurely back and forth until, after a few minutes, the older one pretended to check the dead clock and nodded to his partner. They moved the sawhorse barriers aside and waved people through.

Nhung and Coi followed the crowd. The sky behind them glowed coral pink. Thatched bungalows lined the roadside leading to the garrison in the middle of a rice field, visible from the road. Tiger cages next to the guardhouse held several prisoners. Soldiers were gathering in the dining hall, large enough to seat fifty men. Behind it were the kitchen, the workers' quarters, and the latrines up against the north fence at the rear. Legionnaire barracks were located along the west fence, opposite the parking lot and the Viet troops' barracks flanking the east fence. At the center of the compound, the two-story white villa looked out of place among the other crudely built structures.

The crowd moved on to town. Nhung and Coi stopped at a hut within shouting distance of the garrison gate. A pretty woman with high cheekbones and large cat eyes was preparing breakfast porridge over a small woodstove. She was humming a tune to a baby asleep in a basket set on a table by the front door. Nhung introduced Suong as a "friend from the mountains," which meant a Resistance supporter. They helped her set up a long coffee table and stools. She finished cooking her porridge while Coi and Nhung stacked bowls and condiments on the tables.

"Sister Suong, who are those people?" Coi asked.

Across the road, scrawny figures rose from the ground, raising their heads out of the weeds, throwing off straw mats, and crawling out from under heaps of hay. Coughing, they tottered to their feet and gathered their things. There were some two dozen of them, mostly elderly and children, camping in the open. Some wandered off to relieve themselves in the weeds.

"Families of conscripted coolies, like yourself. They're waiting to see the head administrator. They hope he will release their relatives."

"Has he ever released anyone?"

"A few severely injured people. I don't think he has ever released anyone because of a petition. He didn't even take the money I offered for my husband."

"Your husband was conscripted?"

"My husband was one of the fifteen men taken from our village. We formed a support group and came here in rotation to feed and take care of our men. Back then, before some coolies escaped, they allowed people to bring food and medicines for family members. Now they don't allow any contact, but people still gather here to bring food to their relatives via the guards."

Coi grumbled, "This is unbelievably cruel. How can they deny people a little help from their families? Are we slaves?"

"Slaves have value. We're disposable. There's an endless supply of poor peasants."

Nhung quoted the Resistance party line: "The French have ruled this land for three generations. They believe Indochina belongs to them and we are subhuman."

Suong added, "Worse, the Viet troops tell everyone that coolies are Resistance sympathizers and forced labor is their punishment."

"People believe that?"

"Oi, people believe anything that spares them the same fate," Nhung snapped.

Suong nodded. "It's true. Townies call us beggars and troublemakers."

"Is your husband still in there?"

"He died. Crushed under a log. The medic said there wasn't anything he could do. He didn't even have morphine to give him. I was here when the accident happened. They brought him out to me. He died right over there." She gestured toward an open patch of ground where mounds of garbage were festering next to a stunted tamarind tree.

"Heavens!" Coi touched the woman's forearm.

Suong looked away. "At least we had a chance to say good-bye. I stayed with him under that tree half the night until he passed. I was eight months pregnant."

"Please forgive me," Coi said softly. "I did not mean to remind you."

The baby began to cry but stopped when Suong picked him up and carried him in a sling on her back. After her husband died, Suong had decided to stay. She had set up the small food stall so she could help others. It had been a good move as she had made many friends during the months she had camped outside the compound, and as she had sold their farm in an attempt to buy her husband's freedom, she had nowhere else to go.

Four women from the encampment came over. Coi recognized one of them from the market and greeted her. The woman said both her son and daughter-in-law had been conscripted. Suong ladled porridge from the great vat into two buckets. Nhung prepared a kettle of hot tea for them. The four then carried a basin with bowls, cups, and utensils back to share with the others.

"Why don't they eat here?" Coi asked, nodding toward the stools at the long coffee table.

Nhung whispered, "Paying customers don't like seeing other

people eating for free. Suong needs real customers with real money to support herself."

"Oi! I'm blind as a bat," Coi cried.

The sky brightened to a pearly gray and more people on foot appeared on the road. A procession of oxcarts was heading to town, laden with fresh produce. There was no one in the shop when a heavyset woman in her fifties walked in from the direction of town. She had a round face with a mango-shaped birthmark on her cheek just below her eye to the jawline. Her gray-streaked hair was pulled back in a tight chignon. Suong introduced her as Second Sister, the head of the garrison kitchen crew. She ladled out three bowls of porridge and suggested Nhung and Coi sit with the woman.

"Pretend we're just customers sharing a table," Nhung said, eyes darting about.

Coi squatted on the low stool opposite the woman and discreetly placed a photo on the table. "I'm looking for my niece, Le Tuyet."

Second Sister picked up a cube of blood pudding with her chopstick and flicked it toward a stray dog in the road. She glanced at the photo but didn't pick it up. "She took a heavy beating a couple of nights ago."

"What happened? What did she do?"

"She resisted," she said with a sigh.

Nhung put down her spoon and looked away, her lips a thin line. Uncomprehendingly, Coi turned back and forth between the two women.

Second Sister explained, "A lieutenant raped her. She fought back and he beat her badly. The medic said she has some broken ribs. She'll live, but it will be sometime before she can move without pain."

Coi wailed, jamming her fists into her mouth to stifle the cries pushing against her throat. Tears ran down her face.

"I'm sorry to bring you bad news," she said without looking up and continued slurping her porridge. "Some of the legionnaires force themselves on coolies regularly. LaGuerre raped your niece. She clawed his face."

"Her totem is the tiger. She's a fighter," Nhung said.

"Well, she gave him a souvenir to keep for the rest of his life," Second Sister replied with a cold smile. "I put a little soda powder into the salves. The skin will scar unevenly. LaGuerre will have three ugly scars on his left cheek."

"I want to see her. Can I come into the compound with you?" Coi said, sniffling.

"No. It's too risky."

"Please, Second Sister, I beg you to help me get her out!"

"Impossible. They never release the good-looking women until they get bored with them or until they capture new ones."

"Why do they rape?" Nhung asked with disgust. "There are plenty of tea-house women, even in this small town."

"Most of them don't rape, but they don't stop the ones that do either. The Africans say rape was one of the methods the colonizers used to control the natives."

Coi's voice rose in panic. "Please help me bribe someone. My niece is all I have."

Second Sister sighed, shaking her head. "I have helped people with small things, but I have never arranged a release."

"Is there any other way at all to get her out?"

The woman flicked a piece of food from her chin to her mouth, frowning. "Only three kinds of coolies leave that place: the dead, the badly injured, and the diseased."

"I have gold."

Second Sister raised her head with a look of cool self-possession. She stared intently at Coi as though she was about to say something but thought better of it. Across the street, guards were opening the garrison gate. The crowd stirred and gazed down the road as a solo bicyclist came into view. A hubbub spread as people rushed to meet the cyclist. The administrator was a tall, pale man in his early thirties. He looked professional in a white short-sleeved shirt, charcoal-gray slacks, and leather sandals. The elderly people pressed toward him in a pitiful throng, pleading and begging for attention, waving sheaves of documents at him.

Second Sister said, "That's Nguyen Liem, the garrison administrator."

"He's a Catholic from Hue," Nhung added.

"A French shit-eater," Second Sister hissed under her breath. The birthmark on her face darkened like a fresh wafer-thin slice of meat. "You see how he smiles and listens to them as though he cares. He only pretends to be helpful so he can preach Christianity on both sides of the fence." Abruptly, she turned to Coi. "I will help you on one condition: you don't bring this up with anyone else. Do not show your face to that shit-eater over there. Do you understand?"

"Yes, but why?"

"There are informers everywhere. I don't want to get caught because you mentioned gold to the wrong person. Agreed?"

"Agreed."

Nhung said, "Thank you, Second Sister, for your help." She slipped a well-wrapped package into the basket at the woman's feet. "A small token of gratitude for your trouble and some medicine for our people inside."

Second Sister said she would come by at the end of her shift that evening. She picked up her basket, paid for her meal, and strode into the compound, giving a wide berth to the cluster of people crowding around the administrator.

Watching the woman go, Coi wondered if she had made the right decision. She asked Nhung, "Is she on our side?"

"She's on her own side," Nhung replied with a rueful smile. "But she has been useful to us when she profits from it."

Many people like Second Sister sympathized with the Resistance but did not join because they were afraid they might receive orders they could not refuse. Under Ho Chi Minh and Giap, the Viet Minh were so brutal and uncompromising that most ordinary people thought it better to stick with the tyranny they knew.

Coi bade Nhung and Suong goodbye to walk into town. There was one place she always visited for wisdom and solace.

40

Nun

THE ROSE SHRINE OF THE LADY BUDDHA WAS A large brick house. It sat on a quiet road between the town center and the sea, a green oasis amid vacant fields and homes on modest plots, hidden from the street by a dense hedge with tall trees. Four majestic giants—an ancient mango, a banyan, and two flame trees—sheltered the entire place, their branches weaving a dense canopy. Named for its rainbow of roses, the shrine was renowned for its blood orchids, violet wisterias, tangerine cups, emerald ferns, birds of paradise, gardenias, and rare blooms brought by travelers from throughout the region.

Squirrels, cats, and other small animals found sanctuary at the shrine. Songbirds flocked in the foliage from dawn to dusk. The well gave clear water year-round and fed a small clay-lined fishpond filled with potted reeds and water lilies, which Coi had planted herself some years earlier. A family of turtles shared the pond with a chorus of frogs and toads, as well as fish and the occasional visit of wild ducks.

The walk from the garrison took Coi the better part of an hour. With a bow, she entered past two large slabs of pink marble. The garden was quiet, deserted. Foliage filtered sunlight that gave the blooms a pastel glow. Setting her baskets on the swept path of white river stones, she mopped her brow and sighed with relief at seeing the sanctuary again after a long year away. On the altars, the incense sticks, though extinguished, were still warm. The morning visitors had left, and the shrine would now remain empty for most of the day until people stopped by to offer prayers on their way home from work.

She mounted the three steps up to the sanctuary and stood outside the front room, which opened to the garden via three sets of removable wooden panel doors. The floor of the chamber was of blue ceramic tiles. It served as the prayer hall. The main altar, with a life-sized statue of the Lady Buddha, stood at the rear. Smaller statues representing ten deities lined the walls. A door at the far corner led to two bedrooms and a kitchen at the back. Coi made her obeisance to the Lady Buddha from the threshold. She took her baskets around the side of the house to the kitchen and left her donation at the pantry: a bag of rice, jars of pickled radish with soured bitter-greens, and a string of dried fish she had bought at the market. Taking a few minutes to tidy the kitchen and water the vegetable patch, Coi bustled about the shrine as though she had never left Phan Thiet. There was enough food, she noted with satisfaction, in the pantry and the garden, to feed any needy family for a few days.

Some of the fruits on the altar were a day old but still edible, so Coi replaced them with fresh tangerines, rambutans, and mangoes from her baskets. The fruits she moved went into a large wicker tray with ripe mangoes and squash picked in the garden. She placed the tray of food for the poor on a wooden box by the front entrance. Chores completed, she returned to the altar chamber and lit three incense sticks for the Lady Buddha. At length, she struck a small gong with a small wooden mallet and knelt on the straw mat to pray.

Coi looked up at the sound of sandals crossing the gravel. With mincing steps, a tiny nun came up the path. The seventy-five-year-old founder of the shrine, she was dressed in pristine white attire, a palm hat, and rope sandals.

"Mother Nam!"

"I have been expecting you, Daughter Coi," said the nun, using a title of endearment. Her small beatific face and high forehead were more pronounced for her shaven scalp. "I had a feeling you would be here today."

"I have been dreaming my thoughts to you."

"I have done the same."

Mother Nam had been a wealthy widow who had renounced the world after she had lost her entire family in a tragic road accident. After giving away her possessions and selling all her assets save two houses, she had donned the white robes of a Buddhist nun at the ripe old age of sixty. The abbots of the town's two competing sects, the Brown Order and the Saffron Order, had personally invited her to their temples, but she wisely had declined. Instead, she had made equal donations to both, reasoning that it was better to have two allies than one adversary. The remainder of her fortune she had entrusted to a family banker in Saigon to manage. In a flash of foresight, she had made her own home into a shrine and another larger property nearby into a convent. There she now lived in a spartan dormitory with several lay followers and nuns like herself.

"I've missed you, Mother Nam."

"It has been too long," the old woman replied.

They stood and held each other's forearms in the intimate manner of dear friends. Both born in the years of the Monkey, separated by two cycles, twenty-four years in all.

"Come sit with me," Nam said, leading Coi by the hand out to the banyan tree. "Your heart is heavy. Tell me everything."

They sat on Nam's favorite marble bench. As she took the younger woman's hand in hers, words poured from Coi as she unburdened herself in a long torrent, relating all that had happened since the last time they had seen each other. Nam comforted Coi, who wept as she spoke. When she had finished her story, they sat in silent meditation. The afternoon had grown warm. Birds sang loudly overhead. An orange tabby curled up at their feet.

Nam sighed as she opened her eyes. "Daughter, did that woman from the garrison say that only the disabled, the dying, and the dead leave there?"

"Yes, Mother. She also said that the administrator won't take a bribe."

The old nun's eyes narrowed, her face crinkling like parchment. She mumbled, "The altar fruits we leave outside for the poor."

"Yes, Mother. I arranged them just now."

"Are they any less tasty or nutritious for the small bruises and imperfections?"

"Of course not."

"I was a fruit seller in my previous life," Nam said, remembering.

Coi nodded. She was not sure whether Nam was talking about her current life or one of her previous incarnations.

"One of my customers was a rich but miserly woman. She used to intentionally bruise my fruits and then demand a discount for the imperfections that she had made with her fingers and knew to be only superficial."

"That's nasty."

"Yes, but remembering it now gave me an idea."

"What is it, Mother?"

"Do you have any of the Japanese's gold left?"

Coi nodded and showed the gold slabs she still had in her pouch.

"You don't need that much," the nun said. "Go see Master Woo."

"The Chinese apothecary?"

"Yes, that chubby womanizer," she said, gazing at Coi as she squeezed her forearm firmly. "I know you dislike being manipulative, but you must do exactly as I tell you."

"Master Woo is a friend. He has been good to us."

"He won't like this plan, but the gold will soften the sting some," Nam replied with a cynical smile. "Stop fretting about details. Tuyet is in danger. We must do everything in our power to help her even if this means twisting a few arms. Understand?"

"Yes, Mother Nam."

"Now, listen closely," the nun said as she scribbled something on a small notepad she pulled from her pocket. "I have a plan. It's dangerous, but it's the best chance we have."

41

Apothecary

MASTER WOO MEE WAS A ROTUND LITTLE MAN IN his late fifties with pinkish hands and pudgy sausage fingers. A fastidious dresser, in his shop he always wore a dark blue silk shirt with embroidered clasps, black cotton slippers, and a gold-threaded Chinese cap. His beady eyes sat in a round face with a full head of salt-and-pepper hair and a distinctive beard of the same coloration. He had a disarming smile that radiated good humor. As a moderately wealthy widower with a honeyed tongue and known for giving generous gifts, Master Woo discreetly enjoyed the company of many widows and single mothers.

"Sister Coi, where have you been? We have missed you. A year now, isn't it?" Woo opened the rear gate to his shophouse, beckoning Coi into the yard.

"Greetings, Master Woo! It's a blessing to see you strong and healthy. I heard you working in the backyard," Coi said with a bow. She had come by the back alley to avoid meeting anyone she knew.

"Come in. Lee and I were working the large mortar and pestle," said Woo.

Coi bowed to a slim, handsome Chinese-Viet who rose to meet her. "Greetings, Brother Lee. It's good to see you."

"Sister Coi!" Lee gushed, squeezing her forearm. He towered over Coi. "I have to get Loi. He would love to see you." He went in to fetch his partner, who was minding the shop. Lee and Loi were a handsome male couple in their early forties who lived in modest quarters at the rear of the building.

Coi turned to the smiling apothecary. "I need your help, Master."

He raised his eyebrows at the walls separating the court-yards, wary of eavesdropping neighbors, an opium den on one side and a brothel on the other. He guided her down a narrow path between a row of rainwater barrels and a wall of wooden crates into the narrow kitchen. The room was a small warehouse, crammed with trunks, urns, cardboard boxes, and floor-to-ceiling shelves sagging with jars and tins. The once yellow walls were covered in a thick layer of greasy soot. In areas, the plaster had peeled off in leprous white patches. From the high wooden ceiling, ropes of sausages, garlands of garlic, and bouquets of dried herbs hung haphazardly. A large pot was simmering over a woodstove, filling the room with the steamy waft of star anise, berries, and bitter roots.

Woo and Coi sat on hard teak chairs at a round marble table. Lee and Loi traded pleasantries with Coi, Lee busying himself in the kitchen for a fresh pot of tea, Loi plating fruits and candied lotus seeds. After Master Woo thanked them, Loi went back to minding the shop, and Lee returned to his mortar and pestle in the courtyard.

Woo nudged a lacquered saucer of candied lotus seeds toward Coi, smiling indulgently. "These are fresh. Loi remembers that you like them."

"I love them. Thank you," she said, putting one in her mouth slowly to savor its sweetness.

"Now, you didn't come all this way to chat. What is troubling you?" Woo inquired solicitously in the soothing way of a doctor.

"My niece was captured," Coi said. She told him about Tuyet's conscription and the contact she had made inside the garrison.

Woo stroked his beard. "I hope your niece didn't use her real name. That rich Frenchman, Feraud, placed a big bounty on Major Yamazaki's head."

"She's not that foolish."

"I suppose you want me to do something."

"Could you make me a tincture and a potion?" she asked, handing him the piece of paper the nun had given her.

He put on his reading glasses and held the paper to the light from the doorway. Scowling suspiciously, he puckered his thick lips with a look of distaste. "What do you need blue nettles for?"

"Do you really want to know?"

"A single drop of this tincture will cause a nasty rash over your entire body!"

"Would the rash look like . . . that French thing . . . *clapier*?"

"Gonorrhea? Yes, I suppose so. Similar but very itchy."

"Perfect."

"Aiya! You're not thinking about . . ."

"Of course. Those demons would rape a dog if it didn't bite."

The apothecary cleared his throat, glancing at her. "If this ever gets back to me . . ."

"It won't, and I promise it will be worth your while." Coi reached into the secret pouch at the small of her back. She placed a gold slab on the table.

He stiffened, alert, like an animal smelling bait. Licking his lips, he paused, then averted his face. "I won't risk my neck for a bit of gold."

Coi seized his hand. "You've always been kind to me, and I'm sorry to burden you with this, but I have no choice. My niece's life is at stake. You have the power to help her."

"Don't you put that on me," he protested, pulling his hand away. He shook his head so vigorously his cheeks jiggled.

"He who has power also has responsibility, Master Woo."

"It would be irresponsible. You have no idea what you're asking me to do. Blue nettle is harmless enough, but the Long Sleep potion is a poison. An overdose could be fatal."

"Imagine yourself in her place. What choice does she have?"

He folded his arms across the dome of his stomach. "If anything went wrong, they might trace it back to me. I'm offended that you would think I might consider this. I think you should leave now."

"Are you sure you won't reconsider? Two slabs of gold?" She added one more.

"Do I look like I'm poor?"

"Mother Nam said you might feel that way."

"I knew it!" He slammed his hand on the table, upsetting the teacups. "That meddling, conniving nun! Always sticking her nose into other people's business."

"Master Woo, you are a fine one to talk about interfering," snapped Coi, placing a second piece of paper on the table.

The apothecary would not touch it, but his eyes glanced at the two names. He let loose an apoplectic groan. "This is blackmail!"

"I suppose so."

His voice quivered with both anger and hurt. "I thought we were friends. How could you do this to me?"

"How could you have gotten married women pregnant? All the while running about town, boasting about comforting widows. Just wait until those cuckolded husbands catch on to you."

He wrung his chubby hands in anguish. "That witch put you up to this. What does she want?"

"She wants you to help me."

Woo puffed out his chest, a trenchant look on his face, trying to hold on to a little dignity. "What if I don't?"

"She will put a curse on your precious jade stem to put an end to your bed-hopping. And then she will help those poor husbands discover your adulteries. The rest—well, we can leave it to karma."

He moaned, "How did she know?"

"She's a witch, you said so yourself."

"She knew all along," he gasped, slumping in his seat.

"And she never interfered."

"Until now."

"There is a time for everything."

Grim-faced, the apothecary swept the gold off the tabletop. In one smooth move, he disappeared them into the sleeve of his gown. Straightening up in his chair, he said in a dignified tone, "Sister Coi, against my better judgment, I am at your service."

··· 42 ···

Potion

THE STORAGE ROOM WAS HOT AND STUFFY THAT afternoon. Tuyet was lying on a straw mat on the cool concrete floor, looking out the barred window at a square of blue sky. Stench from the sewage trench wafted in. She listened to sounds from the kitchen, the clattering of dishes and the chatter of women voices. Noise from the dining area had died down as the lunch crowd drifted off for their noon break. She heard faint shuffling footsteps approaching her cell.

Second Sister unlatched the door and entered. She set the lunch tray down by Tuyet's side. "Try to eat something."

Tuyet looked at the food.

"You will need your strength if you are going to survive," Second Sister said, helping Tuyet sit up against a crate.

Tuyet hissed. Sharp pain stabbed her ribs, her whole body protesting. Her long hair was matted; bits of grass clung to it. Thumping pain racked her head, her left shoulder was tender and swollen, her insides ached, and her split lower lip stung, making eating or speaking difficult. One eye was swollen shut, the other a cracked marble of blood. The bruises on her cheeks were solid purple, those on her neck mottled. The thick bandage around her ribs made breathing difficult. Hand trembling, she took hold of the spoon.

"I have a message from your aunt," Second Sister said, showing Tuyet a red jade bracelet.

Tuyet recognized the flowering swirl in the stone. She had bought it for Coi as a gift when they first moved into the Yellow

House. Another time, another life. A wave of both relief and shame washed over her.

"Have they taken you again?"

Tuyet gulped several times to find her voice. "Ali was here last night. He didn't let them. The medic said I have internal bleeding."

"Ali is a good man," Second Sister said, glancing about. "But he's only one man. Those dogs will come again. He won't be able to stop them."

Tuyet knew that already. She stared forlornly at her hands.

"Listen, your aunt has a plan. It's not a good one, but it's all we have. You will have to take a poison that will make you very sick. She wants me to make sure you understand the danger. It could kill you."

Tuyet turned her mangled face to the other woman. "There are worse things than death."

"True," said Second Sister, not averting her gaze, her face inscrutable, the mango-shaped birthmark on her face like leather. From her pocket, she took a small matchbox containing two tiny glass vials.

Tuyet closed her eyes for a long moment. "I'm not the only one they raped."

"We're all going to the same place, but every woman's journey is different. You can't save them unless you save yourself first," Second Sister said, slipping the matchbox into Tuyet's pocket. Then she whispered the instructions.

A LONG TIME after Second Sister had left, Tuyet lay on the mat and composed herself. She prayed to the Lady Buddha for guidance to the far shore if she died. She did not want to become a hungry ghost, condemned to wander in the gray mist between worlds. Yet even that was less frightening than the thought of being violated again. Once she had made up her mind, her fear subsided. She opened the yellow vial and rubbed the tincture on her groin, the inside of her thighs, her abdomen, breasts, and neck as instructed. A warm sensation spread over her skin. A few minutes later, it began to itch. Soon the rash spread all over her chest and abdomen. Her skin turned bright red, burning. Little red water blisters formed everywhere.

When the supper bell clanged, she opened the red vial and swallowed its contents. The potion was thick and bitter. Her stomach tried to heave it back up. She clamped a hand over her mouth and gulped it back down, fighting her gag reflex. She drank some water. Her mouth became numbed, her lips felt swollen. She crushed both glass vials with a brick, tore the matchbox into tiny bits, and scattered the pieces among the debris at the far end of the room. Her belly began to cramp. She curled up on the straw mat and closed her eyes. The lines on her palms, she concluded, did not matter. No matter what happened, she swore a silent oath to herself, in the name of the Lady Buddha, she would fight the French until her last heartbeat. She groaned. Her insides clenched and began twisting into a knot.

"*MERDE!*" CRIED the legionnaire, holding a lantern.

"What's wrong with her?" asked another.

Voices penetrated her drugged sleep. Tuyet's mind struggled awake. She shivered. Night stood at the door. Light flickered across the drunken faces of the four men crowding the dark cell. One of them was bending down, hands on his knees, leering at her. She knew that face: the blue-eyed monster. He reached down with both hands and ripped her shirt apart, exposing her breasts.

"The filthy whore!" cried one of the men, pointing at the rash on her chest and neck.

The second lieutenant shoved another man toward the door. "Get Bernard!"

They pulled off her pants. The three of them stood over her with the lantern, revolted by the angry red rash on her body. Tuyet moaned, barely aware of her surroundings. Their words were meaningless garbling in her ears. The darkness was dragging her down again.

"That looks bad," one man said.

"The bitch put up a real fight, didn't she?" asked the second lieutenant.

LaGuerre fingered the lumpy lines on his face, his lips curling into a feral snarl. "If I get that, I'll kill her."

Bernard, the medic, shuffled into the room, carrying a grimy leather satchel. A scrawny corporal in his early twenties with an unruly head of curly blond hair, he was dressed only in his shorts and undershirt. They pried her legs wide and pinned down her arms. He knelt between her thighs. He took a probe from his bag. The swaying lantern shed a ghostly light on the group.

Tuyet felt his fingers and something cold, metallic. She moaned, stomach cramping. Her mouth all bitterness. The poison was throbbing like hot lava in her veins. Her flesh seemed to be crawling with spiders. Her vision spun. She shut her eyes and gritted her teeth. Darkness welled up. She slipped back into the grip of the poison. The sounds of ocean waves filled her head. She drifted into the night. From that moment on, she heard, felt, and remembered nothing.

The second lieutenant pried open her eye and said, "I think she's out."

The medic said, "She's running a fever."

"What is it?"

"The clap. Maybe with malaria or dengue," Bernard answered with a shrug. "What do I know?"

The others grunted, aware of the corporal's limited medical training. All the legionnaires were treated at the town's hospital.

LaGuerre asked the medic, "You think she might have given it to me?"

"You have any symptoms? Itches? Rashes?"

"No, not yet."

Bernard stuck out his chin and shrugged. "Patience. Give it a few days."

"Your mother!" LaGuerre made a crude gesture and stormed off with the others.

Ali stepped out from the dark kitchen. Bernard motioned for the Moroccan to help him. Silently, the two men dressed her. They set up a folding cot, lifted Tuyet on it, and covered her with a blanket.

"I'll check on her in the morning," said the medic. He picked up his satchel to leave.

"Thank you, Corporal," Ali said.

"I didn't enlist for this shit," Bernard replied, sadly shaking his head.

SECOND SISTER arrived for work at dawn. Entering by the gate, she saw the whole kitchen crew in an agitated state gathered at the wash basins.

"Second Sister! Second Sister!" they beckoned her.

"What's wrong?"

"She's dead!" They went to the storage room.

"She won't wake up," one girl cried. "I went to see her this morning."

"Did you check her pulse?"

They all shook their heads, frightened. The oldest woman said, "She has some kind of disease. Just look at the boils on her skin."

Tuyet was curled in a fetal position on the floor by the cot. Her skin was pale, the bruises on her skin dark as ink. Second Sister put her hand under Tuyet's nose. She felt no breath. Touching the carotid artery of her neck, she felt nothing. Pressing harder, she detected a faint heartbeat and almost sighed aloud with relief. Composing herself, she rose and shook her head.

A cry of grief swept around the group. Curious soldiers came to see what was going on. Someone mentioned disease and the rumor went quickly around the camp. Ali pushed through the crowd and stopped at the threshold, blocking the doorway.

"Is she dead?" he asked.

"The Lady Buddha has her now," Second Sister muttered and covered her nose with a handkerchief, making way for the big Moroccan. "I hope whatever killed her is not contagious."

Ali wrinkled his nose at the stench of urine. The ground under the body was damp. He bent over and placed a finger under her nose, careful not to touch the skin. He shook his head, his face dark with anger.

Second Sister draped a blanket over the body. She said, "Someone, please, find a tarp. We don't know if it is contagious."

"LaGuerre will piss himself," said Ali.

"Let's hope he doesn't take his anger out on the other women."

Ali told a teenager nearby to fetch the commander. Turning back to Second Sister, he said, "Last night, LaGuerre and his men came again. They left her alone because she was too sick. Do you think he got whatever that is?"

"God willing!" she hissed under her breath.

"The medic thought it might be the clap or syphilis."

"People don't die from that overnight."

"True." He nodded, nervously wiping his hands on his apron. "I've seen disease wipe out an entire village."

"Let's send the body to the hospital. The sooner the doctors figure it out, the better for everyone."

A restless crowd gathered. Ali barked at a soldier to find a tarp.

The teenager returned saying that the commander had gone into town the previous night with LaGuerre and was not expected back until evening. Second Sister said the body was stiffening and the day was going to be a scorcher. Flies would be all over the body in no time. Ali looked out at the empty parking lot. All three vehicles were out on patrol, not due back until sunset.

She brightened. "Have someone with a cart take it to the hospital. The sooner we get that body out of here, the sooner we can burn the bedding and clean out that cell."

"Good thinking." He nodded.

"Look over there. An oxcart just came through the gate," she said, pointing to the road where a young man was peddling homemade charcoal.

Ali bellowed orders. Two men fetched the cart. The kitchen women lit incense at the door and prayed that Tuyet's spirit would remember their suffering. A soldier brought a tarp and helped Second Sister wrap the body. Finally, they lifted the bundle onto the charcoal mound in the cart bed, ordering the carter to deliver it to the hospital.

TANG SWATTED the ox with his bamboo crop, urging it on, but the old beast ignored him. Beneath his palm hat, the youth was sweating profusely. He reminded himself that he must not turn around even though, at any second, he might hear an order to halt or a gunshot. Neither came, so after a few minutes, he rounded the bend, and the garrison disappeared from view. He heaved a loud sigh of relief.

The road into town was sparsely traveled at this hour as the market traffic had already passed. At a stand of willows by the river, he urged the ox onto a faint wagon trail.

"Oi!" His grandfather stepped out from the thicket, followed by Coi. They waved for him to bring the cart around to where Old Binh had halted his cart, out of sight from the road.

They lowered the bundle to the ground and unrolled the tarp. Coi nearly fainted when she saw her niece's swollen face. Binh placed two fingers along the side of her neck and said he'd found a pulse. Sobbing, Coi found the glass vial in her pocket, but her hands shook so violently that she gave it to Tang. Binh held Tuyet's head and told his grandson to pour the vial's contents into her mouth.

"What's this?" Tang asked.

"The antidote," said the grandfather. "I hope we're not too late."

They lifted Tuyet onto Binh's cart, curled up as she was on her side, draped a canvas over her, and covered it with offal from the fish sauce factory, which farmers used as fertilizer. A cloud of black flies buzzed around the cart.

The boy complained about the stench. "Why didn't you carry something else, like turnips or cabbage? We'll never get rid of this smell."

"Nobody wants to search an offal cart."

They rolled two sacks of charcoal in the tarp to make it resemble a body and hoisted it back onto Tang's cart. Binh told his grandson, "Take it straight to the temple. The crematorium supervisor is waiting for you. Help him burn it and then leave the cart there. The owner will come for it himself. I'll take Aunt Coi and Miss Tuyet to their village. See you at home tonight."

"Good luck going out the town gate, Grandpa."

Coi wiped her eyes and pulled the rim of her palm hat lower over her face. She sat up front on the carter's bench with Binh. The ox ambled along without being urged, back toward the garrison and the town gate. An old provincial bus chugged past, full of passengers and crates of livestock, trailing a cloud of exhaust. Binh clicked his tongue to soothe the ox. As they rounded the last bend, the garrison came into view. Smoke was rising from behind the kitchen where the cleaning crew was burning the bedding. As they pulled closer, Coi saw soldiers breakfasting in the dining hall. Across the road, Suong was serving rice porridge in her shop. Their eyes met. Suong looked away, a faint smile on her lips.

At the town gate, the bus was idling by the side of the road. Passengers were squatting in the dust with their belongings as guards checked their documents, shaking out some tea money. As Binh halted the cart at the checkpoint, a soldier scowled at them, wrinkling his nose at the stench. He waved them through. Coi kept her head low, giving thanks to the Lady Buddha.

◆

FOR TWO nights and a day, Tuyet floated in the void as the antidote threaded its way slowly through her body. It drew her back in gradually toward the realm of the living. On the return journey, she passed through the middle realm of dreams.

Here, the dream-walker met her third child. He was a four-year-old. They were standing on an island in an ocean of glass, under a luminous yet sunless sky filled with persimmon clouds stretching to an infinite horizon. Light suffused his strangely familiar face. A plant sprouted from a boulder of green jade and grew into a tree with white blooms. Birdsong filled the air, rhythmic like a beating heart. The beige curls framing his face were brushed through with blond highlights. He had her brown eyes, not blue like his father's.

Sorrow, streaked with joy, welled up in her like early spring, like a warm rush of blood, full of bittersweet love.

He put his tiny, soft hand in hers, and she let him, and with this smallness, he took hold of her life.

PART VI

Death

1948–1949

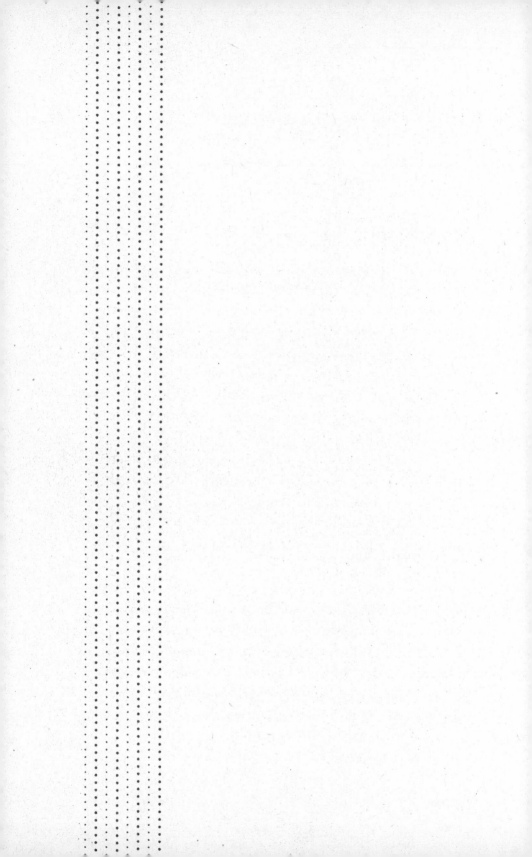

43

Wish

THE MORNING SKY PROMISED RAIN, AS DID THE wind, but Coi would not stay home. It was her birthday, and she wanted to make a wish at the Rose Shrine of the Lady Buddha. It was her fifty-second. Still sharp of mind and strong of body. The decades of labor were beginning to catch up with her, but instead of slowing down, she found herself working harder than ever.

Without breaking stride, she shifted the bamboo yoke behind her neck from one shoulder to the other. The baskets were heavy today, each laden with a dozen glass bottles of mango and rice wines, Takeshi's homemade specials. *The gods do have a sense of humor,* she chuckled to herself. Certainly, her late husband, the boozy gambler, would be turning in his grave to see her peddling alcohol.

When they had first moved into the area, Takeshi had complained that all the local rice wines were terrible, the government-sanctioned ones worse. Coi had quipped that being a connoisseur he should brew some himself, miffed for she had bought and carried the bottles twenty-five kilometers home for him. Takeshi had scratched his big nose and laughed out loud, praising her for the idea. He had remarked that they had a surplus of fruits from the orchard and plenty of rice from trading with the farmers. It wasn't difficult. After all, he had brewed sake with his father in Hokkaido. It had not taken him long to build a fermentation hut in the woods behind the farm. In no time, he had more sake than he could drink. He offered bottles of it to any Resistance fighters passing through the village. Some accepted, but others declined because the Viet Minh generally frowned on alcohol as a vice. The wine stockpile kept growing. Coi had no choice but to sell the surplus to village shops in the area. Although Takeshi's premium product would fetch higher prices in town, Coi didn't dare risk running afoul of the tax authority.

Instead of taking the main road and crossing the bridge, she detoured via a narrow track through the forest, a longer route that bypassed the checkpoints. Lately, no one used the main roads unless it was absolutely necessary. Being intercepted by the Viet troops would ruin her day. No doubt they would help themselves to her wine.

Approaching the riverbank, she smelled smoke before she come upon a shirtless, barefoot old man squatting by a campfire. He was in his sixties, bald and wiry in a muscular way. His scraggly whiskers were white, as were the wisps of hair around his ears. His ribs and spine seemed about to poke through his dark leathery skin.

"Good morning, Uncle Nuoc," Coi said, lowering her baskets.

"Aiya!" he cried, tipping backward. He stared up at her with rheumy eyes, his mouth a maw of missing teeth. "Sneaking . . . sneaking up on me like that! Don't . . . don't you have any manners?"

"So sorry! But I made a racket coming through the bushes. Are you losing your hearing already?"

With an indignant harrumph, he lumbered to his feet, towering over her, a two-meter giant, uncommonly tall for a Viet. His height had made him an easy target for the French, who loathed having to look up to a mere peasant. Shy and with a stutter, he had become a recluse as a young man. During one dry season, he had stumbled into his job as a river-man when he carried women and children across. Realizing that people would pay for his service, he built a hut by the river and had lived here ever since. He noticed the rags covering her baskets. "That . . . that is what I think it is?"

"Think it right out of your head. You still owe me for the last bottle."

"Can't . . . can't you give it to me . . . on credit?"

"Not when you can afford to buy a new boat!"

"This leaky old dinghy? My . . . my cousin died and left it to me."

"Well, it's better than your scary bamboo raft."

"Yes! And . . . and it's at your service if . . . if you could spare a bottle."

"I can't have everyone running up big tabs."

"Have a heart. Just . . . just a little fire in the gut. Old . . . old man freezing here, all skin and bones."

"Then, eat more and drink less."

"Don't be unkind. If I want a sermon, I'll . . . I'll go to church," he whined and made a face. "Look, it's fixing . . . fixing to rain. Spare a little wine. Save . . . save an old man from a cruel death. Bank some good karma."

"Oh! You're such a good actor. You should join the street theater the next time they come through."

"Come on, they're all Viet Minh in . . . in disguise. They'll use an old man like me for . . . for cannon fodder."

"Oy, oy, hush up already. Only one on credit," she said, feeling charitable on her birthday. She chose a bottle of mango wine.

"May the Lady Buddha bless . . . bless you a thousand times," he crooned, reaching greedily for it with both hands.

"Don't take me for a fool." She laughed, hiding it behind her back. "I give it to you now, you won't be sober enough to take me back across later. Take me over and I'll pour you a cup. You'll get the rest of the bottle when I come back, not before."

He howled at the injustice, but Coi turned a deaf ear. She climbed into the little boat with her baskets and sat there with her arms folded across her chest until he resigned himself to pulling them across the river on the guide rope.

◆

"I THOUGHT you might come today," the old nun said with a smile. "Let's have tea before we pray."

"Tuyet didn't want me to go because it looked like it was going to rain."

"It will. You're welcome to stay here for the night."

Coi thought about it, then shook her head. "Thank you, Mother Nam, but they need me at home."

In the muddy light, starlings swooped over the trees. They were sitting under the eaves at the main entrance to the prayer room. The shrine was quiet with only a couple of worshipers. A pair of old nuns was puttering about in the garden. Mother Nam lifted the lid of the porcelain pot to check the lotus tea. Satisfied with its color, she poured them little steaming cups, inquiring about Tuyet.

Coi raised the teacup in both hands and bowed to the nun. She took a sip, heaved a long sigh, and unburdened her heart. It had been a very difficult seven months since Tuyet's conscription. After her niece had returned home injured and pregnant, Coi had been running the entire household, including the shop they had decided to operate and the orchard, by herself. Tuyet had been bedridden the first month, broken in body and spirit. She had barely eaten and had spoken little. She had told Takeshi that she had been beaten and raped at the garrison, but she had refused to talk about it. Coi would find her some afternoons, sitting quietly alone, staring out the window, tears rolling down her cheeks. Several times, Tuyet had screamed out in her nightmares, waking up the whole family. They had lain in the dark listening to her inconsolable sobbing as Takeshi tried to comfort her.

Day after day, for weeks on end, the two of them had moved along like invalids. Takeshi's wounds had healed, but something dark had come over him. Coi could tell he no longer was quite the same man. With Tuyet, he always was very tender and solicitous. He refused to rejoin the Viet Minh even after Ha and Xuan begged him repeatedly. He said his duty, for now, was to care for his wife even though there was little he could do. Sometimes, Tuyet allowed him to wait on her and feed her; other times, she did not want to be touched. For hours, she would lie in silence, facing the wall. She took cold baths, using coarse soap, scrubbing herself raw as though she could never be clean. Once in a while, Coi heard them talking playfully and laughing like in old times, as if none of this had ever happened, and she told herself that there was hope. The shroud of sadness would lift for a few hours but then fall back again over the entire household.

The nun refilled their teacups and asked, "How are the children?"

"Anh understands a little about what happened to her mother. She is doing her best to help me. She's only a child, but she can make dinner for everyone. She's good with the animals and takes care of our chickens. She is smart enough to watch the shop for me."

"What about the little one?"

"Hoang has a big heart and a strong sense of empathy. He suffers when he sees his mother suffer. He doesn't go out to play. He stays around the house all day, never losing sight of his mother."

"Has Tuyet been meditating?"

Coi nodded. "Yes, since her second trimester. She meditates in the morning and before going to bed. She does it whenever her mood spirals."

"Has she talked to you about adoption?"

"No, I'm afraid to ask her. It might push her toward a dark place. I don't think she's able to discuss it yet."

"She's a dream-walker. The time will come."

"You've seen it?"

Mother Nam nodded but would not say more.

AT THE town market, Coi bought taffy for the children, tapioca pudding for Tuyet, tobacco for Takeshi, some salves for her feet, and spices for the kitchen. She also bought ingredients for her heirloom spring rolls—the family's happy-time food reserved for festivals and special occasions. She figured they all needed something delicious to remind them of better days.

Her errands done, Coi sat down on a footstool at the rear of the market for a quick bowl of beef noodle soup. Two customers were slurping noisily. Coi greeted the thirty-year-old owner, a northerner like herself, who served Hanoi-style *pho*, a rare thing in the south.

"How is the beef broth today?" Coi asked, using a code phrase to ask whether the meeting was safe.

"It's tasty and clear. Have a look," she replied in a thick Hanoi accent, concentrating on the bowl of noodles she was preparing.

"Good. I'll have a bowl, please."

"Right. Do you want some mung bean dumplings too?"

"As many as you can spare. I'll resell them on the way home," Coi said, meaning that she could carry a full load.

After Tuyet's escape, the family had joined the Resistance's underground supply network to support the fight against the French. From the beginning, the Resistance mountain base had been in dire need of antibiotics, morphine, and other medical supplies due to the colonial government's restrictions on the sale of medicines, especially penicillin, intended to cripple the Resistance. Many volunteers sought treatment at the hospital for fake ailments. They then took the medicines to a collector, who would reimburse them. The collector would package the medicines and turn them over to couriers, who would then smuggle them out of the French-controlled zone. That was the most dangerous part of the operation.

With a full belly and the special dumplings in her baskets, Coi hastened on her way as the sky began to rumble. People rushed onto the road, hurrying to shelter. Weaving through the crowd, Coi strode on as fast as she could. An apprehensive murmur rolled down the street just before the first few fat raindrops landed in the dirt. Lightning flashed a white whip by the corner of her eye. The boom startled Coi. She dashed for the cover of the closest townhouse just as the clouds opened. The rain came down hard, a pounding din, unleashing a curtain of water.

Huddling in the doorway of the big townhouse, Coi quickly wrapped herself in a tarp she used for a raincoat, then checked her precious loads. Setting down her baskets against the wall, she pulled down the brim of her palm hat and curled herself into a ball to keep warm. It was just as well to have a break, she thought, because she couldn't walk fast on a full stomach anyway.

"Auntie! Please, come inside. You'll catch cold out here," said a young woman who had opened the front door and was beckoning to her.

"Oh, the rain will pass soon. No need to bother about a stranger in your doorway."

"Please, Auntie. My husband will be very upset with me if he sees you out here like this."

"I don't want to be a bother."

The young woman insisted until Coi stepped inside. They sat on hardwood chairs in the front room. A housekeeper brought hot pandan tea with butter biscuits. Coi fidgeted self-consciously. She wasn't used to being served in such a fine house. The sitting room was spacious with a high ceiling of wooden beams. Silk paintings decorated the plastered walls.

There were heavy bookcases, marble sculptures, and giant porcelain vases, all the trappings of an upper-class home. A tabby cat meowed and curled up around Coi's ankle.

Nguyen Thanh-Ly was twenty-six years old, a northerner from the port city Hai Phong. Her husband, a southerner from Phan Rang, was a doctor at the town's hospital. They had been in Saigon during the Hai Phong Massacre just a year and a half earlier. She had lost her entire family when an artillery shell hit her ancestral home, killing her father, mother, and younger brother. Thanh-Ly and her husband had been married six years but, to their deep sorrow, had not been blessed with a child.

As they talked, Coi felt a deep calm settling at the back of her mind. A simple soul attuned to her instincts, she felt the rain had guided her into this house.

Reaching out, Coi touched the woman on the forearm and said, "Little niece, I'm so happy to meet you. I believe it was more than chance that guided me here."

"So am I, Auntie. I have been rather lonely here. I don't know any northerners at all in this place."

"Have you been to the Rose Shrine of the Lady Buddha?"

"No, we moved here from Saigon only a month ago."

"It's where women go for fertility blessings."

"Thank you, Auntie! I'll go first chance."

"There is someone there I think you should meet," Coi said with a bright smile, her eyes crinkling with joy, suddenly oblivious to the storm outside.

COI TOLD no one about Thanh-Ly. The following week, she made an excuse and went into town to see Mother Nam. The couple had been to the shrine to request fertility blessings. Mother Nam read their fortunes and advised them to adopt "a blighted one" to prove their good hearts and worthiness. The Lady Buddha would bless them with not one but three children of their own. She urged them to take time to consider well their reply as the baby would be of mixed race, conceived in violence. Three days later, they had returned and confirmed their decision to adopt. After hearing the news, Coi wept with joy, for the Lady Buddha had heard her birthday wish.

ONE DAY in the final month of her pregnancy, Tuyet told her aunt that in her dream, she had seen a happy young couple playing with her baby boy.

44

Gambit

A SQUAD OF RESISTANCE FIGHTERS LAY FLAT IN
the dry grass. The sun seared their backs. The heat was at its
worst in the early afternoon. The open field offered no protection. Panting, they shut their eyes against the blinding light,
trusting their spotter to tell them what was coming down the
road. It should not take long. The radioman said the supply
truck had left the railway station, en route to the garrison.

Takeshi stifled a yawn. By his side, Xuan was sprawled on
his back like a corpse, a scarf draped across his face against the
sun, hands folded on his chest. The grass was so dense the only
other person Takeshi could see was one of his ten teammates
directly in front of him. All the men wore beige shirts resembling the uniforms of the Viet troops. The black cotton shirt
he wore under the fake uniform was damp and itchy. He was
glad to be wearing the regulation Viet troops' leather sandals
instead of cumbersome army boots.

Takeshi pinched the bridge of his nose, forcing himself to
remain alert in the listless heat. Flies landed on his neck, sipping beads of sweat. The air was steamy, heavy with the scents
of frazzled grass and scorched earth. He nodded off and jerked
awake. The heat lay on him like a punishing burden, the sky
a limitless bowl of light. For days, rain clouds had been rising from the horizon only to traverse the sky without shedding a single drop. Blackbirds cawed from the trees lining the
meadow. A cricket chirped near where he lay. He felt the baked
earth under him, the grit in his hands, the presence of men
around him, the faint scent of decay on the breeze.

"Who chose this location?" Yamazaki asked Xuan.

"Major Tran, he's in charge," Xuan mumbled groggily.

"It's barely two kilometers from the garrison."

"That's why they'll feel safe," Xuan muttered, waking up.

"What do you mean?"

"They're almost home; they won't expect anything."

"How will the breakdown happen?"

"The driver fixed the distributor so he can stall the engine any time."

"Brilliant. What's your battle order?"

"I will stay with the sniper team. Once the garrison is under attack, they will radio their patrol units to return to base. We'll plant landmines on the road and pick off the survivors so you boys won't be attacked from the rear."

"You always have my back, Brother. I want to thank you for including me in this operation. I owe you for this."

"Just do me a favor: have your revenge but get out alive."

"I will."

Rolling onto his back, Takeshi thought about the man who had raped Tuyet. She had refused to talk about the monster, but he had discovered the Frenchman's identity through the Resistance network. He had a name, and he would get his revenge or die trying. Two weeks earlier, at the Resistance camp in the mountains, he had received news that Tuyet had delivered a healthy baby boy at the town's hospital. She had told him that she would be staying with the adoptive family for a few weeks until the baby settled with the wet nurse. It had never occurred to her to have an abortion; perhaps, he thought, she had wanted him to urge her to keep the baby. He had never suggested it, and he had never told her of the storm that raged in his heart or of his vow of revenge.

The spotter whistled. They heard them before they saw a jeep and a tarpaulin-covered truck coming over the slight rise. Three French soldiers sat in the jeep. One French and three Viet soldiers rode in the old six-wheeler. With a bleat of its horn, the truck slowed and rattled to a stop thirty meters from the lone tree. The engine sputtered and died. The jeep reversed to the truck. The three French soldiers, sharing a bottle, cursed loudly at the delay. A swarthy, middle-aged Viet driver and a young French private jumped out of the truck's cab. The driver stepped onto the fender and raised the hood to check the engine. A cloud of steam hissed upward. Two Viet soldiers came around from the truck bed to watch, standing around helplessly as non-mechanics do.

"Ah! She overheated again. Give me a minute. It won't take long," the driver said in French.

Towering over the driver, the French private frowned. He was twenty-one years old, handsome with wispy blond hair and boyish pink cheeks. He sighed, "We're practically there. Lousy luck."

"Sorry, monsieur," said Driver, wiping his brow with his sleeve.

"Didn't you check the engine?" Handsome asked.

"I did. She's a fickle old bitch." Driver shrugged. "The mechanic said we're short of parts, so he doesn't want to replace anything until it actually breaks."

"Just fix it! The captain is going to put us on night watch for being late again," he complained. Handsome slouched off to drink whiskey with the other French soldiers.

"Right away, monsieur!"

"It's a scorcher today," said a Viet soldier sporting a trendy pencil mustache and slicked-back hair. Standing on tiptoes, he peered into the engine well. "Is it the hose or the radiator?"

"Shut your trap!" Driver pointed a spanner at Mustache. He hated Catholics. "Damn grunt! You're biting my ass too?"

"I was only trying to be helpful," Mustache said, throwing his hands up.

Driver turned to the second soldier, a chap with a pock-marked face. "Get this fool away from me!"

Pockmark draped an arm around Mustache's shoulder, steering him to the rear of the truck. He cooed, "Relax, don't mind that geezer. He's a cranky son of a bitch. Best to leave him alone. Get involved, get blamed."

THREE VENDORS came around the bend ahead, from the direction of the garrison, their arrival perfectly timed by a spotter on the radio. The French soldiers in the jeep whistled, recognizing the pretty women who every day sold snacks, whiskey, and tobacco at the garrison gate. The soldiers stepped out of the jeep and, along with Handsome, sidled over to the women, steering them toward the shade of the lone tree, thirty meters away from the truck. They bantered in pidgin French as they made themselves comfortable on the ground. The men teased and groped the women, who coyly fended off their advances. Handsome grinned and winked at the bustier of the girls, nodding toward the bushes. She whispered to her giggling friends, who translated that she was game if he didn't mind that she was menstruating. He blanched. His comrades hooted encouragement. Taking that for an affirmative, she grabbed his arm to drag him into the field. Prying his arm free, he got to his feet, dug out a fistful of piasters from his pocket, and thrust the money at her, announcing that he much preferred some fruit. His comrades howled with laughter.

AT THE back of the truck, Pockmark offered Mustache a tobacco pouch. The younger man set it on a ledge and pinched off some tobacco to roll a smoke. Pockmark drew his knife and came at him from behind. Cupping one hand over Mustache's mouth, he pulled the man's head back and slit his throat. Mustache's eyes widened. Blood gushed from his carotid artery. He shuddered in Pockmark's embrace, his hands clutching at his throat, trying to stem the bleeding.

Takeshi, crawling through the grass, followed the squad leader. One by one, they darted to the truck as two men carried Mustache's body into the grass. Takeshi climbed onto the truck bed first and worked his way deep into the crammed cargo space. The rest of the men followed him, wedging themselves awkwardly among the wooden crates, and Pockmark and Squad Leader brought up the rear.

No sooner had the last man climbed in than Handsome returned to the truck with an armful of fruit. "Anybody want some?"

"Those custard bananas look good," Driver called out.

Handsome handed him a bunch.

Driver winked and asked, "None of my business, but are you going to flatten the hay with that girl? I can drag out this repair job as long as you want."

"She's on the rag, but she doesn't mind doing the dirty."

"A tigress! One in a million. Take her the first chance you get." Driver grinned. "Never let the thorns keep you from the roses."

"You pervert!" Handsome chortled and made a face. He turned away to the rear of the truck with his fruit.

"Oy! Oy, back there!" Driver called to the back. "You monkeys want some bananas?"

At the rear of the truck, the men froze. Squad Leader pointed at Pockmark's blood-stained shirt and drew his stiletto. Waving Handsome back, Pockmark thrust his head out the side of the truck, keeping his shirt out of sight.

"None for this monkey," Pockmark replied, turning his head as though speaking to his companion. "You want some bananas?"

Squad Leader grunted that he did not.

Driver shrugged and turned to Handsome. "Monsieur, if you're not going to tame the tigress, would you mind if I start the engine?"

Handsome climbed into the cab. The engine roared, spewing a cloud of black smoke. A round of cheers rose from the three other French soldiers as they lumbered to their feet and returned to their jeep. Both vehicles continued down the road. Driver was the only one to notice that the truck was riding lower with its extra load.

45

Vengeance

SENTRIES SALUTED AS THE SUPPLY DETAIL ROLLED through the garrison gate. Both vehicles proceeded to the left of the yard and parked beside a row of wooden planters in front of the dining hall. The supply crew joined a dozen legionnaires waiting for the mailbag from Saigon. They were in a cheerful mood, passing around bottles. Four barefoot male coolies made their way toward the parking lot to unload the truck.

Driver went around to the back of the covered cargo space and dropped the tailgate. It was sweltering under the tarpaulin. The ambush team was sweating in their colonial uniforms. Silently, they extricated themselves from the tight spaces among the crates and climbed down. Pockmark and Squad Leader jumped out first. One loped toward the rear watchtower at the southwest corner of the compound. The other ran in the opposite direction, to the watchtower at the northeast corner. Driver sauntered toward the gate with a pack of cigarettes, one hand checking the pistol wedged at his waist. Next a two-man sapper team walked toward the dining area, each man holding two live grenades behind his back. The rest of the group were clambering over wooden crates to get out of the truck. Last to exit, Takeshi waited for a young cadre to untangle himself. His rifle's shoulder strap had caught on a nail. When he tugged at it, a crate slipped off the stack, pinning him down. Everyone else was gone. Takeshi slashed at the strap with his knife.

Coolies crossing the yard stopped in their tracks, perplexed at the sight of armed troops coming off the truck. One of the fighters held a finger to his lips and dispersed them with a wave of his hand. Nearing the hall, the sappers tossed their grenades into the crowd of legionnaires and ducked behind the heavy wooden planters. The metal canisters clattered across the cement floor.

Someone shouted, "Grenades! Grenades!"

A moment of confused yelling was followed by a chaotic scramble. Legionnaires bolted, barreling into one another. Benches were overturned. Several men tripped, tumbling onto the floor. Two red-faced drunks fell backward in their chairs. One man picked up a grenade. It exploded in his hand, shredding his body into a red mist. Three more blasts came almost simultaneously, the concussion as powerful as a direct mortar hit. The smell of cordite filled the dining hall.

Several dead and wounded littered the floor. The sappers drew their sidearms and opened fire on the survivors. The rest of the team divided into three groups to secure the gate and the main yard. Meanwhile, in the cargo bed, Takeshi freed the young cadre. An alarm siren howled.

In the front watchtower, a soldier swung the FM 24/29 machine gun to aim at the invaders by the dining hall. Bullets rained down around the vehicles, mowing away the sappers. The machine gunner aimed at the truck. Below him, Squad Leader was climbing up the ladder. At that same moment, Driver shot and killed both sentries at the gate. Across the road from the garrison, Viet Minh fighters in black clothes emerged from behind the shophouses.

THE YOUNG CADRE moved to the tailgate, Takeshi right behind him. The machine gun coughed violently from across the compound, a staccato percussion: *Pfft! Pfft! Pfft!* Bullets zinged past his head. Takeshi ducked. *Pfft! Pfft! Pfft!* Holes appeared in the canvas covering. Floorboards and wooden crates splintered. A wet, smacking sound. The young man in front of him rocked backward. The next bullet split his head open like a melon. Blood spattered onto Takeshi's face. A mouthful of mushy brain matter, a coppery taste. The man toppled on him, taking them both backward. Takeshi lost his rifle and landed on the floorboards, the lifeless body in his arms. Above, on the canvas ceiling a constellation of blood.

Takeshi scooted back, wiping the warm, sticky fluid from his eyes. More rounds struck the corpse, making it twitch. Exiting by the tailgate now impossible, he drew his knife, slashed an opening in the tarpaulin, and slipped out over the sideboard, landing between the truck and the jeep. He looked toward the northeast watchtower where Squad Leader had shot the gunner and seized the machine gun. A cheer rose as Resistance fighters charged through the gate. Splitting into two groups, they swept into the barracks on both sides of the compound. Fierce fighting broke out as the garrison forces swung to the defense.

A half-dozen legionnaires scrambled behind the water cisterns on the far side of the dining hall and returned fire with their pistols. Several severely injured men lay scattered in the hall. A big Algerian sat with his back against a post, pressing a flap of red skin over his exposed intestines. A young man with curly brown hair shrieked for his missing leg. Clumps of pink flesh were strewn everywhere, the concrete stained crimson. As the thatch roof caught fire, smoke began threading skyward.

Behind Takeshi, by the jeep, one of his teammates was taking off his beige colonial uniform, revealing a Resistance black shirt underneath. Takeshi was about to do the same, but heavy gunfire from across the yard raked the ground around him. He crawled for cover between the truck and the jeep. A volley from legionnaires on the other far side of the hall rattled across the vehicles. Takeshi lobbed his only grenade through the hall at the legionnaires. Exploding, it shattered three cisterns. Water splashed over the dusty ground. The legionnaires retreated to the kitchen. Pursuing them, Takeshi drew his pistol.

Someone shouted his name from the direction of the barracks, thirty meters to his left. He recognized Den, the blacksmith, waving at him from behind a stack of lumber. The old
man was their insider for this operation—the one who had discovered the name of Tuyet's rapist. Den mouthed "LaGuerre"
and pointed at the whitewashed administration building that
served as the officers' quarters. The two-story mansion had
rows of windows on both floors. Legionnaires were fortify-
ing the entrances. Shooters inside the building were picking
off Viet Minh fighters with deadly accuracy. He considered his
chances of getting through the front door alive to be poor. Den
shouted again and gestured for him to go around the back.
Takeshi nodded and dashed for the kitchen, bullets whining
around him.

FIERCE FIGHTING engulfed the compound. Viet Minh
fighters killed several colonial troops before they were able to
barricade themselves inside their barracks. Most of the surviv-
ing legionnaires withdrew to the main building.

"Kill! Kill! For the Motherland!" yelled a squad of Resistance fighters as they charged through the gate. Several were
instantly mowed down by machine-gun fire from the southwest watchtower. Pockmark lay at the foot of the ladder,
fatally wounded.

"Follow me! We must take out that gun," a cadre screamed,
leading two men at a sprint by the inner perimeter.

On the front tower near the gate, Squad Leader repositioned
the light machine gun, aiming it diagonally across the compound at the rear watchtower, one hundred fifty meters away.
He struggled with the unfamiliar weapon before he could get
off a volley. The gunner in the other watchtower frantically
swung his weapon about and returned fire. For several seconds, two streams of bullets crisscrossed back and forth like

hot whips, zeroing in on each other. At the far side of the compound, the cadre reached the rear tower alone, having lost both
his men in the charge. He threw a poorly aimed grenade at the
tower. It exploded midair, distracting the gunner for a fatal
second. Squad Leader sprayed bullets into the rear watchtower,
shredding the soldier as well as the parapet. Viet Minh fighters
had cornered a group of defenders in a warehouse and another
in the administration building.

"HELP! HELP ME!" someone cried in French at Takeshi.

He spotted two legionnaires on the ground, one dead with
a neck wound. The other man raised his blond head, again
pleading. Half of his face was raw flesh, the skin scraped off,
one eye missing, teeth and jawbone exposed. The right side of
his body from head to foot had been mangled by shrapnel.

It took Takeshi a second to realize that he had forgotten to
remove his colonial uniform. He holstered his revolver pistol
and ran over to the scrawny Frenchman. Takeshi helped him
up, saying, "Put your weight on me."

"I can't feel my leg!" the legionnaire groaned.

The Frenchman collapsed as they took the first step. Takeshi
heaved the man onto his shoulder like a sack of grain and ran
to the main building's back entrance. Bullets kicked up clumps
of dirt around his feet. He didn't look to see who was shooting. As he neared the entrance, he stiffened at the sight of rifle-
men in the windows. They fired a volley past him at Resistance
fighters on the perimeter. Through the cloud of cordite smoke,
he charged into the building.

"Medic! Medic!" Takeshi went room to room, the wounded
man on his shoulder. He was looking for a red-haired man with
facial scars. Bullets zinged through the window, gouging lumps
of plaster from the walls. Window glass shattered, showering
the floor with splintering fragments.

A man shouted, "Where's Bernard?"

A soldier with blood on his face pointed to the other end of the house. "Over by the kitchen."

A dozen legionnaires were spread out on the first floor. Some were shifting furniture to barricade the doors. Others were exchanging gunfire with the invaders outside. No one challenged Takeshi. Face smeared with blood, he moved through the hallway unnoticed, looking for LaGuerre. In the small dining room off the kitchen, a medic was helping injured men on the floor. Takeshi lowered the wounded soldier off his shoulder. The medic said something about bandages, but his words were lost in the noise.

Takeshi shouted, "Where's Lieutenant LaGuerre?"

"Second floor. Are you hurt?"

Takeshi shook his head and left, ignoring the medic's plea to find more bandages. Instead, he grabbed an MAS-36 rifle discarded in the hallway and ran upstairs with it, keeping his head down. In an office next to the landing, a legionnaire was shooting from the window.

He turned and yelled at Takeshi, "*Merde*, I'm out! You have ammo?"

"Yes, Sergeant!" Takeshi pointed the rifle at the man's chest and squeezed the trigger. The man fell back against the wall then slid down to the floor, leaving a vertical trail of blood.

Takeshi dropped the empty rifle and drew his revolver. Six rounds. He sneaked down the hallway, peeking into the officers' quarters. In a darkened room, a defender with a scoped rifle was picking off attackers through the shutters. He executed the man with a shot to the head.

He followed the jabber of submachine guns to a corner bedroom at the end of the hall. Two men were firing MAS-38s, their backs to him. One was bald, the other a redhead. Takeshi shot the bald one in the back of the skull. As the redhead turned, Takeshi fired twice, striking the right arm and left shoulder. The man stumbled back against the wall. The MAS-38 slipped from his grasp.

"Lieutenant LaGuerre," Takeshi growled as he stepped into the room.

"What . . . ?" LaGuerre groaned, wide-eyed with shock.

Takeshi shot him in the knee. LaGuerre crumpled to the floor. Takeshi drew his knife and came at the man. He turned LaGuerre over onto his back and pinned him with one knee on his chest. LaGuerre struggled, helpless. Takeshi straddled the Frenchman across his abdomen.

"So, you are the Blue-Eyed Demon."

"Who?" cried LaGuerre. "Who are you?"

"Another demon," Takeshi replied in a low rumble. He leaned down, stony-eyed, face to face at last with the man who had blighted his thoughts for nine months. He grabbed a fistful of curly red hair and sliced LaGuerre's cheek four times with his knife, reopening the scars Tuyet had made. He waited until comprehension dawned in the Frenchman's eyes, terror dilating the pupils.

"Yes, you remember my wife." He sighed and pressed the tip of the knife on the man's chest, both hands on the handle. Then, slowly, he pushed the blade into LaGuerre's ribs, burying it to the hilt.

LaGuerre's cry was drowned in the din of battle. His body jerked in spasms. His breaths came out in bloody, foam-streaked puffs. His face turned crimson, the arteries of his neck taut, eyes bulging from their sockets.

"That's you drowning in your own blood," Takeshi said and wiggled the knife loose.

He pressed the blade in again, almost tenderly, puncturing the other lung. He peered into LaGuerre's vibrating eyes. The whites were riddled with red scrawls. His last breaths rattled, mixed with blood gurgling in his throat. Takeshi pulled the blade free and plunged it into LaGuerre's heart. A final shudder went through him. His blue eyes turned dull.

With his knife, Takeshi began cutting the corpse's trachea, vertebral ligaments, and neck muscles. The blade was sharp but unsuitable for the task. He had to hack and rip at the flesh. Blood made the handle slippery. He met resistance severing the spinal cord. Finally, he drew his revolver and fired the last bullet into the neck, shattering the vertebrae at the base of the skull. The head rolled free. A bright red pool spread around the headless corpse.

A sense of sublime satisfaction came over Takeshi. Then bone-deep fatigue. He looked around. Outside, the fighting had intensified as the Resistance fighters attempted to breach the building. An explosion downstairs rattled the floorboards and windows. He wanted a cigarette, but his hands were soaked in blood. He took off the colonial uniform shirt and wiped his hands on it. Lighting a cigarette, he reloaded the revolver and picked up LaGuerre's head by the hair.

As he crossed the threshold, something sailed through the window and thumped onto the floor. The grenade blast slammed him into the hallway wall. Everything went black.

"KI! KI! Can you hear me?" Xuan called, squatting at his side.

Takeshi opened his eyes, vision blurred. He lay flat on his stomach, face pressed to the floor. Grainy plaster dust filled his mouth. A high-pitched sound rang in his ears. He could barely hear his friend's words. His head hurt, his thoughts were fuzzy. Pain racked his entire body.

"We took the garrison," Xuan said, his face bleeding from a scalp wound. He placed LaGuerre's head on the floor facing Takeshi. "I see you've got what you came for."

Takeshi grunted, one corner of his mouth twisted in a sneer.

"What do you want me to do with it?"

Takeshi wheezed, "Hang it . . . on the gate."

Xuan nodded. "A proper warning."

Takeshi struggled to rise but couldn't move.

"Stay down. You have shrapnel wounds all over your back. I sent for a stretcher."

He closed his eyes, shivering as nausea rolled over him. As darkness reclaimed him, he thought of his wife and son.

46

Raid

THE SHRILL TOWN SIRENS SENT PEOPLE PANICKING into the hot afternoon. Scattering through the neighborhoods, they raised the alarm about a Viet Minh attack. The commotion reached the Nguyen home, waking a two-week-old infant who promptly started bawling. Thanh-Ly, the adoptive mother, and Tuyet, the birth mother, entered the nursery. Tuyet picked up her baby and cooed to him. Since the delivery, she had been recuperating at the home of the adoptive family. The wet nurse had arrived the previous day and, after meeting her, Tuyet was now relieved to know that her baby would be in good hands.

An urgent knock rattled the front door. Tuyet passed the baby to the wet nurse and followed Thanh-Ly to the entrance.

"Mister Bun, what are you doing here?" Thanh-Ly asked the balding middle-aged man.

"Madame Nguyen," he wheezed, out of breath. "There was an attack at the garrison. Your husband sent me to tell you not to leave the house. Many wounded are arriving at the hospital. There are not enough doctors. He said he won't be able to come home tonight."

"Give me a minute to get a few things for him," she said, gesturing for Bun to come inside. She told the housekeeper to ready food for her husband and went upstairs to pack an overnight bag.

Tuyet brought Bun a cup of pandan water. The sirens quieted. They heard the hum of a reconnaissance plane passing overhead. The orderly said that some of the wounded had told of a horrific battle with many casualties. He had overheard some gendarmes saying that the army suspected villagers in the Twilight Territory had helped the Viet Minh. The army was mounting a reprisal. A chill ran down Tuyet's spine.

"I must go home right away," she told Thanh-Ly when she returned.

The orderly said, "Ma'am, there's a curfew. No one can go anywhere."

"If they start raiding the villages, I need to warn my family," Tuyet cried.

"Let me ask my husband. He might have an idea." Thanh-Ly scribbled a note and handed it to the orderly.

IN THE NURSERY, Tuyet gathered her things, pained that she could not stay a full month to nurse her adorable infant. He was asleep, his skin creamy white, his face pink, with wisps of very light brown hair, neither Viet nor French. She remembered Captain Moreau's children, *les petits café au lait*. Her son would have no name until the one-month blessing at the temple. She whispered to him, "You are a very lucky boy. You have a good family, a good life. Your parents are kind people with good hearts. Love and obey them. I love you, and I will always be near. Think of me, and I will come."

THE NEXT DAY, Tuyet left town in a supply truck, the ride arranged by Dr. Nguyen. The driver, an amiable young man in his twenties, drove barefoot. One of his front teeth was missing. He had the unsightly habit of using the gap as a cigarette holder. Tuyet sat in the front passenger seat. Two porters rode on the flatbed, guarding the cargo. Soldiers were patrolling the town. The streets were quiet. At the market, guards had surrounded a group of peasants squatting in the sun. Soldiers moved through the rows of shops harassing vendors and round-

ing up known Viet Minh sympathizers. The driver stopped at
the bridge checkpoint, grinned at the soldiers, and flashed his
road permit. They bantered back and forth, then waved him
through.

As they neared the edge of town, the driver said, "Yesterday,
I drove a truckload of dead and wounded men from the garrison. That was my first battle cleanup. I don't ever want to see
that again."

"You were inside the compound?"

Nodding, he fussed with his lighter, took a long drag on his
cigarette, and blew the smoke out the window. "I wish I hadn't,
but they ordered me to help load the truck. It was ugly. Blood,
flesh, bones, and intestines everywhere, like a meat market.
Fire and smoke. Hellish! People crying, moaning all around.
I'm never going to get that out of my head. It was horrible.
Somebody put a Frenchman's head on a pike and set it on top
of the gate."

Tuyet averted her face, one hand pressed over her mouth.
Bile rose in her throat. She felt light-headed. The driver did
not notice her unease and kept up the chatter until they neared
the garrison.

"Look, over there by the gate. They removed the head
already," he said. "It was like that of a demon with flaming red
hair. The face was all sliced up. Gruesome. People said he was
a real bastard."

From the road, she saw little besides heaps of charred timber and trash. The dining hall was gone, along with some of
the barracks. Parts of the mansion had been destroyed, part
of the roof missing. The garrison was overrun with laborers
clearing debris, sawing fresh lumber. The army had taken over
the petitioners' campsite, using it as a parking lot for military
vehicles and equipment. Hundreds of coolies, Viet soldiers,
and legionnaires were busy erecting new barracks and rein-
forcing the perimeter fence with concertina wire. Shops and

cafés across the road were bustling. Tuyet did not recognize the garrison that had been the site of her terror. The past nine months rushed back in cascading waves, from the day she had been conscripted to the day she had been raped, to her escape, to the limbo months, to the birth—all the pain, and the hours of infinite darkness.

THE TRUCK DRIVER dropped Tuyet off at the outskirts of her village, a few kilometers from her house. Wary of patrols on the main road, she chose a trail that led through the woods. A handful of peasants were laboring in the green rice fields, bent over, faces to the earth, backs to the sun, taking no notice of a lone traveler passing along the hedgerow and into the trees. The morning heat had not penetrated the forest canopy.

Tuyet made good time on the well-trodden dirt path until she came to one of her favorite shrines. It was a crude wooden altar under a banyan tree near a stream. She made an offering, sounded the brass chime, and prayed. Afterward, she washed her face in the clear spring water. Sitting down, she washed her legs, then rested her feet on the velvety green moss. Sunlight glittered in the water. A fragrant breeze cooled her wet face. Peering down at her reflection in the still pool, she grimaced at the stranger. Who was this tired woman with hollow cheeks, worn out at thirty-four? Her best memories seemed distant, as if they had happened in another lifetime: her brilliant years as a cheery socialite in Saigon with fine dresses, fancy parties, and well-heeled friends. Not so long ago. Now she was a middle-aged mother of three, drained and bare. All her superfluous and decorative parts had been cut away, leaving only sorrow, anger, regrets, and a deep ache. Her heart was heavy, her mind distracted by conflicting thoughts. She mourned all that had been lost.

The wind wrestled noisily in the trees. Yellow-jacket bamboos creaked and groaned against one another. Falling leaves flashed like bright coins in a shaft of sunlight. She inhaled the scent of trees and earth, felt the low hum of the forest. The knot in her chest unraveled, tension ebbing from her limbs. She took solace in the Buddhist's universal truths. *Nothing is lost in the universe. Every action, good or bad, has consequences.*

His karma had found him. So be it. Her baby would never know his father, never from her lips. Dust to dust, ashes to ashes. No legacy of anger or bitterness. The son shall be free of the sins and the shame of the father.

THE NEXT DAY, fog smothered the village at dawn. Tuyet and Auntie were preparing breakfast in the kitchen when, in the distance, dogs started barking. Within moments, all the village dogs sounded the alarm. Hackles raised, Mimi and Momo bolted out front, barking ferociously at some unseen threats way down the road.

"The soldiers are coming! Anh, get the dogs. Hoang, come out front with me," Tuyet called to the children, who had been washing their faces at the rear patio.

"I'm going to check the house again," said Coi.

"I'm sure we found everything yesterday."

"Better safe than sorry."

The previous evening, she had asked her aunt to help scour the house for Takeshi's personal effects. They had gathered his things and the family's valuables—jewelry, jade, diamonds, and the gold that Takeshi had entrusted to Tuyet—and had put everything into a large ceramic jar and sealed the lid with wax. Using a wheelbarrow, they had hauled it to the fire pit, where they had raked the ashes aside, dug a hole, and buried the jar. After burning Takeshi's clothes, they had swept away any traces of their work.

Anh tied their two barking dogs to a tree by the side of the house. Tuyet doused the cooking fire. She smeared soot on her cheeks and donned an old gray work jacket. The thought of being conscripted again terrified her. Coi came back out and all four of them waited together in front of the house. As a way station on the Resistance supply route, they had to appear calm and cooperative.

A single gunshot startled them. Three more shots rang out over the next several minutes. They had no idea whether the soldiers were shooting people. The urge to flee was overwhelming. Coi wanted to hide in the woods, but Tuyet said they could never outrun the soldiers. There was nothing they could do but pray.

Since the main road ran straight through the middle of the small village, it was easy for the patrol to split into several squads. They swept both sides of the street at the same time. Several minutes passed before Tuyet saw a group of seven men come marching over the slight rise, six Viets and one legionnaire with a dog on a leash. Their dogs snarled at the large hound. The squad leader told two soldiers to search Tuyet's shop and sent the others to a farm across the road.

"Let's see your papers," a chubby sergeant with a pencil mustache said curtly. He motioned for his men to search the house.

Tuyet bowed respectfully, but he did not acknowledge it. She handed over their documents. Their dogs barked. Coi told Anh to keep them quiet.

"Are you Viet Minh sympathizers?" the man asked.

"Of course not, sir," Coi said.

"Do you know of anyone involved in the garrison attack? We give rewards for good information."

"No, sir. We're just poor shopkeepers. We don't know anything," Tuyet replied. "We heard shots in the village. Did you catch some Viet Minh?"

"Be quiet! I'm the one asking the questions," he snapped, handing back their papers.

Shouts came from across the road. The hound barked excitedly. A soldier yelled for his prey to come out of hiding. Coi looked at Tuyet; their neighbors were in trouble.

A soldier loped across the road to report that the hound had found an underground hideout behind the farmhouse.

"Excellent! The captain will be happy if we bag a cache of Viet Minh weapons."

"No, no!" Tuyet cried. "They're just farmers. They have three small children."

"Farmers don't have underground shelters," the man scoffed.

Tuyet had no reply. She had not known her neighbors had a secret hiding place.

"Let me talk to them. They're just frightened. Please, sir," Coi begged, kneeling before him. "Show mercy, make merit."

He frowned, irritated. "You'd better be quick about it."

A pistol report cracked across the road. Coi ran toward the sound. Anh sprinted after her. Tuyet grabbed Hoang's hand and followed them. Approaching the tiny knoll behind the farmhouse where the men had gathered, they heard the legionnaire shouting in French. A translator hurled threats into a dark crevice in the exposed roots of a large tree stump. The soldiers had cleared away the bushes. The opening was hardly big enough for a person to wriggle through.

The legionnaire, a tall, stiff man, stood facing the crevice, his back to them. Tuyet heard him counting down. Three. Two. One. The men backed away from him. Suddenly, she saw a grenade in his hand. He pulled the pin and tossed the grenade into the hole. Coi screamed. A soldier saw her and scooped both her and Anh into his arms, forcing them down to the ground with him.

The crevice exploded outward in a cloud of smoke and debris. Tuyet sank to her knees. Her son hid behind her. Coi wailed. Anh froze in shock. The bitter smell of cordite drifted over them. The legionnaire tossed a flashlight to the scrawniest man in the squad and pointed him into the cavern. The soldier sighed, wrapping a piece of cloth around his nose and mouth. He crawled in. A minute later, he backed out, covered in blood and mud, ashen-faced, shaking his head. There had been no weapons in the cavern. He had counted five dead, one man, one woman, and three children.

Coi got to her feet and stumbled toward the opening, but the man stopped her.

THE SOLDIERS REGROUPED, and the entire patrol marched off to the next cluster of houses, a line of prisoners in tow. Some people followed cautiously at a distance, venturing to the edge of the village to investigate the explosion. Coi called into the dark crevice. There was no answer. Not a groan, not even a sound. Anh hadn't moved, her eyes fixated on the crevice. Hoang whimpered. Tuyet ran to the house for an oil lamp. Coi crawled into the dark hole. Her wails of bereavement rolled out into the daylight. Tuyet returned with the lamp and tried to follow her aunt, but Coi was already backing out, dragging Hoa, the youngest child, Anh's best friend.

"Oh, heavens . . . oh, heavens! Look at her," Coi sobbed, her face streaked with tears and blood. "Her hand is missing. I can't find her hand."

"Stop! Stop, Auntie. There's nothing we can do now."

Coi's face twisted, her eyes darting wildly. She bawled, "Somebody, help me. Her belly is hurt." She tried to stuff the intestines back into the child's abdomen.

Anh shrieked, a heart-wrenching cry of horror, then sprang to her feet and ran into the orchard behind their house.

WORD OF the killing spread swiftly, and the villagers came running. The headman took charge of the scene of the mur-

ders. The senior women prepared the funeral. A neighbor volunteered to go into town to notify the relatives of the victims.
A runner was sent to fetch a monk from the closest temple.
Men went into the forest to cut firewood for the pyre. Women
cooked food for the spirits and cleaned the house for the ceremony. The headman and his deputy crawled into the tunnel
and brought out the remains of the family, one by one: the
thirty-three-year-old father, the twenty-nine-year-old mother,
the eleven-year-old daughter, and the ten-year-old son.

Villagers laid garlands of wildflowers on the bodies, now
wrapped in white sheets and resting on freshly cut palm fronds.
They lit incense and prayed. The headman recounted the life
stories of the victims. Three saffron-robed monks sat themselves on the straw mats next to the dead family. They struck
their brass gongs and chanted through the day and into the
evening to soothe the living, to bless the dead, and to protect
the village from evil spirits.

IN THE CLUSTERS of sugar canes behind the orchard, Anh
was curled up in the soft grass with her cat, Nunu. Chewing
on a section of cane for comfort, she dragged her shirt sleeve
across her face, crusty with dried tears and snot. She had been
crying and talking to herself, her cat, and her friend. "Too bad
you're not here, Hoa," she mumbled, "the canes are very sweet
right now. I'm so sorry we're not going to finish weaving the
jump rope together. And what a shame, too, I saved up a bagful
of rubber bands. What fun it would have been—a rubber band
rope long enough for three people to jump at the same time!
Everyone would have wanted to play with us at school. I'm so
sad now. Well, you take it with you. Find some friends to play
with wherever you're going. And I'm giving you the silk parachute we found in the tree with the burnt-out flare. It's no fun
making silk blouses without you. I hope you won't be lonely.

I'm going to send Bim-Bim with you. She's a good doll, and she will be your friend. I miss you, Hoa. You're my very best friend, forever and ever."

Anh felt a comforting presence, a familiar glow in the air. She knew this presence from her dream. She had felt it since her earliest memory. Anh tilted her head and heard the monks chanting on the breeze. She went to find her gifts and carried them to the pyre where everyone had gathered. She laid the rubber-band jump rope, the silk parachute, and the doll on her friend, the smallest of the five bodies wrapped in white cotton. Anh said her prayer as the flames rose sky high, taking Hoa and her family to the next realm.

47

Typhoid

IN THE WEEKS FOLLOWING THE ATTACK, THERE were skirmishes throughout the twilight around Phan Thiet. During the day, the French ventured out from their positions to patrol and raid. At sunset, they retreated to the safety of their fortified encampments. At night, Viet Minh units emerged from the wilderness. Every other night, they attacked one or more French positions. Even when they had no intention of fighting, they fired mortars into the encampments to harass the French. In return, the French launched parachute flares and fired wildly at anything that moved outside their perimeters.

The French knew that some peasants were helping their enemy so they treated all of them as hostiles. The Viet Minh were hiding among the villagers and getting supplies from them. Most people sympathized with the Resistance and believed in the Cause, but the constant fighting resulted in numerous civilian casualties. Farming, a marginal livelihood at best, became even more precarious as people had to work the land without getting caught in the crossfire. Productivity and crop yields plummeted. Hunger stirred memories of the great famine that had ravaged the country a few years earlier in the Japanese time. One by one, villagers were abandoning their homes for safer havens elsewhere.

Tuyet's neighbors, the Trans, boarded up their house early one morning, the day after a patrol had arrested three men on suspicion of hoarding food for the Resistance. The Trans had sold their livestock and had entrusted their farm to the village chief. Tran, a strong forty-year-old, had fashioned a harness to tow his handcart, loaded with all their worldly possessions. Neighbors gathered, bringing small gifts.

"We're not going far. I have a sister in Mui Ne," Tran told the small gathering. "They're fisher-folks with their own boat. We'll make a living with my in-laws. Coastal land is salty, nearly worthless, almost free for the taking. We will build a simple thatch hut and live there in peace."

A bucktoothed woman chimed in, "Good choice. There is no fighting out that way, too far from the Resistance's base. I'm thinking about leaving, too."

Tran said, "You should. How many of our neighbors have been arrested or conscripted for labor? The French have killed two whole families. They beat up innocent people for nothing."

Another woman nodded. "If it gets worse, we'll go into the mountains. The Resistance has many jungle camps. Real villages with schools for the children, farms, and workshops too. Everything is free. They welcome everyone."

A woman with a large mole on her cheek was wary. "Nothing is ever free, Sister. You'll have to join the guerrilla forces. I support the Cause with food and money, but I don't want my husband to die in battle. My brother already gave his life for the Cause. One sacrifice per family is enough. We'll take our chances in town."

A white-haired woman added in a singsong voice, "My husband and I would live in town, but we're too poor. Who will hire old people? This plot of land is all we have. If we leave, squatters will claim it."

"What are you going to do, Aunt Coi?"

"The village elders say that the monsoon will put a stop to the fighting," Coi replied with a shrug. "I hope so, but I'm not sure. I'll wait for my son. He always knows what to do."

"Don't wait too long," said another. "Bandits get bolder every day."

"That's life in a war zone. If neither side gets you, the wild dogs will."

A WEEK LATER, the first monsoon storm rolled in, wreaking havoc on the village. Tuyet and her family huddled in the large bedroom as a wild gale knocked a tree over, dumping it into the far end of the house. Half the roof caved in. The shop was flooded. Dried seafood, peanuts, seeds, salt, soap, bolts of cloth, and incense sticks were ruined. The chicken coop collapsed, killing many hens and chicks.

No family in the village remained unscathed. More people abandoned their homes. Everyone was busy repairing what they could, so Tuyet and Coi had to do the work themselves. It took two days of back-breaking labor to remove the fallen tree and string up tarpaulins for a makeshift roof.

First Hoang and then Anh fell ill with fever and stomachache within a day of each other. Coi believed they had caught a bad wind, but Tuyet thought their wretched living conditions were to blame: a collapsed roof, muddy floor, damp clothes, and drafty sleeping area. Worse, they were living with the dogs, cats, chickens, and even a few mice, all in the same space. There was no choice but to eat soiled food salvaged from the deluge. Despite the rain, there was little clean water to drink. The fallen tree had shattered all the rainwater cisterns. They had to use water from the well, which had been fouled with mud. It had to be filtered through cotton cloth and then boiled one pot at a time. After the children fell ill, both Coi and Tuyet followed suit with stomachaches, diarrhea, and low-grade fever.

A local medicine woman treated them with herbal remedies. Coi, Anh, and Tuyet recovered, but Hoang worsened. He was feverish and was unable to keep anything down. On the fifth morning, Tuyet and Coi left Anh with a neighbor and started out for the hospital with Hoang. They carried the five-year-old in a large basket between them on the bamboo yoke. The road was deserted, not even an oxcart going to market. They had no choice but to walk the entire twenty-five kilometers.

Staying off the main road, they took the foot trail, reaching the swollen river around noon. Seeing neither the boat nor the river-man at the usual crossing, they went upstream toward his house. They found him picking through the pile of charred rubble that had been his hut. A French-led patrol had sunk his boat, set fire to his hut, and threatened to arrest him if he continued to ferry people across the river. Now everyone was required to cross by the guarded bridge.

Coi pleaded, "Please, Uncle Nuoc. You must help us. There is fighting near the bridge. We don't dare use the road. Please, help us get across."

"Dangerous now. Look . . . look at the current." He gestured at the basket they were carrying between them. "What's that?"

"My son. We must get him to the hospital!"

He looked at the unconscious child and clucked his tongue. "There is one way . . . I have a second guideline, but . . . but it's very risky."

"You have a rope across the river?"

"A backup, of course. It's too difficult to lay a new line if . . . if . . . if something happens to your main," he said. "Damn those big-nose demons! To hell with them. This is my river. Follow me."

He led them a short way upstream to where the river was about fifty meters wide. The sky was dark with leaden clouds. "Miss Tuyet, since you are heavier . . . heavier than your aunt, I will take you across first. Then . . . then I will take her and the boy together. You will . . . you will need to hold a safety rope . . . for me from the other side."

He lashed Tuyet to his back and attached himself to a wooden roller that slid along the guideline spanning the river.

The cold current tugged at them. Tuyet clung to his back as Nuoc waded in, sinking deeper with each step. With sinewy strength, he pulled himself along the guideline, treading carefully across the rocky bottom. The water quickly rose chest-high. The current pushed them about, and Nuoc struggled to stay on his feet. Tugging the rope firmly in his vise-like grip, he hauled them across one step at a time, Tuyet's arms and legs wrapped around his torso.

At the halfway point, the water began splashing over Nuoc's head, but he held his breath and kept going, arms above his head, continuing to pull hand over hand on the guide rope. Tuyet's thighs rode up into his armpits. She was pushing off on his shoulders to keep her head above water. When it seemed almost impossible for him to stay under any longer, Nuoc stepped onto a submerged stone and raised his head out of the water, gasping for air. A moment later, he submerged again, advancing a few more meters before coming up for air. It took several minutes for them to reach the far bank. They crawled onto the gravel bar, utterly exhausted. After Nuoc had caught his breath, he walked to his shelter to fetch a long rope. Tying one end of it around his waist, he passed the other end to Tuyet, showing her how to pull and use a tree trunk for leverage.

With the rope around him, he recrossed the river again. On the far bank, he collapsed onto the ground. He shivered with fatigue, looking like one newly drowned. Coi gave him a drink of rice wine from a bottle she had brought for just that purpose. When the color had returned to his face, Nuoc fashioned a loose rope harness for Coi and told her to follow him into the river. He lumbered to his feet and lashed the boy to his back. Once they reached waist depth, he crouched down, telling Coi to climb on his back and wedge the boy firmly between them. Clamping him between her legs, Coi struggled to keep Hoang's head above water. Nuoc inched along on the guideline as the current buffeted them.

304 Andrew X. Pham

A leafy green island of branches glided toward them. Coi yelled, "Tree! Tree!"

"Mercy, Old One!" Nuoc cried to the river spirit. "You can have me, but not . . . not the little one. Not today!"

He redoubled his effort, putting his whole body into his grip on the rope, willing them closer to the far shore. The current resisted. He gritted his teeth, growling with massive force. Sinewy cords strained on his neck as he fought the current with his might. He gained a meter toward shore for every ten that the tree gained on them. Coi clamped her eyes shut and, with all her strength of mind, sent a single plea: *Mother Buddha, save us!*

At the last moment, the tree turned midstream as though it had hit a boulder on the river bottom. Nuoc hauled them clear just as the tree rode into the guideline. The thick rope creaked loudly and snapped. The current wrapped itself around their unwieldy bodies like a mighty serpent, yanking Nuoc off his feet. They tumbled blindly into the roiling river. A sharp jerk on the backup rope nearly snapped Nuoc's back. Miraculously, the current swung them on the rope like a pendulum toward the shallows where they rolled onto submerged rocks. Somehow Nuoc regained his footing.

THEY STAGGERED into Nuoc's shelter, a thatched lean-to in a crevice in the cliff, a narrow space, three by five meters, full of ropes, tools, tins of rusty nails, earthen jars of rice and beans, and salvaged odds-and-ends. A string of dried fish hung from the peak of the roof. Nuoc had built this hideaway after the patrol torched his boat and house across the river. Squatting, he lit a small fire. Coi and Tuyet undressed Hoang and rubbed herbal ointment on his chest to bring back some warmth. They wrapped him in a dry blanket. His red-rimmed eyes flickered open. He moaned at his mother and sank back into a fevered sleep.

"I'll make us some tea," said Nuoc, holding his hands to the flames. Blood dripped from his fingers from where the rope had cut across the palm.

"We'll drink some tea, but you should have this," Tuyet said as she unwrapped a cloth bundle she had carried across the river. It was a bottle of Takeshi's sake.

Nuoc sighed with pleasure. He cradled the bottle in his hands and mumbled, "You have no idea . . . no idea how much I need this. Thank you!"

"We owe you our lives, Uncle. I will never forget it."

Coi gave him the other bottle as well. "Uncle Nuoc, come with us to town. I know of a doctor's family who might be able to give you work. Get yourself a roof over your head and three meals a day. You're not young anymore."

"Ha! The good thing about . . . about old age is . . . it doesn't last long."

"But surely, you can do with a little more comfort."

"I'm living . . . living like an animal . . . but at my age, I don't care about comfort." He smiled sadly. "Been here most of my life. No . . . no . . . no point going anywhere. I'll help people cross the river . . . as long . . . as long as I can. When it's my time, the Old One . . . the Old One will carry me to the sea. I've promised . . . promised Him my bones. I've made peace with that."

"So be it, so be blessed," Coi intoned and bowed.

"Chase the chill with some hot tea. The sky is fixing . . . fixing to rain and you . . . you still have a long way to go." Nuoc lowered his voice to a whisper, eyes casting about warily. "Evil spirits are abroad. That tree was meant to kill us."

The sky rumbled. They fell silent in the gloom. A gust of wind reached through the thatch sidings, causing the flames in the fire pit to dance and swirling smoke into their eyes. The rain began with a roar.

"I sensed the Lady Buddha. She saved us," Coi said over the thrumming downpour.

THEY STAYED at Nuoc's shelter for several hours until the rain stopped. Hoang was unresponsive the whole way as they carried him between them in the basket strung on the bamboo pole. By the time they reached the end of the trail near the town gate, it was pitch dark. They found a flat area and set Hoang down.

"Auntie, he's burning up."

"We have to go by the road through the town gate," Coi said.

"We're too late. They close the gate at sunset. Those are the rules, and they won't break them for us."

Tuyet bit her lips. Shaking with exhaustion, she slumped to the ground. The damp soaked her pants. She massaged her legs, which were on the verge of cramping.

"There's a trail. I've taken it during the daytime. I don't think I can find it at night though," Coi said, cradling Hoang in her lap.

They drank some water as they decided what to do. Worried about Hoang, who clearly was getting worse, Tuyet wanted to try the town gate and offer the guards some money to let them pass. They would see that her boy was very ill. Coi suggested that she go alone first because the soldiers might have orders to shoot anyone approaching the gate at night. Tuyet was about to reject that idea when an owl hooted nearby. Two more hoots. Then something moved in the bushes a few meters from them.

"So sorry to be listening in on your conversation, aunties," someone said, a man's voice. Figures in black clothes came out from hiding. "My name is Ut," said the slim man in his late twenties. "These are my comrades. We're the local guards."

Tuyet made the introduction and told Ut of their situation. He motioned one of his group forward. A woman checked Hoang and agreed that his best chance would be at the hospital.

Ut said, "Don't worry. I will have two of my men carry the basket for you. Sister Chung will show you the way."

A dull sound rang in the distance. A tiny yellow sun lit up the starless sky. The flare parachuted slowly down to earth, illuminating the ground. Shadows shifted, elongating. Briefly, by the guttering light, they glimpsed each other's faces. Tuyet was surprised to see that, except for Ut, the others were in their late teens or early twenties.

"Quick, follow Sister Chung," Ut ordered as he turned to his men. "Brothers Cau and Len, you two carry the boy. Rejoin us later."

They moved through the woods at a pace Tuyet had not thought possible. Sister Chung was in the lead, Coi next, Tuyet in the middle of the column, and the men with Hoang in the basket bringing up the rear, all of them moving exactly in step with the one in front. Several times, they slowed, carefully avoiding some unseen obstacle, feeling their way in the darkness. Chung whispered to mind the traps along the trail. Once, they stopped as Chung hooted at a lookout in the trees. A reply came from the inky foliage, telling them to proceed.

Tuyet was exhausted, but fear for her son kept her going. Adrenaline heightened her senses. She saw the night forest with intense clarity and could smell the wet earth, moldering leaves, tree barks, and even the bodies of those around her. The wind was picking up, bringing the scent of rain. The sky rumbled. Purple flashes bruised the clouds' underbellies. She remembered the omens and the dangers the fortune-teller had mentioned years earlier. Still, she had chosen life with Takeshi. *The heart wants what it wants*, she reminded herself. *I could not have done anything differently. Oh, Mother Buddha, save my boy. Please save my boy, my innocent boy.*

———

IT WAS almost midnight. The town was asleep. The cadres wished them luck and left them at the edge of the houses, a kilometer away from the hospital. A light rain began to fall. Tuyet and Coi picked their way through the dark, empty streets, with the bamboo basket swinging on their shoulders. They ran into the lobby to find two nurses napping at the front desk. After carrying Hoang into one of the examination rooms, the nurses roused the doctor resting in a back room.

A nurse had Coi and Tuyet wait in the lobby. They sat on a wooden bench, overcome with fatigue. Coi took out her Lady Buddha amulet, and they held it together and prayed. The nurse came out to tell them that Hoang was in critical condition. The doctor had given him penicillin and other medicines to lower his fever. There was nothing left to do but wait.

Several hours passed. They fell asleep on the wooden bench. Tuyet dreamed about Hoang. When she woke, tears were rolling down her cheeks. A nurse was waiting nearby as if about to say something. A formless wail escaped Tuyet's throat. She slid off the bench onto the tile floor. She already knew. Her son had passed away.

48

One for One

THE MOUNTAIN WAS DRENCHED. THE TRAIL HAD
melted into treacherous mud slicks. Two men descended to the
lowland at frantic pace. Takeshi, in the lead, negotiating the
uncertain path as it zigzagged along a ravine, steadied himself
with a walking staff in one hand, a machete in the other slash-
ing at the dense underbrush. He forced the pace even though a
part of his logical mind knew there was no need to hurry. His
son was dead. A messenger had brought the news the previous
night. Tuyet would wait for the funeral.

Takeshi was moving as if in a trance as he hastened down
the narrow trail, his mind dark, blind with grief. He slipped on
a mossy rock, fell backward hard, and slid down the muddy
track. His feet caught on a root, sending him careening through
the air, off a tree trunk, hitting his head. He blacked out as he
landed upside down into a scrub.

Mong, the wiry guide in his twenties, found his charge
entangled in nettles and shook his head disapprovingly. He
checked Takeshi for broken bones and, finding none, dragged
him from the shrub to a nearby bed of moss. After inspecting the gash in Takeshi's forehead, he cleaned the wound with
water from his flask.

As Takeshi came to, he fended off the guide's hands. He
grumbled, "I'm fine."

"I told you to slow down, didn't I? You're lucky you didn't
break that gimpy leg, Ki." Mong frowned.

"I'm sturdier than I look," Takeshi replied blandly, cuts all
over his forearms, face, and head.

"I'll get blamed if you break your neck," Mong grumbled, none too gently dabbing a cloth on the bloody gash on Takeshi's forehead. "From here on, I'll lead. Either you follow at my pace or you're on your own."

Takeshi nodded begrudgingly. Mong knew the secret pass phrase for the checkpoints ahead, and he wasn't about to share it. Takeshi sat still as Mong applied a poultice from their first-aid kit.

"How much farther?"

"We'll reach the main road around sunset. If the weather holds, you will be home before midnight." He handed Takeshi some bananas and a lump of sesame rice. "It's a long way. Eat and rest. Conserve your energy, old man."

Closing his eyes, Takeshi leaned back on the damp moss. He felt his age, his decade of fighting. He cursed the wars. His old nightmare was pursuing him even by day. No matter how fast he ran, he could not escape his fate. He had witnessed neither the birth nor the death of his son. He had failed as a father and as a husband. Every success had unraveled, no matter how hard he had tried.

◆

"Tuyet, you must sleep," Coi said, sitting up, rubbing her eyes.

The night was eerily quiet, the house dimly lit by a single oil lamp, the air stale and cloyingly sweet with incense and perfumed with embalming fluid. Coi, Anh, and Tuyet were sharing a divan in the shop through the wake for Hoang, his body wrapped in scented sheets on a table in the middle of the room. Coi saw that Tuyet had already lit new incense sticks on the altar. A portrait of Hoang sat by a framed photo of her late mother and a ceramic statue of the Lady Buddha.

"You don't eat, you don't sleep. You can hardly stand up straight. Anh is still ill. What am I going to do if you get sick too?" Coi was weary beyond her limits. She knew her niece wasn't half as strong as she herself was. It had been five nights since they had set out on foot to take Hoang to the town hospital. Neither of them had rested or slept much since, and Anh was still bedridden with typhoid.

"I had a dream," Tuyet mumbled, staring blankly through the mosquito net, her eyes bloodshot, absently brushing her hair, her face drawn and sallow. On her legs and feet, the cuts and blisters from their journey were still raw. "He's coming."

"It must be almost midnight," Coi groaned, closely eyeing her niece. She doubted that Tuyet was strong enough to survive the tragedy.

The dogs sat up, turning toward something beyond the walls. Tuyet listened but heard nothing. Mimi wagged her tail. Momo barked, pawing at the door. Tuyet rose from the divan and raised the wooden beam that barred the door. The dogs darted out into the night.

It was Takeshi standing in the dark like a gaunt apparition, the dogs whining at his feet. She rushed into his arms, her long hair streaming behind her like a mourning shroud. They sank to the muddy ground, holding each other in the starless night.

THROUGH THE first cock's crow, Tuyet and Takeshi prayed over their son's body. At the second crow, by torchlight, they began building the pyre. They hauled firewood from the shed and stacked it in a clearing at the center of the orchard, a place where Hoang had often played with his sister and the neighborhood children. The logs were damp, the ground still sodden from the rain. Fretting that the fire might not catch, Coi doused the woodpile with peanut oil. Takeshi secured a corrugated metal sheet from the rear patio over the pyre. They labored through the early hours. As night paled, they washed and donned white garments. As he lifted the small bundle of white sheets, Takeshi was startled at how little the body weighed. He remembered Hoang heavier, riding on his shoulders to go fishing by the river, not two moons ago. His face quivered, but the tears would not come. A giant boulder weighed on his soul. Had karma found him? Why did he feel dead inside? *Why can't I mourn?*

He carried the package to the pyre. Coi and Anh covered the metal sheet with banana leaves and ferns. Then Tuyet and Takeshi laid their son on his final bed with his toys and fishing pole. Coi added Hoang's favorite peanut taffy, paper money, and gold coins. Anh brought her brother his books and cricket box. They covered him with flowers.

Tuyet looked expectantly to the road. "Is anyone coming to bless the ceremony?" she asked her aunt, almost inaudibly.

"No, all the monks have been summoned to the temple in town. I know the rites. We should start. It will rain this afternoon."

Coi sat on the straw mat with meditation beads in one hand, brass chime in the other. Taking a deep breath, she closed her eyes and began the ceremonial chant. Anh knelt and prayed to the Lady Buddha to protect her little brother. As one, Takeshi and Tuyet held the burning torch between them and raised it to the sky before touching it to the kindling at the base of the pyre. The oil-soaked wood caught quickly. Flames swirled, licked at the white fabric, and, in an instant, wrapped themselves around the tiny bundle. Crackling sparks rose and climbed to the dark sky. Tuyet's knees buckled and she collapsed sobbing to the ground. Stinging smoke swirled, the bonfire roared. Takeshi pulled Tuyet away from the intense heat. Her wails echoed in the woods. Birds took wing and a gust of wind shook the trees, bearing the scent of approaching rain.

FROM MIDDAY to nightfall, the rain poured steadily without thunder or lightning. Dense sheets of it drummed on the thatched bungalow, flooding the yard and the vegetable garden in a foot of water. A stream off the road flowed past the house to the orchard in the back. The brick floor set on a foundation of packed earth kept them dry even as the roof leaked. Huddled around the table, they ate a dinner of cold rice and pickled eggs. A meal had been set on the altar for Hoang, between the brass urn and his portrait.

The rain abated during the night. Tuyet and Takeshi lay sleepless on their hard bed, listening to dripping raindrops off the roof. Their backs turned to one another, the gap between them a chasm. Haltingly, she told him about the French raid on the village and the deaths. Their neighbors killed in their bomb shelter by a legionnaire's grenade. She spoke of the storms and ensuing crisis, of the children becoming ill in the weeks that followed the raid. She told him how their son had died.

"This place is cursed," he mumbled, staring at the ceiling. "I am cursed. I did everything I could. I tried my best."

"I never blamed you for anything, but I wish you had listened to me and had left the past behind us. I wish you hadn't attacked the garrison," she said, turning to him with reproachful eyes. "Why didn't you tell me?"

"I knew what you would have said."

"Before you embark on a journey of revenge, dig two graves."

He flinched. The Confucian proverb stung. Then, slowly, the full horror of their loss, her double tragedy, struck him. He gulped to keep down the bile. He wanted to reach out to her, but he couldn't. He felt unworthy.

"I knew it would make you unhappy," he said hoarsely.

"But you did it anyway."

"That is war."

"You are no different from Xuan and his men. You're blind to the people's sufferings."

"Never tell a soldier he doesn't know the cost of war."

"I think you know now."

"It was a matter of honor."

"Honor," she groaned.

"That's who I am."

"It is, isn't it?"

"You know this."

"I know we are marked by our choices."

"I cannot go against my code."

"I am glad you have been able to be true to yourself."

He stiffened at the coldness in her voice. "I'm sorry it offends you."

"Do you have any idea how selfish that is?"

He stared at her, open-mouthed.

She said, "I will become whatever, whoever I must for our family. I gave away the baby to save us, to save our family."

"I never asked you to give him away."

"Can you look at that child and not see his father?"

He averted his eyes.

She gritted her teeth. "Tell me about how the rapist soiled your honor. How did you suffer? Were you beaten?"

He touched her shoulder, but she shook off his hand. He whispered, "I would have changed places with you."

"But you couldn't, could you?"

He swallowed. A void opened between them.

"In your world, there is little room for me or what I might want."

"I'm sorry. Sometimes, a black rage comes over me and I want to burn everything. Destroy it all. The urge is so strong, I can't control it."

"You controlled it well enough. You planned your revenge carefully, pretending that everything was normal."

He did not reply.

"You are a private man. I never pried into your business.

I never demanded to know your secrets. When we married, I asked you to promise me one thing: honesty."

"I was wrong to deceive you. Forgive me. I have promised you the world and given you nothing but pain and sorrow."

Bitterness surged up her throat. She cried, "You take a life, and one is taken from you."

She curled into herself and sobbed, inconsolable, unaware of the pain in his face, her words like a dagger in his heart. He knew his sins. He embraced her. She shook him off, but he clung on, pulling her into his arms. He held her tightly as she wept. His eyes remained wide open all night. He would not sleep, he would not meet the nightmares.

SOMBER, LISTLESS DAWN. With swollen faces, Takeshi and Tuyet sat at the wooden plank table. Coi made a breakfast of rice porridge and retreated to the garden with Anh, throwing open the doors to air out the scent of death. The cat meowed and brushed up against his leg. They stared at their breakfast.

Tuyet wore her long hair pulled back in a tight knot, her complexion wan. Her red-rimmed gaze drifted out the window to the starfruit tree where three men squatted, discreetly waiting for her husband. She felt powerless, directionless.

A chicken wandered through the back door, searching for any dropped grains. Tuyet lacked the energy to shoo it away. She muttered, "Will you rejoin the Resistance?"

Mechanically, he spooned porridge into his mouth. "It's not my war anymore. I don't have any fight left in me. I am a pawn. Useless."

They looked at one another, the old question hanging between them. Neither felt the need to ask it.

Tuyet sighed. "I think it's time to look for a passage to Japan."

The cat chased the chicken out of the house. He asked, "Will you come with me?"

She stared into space, then nodded. "My heart yearns for peace. I don't know what to do or even where to begin."

There is a pain that hurts and another sort that alters a person. He wondered if he would ever recognize her when this season had passed. "Take time. Heal. Find your center."

She looked down at her hands, the confusing web of lines in her palms. "What's next for you?"

He glanced through the open door at the men waiting under the tree across the road. "I have one mission left. Then, I will find a way for us to go to Hokkaido."

She gave him a hard stare and weighed his words against the look on his face. "Finish your mission. When you've settled your affairs with the Resistance, look for a way out of this hell."

He turned to her, sensing a glimmer of hope. It was the most she had ever said about going to Japan. If only she saw his homeland, she might see that a good life was still possible there. With his buried gold, he thought he could change her mind. He would fetch the hoard and show it to her. He donned his tattered cotton jacket. She straightened his shirt and threw her arms around him, hugging him tightly. They stayed in each other's embrace without moving, silent, barely breathing.

She wrapped his lunch in banana leaves, put the bundle in his rucksack with a flask of rainwater, and handed them to him. He put on his peasant hat and left without a word of parting, not even a nod. She stared at the floor, willing herself to remain strong as he crossed the threshold. They never said goodbye. People said evil winds always listened for tearful farewells.

He stopped at the edge of the road and turned to see his wife standing in the doorway, bracing herself on the bamboo frame, a solitary figure of grief, slim as a vine, pale as ivory. The heartbreak on her face wrenched him. He couldn't help himself glancing back again and again. With piercing clarity, he saw that her capacity for love and forgiveness outweighed all that he had thought honorable and holy. He chewed the inside of his cheeks, wanting to shout out something but lacking the words, wanting to enfold her in his arms, absorb her pain, take away her grim memories.

He nodded to the men. They set out toward town beneath an overcast sky. The cold mist of night still hung thick on the ground. Hugging his ribs, Takeshi followed them, the rucksack on his back, the hat's fabric chin strap over his mouth to hide his face. His sandals were soon slick with dew. He was dragging his feet. At the road's end, he hesitated, anxious. A sense of foreboding loss nagged at him. He cast a melancholy glance back, hopeful, for what he did not know. A change of heart, perhaps, a hand raised in parting. Tall weeds seemed to swallow the house. Tuyet had remained at the door, a solitary figure. Their glances met across the field, two people caught at the crossroads of diverging fates.

In that instant, their entire life together flashed by him, this journey of seven revolutions around the sun from the very first moment he had met her. The fearless young woman who had faced a corrupt official. The romantic girl who had handed him her heart on the dunes of Mui Ne. The proud mother presenting his newborn son to him. She had woven her essence into every thread of his being. He knew the soft strands of hair at the nape of her neck, the cheerful tinkling of her voice, the playful humor in her eyes. The scent of her skin. The comfort of her head on his chest. Yet at that very moment, in the cool air, there was nothing between them. Still, all of it remained in the depth of his mind: a home warmed by the love of his son, ringing with the boy's laughter, that wholeness that had come with having a family.

He could not breathe. A groan escaped his cracked lips: the sound of a drowning man. His sight blurred. At last, when she was too far to see his face, he looked back, tears rolling down his face.

PART VII

Dissolution

1949–1951

49

Courier

DAWN WAS STILL FAR OFF. ALONE IN THE BED, Tuyet was listening to the hollow hum of deep night, her mind roaming the years, drifting from one good moment to the next, from season to season, revisiting the sunny memories. Her son's laughter still echoed within her mind. She only had to close her eyes to see him. Sometimes, he visited her in her dreams.

It had occurred to her that, perhaps, she was going mad. She did not recognize herself in the mirror. The thoughts in her mind might not be hers. Some days she wished to be alone with her grief. Some nights she yearned for her husband to remind her that it had not all been a dream. The idea of retreating to a Buddhist nunnery often tempted her, but she dismissed it as selfishness. She had obligations to her family. There also was her vow to support the Cause, to prevent others suffering as she had. Even as she felt darkness gathering, it was not in her to give up. Wounded Resistance fighters were dying in the mountains for lack of medicine. She had sworn to stay at her post, so she could not simply run away to save herself. But she could save her daughter.

Birds were shrilling in the trees just before first light. She heard her aunt shuffling out to the back patio to wash her face. Sitting up on the bed, Tuyet hugged herself as she watched first light from the window suffuse the room in the lavender glow of fading night. Her mind shifted randomly to another dawn, not so long ago, in this room, on this bed, when Takeshi had gathered her in his rangy arms. She remembered his peculiar scent of sandalwood and ocean brine. A sharp pang of loneliness prodded her out of her reverie. She sighed, wishing she did not have to deceive her aunt. Coi would never agree to sending Anh away from home.

Coi went through the morning routine of building a fire in the clay-pot stove to make tea. She ate a bowl of cold rice, pickled radish, and salted egg, her thoughts on the day's tasks, the safest route to follow, who to visit, at what time. Delivery day always excited her even though it meant a long hike to the outer settlements. Gossip over many cups of tea satisfied her need to socialize, never mind the messages she would carry for the Resistance.

While Coi ate, Tuyet loaded the baskets with dry goods from their shop and double-checked the order list they had compiled over the past week. She packed a lunch for her aunt. After Coi had shouldered her baskets and padded off into the glow of dawn, Tuyet roused Anh for breakfast.

"Would you like to go to school again?" she asked her ten-year-old daughter, who was now sitting on a footstool by the warm stove.

"Yes, please!" Anh cried, perking up, excited. The village one-room school had been closed for four months since its only teacher had been conscripted for manual labor.

Tuyet shook her head. "Not here. I'm sending you to a village in the mountains where Uncle Ha works. There is a big school there with many children. You'll be safer up there."

"I want to stay home."

"Do you remember Uncle Ha's friend, Miss Nhung? She will look after you. Some of your schoolmates will be going today, too. Let's gather your things. They will be here soon," Tuyet said as she led her daughter inside to pack for the journey.

"I don't want to go!"

"You have to go. It's not safe here."

"When can I come back, Mother?" Anh asked, hesitating

at the bedroom door. After the death of her brother and best friend, she had lost much of her vivaciousness. She fidgeted, unhappily, for she had never been away from home.

Tuyet could not bear to look at her daughter. "Soon, when it's safe."

DAWN SWEPT across the sky. A group came up the road. A man and two young women leading eight children. They waited politely by the roadside. Ha's girlfriend, Nhung, approached, her round face lit up with excitement. She smiled, crinkling her perky nose at Anh, who skipped out to greet her. Tuyet invited the group to tea and biscuits, but Nhung said they should hurry while the morning was still cool.

She asked, "Are you ready, Anh?"

Anh turned to her mother. "Will you and Granny visit me, Mother?"

"I don't know," Tuyet said, turning away to hide her tearing eyes. "If we can, we will."

"When it's safe," Nhung said, patting Anh on the shoulder. After becoming Ha's girlfriend, she had developed into a promising Resistance leader. She had been assigned to moving the children to the safety of the mountain camp while their families continued to cultivate the land. Nhung's tone changed to playful. "But I bet you won't want to come home after you see the camp. There are so many fun things to do there—classes and games from morning to night. No one has time to be bored."

"Can I bring my cats?"

"It's a very long way. There are many cats at the camp. You can play with them."

"Mother, will you take care of Nunu and Pinky for me? Mimi and Momo too."

"Of course!" Tuyet hugged her daughter, suddenly overwhelmed with pity for Anh who, like herself, had never known her father. As Tuyet released her hold on Anh, she wanted to tell Anh that she looked just like her father; but she did not want to darken the moment because her ex-husband had been bad luck, a philanderer who had abandoned them. Since her daughter was still in the womb, Tuyet had sensed that her child was blessed. *Precious daughter*, she thought, *I entrust you to the care of the Mother Buddha.*

With a child's intuition, Anh sensed her mother's unease. Biting her lip, she pressed herself back into her mother's arms, hugging her with all her strength. It was the first time Tuyet had truly embraced Anh since she had returned from the garrison. In that moment, Anh felt the fullness of her mother's love. She would remember that for the rest of her life.

Tuyet kissed her daughter on the forehead, urging her to go with the other children. Sniffling, Anh mustered a smile and shuffled to join the group, her little cotton satchel at her side. "Put on your hat," Tuyet called after her.

The sun was still climbing behind the trees, but the breeze was already warming up. It promised to be a very hot day, not a good one for a long journey on foot. The cadres led the children down the road in single file, singing a school rhyme. At the bend, Anh turned and waved, smiling, pleased that her mother was watching. Tuyet raised her hand. Anh waved again with both arms, then trotted after her classmates.

As the children disappeared down the road, their voices lost to the distance, Tuyet sank onto a stool by the doorway. Mimi, the old dog, licked her hand.

"TUYET! TUYET! What have you done?" Coi shouted, barreling through the door, dropping her yoke-baskets. She stared at her niece, whose face confirmed her suspicion.

"Anh! Anh!" Coi ran through the house and out the back

door. She looked in the shed and the orchard. Not seeing her grandniece, she ran back into the house to confront Tuyet. "Where is she?"

"I sent her up to the mountain camp with Nhung and the other children."

"I heard that on the road coming home, but I didn't think you could do something so callous. She's just a child!"

"I had a dream."

"No! You're not in your right mind. You're not thinking straight. Why didn't you talk to me?

"I knew you'd try to stop me."

Coi said shrilly, "This is wrong! A family makes decisions together. How could you do this? She's just a little girl. She has never been away from home. Who is going to protect her?"

"Ha and Nhung will look after her."

Coi wrung her hands in frustration. "He is never at the camp more than a few nights at a time. Nhung has her duties!"

"Do you think I wanted to send her away?"

"I swore to your mother that I would take care of you. I've raised Anh since she was born. I've earned the right to have a say in this."

"Forgive me, Auntie," Tuyet said, her voice breaking. She curled up on the divan. "I'm scared. Something terrible is coming. I feel it. I'm so sorry!"

Angry, Coi gathered necessities: matches, bananas, rice balls, a straw mat, a blanket, a small knife, a bottle of water. Into the front pockets of her brown shirt, she put lumps of brown sugar and a bag of betel chews, the first for energy, the latter to numb the pain. She grabbed her palm hat off the floor. Turning to Tuyet, she shook her head with a look of deep disappointment.

"Don't, Auntie," Tuyet said as Coi stomped toward the door. "You won't catch them. They left early this morning."

Coi glared at her niece. "Do you realize what you have done?"

"Don't go . . . please," Tuyet pleaded.

A resolute look hardened in Coi's eyes. "Either I'm bringing her back or I'm going with her. You've made your decision, and now I make mine."

Tuyet shook her head, knowing her aunt too well to argue. Coi spun around on her heels, took a deep breath, and straightened her back with visible effort. Then she strode out the door with the yoke-baskets on her shoulders. There was neither time nor energy to argue. Her feet ached. Her legs were shaky. She needed to rest, but she had to catch up with the children before they reached the mountains, where the trails were dangerous and unfamiliar. The sun was sinking toward the horizon. A few hours of daylight remained. Her stomach growled. She peeled a custard banana and ate it as she hastened down the road to the foothills in the direction of the main Resistance base.

THE NOON sun throbbed in the stark blue sky, baking the crumbling road that cut through the woods. Huyen Lam was walking along the edge, trying to keep to the shade. Mopping her brow with her cotton scarf, she was wheezing under the weight of her yoke-baskets filled with supplies from the town market. Sweat soaked her shirt, but her lips and throat were parched. A healthy fifty-three years old, she was weary from a lifetime of farm work. What she lacked in stamina, she compensated for with willpower.

She sighed with relief at the sight of the twin banyan trees that marked the halfway point. Almost home. *Silly buffalo,* she chided herself, *you've been afraid of your own shadow all day.* Her thoughts turned to her lunch of leftovers from the previous night, caramelized fish, morning glory soup, and rice. A long, well-deserved nap would follow the meal. There was no rush. The package of medical supplies would be delivered in the afternoon to a shop in the next village down the road.

It was only her third mission for the Resistance, and she still worried about being caught. She had been looking over her shoulder all day, unable to overcome the sense of danger that had nagged at her since dawn. Still, Huyen had pushed on, for it gave her, a childless widow, satisfaction to be striking back at the colonialists in a way that did not go too obviously against her Buddhist beliefs. Her late husband, who had been arrested during a political protest and sentenced to forced labor, had died in prison of illness.

Her knees protested as she lowered her yoke-baskets to the ground at the clearing under the banyans where travelers often rested. She rolled her head and arched her back, straightening out any kinks. After gulping some tepid water from her bottle, she glanced down the empty road, then left her baskets to step behind the bushes to relieve herself. No sooner had she finished than she heard the rattle of an approaching automobile. She froze. The vehicle crunched to a stop under the trees a dozen meters from where Huyen was squatting. Fear knotted her stomach. She pulled up her pants and slunk deeper into the bushes to peek at the newcomers. Four soldiers got off the vehicle, three Viets and one French. Two went off to urinate. The others lit cigarettes. The Frenchman had a large brown dog on a leash. Sniffing around the area, the dog pulled at its leash, leading the legionnaire to the baskets set a little way into the undergrowth where Huyen had left them. He said something in French. The others guffawed. The dog sniffed the ground, raised its head, and barked at the bushes where Huyen was hiding.

One of the Viet soldiers shouted into the trees, "Come out, little sister." He waited a moment and added irritably, "Come out or we'll send the dog in after you!"

Huyen rose from behind the bush, hands raised. Her throat was dry, her heart thumping like a drum. The dog barked, lunging against the leash.

Another man chuckled. "Little sister is a granny!"

A chubby Viet sergeant with a pencil mustache ignored the comment and said amiably to her, "Don't be afraid. You can lower your hands. We have orders to check everyone on this road for contraband."

She nodded, hands wringing the hems of her shirt. The brown hound was nuzzling the baskets.

"Why are you so nervous? You have something to hide?"

"No, sir." She gulped.

"Good. If you have nothing to hide, you have nothing to fear."

The Frenchman clucked his tongue, motioning a man toward the baskets. The soldier spilled the contents on the ground: spices, dried shrimp and cuttlefish, lumps of cane sugar, bars of soap, lard, and shrimp paste. Another soldier frisked Huyen. As they were checking all this, the dog pawed at the empty baskets, biting the bamboo weave. A soldier took the basket and sliced away the binding with a knife, tearing up the false bottom. Out came a dozen pouches of pills and vials of morphine wrapped in cotton.

Huyen shook her head and stumbled backward. The forest canopy spun around her. They seized her by the arms. She screamed, jerked away. They forced her to the ground, pressing her face into the dirt, and roughly bound her hands behind her back. She wailed, bawling loudly. The legionnaire snarled and kicked her in the mouth. Writhing on the ground, she coughed up blood. They dragged her to the vehicle, bantering among themselves. The Frenchman stroked his hound, grinning. The driver reversed the jeep to return to the base.

◆

A DUST devil danced around the yard in a whirling skirt of dry leaves. The heat was crushing, the cicadas' chorus deafening. Lying listlessly on the divan, Tuyet watched from her shop. A pair of black flies worried her cheek, licking tracks of dried salt. Her stomach felt hollow, but she was not hungry. She hadn't eaten since her aunt had stormed off the evening before. Hissing, Nunu, the calico cat at her feet, leaped from the bed. The dust devil spun toward the front door. She shut her eyes just as grit and debris burst into the room. The scorching gust smelled and tasted like the dragon-bone wind of yesteryear in Phan Thiet. *Of course*, she thought, *that day, we were about to make some* banh cang *when Takeshi walked in the door with his ridiculous present.* A tremor passed through her. Déjà vu. She had seen all this.

Mimi's floppy ears perked up. She trotted into the yard, looking down the empty road. Napping under the shelves, her pup, Momo, yawned, confused. Hackles raised, Mimi barked. A military truck and a jeep appeared over the slight rise and slowed to a stop in front of the house. A squad of Viet soldiers spilled out from the vehicles. They quickly surrounded the property. Tuyet walked out of her bungalow, a cold feeling gripping her belly. She called Momo back, but the dog stood firm in front of the shop, barking at the intruders. A French legionnaire came around the jeep holding a brown hound on a leash, a short-haired, muscular animal with a sturdy Rottweiler muzzle. She recognized the dog, the same one that had found her neighbors hiding in their secret cave.

The group's sergeant pointed at Tuyet. "You are under arrest!"

Two men approached to seize Tuyet. Her dog, Mimi, attacked them. Another soldier drew his pistol and shot the dog. Mimi slumped to the ground, whimpering. He finished her with another bullet to the head.

Soldiers scattered to search the property. The hound and its handler worked the house over from the outside in, one room to the next.

Tuyet lowered her head in dismay. "She's just a harmless old dog. You didn't have to kill her."

"Shut up," the sergeant snapped. He twisted the tips of his pencil mustache, scowling at her. "I remember you. The lieutenant finished off your neighbors with a grenade."

"They were innocent!"

"They shouldn't have been hiding."

"Their blood is on your hands."

"In war, every hand is bloodied. Including yours. Where are you hiding the contraband?"

Defiantly, she raised her head, her eyes full of contempt. She shook her head, dismissing the men.

The sergeant stared, mouth agape at her audacity. In the house, the hound barked excitedly. The sergeant scowled. "It found your stash."

Tuyet's heart sank as she watched soldiers hauling bins of rice, beans, and spices out of the shop and upending them on the ground. The hound sniffed, pawing at the brick floor, which had been laid on the tamped earth in a herringbone pattern without cement. The men pried up the bricks with their knives. They found the clay jar in which she had hidden medical supplies and the Resistance's messages.

Looking down at her hands, she saw the line of destiny on her palm in a pattern of congealed blood. Something awoke within her, lifting the year-old fog that had that ruled her life since the rape. Now, she sensed the path ahead, her purpose in life. All of it had all been leading up to this. The inevitable had arrived. The uncertainty of waiting was gone. She was ready. She had been ready a long time.

From the house, a man shouted, "It's empty!"

"Of course it's empty. The traitor is waiting for another lot," he yelled, signaling a soldier waiting by the truck. "Bring the prisoner."

Two soldiers dragged Huyen from the truck. She collapsed in the dirt, unable to stand on her bleeding feet. They hauled her by the armpits and dumped her next to Tuyet. Her face was bruised, her eyes swollen shut. Lying face down, she mumbled something unintelligible.

"No, you have nothing to apologize for," Tuyet said, bending down to touch Huyen's arm.

"I betrayed you."

"No, you didn't."

"I tried to hold out as long as I could."

"I wish you hadn't. I'm sorry they did this to you."

"It was my choice. I wish I could have done more."

The sergeant snarled, "Both of you are going to name all the traitors you know."

Tuyet said, "I'll cooperate if you let her go. She's just a hired courier. She's a widow with no one to support her. She had to take the job to survive."

"That's not for me to decide."

"Then I will tell you nothing."

He slapped her savagely across the face. "Then you will tell it to the interrogator!"

The legionnaire ordered his men to confiscate everything and torch the house. They emptied the shop, loading the store's valuables and stock on the truck. Two soldiers went into the chicken coop and caught half the laying hens before the rest fled into the orchard. They ransacked the bedrooms and tore apart the dressers. They pocketed the little pieces of jewelry Tuyet kept in a box behind the mirror and took Aunt Coi's stash of money hidden inside her pillow. One soldier tossed Mimi's body into the well to ruin the water. They doused the house in kerosene and set it on fire. One by one, the barn, the tool shed, and the outhouse were put to the torch. Flames quickly consumed the wood and thatch structures, roaring out of doors and windows and up to the roof. Heat radiated outward in waves. In an instant, Tuyet watched her home of nearly two years swallowed by a giant bonfire. The wind shifted and blew the smoke into their faces. At last, the legionnaire ordered the squad back to base. They put Tuyet and Huyen into the back of the truck.

A crowd had gathered across the road. A bitter murmur passed among the people, for many had helped build the house. Scowling, old peasant women shook their heads contemptuously at the soldiers.

Addressing the crowd, the sergeant shouted, "Let this be a lesson to traitors! If anyone has information about Viet Minh collaborators, come to the garrison. You'll be rewarded."

As the truck lurched onto the road, Tuyet recalled her son's cremation, how the fire had devoured her entire world. His urn had stood on the altar in the house. Ashes to ashes. All she treasured was now locked away in the chamber of her mind. She sent a silent prayer to the Lady Buddha: *Mother, I am in your hands.*

50

Bed of Ashes

IN THE GATHERING DUSK, COI RETURNED HOME
alone four days later. Trembling, she was unable to recognize the
space where her house had once stood. The longan tree had been
burned, the branches leafless, skeletal. The smell of fire lingered
in the air. She dropped her yoke-baskets and sank to her knees
in the doorway. The house posts had been reduced to charred
stumps jutting out of the ground to knee level. She ran her hand
over the undamaged brick floor, expecting heat, but it was cold.
Powdery ash slipped through her fingers like smoke. She buried
her face in her hands, her shoulders heaving. For the first time
since her husband's death two decades earlier, she howled her
loss to the heavens, weeping uncontrollably like a child.

Up the road, the neighbors' dog barked. The sky darkened,
the mosquitoes swarmed. Mrs. Sang came over from her farm,
her dogs bounding ahead, tails wagging. Momo, the puppy,
yipped and wriggled into Coi's lap, licking her face.

"What happened to Tuyet?"

"She's alive. They beat her and took her to prison. They
burned down the house. They killed Mimi and threw her
down the well, but after they left, we buried her in the backyard. The soldiers took your chickens and most of what was
in your shop. Momo and the cats are staying with us," Mrs.
Sang said, kneeling down to embrace Coi. "I'm so sorry. We
tried to save the house, but the fire was too fast. Did you find
your grandniece?"

Coi nodded. She turned away and wiped her face with the
hem of her shirt, leaving black streaks on her cheeks, her voice

hoarse with grief. "We were on the way up to the mountain camp when a messenger caught up with us. I sent Anh on with the group and came back."

"You did the right thing. This war zone is no place for a child. It's a good thing you weren't here during the raid or you would have been caught too."

"Tell me what happened."

"Later, you must come for dinner first."

COI ATE with the neighbors, but she declined a bed for the night. She wanted to be alone with her grief. They gave her some fruits and incense for an altar. Walking home under a clear, starry sky, she listened to the forest spirits whispering. She set out a bowl of fruit, lit the incense, and sent prayers to Lady Buddha, her patron saints, and Hoang's spirit. Then, unrolling her straw mat under the burnt tree, with a groan, she curled up to rest. Momo, the puppy, nestled against her for warmth. The ground was hard, and her body ached. She sighed, feeling all her fifty-three years, her face gaunt, prematurely aged, her body worn from use, no fat anywhere. Her hair was streaked with silver. Her skin had become leathery from exposure to the elements. Every part of her body throbbed from five days on the trail. But the pain was a mercy, the exhaustion a blessing. She surrendered easily to sleep, clutching her prayer beads. Crickets sang her to the dreamworld, carrying Coi to her timeless village. She found her sister and her grandnephew Hoang in a golden rice field, the tall stalks shimmering, undulating beneath a honey sun. All the ancestors had gathered for the Harvest Festival. Coi was home at last, and she wanted to stay, but she couldn't.

AT FIRST LIGHT, Coi met her heartache anew. She searched the charred debris and found Hoang's urn. It was dented, half of the ashes spilled out, mixed with that of the house. With her hands, she scooped up what she could. The puppy barked, pawing the dust.

Coi wrapped the urn in a blanket and put it in her basket. She sifted through the debris but did not find Tuyet's jewelry box. Remembering the gold they had buried, she found a shovel, its wooden handle burnt to a nub. Running out to the orchard, she fell on her knees in despair. The fire pit had been dug up. An empty hole, their jar of money and gold gone. Boot prints marred the newly turned soil. A terrible realization dawned on her. A chill shot through her body. She put her hands over her mouth, eyes wide with horror.

"They tortured my poor child!" Coi rocked back and forth on her knees, beating her fists on her thighs.

Taking the prayer beads from her pocket, she forced her mind to focus. If the interrogator had wrung this information from Tuyet, then Coi, too, was in danger. Once she had calmed down, Coi rose, shouldered her yoke-baskets, went over to her neighbors' house to give them the puppy, then walked into town to find her niece even though she had no idea what she could do. She just knew that Tuyet needed her.

PHAN THIET was a thousand miles from her birth village, Binh Suong, in the Red River Delta. Far from family and relatives, Coi was utterly alone. She dared not contact her former neighbors and friends for fear of implicating them. Some might be tempted to report her to the police for a reward. Informers were everywhere, on both sides. So Coi sought refuge at the only safe place she knew, the Rose Shrine of the Lady Buddha.

"TUYET'S ALIVE," Nam, the old nun, told Coi as they sat in the garden, the late afternoon sun slanting through the foliage. The last visitors had left, and they were alone by the carp pond. "One of your contacts told me before she escaped to the south."

"I know they're torturing her," Coi said and told the nun about the gold. "I'm sick to my stomach, thinking about what the interrogators do to prisoners . . . to women."

"You must not think about that. It's out of our hands."

"She already suffered enough when those animals con-scripted her at the garrison."

"It has been nearly a week since she was arrested. I think the worst is over. Remain positive: she's still alive. That's a good sign."

"I was angry at her for sending Anh into the mountains. I was wrong. I didn't know she was sacrificing herself to save us."

"We each have our destiny," said Nam, taking Coi's hand in hers. "Listen, I have arranged things for you. Stay here as long as you want. There is a spare room next to the kitchen. Tomorrow morning, go to the prison. Stop at the market to pick up some fruit and snacks to sell from your baskets. You'll be like the other vendors at the prison gate. Wait for a guard named Mu at the Full Moon Café. He is an agent and handles all the clandestine deals for the prisoners. I have already spo-ken to him."

"Can he be trusted?"

"When it comes to money, he can be trusted to fulfill his end of the bargain." She pressed a roll of piaster notes into Coi's hand. "Take this. I know you've lost everything."

"I can't accept it."

"Yes, you can, and you will. The agent does not work for free. The nunnery is self-sufficient. This shrine is just a place of solace. We don't need money, you do. Take it with my blessings."

"Thank you, Mother. I will repay this."

Nam shook her head. "Think of it as a small return for the donations you and Tuyet have made to our shrine."

Coi bowed and thanked her mentor again. She sighed. "There is a favor I need to ask."

The old woman nodded. Coi removed Hoang's urn from her basket.

"Of course. He will have peace here among the guardian spirits."

"Thank you, Mother. He loved the fishpond. When he was a toddler, he liked to come here to feed the carp."

PHAN THIET PENITENTIARY was a group of rectangular buildings within a high brick wall and guard towers at the corners. The main entrance was through heavy steel-reinforced doors. Inside the compound, several smaller buildings housed the main prisoner population. There were two separate courtyards, one for assembly and visitation, the other for bathing and washing. Male inmates outnumbered female, by four to one. Women were kept to a single building at the far end of the complex. At any one time, the prison held between three hundred and five hundred inmates.

It was late morning by the time Coi arrived at the prison. She squatted under a shade tree within shouting distance of the gate, waiting with two dozen others outside the Full Moon Café. She struck up a conversation with some older women and learned that there were three visiting days per week. Each prisoner was allowed only one visitor a week. Inmates relied on their outside contacts for support because the warden skimmed the food budget, providing his wards with only a minimal diet. Lucky inmates had relatives who brought them extra food, medicines, and other necessities. The unlucky ones had to trade their labor for food. The prison agent made a healthy profit from whatever he took in to the prisoners as well as from any messages.

Coi waited until a boy from the café came to fetch her. She followed him inside through the back door. The Full Moon was

338 Andrew X. Pham

a dingy wooden shack with a tin roof with some crude wooden tables. Mu, the agent, who was also the head prison guard, sat on a stool at a table near the kitchen, conducting business. He had a notebook and a wooden cash box open on the table. Spread out in front of him were little saucers of dumplings and sweetmeats and a basket of steamed white pork buns. The aromas made Coi's mouth water. Her stomach growled, reminding her that she hadn't eaten anything all day.

"I beg to offer you greetings, Officer Mu," Coi said, bowing deeply to a portly man barely older than her son. "Mother Nam sent me. Do you have any news about Miss Le Tuyet?"

"Ah, yes, the nun told me you were coming," he mumbled, his mouth full of dumpling. He swallowed and took a swig of tea. He had a florid oily face with cold eyes.

"How is she?"

"Alive. She went through interrogation. It will take some time for her to heal."

"Oh, heavens. What did they do to her?"

He made a vague gesture with his chopstick. "It's always the same for low-grade prisoners."

"Can you be more specific? I need to know so I can get the right medicine for her."

He rubbed his unshaven chin and looked down in a way that worried Coi. "She has some burns and lacerations. Bruises, you know, the usual. Go buy salves and something for her lungs. They waterboarded her. She has a bad cough and a fever."

Coi gasped as she sat down on a stool without asking his permission.

"Calm down, Auntie. She is lucky compared to the Viet Minh prisoners. Get her some medicine from the Chinese shop at the market, the one run by the old herbalist. Tell him your situation, he will know what to prepare."

"Can I see her? I'll treat her myself."

He shook his head. "That's against the rules. Bring me the medicine and food. I'll arrange for someone to help her."

"When can I see her, then?"

"After interrogation, every prisoner is on probation for three months. With good behavior, she will get visitation rights. There is no chance of you seeing her before then. In the meantime, if you want to give her messages or send her something, give them to me. If I'm not here, see the café owner. The usual fees. That's all I can tell you," he said, dismissing her with an impatient wave of his hand. He nodded at the boy to bring in the next client.

Coi went out into the dazzling sun to stand staring at the forbidding prison wall, impenetrable like a medieval fort. Her niece was in there, one of several hundred souls, condemned, trapped behind concrete and iron bars. She forced herself to focus on the task before her: get Tuyet the medicine.

51

Prisoner

THE TWO-BY-THREE-METER CELL WAS WINDOW-less. A ray of light passed under the door, a subterranean glimmer. The stagnant air was sour, fetid with human waste, but Tuyet no longer noticed the stench. She lay in filth, curled up on the wet stone floor by the overturned toilet bucket. Her clothes were now rags, encrusted with blood and salt. Her body was a cage of pain. On her legs and arms, open sores oozed pus. Her ribs broken, she drew shallow breaths, taking in the hot air in small gasps. Her face was discolored, misshapen with bruises, mouth open, lips blistered. Fever burned in her throat, raw from days of screaming. Her bloodshot eyes stared vacantly, along the floor, at the cells across the passage. She heard other prisoners murmuring. Screams from the interrogation chamber far down the hall, at the other end of the dungeon.

Time was shapeless. Days and nights fused into a long landscape of terror and agony. She had confessed everything—her husband, the enigmatic Japanese and his secret fortune; her cousin and his Viet Minh connections; and her role in the medical supply chain—but the torture had not stopped. She had confessed all her love, hate, and pettiness, surrendering anything the demons wanted, real, imagined, or suggested. She had told them her entire life story, all her secrets, the conscription, the rape, the half-French son, the death of her half-Japanese son, and even her daughter now in the Viet Minh camp. Still, the demons showed no mercy. She prepared for death.

———

TWO VIET guards opened the cell door and found her unconscious on the floor. One of them checked her pulse. They carried her to another chamber where they stripped her and threw buckets of water on her raw wounds, which shocked Tuyet into consciousness. Whimpering, she curled up into a shivering ball. They wrapped her in a piece of cloth and told her to walk. She could not move, too weak even to stand. The burly guard picked her up and hung her over his shoulder like a sack of flour. She passed in and out of consciousness, aware that she was being carried in daylight through the courtyard, the sun on her skin.

WHEN SHE WOKE, her eyes were sticky, her vision blurred. Indistinct figures hovered around her, muttering in a warble of voices. A woman was wiping her face with a cool wet towel. All four of the beds were occupied. The infirmary was a dank room with mildewed walls, iron bars on the windows. Outside, dusk was settling.

She had been dressed in clean clothes, her ribs bandaged. The sores on her arms and legs had been cleaned and dressed. They had also shaved her head. A man came in. It took her a moment to recognize him, the man who had adopted her half-French son.

"Doctor?" she whispered hoarsely.

"I'm here, Miss Tuyet. I'm so sorry to see you like this." He took her hand and felt her forehead. "You have a very high fever."

"Is it over?"

"I think so. I hope so." He didn't tell her that this was the first time he had been summoned to the prison's infirmary.

"I told them everything. They know about the baby."

"That's not important. Put it out of your mind."

A hacking cough racked her frame. She hugged herself, doubled over, bringing up blood-speckled spittle. Beads of sweat formed on her forehead and trickled down her temple. Light-headed with pain, she wheezed, "Tell my aunt I'm sorry. Tell my children I love them."

"I'm going to give you something to help you sleep."

He gave her aspirin for the fever and penicillin for the infections. He feared her lungs had been damaged by the water torture. From the hidden compartment of his satchel, he took a vial of morphine, his secret stash, and granted her the oblivion of deep sleep.

A SOLDIER had been ordered to take Doctor Nguyen to the warden's office. Night had fallen. The lights were on around the perimeter walls. Walking down the rows of cells, he shuddered at the muffled voices from beyond the iron bars on the high windows. In the gloom, the pervasive stench of sweat, urine, feces, and decades of grime made the compound not only oppressive but sinister. Nguyen swallowed his fears, telling himself that it was all too new to him, that he had never seen the inside of a prison until today. He was a scion of an upper-class Vietnamese family, the backbone of French colonialism. People of his class believed in the French system and its ideals.

In the cluttered office full of aromatic cigar smoke, a thin, bearded man introduced himself as Warden Cadart and another man as Inspector Renier. At Cadart's urging, Nguyen detailed Tuyet's condition and made recommendations for her care. They questioned him about the adoption of her half-French baby.

Cadart asked, "Did you know she was part of a supply chain for the Viet Minh?"

"No, I had no idea. She would not have told me that. Believe me."

"She did not name you as a sympathizer."

Nguyen was relieved but kept a straight face for fear of needlessly arousing suspicion. He asked, "Are you going to take the baby?"

Cadart turned to Renier, who stood at the window, lost in thought as though he hadn't heard. At last, he replied, "No, his father is dead, and his mother has given him to you. Unless someone comes forward to contest your parental rights, he is yours to keep. It is out of kindness that you are giving the child a home, Doctor. Thank you for your effort today. You may go."

Doctor Nguyen bowed and left.

Renier turned to the warden and said, "Clean her up and put her with the main prison population. She is not to be harmed."

"We're not done with her yet," Cadart protested, flustered, for he was a stickler for rules.

"Did I ask for your opinion?" Renier snapped.

"Forgive me, Inspector," Cadart replied obsequiously. "May I ask what you intend to do with her?"

"I need her to catch a bigger fish."

52

Watcher

COI LINGERED IN TOWN FOR A MONTH UNTIL SHE learned that Tuyet had recovered from her wounds. Once her niece was transferred from the dungeon to the main cell block, Coi sent a message to her son with a request to bring Anh home. Lacking reliable means of communication, she had no way of knowing whether her son received the message. She decided that the best she could do was to go back to what was left of their home and wait for Anh there. Once a week, she would trek into town to send supplies to Tuyet via the agent.

The village had changed dramatically in two months' time. Its population had dwindled to less than half. It seemed as if every other structure had been abandoned or destroyed. The village chief had passed away. No one wanted to take his job, so his eldest son, a shy farmer in his mid-thirties, reluctantly became the village deputy until someone else could be appointed. Coi's neighbors, the Sangs, were still entrenched at their farmstead, hoping for the best. Although there were unoccupied houses nearby that she could have used, Coi reasoned that if Anh did not find her at home, she might panic and do something rash like returning to the mountains or going into town to look for her mother. Coi had no choice but to camp at what had been their home.

The site was overgrown with weeds. Rain had returned the ashes to the soil. Grass had sprung up knee-high around the yard. Undaunted by the mess, Coi cleared the debris from the center of the house to the perimeter. In the orchard, she found the worktable with two legs missing and dragged it to the place she had cleared. Resting on its legless side, the table was canted on its two remaining legs to form a triangular shelter. The rectangular tabletop served as a slanted roof, allowing just enough space underneath for a small person. She dug up bricks from the bedroom area to build a raised sleeping platform under the table, hoping that it would be enough to keep her dry when it rained. Unrolling her straw mat, she judged her shelter adequate for the night. The next day she went to the other abandoned homes in the area and salvaged panels of roof thatch, ropes, nails, and wooden boards. Bit by bit, she reinforced her nest, adding side walls and rainproofing the tabletop. The shelter was barely long enough for her to lie down outstretched and just high enough to sit with her head touching the underside of the table. From the road, her shelter was indistinguishable from any other mound of debris.

Like a crow, she picked through deserted homesteads for usable things: a discarded blanket, an old coat, straw mats, clay pots. She had a sack of rice brought from town. There were fruits from her orchard, wild greens that grew along the creeks, and the neglected vegetables from the gardens of vacant homes. She ate a steady diet of sweet potatoes, radishes, string beans, eggplants, peppers, morning glory, bamboo shoots, and mushrooms. Sometimes, her neighbors gave her a fish caught in the river. They invited her to join them and share their food, but Coi did not want to burden anyone, telling herself that in wartime, no family needed another mouth to feed.

In the early morning hours, when there was no patrol to notice her, she cooked enough food for the rest of the day. She learned to be content with what she had, without desire for more, even when she went into town. Meats, sausages, and dessert sweets did not tempt her. What little money she had, she saved for Tuyet's supplies and for bribes for the guards.

———

"AUNTIE. AUNTIE COI."

Coi was in the garden digging for potatoes. She rose to her feet, recognizing the voice.

"Ki! Ki!" she cried.

In the cool morning air, they sat on tree stumps in the orchard. She told Takeshi all that had happened and described the peaceful spot at the shrine where she had placed Hoang's ashes. Takeshi thanked her. He had visited the shrine only once but remembered his little boy feeding the colorful carps there. Sighing at the ache in his heart, he changed the subject and talked about his journey north to the military academy. Tuyet's incarceration weighed heavily on his mind, and he blamed himself for not having been present at the time.

Coi said, "They sentenced her to two years in prison. Is there any chance of getting her out early? Do you think we can bribe someone?"

"We must try. Gold opens many doors."

"Be careful." She grasped his arm, her brow furrowed. Lately, she had not seen him in her dreams, and this disturbed her more than she dared admit.

"I will," he promised and looked out to the road. His men were collecting sacks of food and supplies donated by villagers. The squad leader called out that they had to get moving. A patrol was approaching. Takeshi signed that he needed another minute.

Smiling, he turned to Coi with evident affection. How much she had aged in just a few months. Her face had become weathered and lined by suffering, but her eyes still sparkled with kindness. Her sacrifices and endurance were boundless. "Auntie, I'm so sorry things have come to this. Everything I have touched has turned to ash. I wanted to give you and Tuyet a good life."

"I know," she said, patting his forearm. "We had a fine time while it lasted. You made Tuyet very happy."

His face twisting with emotion, he gazed intently into the orchard as though memories were hiding there. "Auntie, it pains me to see you living here alone like this."

"Don't worry about me. I have everything I need."

"I have to go. Please forgive me, Auntie. I wish I could do something for you."

"Never mind. Go on, before it's too late," she said, shushing him. As the words left her lips, she felt something changing in the air.

◆

DAYS BECAME weeks and weeks turned to months, bringing winds, sun, and rain. She endured nature's fury under the broken table, watching the village unravel around her. One by one, the farming families, including her neighbors, the Sangs, gave up and moved away. They had learned to adapt to the ebb and flow of war, but they were unprepared for the sudden rise of savage bandits roaming the Twilight Territory like packs of wild dogs, robbing and raping with impunity. Day after day, French patrols marched by toward the mountains, passing Coi's shelter without even noticing it. At night, Viet Minh fighters moved silently through her orchard in the direction of the garrison. The sound of gunfire was carried on the breeze. Evening storms passed at the horizon with violet flashes. Beyond the green hills, mortars rolled like thunder. She watched the starry sky for airplanes, comets, and, especially, flares, which she would retrieve at sunrise for their prized silk parachutes, which her grandniece adored. Even as the fighting swept through her village, none of it touched Coi. She lived in solitary silence, days at a time without speaking a single word. She lived like a field mouse, careful, quiet, resourceful.

———

"AUNTIE! WHERE are you?"

Curled up on her mat, Coi thought she was dreaming, but she knew that voice. In the predawn glow, she crawled out from her shelter and made her way through the debris to the three figures standing by the road.

"Is that you, Anh?"

"Auntie!" Anh shouted and ran into her arms.

They had walked through the night to avoid any French patrols. Comrade Lai and Sister Nhung, on a mission to the south, had brought Anh down from the Resistance mountain camp. The journey had taken the better part of a week. They had rested during the day and walked mostly at night.

Comrade Lai said, "It was still dark when we came by earlier. We saw that . . ." He gestured at the rubble.

"I must have been asleep. Did you call out?"

"No, we didn't think anyone could possibly live here, so we went on to see the village chief. He told us you were here."

Nhung explained that when they had received Coi's first message, there had been heavy fighting along the route, making travel impossible. While they were waiting for a lull in the fighting, an outbreak of dysentery had affected the entire camp. All the children, including Anh, had fallen ill. Two toddlers had died. Anh barely had recovered when she came down with malarial fever. It had taken months for Anh to regain enough strength for the journey home.

Coi went back into her shelter and returned with three baked yams on a clay plate. She offered them to her guests as she invited them to sit while she boiled water for fresh mint tea. Nhung and Lai exchanged glances. They were hungry, but it was clear that Coi was serving them her breakfast. They said friends up the road were waiting to eat with them. Comrade Lai said they should get to where they were going before sunrise.

———

DAWN BRIGHTENED the sky. Coi and Anh ate together for the first time in six months. She reassured Anh that her mother had become used to life in prison. Her stepfather was working on a way to get her out. Anh had become talkative during her time at the camp. She prattled on about her many adventures, including a harrowing escape when the camp had been attacked. With an impish grin, she announced that Uncle Ha would be asking for Auntie's permission to marry Sister Nhung. Coi was pleased to hear this, for she felt that Nhung would make a good wife for her headstrong son.

"Oy! I almost forgot your present." Coi clapped her hands and fetched a small bundle from her shelter. "I found three flare parachutes. I've been saving them for you."

"Thank you, Auntie," Anh said, holding them up to the light. "They're perfect, no holes or stains."

"We'll make dresses for your doll," Coi proclaimed proudly.

"I gave her away. I'm too old to play with dolls now."

"Ah . . . what a shame," Coi murmured and wondered why she had risked her life crossing combat zones littered with unexploded ordnance for these squares of fabric.

"We could sell the silk for a good price at the market."

"I guess we could." Coi nodded, ruing the passing of childhood.

"We could treat ourselves to some cakes and soy milk?"

"Oy! I see you haven't outgrown your sweet tooth."

53

Speaker

MOSQUITOES DRONED IN HER EARS. TUYET WAS lying on her side, eyes shut, resisting the pull of dawn. She heard other inmates stirring. Someone coughed a deep hacking cough. Women were lining up at the lavatory at the south end of the communal cell. The toilet lineup had begun earlier than usual, for many of them were in their time of the month. The scent of blood brought hordes of flies.

On any given day, the rectangular cell block housed between sixty and eighty female inmates, sleeping side by side, shoulder to shoulder. Measuring eight by thirty-two meters, the space had two sleeping platforms, raised a foot above the walkway running north to south, the length of the building. Windows with iron bars ventilated the cell block. The door was at the north end of the walkway. The toilet was at the south end, a single hole in the concrete floor without cover. Next to the slimy hole was a square cement tank with a water faucet that dribbled from dawn to dusk but never seemed to fill the tank.

After being tortured under interrogation, Tuyet had clawed back to life in this cell, on a tattered straw mat near the toilet. Two months had passed since the guards had carried her from the infirmary and deposited her in this cell with one straw mat, one towel, one change of gray clothes, and a tin mug, a spoon, and a bowl. Speaker Hoanh, the cell's elected leader, had organized the inmates to help nurse Tuyet back to health. They had shared their stories, advice, food, and other items with her until she was able to care for herself, as they did traditionally with every new arrival. Huyen, the courier who had been caught with Tuyet, was one of her cellmates and a good friend.

"Big Sister," a young woman whispered, sitting on the floor at the foot of Tuyet's mat. "Are you awake?"

"What is it, Sister Chieu?" Tuyet asked, sitting up. Although the women sleeping on either side of Tuyet were awake, they neither moved nor looked up, allowing Tuyet and Chieu a token privacy.

"Anything I can do for you today? Need your washing done?"

Tuyet was taken aback by the desperate look in Chieu's pinched face. She had known her since she had lived in the Yellow House. Chieu had been a well-respected twenty-five-year-old merchant, and she'd been convicted for assaulting a moneylender in a loan dispute. She had a strong, round face and a button nose.

"Are you all right? Cramps?"

Chieu nodded. "It's a little heavy this month. Do you have any work I can do?"

She needed something but only had her labor to offer. Barter was a way of life in prison. Everything had its exchange value: bed positions, labor, cleaning duties, grooming, massages, food, medicine, tobacco, betel nut chew, and clothes. Proud but poor, Chieu had no one on the outside to send her survival packages.

Tuyet had no laundry save her soiled menstrual cloth, but she didn't want to involve someone else in that unappealing task. She said, "Later when the light is better, you can check my hair for nits. What do you need?"

"A menstrual cloth if you can spare one," she whispered, clutching her belly. "I lost mine. There wasn't enough water to wash yesterday."

"The rats?"

Chieu nodded. It was not unusual to be awakened by rats scampering over one's body to get at food or soiled cloths.

Rats were not the worst of their problems. At one time or another, they all had insect bites, rashes, lice, open sores, fungal infections, toothaches, eye irritations, worms, diarrhea, bladder infections, and other ailments. Most inmates kept private stashes of salves, iodine, salt compresses, aspirin, and herbal medicines.

Tuyet nodded. "Of course, let's boil some water. My aunt sent me some herbal tea for cramps."

PRISON LIFE revolved around three main events: eating, bathing, and visiting. The kitchen served food twice a day, mornings and evenings, when guards brought in two giant cauldrons: one of rice, the other of soup, stew, or stir-fried vegetables with bits of meat. The fare was so poor that inmates supplemented their diet with food sent by their families. Those without outside support earned their morsels by washing and cleaning.

Twice a week, the prisoners were herded into the bathing courtyard, one cell block at a time. The courtyard had two long water troughs with tin basins and bowls. The women had one hour to bathe and wash their clothes. Wrapped in cotton cloths, they bathed and took turns washing each other's hair. They always sat the last few minutes under the open sky, soaking up the sun.

Once a week, prisoners with visitor privileges were led into the main courtyard. On visiting days, a portable metal fence was set up to divide the yard lengthwise into two sections, visitors on one side, inmates on the other. Each visitor could bring one basket of food, which was checked by the guards. The guards charged an unofficial fee for each basket. For half an hour, inmates and visitors were lined up along each side of the fence opposite one another, talking, weeping, shouting over the din. Tuyet was always visited by a middle-aged woman named Lieu hired by Coi from a shop outside the prison.

In her fourth month in jail, Tuyet had an unexpected visit from an old acquaintance. It did not happen in the yard but rather at the cell door, which was highly unusual. The guard called Tuyet to the door after the first meal of the day. She was perplexed and more than a little frightened to hear her name called. Curious inmates crowded in behind Tuyet as she waited at the inner door of wrought-iron bars. Looking out across the yard, she beheld a striking scene: a guard escorting a slim woman in a robin's-egg-blue *ao dai*, fluttering in the breeze, seeming to glide over the paved yard under an overcast sky, a vibrant splash of color on a stone-gray background. The air was cool, charged with ions, smelling of the sea. A sense of déjà vu overcame Tuyet. Her knees weakened and she gripped, white-knuckled, the thick iron bars. Where had she seen this before?

Captain Moreau's wife, Tam, was more beautiful than Tuyet remembered. She was in her early thirties, her hair black and lush, her figure as slim as a girl's. Tuyet knew that Tam was well-off from the pearl necklace around her throat, the thick jade bracelets on her wrist, and the extraordinarily fine silk of her dress.

Tam bowed and they exchanged greetings. She said, "Sister Tuyet, I'm so sorry to see you here."

"Don't be," said Tuyet with an easy smile, nodding at the crowd behind her. "It's not so bad. I've never had more friends to play cards with."

The entire cell erupted with hearty chuckles. It broke the awkwardness.

"Are you still living in town?" Tuyet asked.

"No, my husband was posted to Nha Trang last year, so we had to relocate there. I was in town visiting when I heard a rumor about you being in here," she said, holding Tuyet's gaze.

"It's nice to see a friendly face."

"I have not forgotten what you did for us."

Tuyet bowed, remembering that hot March morning when she took a cyclo across the bridge to look for the house on *la rue des petits café au lait.* "That was five years ago. How time flies . . ."

"You saved us. Your husband saved mine."

"It was the right thing to do."

"It's my turn now. I will speak to my husband. He is on good terms with the warden," Tam said with a vague wave of her hand. "That's how I got this visit with you. Perhaps there is something I can do to make your time here a little easier."

Tuyet bowed, moved by Tam's sincerity. "I appreciate whatever you can do."

"In the meantime, can I bring you anything? Food, medicine, whatever?"

"Menstrual cloths," Tuyet replied.

"Menstrual cloths?"

Tuyet nodded. "There's a permanent shortage here."

Understanding dawned on Tam's face. She shuddered. "Of course, I can bring that. Do you want anything else—medicine, food?"

Tuyet shook her head. "Just the cloths and some soap, but can you bring enough for everyone in here? I know it's a lot to ask."

Tam smiled. "I'll see what I can do."

SEVERAL BOXES of cloths and soap arrived the next day, along with many other things, including medicines, ointments, honey, cooking lard, fish sauce, toothbrushes, sugar, tea, and lotus moon cakes. Tuyet shared the bounty with her cellmates and added the medicine to the communal chest. It earned her many friends and marked the beginning of her popularity.

WHEN THE monsoon arrived, wind howled in from the sea and drove rain sideways through the cell block's high windows, drenching everyone. Inmates grabbed their possessions and huddled by whichever wall offered the most shelter. They strung their straw mats like tarpaulins, roped to the bars of the windows. They sat together, hip to hip, shoulder to shoulder, by tiny stoves, boiling tea to dispel the cold. When they ran out of lamp oil for the stoves, they rubbed mentholated salves onto their chests to keep warm. The waterlogged skin on their hands and feet wrinkled and split. Thrumming rain drowned out their words. In silence, they stared into the grayness with rheumy red eyes. Hunger hollowed their cheeks. Their teeth chattered, lips blue. At times the monsoon rain pelted down for days on end.

Whenever debris clogged the courtyard drains, water gushed into the cell from beneath the door, flooding the walkway. In no time, the toilet backflowed into the cell, filling it with excrement. The chamber became a vile cesspool that rose steadily with the downpour. For hours, they cried for help, standing on the sleeping platforms, knee-deep in waste, clutching their belongings. They rolled up food and heavy items in blankets and tied them to the window bars. Hungry, they shivered and moaned, for there were no hot meals whenever rain flooded the prison kitchen.

During the lulls between storms, they slept fitfully in wet clothes, on damp mats, coughing and sneezing, choking on the stink of the black mildew spreading on the walls. Sores festered on their skin. Every day the resident midwife squeezed and dug out pus cores, cleaning wounds with iodine. The long cell became rank with sewage. Little white mushrooms appeared from the crevices between the bricks. Slippery green muck made the walkway treacherous. Swarms of mosquitoes descended to feast on the inmates. Blood-red splotches decorated the walls, the remains of bloated mosquitoes slapped into oblivion. Malaria swept through the prison population, claiming several lives.

Tuyet survived her bout of malaria, but Granny Oanh, the Speaker, caught pneumonia and passed away quickly as though her spirit was ready to escape the prison hell. The women voted Tuyet to be their new Speaker. She inherited Granny Oanh's mosquito net and sleeping place at the northeast corner of the cell, the farthest spot away from the toilet. It marked a new stage in Tuyet's life.

EARLY ONE MORNING, a woman in her fifties rose from her sleeping mat and began stretching in silence, her cellmates still asleep. She moved slowly, flowing from pose to pose, hands expressive, arms like wings, legs like a crane's, graceful in the pale light. Her eyes gazed peacefully beyond the prison confines. She could have been anywhere. To anyone watching, she had escaped to another place.

Days later, two women rose and copied her movements. Tuyet and her two neighbors joined them. The group grew a few at a time until all those physically able rose to their feet and found the will to move together, in quiet solidarity, bending, twisting, turning in slow motion with the ebb and flow of invisible tides, in the half-light like seaweed beneath the water's surface. It became a morning routine that Tuyet would practice daily for the rest of her life.

AT THE HEIGHT of the hot season, the cries of the cicadas filled the prison. Tuyet thought of her daughter and half-French son. She did not know what had become of her husband, but in her heart, she felt he was still among the living, for she had walked many dreams with him.

Dripping sweat, Tuyet lay down on her sleeping mat in the afternoon heat. She closed her eyes, counted her breaths, and shut out the drone of conversation. On a long slender thread, she sent her mind down through layers of sleep to that place where the cicadas beckoned, a mountain cave and a crystal fountain, high in the blinding sky. He was there waiting for her. A part of them had always lived there, on the flat wet granite at the cave's mouth, enveloped in the monotone song of the cicadas.

54

Reckoning

DUSK SETTLED ON THE TREETOPS. SHADOWS stretched over the fields and the scattering of rooftops. The last visitors had left the shrine to hurry home while daylight lingered in the sky. Takeshi was sitting beneath a tamarind tree in a grassy lot across the road from the shrine, waiting for the coast to clear. He rose, dusted himself, and checked the empty road. He felt naked without his pistol, having left it at the safe house as required for excursions into town. There were too many checkpoints and random searches. He carried only a forged identity card.

The Rose Shrine of the Lady Buddha was as he remembered it from the one time his wife had taken him there to donate food during the famine year. He walked down the white gravel path, left his sandals outside, and mounted the steps. The door to the left of the altar opened, startling him, An old woman with a drawn catfish mouth came out. Seeing him, she huffed: another late worshipper. He remembered Coi mentioning volunteer caretakers when he had sat with her in their orchard a few days earlier.

"Are you going to light incense?" she asked, gesturing at the flickering oil lamp. "I'm going to put out the flame. We need to save oil."

"Yes, thank you."

He put some money into the metal collection box, took three incense sticks, and held them to the buttery flame. Then he knelt on the blue tile before the altar with its life-size statue of the Lady Buddha and prayed for protection for his wife. He lit another three incense sticks and went out to the carp pond.

The caretaker reappeared from behind the house and trailed him. She called out in an irritated voice, "Mister, aren't you leaving yet?"

"May I have a few minutes in the garden?"

"It's late. Can't you come back tomorrow?"

He held up the smoldering incense. "Ma'am, I'm just passing through today. Please, if it's not too much trouble . . ."

She gave him a curious look. "You have a strange accent. Where are you from?"

"Ninh Tung, a small village north of Hue," he replied, giving his alias. Since his extended stay at the military academy, he had been affecting a thick Central Highland accent to disguise his imperfect Viet.

"You're a long way from home."

"I am."

"Stay as long as you want. Be sure to close the gate behind you so the stray dogs don't get inside and dig up the garden," she said and left.

HE KNELT on the grass by his son's memorial stone. Poor Auntie, bless her for scrounging up enough money to carve Hoang's initials. He traced the letters: *K* for Kei, *jubilation*; *H-H* for Huy Hoang, *glorious*. It was true: the boy had been a miracle, speaking in complete sentences at two years old, writing his name at three, and doing simple math at four. A cat meowed and jumped down from where it had been lying atop a boulder. It purred and rubbed against his leg. Smiling, he thought, *You've got a cat, Kei. They have always liked you.*

He sighed deeply. The loss ached like a mortal wound. His karma, his fault. He had tried to bury his grief in the war. It kept him busy and kept him from home but not from his

360 Andrew X. Pham

demons. Once in a while, sometimes in the middle of the day, out of nowhere, he would remember the weight of his boy riding on his shoulders as they strolled in the woods. Soft little hands pulling his ears. He hummed an old Edo lullaby.

Hushaby, Hushaby!
My good baby, Sleep
Where did my boy's babysitter go?
Beyond that mountain, back to her home.
As a souvenir from her home, what did you get?

He reached into his pocket for a fistful of shiny brass buttons. *Look, son, your gold coins from Rooster Mountain.* He placed them under a small rock next to the memorial stone. It was quite dark now. He had lost track of time. The incense had burned down to nubs. A half-moon was ascending the night sky.

At the sound of gravel crunching underfoot, he froze, scanning the darkness. The garden was sunk in shadows; moonlight glowed through the trees. To his left, figures silhouetted on the pale gravel. They passed in front of the shrine toward the pond. Something moved close behind him, too heavy to be cats. Hackles rose at the back of his neck. Adrenaline surged through him. He fumbled about his waistband for a weapon, even as he remembered he was unarmed. He grabbed a fist-sized stone. A twig snapped behind him.

He rolled away and came to his feet running by the edge of the pond. Footsteps crashed through the bushes behind him. He made for the rear gate. A flashlight caught his face, blinding him.

Someone shouted, "He's running!"

He veered away and fell into a rosebush. Thorns ripped his shirt and drew blood. A hand grabbed his ankle. He kicked the man in the face and rolled onto his knees, losing his sandals. Another man tackled him, and they tumbled. He struck the assailant over the head with the stone, freeing himself. His vision cleared as he fled along the tall hedge, but he found no way through. He recalled a low wall behind the shrine near the kitchen. Crisscrossing flashlight beams swept past erratically, panning the dark garden.

"Stop! Stop!"

"Take him alive!"

"Which way did he go?"

He hurled the stone into the pond to distract them. Ducking low, he ran barefoot toward the back of the shrine. As he rounded the corner of the house, a huge figure, a bearded Frenchman, stepped into his path and drove a fist like a sledgehammer into his belly. He crumpled. His eyes caught the merest glimpse of a truncheon descending on his head. All went black.

THEY BOUND him and dragged him out to the road. A car pulled up, its headlights shining on the big, bearded man standing over the unconscious captive. A thin Frenchman with a scraggly mustache stepped out from behind the driver's seat. He paused to light a cigarette, frowning disapprovingly at the inert body.

"Victor, what's all that blood on his face? Is he dead?" he asked.

Victor nudged the limp body with his foot. "No, but he'll wish he were."

The old caretaker stepped out from the shadow. She jutted her catfish mouth at them and said in French, "Monsieur Boisson, this is your man, no?"

"Well done." Boisson tossed her a roll of money and dismissed her with a wave of his hand. Turning to Victor, he said, "The inspector is going to be very happy."

"What did he say?"

"He's on his way. Be here by morning. He said not to interrogate the Jap without him."

Disgusted, Victor slapped the leather truncheon into his meaty palm. "Why?"

Boisson sniggered, "He doesn't trust us."

"Bastard!"

"Let's put the Jap in the dungeon. I hate working at night anyway."

"I'm hungry. Steak at the pub?"

"Why not. We've hit pay dirt."

55

Basket Boat

"MAJOR YAMAZAKI, DO YOU REMEMBER ME?"

"Renier. Inspector Renier," said Takeshi from the interrogation chair, his wrists and ankles shackled. Who could forget that shiny, bald head and that champion handlebar mustache? A more compact version of Feraud, he thought, the same bulbous nose, mean beady eyes, but younger, stronger, and more dangerous. "The last time I saw you, you were floating face down in the river."

"I nearly lost a leg."

"You're not the type to hold a grudge, are you?"

Victor and Boisson guffawed from the worktable, preparing their tools. Takeshi recognized the big brute, the man who had knocked him out the night before.

Takeshi asked Renier, "Where is your boss, Monsieur Feraud?"

"In heaven, God rest his soul." Renier crossed himself, glancing upward.

"What happened?"

"He passed away peacefully in his sleep," Renier replied. "Men plan their lives, God their deaths."

"My condolences."

"Thank you. Unfortunately, he didn't leave me anything," he said and paused, raising an index finger. "Except the gold you took from him."

"You think I still have it?"

Renier smiled, his mustache rising a fraction. "Let's not start by insulting each other's intelligence, Major. You may wonder why my men have not started working on you."

"The thought did cross my mind."

"Thirty years I've been in this line of work. It is my experience that it doesn't always have to be the carrot or the stick. Sometimes, it could simply be a very, very large carrot. There doesn't have to be a stick at all. It might be invisible, like an idea. Are you following me?"

"I'm afraid to ask, but what is the large carrot?"

"I release both you and your wife. I keep the gold. As a gesture of goodwill, I give you a generous reward for your cooperation, something to help you return home to Japan."

"And the stick?"

Renier clucked his tongue, shaking his head in mock disappointment. "You had to ask, didn't you? They always ask."

"That's human nature."

Renier gestured to his men. They raised Takeshi from the chair, cuffed his hands behind his back, and led him down a long, dark passageway, out of the dungeon, and up two flights of stairs into an office. The room had a row of filing cabinets on one side and on the other, several windows overlooking the prison courtyard. It was midday, a blustery blue sky, the sun glinting above rippling clouds. Female inmates were bathing, modestly wrapped in brown cotton cloth. They were rinsing themselves with bowls of water from two long troughs. Sounds of conversation, splashing water, and wet laundry being slapped on stones drifted up to the windows.

"Welcome to my prison, Major Yamazaki," said an anemic-looking Frenchman, rising from a desk at the far end of the room. "It's an unexpected pleasure to have you here."

"You're Chief Leroux's lieutenant. I don't remember your name."

"Cadart. I was in the detention camp with the chief when he died."

"That was a bad war. A long time ago, no?"

"Not to me," Cadart said coldly. He walked over to the window and pointed down to the courtyard. "Your wife. In that corner by the clotheslines."

Takeshi recognized her instantly. Tuyet was pouring water for a woman washing her hair. He only saw her face in profile, but he knew her form, the way she moved. Her hair was shorter, shoulder-length. She looked gaunt and wan, years older than the last time he had seen her, only months earlier. He felt weak with grief.

Cadart opened the window wider. "Go ahead, call out to her. You may speak to your wife."

Takeshi stared at Tuyet, his chest heaving, his hands balling into fists. Although he knew that Tuyet was here, he was not prepared for actually seeing her. His jaw clenched. He backed away, shaken, ashamed, suddenly afraid to be seen. All along, he had known that he had sealed her fate, from the beginning, without her being aware of it. His karma had found him.

"She really has no idea of what you've done or who you truly are," Renier said. "We interrogated her for days. She nearly died because we didn't believe her."

"Bastards!" Takeshi snarled.

"Shut your mouth!" Renier backhanded Takeshi across the face, his voice low, caustic. "You should not be outraged. This is all your doing, Major. Take me to the gold or I will have you watch me flay her alive."

Takeshi stared at the Frenchman's beefy face, those stony eyes. He flinched.

"Is that a *yes*, Major? I need to hear you say it."

"How do I know you will keep your word?"

"I will keep my word to put your wife to the knife right now."

His mind was blank as he stared at the floor. He had nothing left to bargain. "I'll take you to it."

THE LATE afternoon sun dipped in and out of the clouds. The car bounced along the washboard road, kicking up a long plume of dust until it squeaked to a stop. Boisson shut off the engine, stepped out, and looked around with disgust at the desert landscape. Victor dragged Takeshi out of the rear seat. Renier donned a white straw fedora and took a quick sip from his whiskey flask. After wiping his mouth with the back of his hand, he twisted the tips of his mustache between his thumbs and index fingers.

Takeshi rolled his aching shoulders. Wrists cuffed behind his back, he nodded in the direction of the ocean. "We'll have to walk the rest of the way, about a kilometer between those hills."

Boisson motioned for Takeshi to lead the way. Victor grabbed a shovel and a sturdy leather bag from the trunk. They could smell the sea on the breeze as they walked.

Renier asked, "Why didn't you hide it in the jungle?"

"Too many eyes," said Takeshi, scanning the ground for thorns. He was barefoot.

Renier narrowed his eyes. "Why didn't you bury it closer to the road?"

"I didn't come by the road," he murmured.

"You used a boat?"

"Airplane. Landed on the beach."

He had passed by this point several times over the years, but an opportunity to recover the treasure had never arisen. Even if it had, there was nowhere else to move the gold. Since he buried it, he had known that the gold would only be unearthed if he settled in Vietnam or left the country.

IT WAS WINDY on the bluff. Nothing had changed, as though no time had passed since he'd buried the stash. No trace of cattle grazing, no traveler's footprints. He noted the path down to the beach where he had landed the airplane years earlier. He found the boulder with the vertical cleft, sighted the line, and measured the distance with his steps. The oval stone had not been moved from where he had placed it.

"It's under that rock. Not deep."

Victor came up with the shovel, but Boisson said, "Let him dig it up. These Japs are clever little devils with booby traps."

Victor tossed the shovel at Takeshi's feet. They unlocked the handcuffs and backed away to a semicircle, keeping Takeshi between them and the cliff. Boisson and Renier drew their pistols. As Takeshi picked up the shovel, an idea occurred to him. He moved the stone and began to dig. When the shovel struck metal, he knelt and by hand carefully scooped away the soil. Without removing the box from the hole, he opened the lid. A black velvet gem pouch and a folded scrap of paper rested on top of the gold. The haiku he had written, full of hope. Bitterly, he crumpled it in his hand and pushed it into the loose soil along with the gem pouch. He took out a red silk sachet, loosened the drawstring, and held up five gleaming gold slabs. Putting the gold back, he tossed the sachet to Renier.

"There it is," he said, standing up as he backed away.

"Take it all out," Boisson said.

Takeshi swallowed. "There is an explosive charge with a pressure trigger under the box."

"You rotten son of a bitch!" Victor barked.

Renier clucked his tongue, wagging a finger at Takeshi. "I'm sure you have a solution."

Takeshi licked his lips. "Take out the gold, a couple of sachets at a time, and replace them with stones."

"You two, gather some stones for him," Renier ordered, stepping back.

Takeshi sank to his knees, head down in a posture of defeat. One by one, he removed the sachets and replaced them with stones. He tossed the sachets to Victor, who checked the contents of each before putting them into the leather bag. Renier had returned his pistol to his pocket and was smoking a cigarette while sipping from his flask. Surreptitiously, Takeshi set aside four sachets of gold.

"This infernal heat! Hurry it up," Renier groused.

"Easier said than done," Takeshi snapped, flat on his belly, arms deep in the hole.

"What's the problem?"

"Too many stones in the box. Can't get the ones at the bottom," he replied, pulling up the pouch of gems and four gold sachets. He reached down with his other hand and slammed the box lid closed with a loud metallic bang. He dove to the ground.

Startled, the Frenchmen flattened themselves into the dirt, covering their heads. Takeshi rolled over, came to his feet, and ran toward the cliff. He jumped over the edge, landing on a ledge two meters below. Stuffing the gem pouch and the four gold sachets into his pockets, he scrambled down the slope, grabbing at shrubs, bare feet slipping on loose rocks, crawling over boulders.

Gunshots rang out. Bullets ricocheted off stones around Takeshi. He tripped and tumbled. Flinging out his arms, he caught a gnarled root, arresting his fall. Looking up, he saw that pressed against the rock face, he was not in their line of sight. Loose gravel showered down from above with the sounds of boots scrambling for purchase.

Renier called out, "That was a low trick, Major."

"I didn't think you're the type to honor a bargain, Inspector."

"Don't run. I'll take it out on your wife."

Takeshi stepped out and shouted up the cliff, "If anything happens to her, I will come for you. I swear it on my life!"

Takeshi climbed down, half sliding on his rear. At the bottom, he moved along the sheltering cliff. Renier's heavies were halfway down the bluff face, carefully making their descent. He hesitated, weighing his options. The rocky headland to his left offered little protection beyond shrubs. To his right, meter-high surf pounded the shore. The long beach offered the best escape route. He recalled flying over lonely fishermen's huts about three or four kilometers to the north. He stumbled across the soft sand toward the sea. The four gold sachets in his pockets hampered his movements, so he carried them in his hands. Shots rang out from above, bullets whined overhead. Renier stood on the bluff, pistol in hand, his white straw hat bright against the sky.

On firm sand now along the tide line, he stepped up his pace to a jog. Still hindered by his bad knee, he could not run. But his stamina, he thought, gave him an advantage over his pursuers. By the time the Frenchmen reached the beach, he was two hundred meters ahead of them. Two pistol reports rang out across the sand. Takeshi neither looked back nor ducked, confident no one could hit a moving target at this distance with a pistol. Speeding up, he lowered his head, arms swinging, legs pumping like pistons, overriding the pain in his knee. His eyes scanned the sand for sharp shells and debris. Somehow, his stride began to lengthen with each step, and he ran as he hadn't run in years, his heart thumping in his chest like a war drum.

Victor was keeping up, step for step like an enraged bull. The other one had fallen behind. Takeshi's lungs were beginning to burn. He was drenched in sweat. Sea spray stung his eyes. He was running at a speed he did not know was possible, yet he could not put more distance between himself and his pursuers.

Pounding harder, he pushed himself more, too much, perhaps, for soon his breath grew ragged. His rhythm was faltering. He was tiring quickly. He hadn't eaten since the day before. A telltale stitch of pain in his side warned him of the onset of cramp.

Two more kilometers to the fishing hamlet. He began to doubt he could outrun the brute. Could he outrun Renier? The inspector would be on his way back to the car, on the dirt road that paralleled the ocean for twenty kilometers. His lungs were drawing on a vacuum. He had to reach the fishing hamlet before Renier did.

As he ran, Takeshi opened one of the sachets and scattered all five gold slabs on the sand, dropping the red silk bag as he went. He emptied another sachet. Moments later, farther down the beach, he turned to see that the Frenchmen had halted, stooped over, gathering the gold. Encouraged, he sacrificed the third sachet, scattering a small fortune. Time had become immensely expensive. All his life, all that had come before and all that was to come, boiled down to this. He ran like a man possessed, depleting all reserves, his hand clutching a single sachet of gold. The pouch of gems remained in his pocket.

CUMULUS CLOUDS boiled up high in the northeast. Above, the sun was weakening behind a pearling sky. Far ahead, he saw the tops of the coconut palms by the fishermen's hamlet rising above the dunes. A jolt of power surged through him. He felt as though his heart might burst. His legs pounded out the meters, feet thumping the sand. His eyes blurred, tunneling.

The hamlet lay deserted, the huts burnt to the ground. He called out. No one answered. Not a soul, not even a dog. Tangled nets hung on bamboo poles. Broken furniture, debris everywhere. Something terrible had happened here. Survivors had long since abandoned the place. He scanned the wagon tracks to the seaside dirt road and the flatland beyond. No shelter anywhere. On the beach, his enemies were closing in to within six hundred meters.

He ran to the coconut trees where half a dozen coracles— round basket boats—were beached upside down, some smashed or burnt. He chose the best of them, stood it up on its side, and rolled it down to the waterline. He took the single oar wedged beneath the bench and pushed the coracle through the surf, maneuvering it through the waves. With a practiced motion, he heaved himself aboard and began paddling.

They were less than two hundred meters away when he cleared the first breakers. Victor fired his pistol and missed. Boisson limped past Victor, stopping at the water's edge. He stood doubled over, hands on knees, gasping, pointing up at the coconut trees.

"What?"

Boisson wheezed, "Fetch a boat."

While Victor jogged off, Boisson checked himself. Taking long, deep breaths, he flipped open his revolver, reloaded the empty chambers. The little round boat was bobbing about seventy meters from shore, Takeshi paddling furiously, his torso above the coracle rim.

Boisson filled his lungs, exhaled halfway, and aimed. He fired twice and missed both times. He lowered the pistol and turned his neck to loosen his shoulders. Taking another deep breath and exhaling halfway, he aimed and fired the remaining four rounds in quick succession. Takeshi jerked upward and fell back into the boat.

"You got him!" Victor shouted.

"Let's go. Get that thing in the water."

They hauled the basket boat into the surf and fought with it briefly until a big wave tore the boat from their grasp and upturned it. The next wave dumped it back on the beach. More waves filled it like a bathtub. Retreating to the beach, they watched Takeshi's coracle for signs of life. Finally, a bloody forearm rose, the hand grabbing the rim of the basket as though the man was trying to get up. A moment later, it slipped back. They did not see any part of him again. From where they were, the boat appeared stationary, but the tide was slowly dragging it away from shore.

"You got him in the chest. He won't be paddling anymore. Look at that storm brewing over there. It'll sink his boat when it gets here."

Boisson said, "Maybe, but the inspector won't be happy about it. You swim out and get him."

The big man grimaced at the rolling surf. "He's bleeding."

"So?"

"Sharks. Lots of sharks this season."

"Don't be a coward."

"Better a live coward than a dead fool," Victor countered.

"Damn it, Victor."

They sat on the sand and divided the gold they had picked up. Boisson fumbled for his pack of cigarettes and cursed, finding it drenched. The sound of a vehicle drifted over the dunes. It stopped by an abandoned shack. Renier limped out and staggered down to the beach, red-faced from the effort. Seeing his men alone on the beach, he shook his cane, cursing at them from afar.

Boisson hissed under his breath, "Keep your mouth shut about the gold."

"Don't worry about that."

Head bowed, Boisson explained the situation. Renier paced the beach, squinting out to sea. By then the current had carried the coracle far out, a mere dot now, rising and falling between waves. Boisson volunteered to find a boat at the next village. Victor wanted to radio for a scout plane.

Renier stroked his mustache. "If we call in support, there will be a lot less gold to go around."

"An inquiry could get ugly," Boisson added.

Victor turned to Renier. "I guess he didn't believe that you were going to let him go."

Renier snorted, "He knew he had it coming."

"What now?" Boisson asked.

"That Jap is as good as dead. Leave him to the sharks," Renier grunted and spat. He heaved to and stomped back to the car.

———

THE BULLET had plowed through his left shoulder, from back to front. He lay on his back, at the bottom of the coracle, legs bent sideways. His breath rattled in his throat. Blood oozed from the wound, trickled down his chest, and dripped off his ribs. He fingered the hole in his shirt, the mangled skin and flesh underneath. His hand came away coated crimson. So much blood. He groaned, lacking the strength even to curse himself. His left arm was twitching uncontrollably. Grunting, he ground his teeth. He was thirsty. The rolling swell of the sea was familiar, soothing, like being in a cradle.

A lone seagull circled high above, spiraling toward the cotton bowl of the sky. He watched it in irrational fear of plummeting upward. No way to swim through that, no way home. He felt light. He felt himself rising, his senses expanding. He saw the world as though from a great height, riding the thermals like a bird.

A blue gap opened in the clouds. Sunlight poured through it like gossamer threads, turning a ribbon of sea turquoise, catching a coracle with a man, curled up in a brilliant pool of blood. All around, the sea was streaked with white.

56

Yam Sellers

THESE WERE LEAN TIMES, THE HARDEST YEARS OF
Anh's young life and her first experience of true poverty. Coi
and Anh lived at the Rose Shrine of the Lady Buddha and sold
yams on the street. Coi shouldered yoke-baskets, one with
raw yams, one with a charcoal grill. Anh carried a woven tray
of roasted yams on her head. They wandered the streets, the
waterfront piers, and the beaches, walking ten, fifteen kilometers daily, squatting at the edge of the town market, unable to
afford a stall, selling house to house, hawking to visitors waiting
outside the prison, napping under roadside trees to hide from
the sun, huddling in doorways to shelter from the rain. They
were always hungry. Anh missed the mountain camp where
there had always been enough to eat, albeit much the same
every day. Here in town, there was everything imaginable—
sweets, cakes, meats, noodles, and fruits—but all they could
afford to eat was yam and the lowest-grade rice with vegetables from the garden, and the occasional fish from Song, the
fisherman whose boat Takeshi had hired regularly. They lived
on the edge, human flotsam of war, relying on the kindness of
the Buddhist nuns and earning the coins of poor people, yam
eaters like themselves.

DURING THEIR stay at the shrine, there were three mem-
orable events. The first was the wedding of Mr. Binh's grandson. They rode his ox-drawn water cart out to his farm where

they stayed three days to help with the preparations for the ceremony and the banquet. It was a modest affair, but it was the highlight of the year for Coi and Anh. There were plenty of things to do: cooking, games, contests, and laughter.

THE SECOND was the arrival of baby Nga, Coi's first grand-daughter. With his mother's blessing, Ha had married Nhung in a private ceremony in the Resistance camp. A few months later, Nhung delivered her baby in Ba Ria, a town near Vung Tau. The Resistance was under attack. Its network of safe houses fell, one after another, in quick succession. Many orga-nizers and fighters were killed or captured. Fearing the worst, Ha sent Coi an urgent message to go to Ba Ria immediately, as the French dragnet was closing around them. Coi left Anh in the care of the nuns and traveled four days and three nights on foot across the province, a fifty-four-year-old woman, alone, armed with only her wits and prayer beads. In Ba Ria, Nhung and Ha asked Coi to take the baby in case something happened to them. Coi agreed, thinking that she would see them again in a few months. Little did she expect that war would shatter her family, nor that she would not see them again for decades.

With one basket holding the three-month-old infant and the other holding water, some food for herself, and two precious cans of condensed milk for the baby, Coi walked back to Phan Thiet by the little-known routes of back roads and trails she had trekked days earlier, covering another one hundred and sixty kilometers in four days and three nights while dodging patrols, bandits, and packs of wild dogs. With feverish eyes and drawn cheeks, Coi arrived at the shrine, her feet blistered and bloodied, her skin cracked and sunburned, barely alive, having walked more than forty kilometers per day for eight consecutive days. At the altar of the Lady Buddha, Coi knelt,

presented her granddaughter, and prayed for Her love and protection. Distressed at having been left behind, Anh was glad
to be reunited with her grandaunt and thrilled at the sight of
baby Nga for now, finally, she had someone to feed, cuddle,
and play with.

THEN A LETTER arrived at the shrine from Japan addressed
to Tuyet.

57

Dunes of Memories

THE DAY OF HER RELEASE BEGAN LIKE ANY OTHER:
tai chi, morning tea, and the first meal. The chief guard came
to the door and ordered Tuyet and nineteen other inmates to
step forward. He announced that the new warden had selected
them for early release, effective immediately. They had five
minutes to gather their belongings.

Someone shrieked with excitement. Tuyet staggered back in
shock. The chosen twenty stared at one another in disbelief.
Cheers went up. Rounds of congratulations and good wishes
rolled around the cell block. Twenty out of ninety-one, more
than one-fifth of their growing number were to be freed. Everyone was relieved because there would now be more room in
the cell. A flurry of activities ensued as the prisoners hastened
to claim the newly vacated spaces and any items left behind.
Tuyet's prized spot would be for the next Speaker, to be elected
the moment she left.

Dazed, Tuyet sat on her mat, counting the time she had
served, fourteen months of a twenty-four-month sentence. Her
hands were shaking. What mementos of hell would she take?
The lice comb or the sharpened seashell they used to cut food?
Someone could use her prayer beads. All that was worth keeping had been stored in her mind: faces, names, stories, poems
scrawled on the walls, moments of kindness. She took only the
pouch with the locks of hair of the thirteen women who had
died on her watch as Speaker.

"Big Sister Tuyet, please let my family know I'm in here,"

said a young woman, pressing a scrap of paper with her address into Tuyet's hand.

Tuyet exchanged bittersweet goodbyes with her cellmates as they handed her hastily scribbled messages. A circle formed around the lucky ones, hugging and whispering good wishes.

"Don't forget us," a woman cried. "Don't forget your sisters in here."

"Send us some harvest moon cakes and fruit candies, please."

"Shampoo! Don't forget the shampoo."

"And don't forget to check on my cheating husband!"

Laughter and cheers sent the fortunate ones through the iron door and toward freedom.

TUYET WENT to see Lieu, her weekly visitor, at the grocery shop near the prison. Lieu swapped Tuyet's gray prison garb for a fresh white shirt, dark farm trousers, sandals, and a palm hat. She treated Tuyet to a tall glass of freshly pressed sugarcane juice with ice to celebrate her release. Tuyet gulped it down. She grinned at the empty glass. It was the most marvelous thing she had ever tasted. Lieu offered to call a cyclo, but Tuyet said she wanted to walk into the brilliantly blue afternoon. The idea of strolling four kilometers into town seemed an extravagant luxury.

LIKE A MADWOMAN, she ambled beneath the noonday sun, unaffected by the heat, taking in the sights, her senses overloading. Her heart was pounding, overjoyed with life. Her mind was bursting with impressions. Everything was huge, the roads, the trees, the street-side shanties. Army trucks rumbled by, showering her in dust and black exhaust. Dogs barked lazily at her from the shade. Drowsy shopkeepers were lounging in their stores, fanning themselves. It was all dazzling, a vivid dream. How had her release come about?

She stopped in the middle of the bridge, feeling the vibration of the traffic through her sandals. The briny scent of sea and fish made her heart ache. Where was Takeshi? Her fisherman-pilot-artist. She could almost smell him: brine, soap, sandalwood, and tobacco. To her left, the sea and Hokkaido beyond. To her right, the river and the past. Behind her, the prison and the sisterhood within. Ahead of her, family.

"MOTHER!"

A girl jumped up from where she had been sitting on the ground with a basket of yams. She ran toward Tuyet, arms outstretched. A small woman rose, a baby in a sling across her chest.

"Anh! You've grown so much. A full hand taller. Auntie, I've missed you."

Tuyet, Anh, Coi, and baby Nga clung together, holding one another in a long embrace.

"How did you get out?" Anh asked.

"They released twenty of us this morning. It's very crowded in there. I think they needed the space."

Coi asked, "How did you know where to find us?"

"Sister Lieu said you might be here at the Catholic school."

Anh added, "I like her. We talk to her every week after she visits you."

"I know," Tuyet smiled, happy to be listening to her daughter prattling on about their yam-selling route and the friends they had made in a year of wandering the streets. Anh was much more talkative and outgoing than before. Tuyet kissed Anh's forehead, her heart brimming over.

AT THE SHRINE, by the carp pond, they lit incense for Hoang. They put out some of his favorite peanut taffy and sat with him as the incense sticks burned.

Coi handed Tuyet a letter. "From Japan. It came a few months ago, but I was afraid to send it to you. If it had ended up in the wrong hands, it might have caused trouble for you."

"It's from Takeshi," Tuyet said.

Tears of relief tumbled down her cheeks as she read the single page, written in his elegant cursive hand. It was the third letter he had sent in hopes that it might reach her. Takeshi was in Hokkaido with his mother. His father had passed away. He described his capture, his escape by sea, and the days he had drifted on the open ocean. A fishing boat had rescued him. After a month, they had put him on a passing Japanese freighter. He had been wounded. Recovery had proved long and painful. The long journey back home had not been his choice. Would she bring the family to Hokkaido? They could make a comfortable life in Japan like Ishigara and Ly, who had settled in Kyoto. His father had left him their ancestral home and many acres of farmland. He had started painting again. Fishing too, with his friend Sakamoto. He reminded her that she had said that she would come, someday. He did not know if this letter would reach her, but he would continue to write until one did.

Coi asked, "What are you going to do?"

"I don't know. Last night, I didn't even know I would be here with you today."

Coi could never leave her son, Ha. She said softly, "Japan would mean a better life than here."

"My soul needs peace. I must find myself again before I can decide."

OVER THE COURSE of three blissful days, Tuyet celebrated freedom with her family and visited her son at the home of the Nguyens. She sent cakes and sweets to her friends in prison and forwarded their messages. Tuyet took long walks with her aunt and played on the beach with her daughter. They cooked some of the food she craved. At dawn on the fourth day, Coi shaved her niece's head. Tuyet bathed, donned the white attire of a novice, and entered the convent of the Lady Buddha.

Coi, Anh, and baby Nga lived at the shrine and sold yams on the street while Tuyet stayed in the convent. Life was easier for Coi now that she no longer had to support Tuyet in prison.

◆

THREE FULL moons later, Tuyet thanked the nuns and left the convent with clear, shining eyes, once more wearing her peasant clothes. She told Coi that she would enjoy a seaside picnic. "Remember, Auntie, that white stretch of sand at Mui Ne where Takeshi took the whole family that day?"

Coi nodded. "Of course, I do. That was a fine day. I remember you were drunk on French wine."

Tuyet chuckled. "Oh, yes, just a little."

Coi said, "He gave Anh a pink kite with a long ribbon tail. You don't remember that, do you, Anh?"

Anh cried, "Yes, I do!"

Tuyet nodded, smiling.

WITH THE FAMILY encamped under the coconut trees, Tuyet strolled alone along Mui Ne beach barefoot, her pants rolled up to the knees, along the surf, the sun warm on her bare shaven head. She remembered her younger self, long-haired and lithe, skipping down the beach, splashing as she went. A white Parisian summer dress with tiny blue flowers. Collecting shells. She could feel him, following her in his white short-sleeved shirt and brown fedora, just over her left shoulder. A few steps away, and nearly a decade in the past. *What was it we talked about, my love? Distance and time.*

The sky burned with gold, orange, and magenta. Now Tuyet

labored up the dunes by herself. No strong hand to help her. She sat on the wind-carved ridge, digging in her feet, sending sand cascading down. The dunes cast long wavy shadows, the breeze cooling fast. Gulls skimmed across the flat sea. Unlike the last time she had sat here with Takeshi, there now were no storm clouds. The horizon was clear, and so, at last, was her mind.

She wrapped her arms around herself, head resting back, feeling the embrace of his strong, rangy arms. A sad smile came to her lips. At last, she allowed herself to grieve, for she knew she would never see the cherry blossoms of Hokkaido. Her vows, her duties were blood-bonded to this land. She remembered the sweetness and the laughter they had shared. Immortal moments.

ACKNOWLEDGMENTS

My wife, Srisuda, has been my light and my foundation of strength. I owe her everything.

I owe my extended family a great debt of gratitude. They have been my pillar of support. My father's knowledge and suggestions have been invaluable. My mother's memory has been a treasure trove of information. My siblings Curt, Tim, and Kay have always encouraged my endeavors. My aunt Hang and uncle Hung Le have shown me great love, kindness, and generosity. I've learned important life lessons from them.

I owe special thanks to my agent, Jillian Manus, for coming out of retirement to represent this book. She has been my steadfast champion. Her perseverance and wisdom have made this book possible.

John Glusman has been a fantastic editor for all my books. It has been my good fortune and honor to have his guidance all these years.

I am grateful to my readers, Richard Ypenberg, Andy Merserth, and Sandra Wright. Their good humor and friendship have kept me in good spirits.